DEEPLY WITH THE SUN IN OUR EYES

Sacrifice, treachery and valour in the shadow of
Britain's greatest military defeat

A. C. Smith

First published in Australia by Aurora House
www.aurorahouse.com.au

This edition published 2019
Copyright © A. C. Smith 2019

Typesetting and e-book design: Acrux IT Services Pvt. Ltd.
www.acruxorg.com

Cover design: Simon Critchell

The right of A. C. Smith to be identified as Author of the Work has been asserted
in accordance with the Copyright, Designs and Patents Act 1988.

ISBN number: 978-0-6486794-3-1 (paperback)

Lightning Source has received Chain of Custody (CoC) certification from:
The Forest Stewardship Council® (FSC®)
Programme for the Endorsement of Forest Certification® (PEFC®)
The Sustainable Forestry Initiative® (SFI®)

A catalogue record for this
book is available from the
National Library of Australia

Distributed by: Ingram Content: www.ingramcontent.com
Australia: phone +613 9765 4800 | email lsiaustralia@ingramcontent.com
Milton Keynes UK: phone +44 (0)845 121 4567 | email enquiries@ingramcontent.
com
La Vergne, TN USA: phone +1 800 509 4156 | email inquiry@lightningsource.
com

Gardners UK:
www.gardners.com
phone +44 (0)132 352 1555 | email sales@gardners.com

Bertrams UK:
www.bertrams.com/BertWeb/index.jsp
phone +44 (0)160 364 8400 | email sales@bertrams.com

How can I prove?
There is no reasoning or asking why.
Only to prove;
I love you deeply with the sun in my eyes.

~B., R. and M. Gibb

Foreword

In 2007, the basic outline for this story was conceived, born out of an avid interest in the history of the fall of Singapore, described as "the greatest catastrophe of World War II" (Peter Thompson, *The Battle for Singapore* 2005, Portrait).

Progress deteriorated over time. "Write fifteen hundred words each evening" was the dictum offered by distinguished former High Court Justice and part-time author Ian Callinan AC QC on being acquainted with my struggle. Legal practice won out.

In May 2013, life-threatening heart disease was found and a triple bypass followed. Mortality's collision with invincibility saw the latter slink off to its sick bed. For the first six months, trying to write a few words taxed every sinew of energy, and completing this work became as forlorn a hope as was a return to the Bar.

Well over a year later, I forced myself back into the novel. So began its quest for form and substance. There were many times when giving up seemed inevitable.

The book wouldn't have been written without the unstinting love, encouragement and support from my wife, Anna. Her suggestions proved to be prescient and her criticism insightful, persisting even when met with frequent disfavour on my part.

One of the most satisfying aspects of telling this tale has involved embracing actual events from history, spliced and woven throughout the narrative.

Psychological torment besets Richard and Greda as they confront reality, much as facing imminent impermanence sent me, nautically speaking, into dry dock for barnacle removal and a refit.

Survival, unselfish love, courage and honour are the enduring themes of this work. They are timeless, immutable virtues and, as the Apostle Paul wrote thousands of years ago, of all gifts bequeathed to humans, the greatest is love.

~A. C. Smith

Dedication

*Dedicated to my beloved sister, Di, selfless, loving and
giving to the end
and to Mum, Stella May Smith (née Greensill),
who instilled in me an appreciation of language and reading.*

Contents

PART I

It was clearer than crystal to the Lords of the state preserves of loaves and fishes that things in general were settled forever.

~Charles Dickens

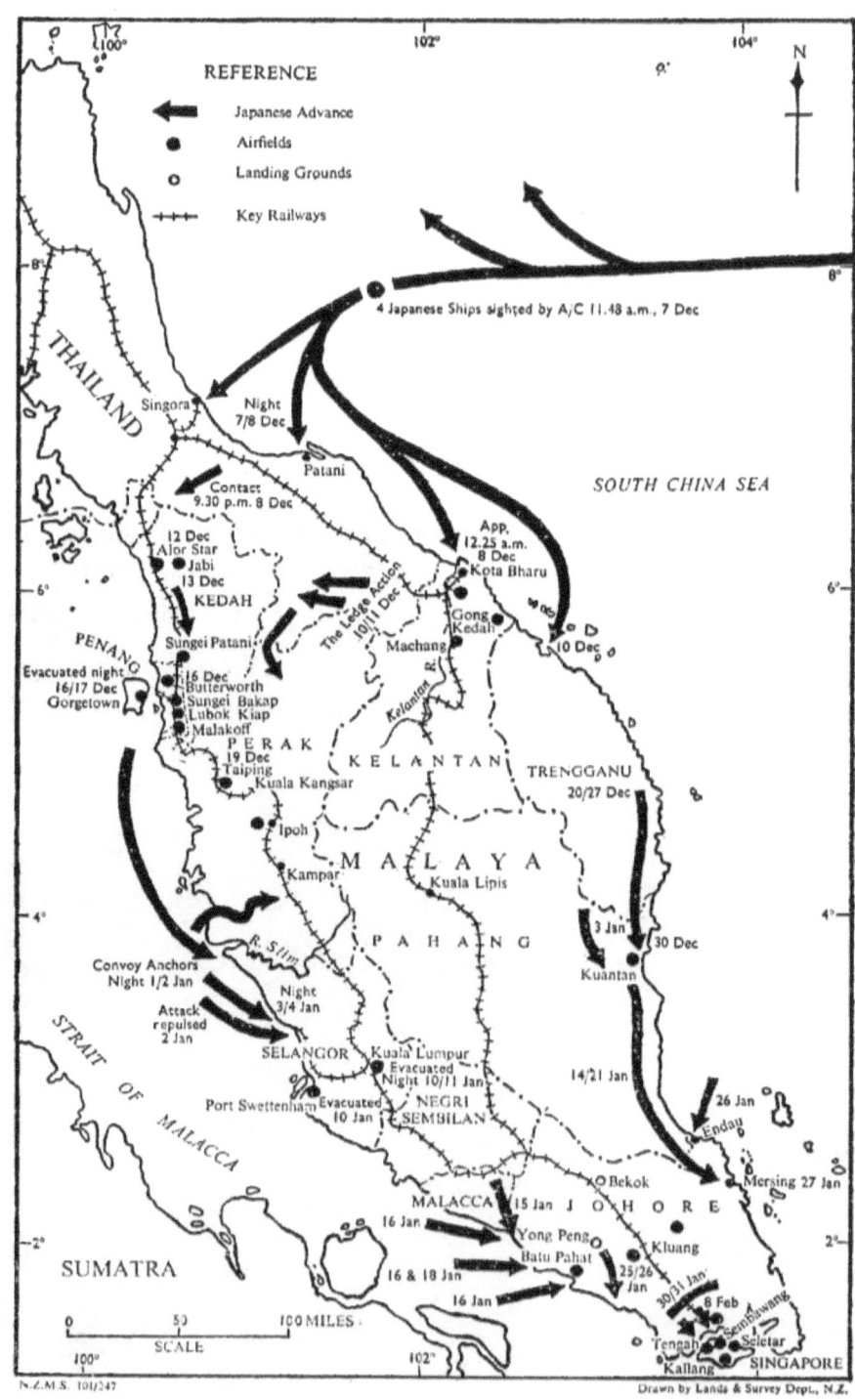

REFERENCE

→ Japanese Advance

● Airfields

○ Landing Grounds

╪╪╪ Key Railways

N

THAILAND

Singora

Night 7/8 Dec

Patani

Contact 9.30 p.m. 8 Dec

4 Japanese Ships sighted by A/C 11.48 a.m., 7 Dec

SOUTH CHINA SEA

12 Dec Alor Star
Jabi
13 Dec
KEDAH

App. 12.25 a.m. 8 Dec
Kota Bharu

Gong Kedah

Machang

Kelantan

Sungei Patani

PENANG
Evacuated night 16/17 Dec
Gorgetown

16 Dec
Butterworth
Sungei Bakap
Lubok Kiap
Malakoff

PERAK

19 Dec
Taiping
Kuala Kangsar

KELANTAN

TRENGGANU
20/27 Dec

Ipoh

MALAYA

Kampar

Kuala Lipis

R. Slim

PAHANG

Convoy Anchors Night 1/2 Jan

Night 3/4 Jan

Attack repulsed 2 Jan

SELANGOR

Kuala Lumpur
Evacuated Night 10/11 Jan

Port Swettenham
Evacuated 10 Jan

NEGRI SEMBILAN

STRAIT OF MALACCA

SUMATRA

3 Jan
Kuantan

30 Dec

14/21 Jan

26 Jan
Endau

Mersing 27 Jan

Bekok

MALACCA
15 Jan
16 Jan

JOHORE

Yong Peng

Batu Pahat

Kluang

25/26 Jan

16 & 18 Jan

16 Jan

30/31 Jan
8 Feb
Sembawang
Seletar

0   50   100 MILES
SCALE

Tengah
Kallang
SINGAPORE

N.Z.M.S. 101/247

Drawn by Lands & Survey Dept., N.Z.

Chapter 1

An energetic young engineer

On any clear night in the Straits of Malacca, in every direction the eye ventures to look, there are sparkles of light from the world's ships powering their way through this narrow passage of water that separates the Malayan peninsula from Sumatra. Such are the numbers of vessels and their movement that any attempt to distinguish which are heading towards the Singapore Roads from those travelling outbound is a fruitless exercise.

Played out perpetually with an ever-increasing number of modern craft in the years since Sir Stamford Raffles planted the British flag in the colony of Singapore in 1819, complacency had begun to set in. Only the weathered sea captains maintained vigilance on the bridge, while the new breed of masters left navigation to their duly assigned watch-keepers.

A novice spectator might have envisaged a high platform on which was perched an inscrutable Malaccan pilot orchestrating the whole timeless operation so that every vessel had been furnished with its position, speed and course. The result produced a furious yet oftentimes harmonious enjoinment of men, rumbling steel, creaking timbers and luminescent wake, where each craft's assignment in the setting was equiponderant with the others and nothing different would ever be charted out on this vast seascape for the future of mankind.

No crew member of the British-registered fifteen thousand ton motor ship *Erakai*, one of these vessels hugging the Malayan coastline, had any inkling of the omens that this eighth day of December 1941 posed to Malaya, Singapore, Australia and, most of all, the British Empire. She was festooned in the company's traditional colours—a seagrass green hull with gold-striped ribbon, a brilliant white superstructure and the funnel, a burnt orange and black affair. Powered by a mighty Sulzer engine that made a steady fourteen knots in favourable seas, the *Erakai*, by no means the fastest tramp afloat, was one of the most reliable. She rarely missed a deadline and defied whatever challenge the weather offered. Comfortable without being pretentious, well-maintained, decks scrubbed spotless, wooden planking evenly caulked, regularly holystoned and four years old, she boasted accommodation for her crew that was the envy of most ships plying Far Eastern waters. Each officer tenanted his own cabin and, apart from the bosun whose ex officio entitlement deemed that he retain solitary quarters, the crew shared one between two.

It was nearly four o'clock in the morning; changeover of the watch for the deck and engineer officers. One could not envisage two more contrasting environments than the bridge and the engine room. One, breezy on the exposed wings, port and starboard, charismatic with moon, cloud and stars, encouraged quiet reflection. Water caressed the bow and hints of salt spray enlivened by gusts of wind spread an intoxicating aroma for the navigators.

The other was an anxious abode. A hotchpotch of energy. A boiling, roasting, enervating cauldron of roaring sound, tolerating speech but rarely, and then only screamed between communicants at point-blank range. Here, the third engineer was finishing the logs in preparation for the arrival of his boss.

On the bridge, the second mate, in the equatorial garb of crisp white, open-necked, short-sleeved shirt with black and gold epaulettes, white shorts, long socks and polished black shoes, was giving way to the affable chief officer; in seagoing parlance, 'the mate'. He nourished his patch and wanted to be loved by those who worked in it and under him, always arriving early for his watch.

Their greetings were, on this particular morning, momentarily interrupted by the dull roar of aircraft passing overhead. Neither their form nor origin was evident.

"Night exercises for our boys, no doubt," observed the Scottish-born mate patriotically, seeming to glimpse the RAF emblem through the layers of dark cloud. "Just making it clear there are no chances of the slanty-eyed Jap bastards getting anywhere near the King's holdings in this part of the world."

Willie O'Connell, an angular Irishman with a shrewd demeanour, was somewhat more reticent. He deemed it judicious to pass off his superior's comment with a feeble aside. "Well, Chief, somebody's having fun up there. Anyway, things are steady, north-easter, ten to fifteen knots and a moderate sea and swell. Just keep an eye on that tanker on the port side; has been a bit erratic in the last half an hour, but I think she's now moving out of the way."

"Right, Willie. At this rate we'll be tied up at Port Swettenham about lunchtime and unloading early this afternoon. The Old Man wants us to be back in Darwin before Christmas, though I don't like his chances."

The traffic was sparse on the narrow starboard side, where the distant mountains of southern Malaya lay silhouetted against the approaching dawn.

As was his usual routine after leaving the bridge, O'Connell descended the outside stairs in time to catch Richard Kirnst. He greeted the Australian, his overalls fluorescent under the superstructure lighting as he focused on the ship's wake. Every morning at this time he could be found with two browned forearms resting on the boat deck railing. He seemed to linger longer than usual. If O'Connell hadn't known him better, he might have questioned whether a touch of the aesthete was overtaking this introspective figure.

Kirnst was the only Australian officer on board and easily recognisable as such. An intense character, he was tall, with a full head of chestnut hair, dark-eyed and as fit a specimen as O'Connell had ever encountered. Now twenty-eight and with a less obvious accent than many of his peers, he had been brought up in western Queensland on a cattle property. From an early age he had acquired bushcraft skills, and by the time he reached fifteen could ride with the best of them. He was a dead shot and worked nearly as hard as men twice his age. Like his father, a legendary axeman, he inherited large hands and rippling, sinewy arms from felling, sawing and splitting logs.

Years of unrelenting drought took its toll, and the farm could not support his education beyond two high school years. Despite never having envisaged a life for his son away from their rural enterprise, Kirnst Senior was driven by necessity to recognise that its time had passed. Richard was boarded with one of the many farming families who had moved to Toowoomba, where he became an apprentice fitter and turner in the local foundry. When his five-year indenture concluded, he found a position as a tradesman in the Kangaroo Point shipyards in Brisbane.

His work ethic caught the eye of the chief engineer of a general cargo vessel that had been undergoing repairs and needed a junior fourth engineering officer. The ship, operated by the Union Steamship Company, was sailing for Auckland, and Richard struggled to contain his excitement at this opportunity. Seven months later, the chief wrote as an aside on his discharge papers: *A very energetic young engineer*, after certifying creditably as to Richard's sobriety, diligence and capacity.

Over the next six years, Richard served on different ships, attaining marine engineering qualifications through a combination of sea-time and shoreside study. He then completed his final examinations, passing all stages with honours, and became the youngest Australian to be awarded his First-Class Steam and Motor Certificates, credentials not usually secured until an engineer was in his thirties.

Richard valued the thought that the top job could not be too far away but took nothing for granted. His appointment as second engineer on the *Erakai* was the realisation of a dream and an unshakeable ambition to become chief engineer was within reach.

"Come on, professor, get your arse down below," O'Connell shouted good-naturedly at his shipmate of the last nine months, rousing him from his reverie.

Richard appreciated the Irishman's caustic humour. "Hey, Willie, I reckon it's time. Did you hear those planes?"

"Yes, I did. Probably the Japs about to give those smug Poms a bit of stick."

Richard turned to face him, like a speaker in a debate responding to an interjection. "Get off it, potata-peeler. I'll not be a party to your republican sentiments, you mad Irishman. I'll stand you for a beer when we hit port tomorrow."

"We'll be lucky. The skipper wants a quick turnaround here, and I think we're going to be working the clock day and night to meet the deadline."

"Serves you right, Willie. Well, I'm off to the hot box."

One last time, Richard recharged his lungs with the balmy air. He was greeted by a thrashing blast of furnace gasses and roaring crescendo of machinery as he opened the fire door. A cursory look at the temperatures on the heads of the main engine satisfied his initial enquiry. Then, he considered the rhythmical sounds of the fuel injectors, snapping like bolts being drawn shut, firing the explosions that in turn punched the pistons down through the crosshead into the big end, turning the propeller shaft at 135 revolutions per minute. Everything was normal as he descended to the floor plates.

Richard acclimatised to the heat and the cacophony of noise as each piece of machinery combined to effect propulsion and power generation. He never ceased to marvel at this self-contained body of steel, encasing water, fuel and oil capable of giving power, circulating brine through the heat exchangers to keep the engines cool and discharging it over the side. Lubricant was force-fed into the main engine, sucked out and sent through purifiers to repeat the process interminably. Refrigeration compressors kept perishable cargo in pristine condition and domestic pumps ensured every cabin had reticulated water. It was like running the utilities of a small city. He relished the responsibility of maintaining mechanical operations on the ship, subject only to the overarching superintendence of the chief engineer.

Richard reflected on the previous incumbent in his position, who had married and resigned from the company to take up a shoreside job running a power station. Although he'd never envisaged abandoning the freedom of life at sea for a family, he felt comfortable knowing that the skills he had acquired could one day take him into secure, land-based employment.

Many of the officers with whom he'd sailed were single, their only notion of marriage being the union with their ship. For Richard, women were beautiful creatures whom he admired and respected, but were to be kept at the protective distance a marine-engineering career demanded.

The sea was an adventurous discipline. In every great ocean he'd experienced weather that tested the ship's seams and men's nerves, cyclones and typhoons with forty-foot waves. There was an air of invincibility about Richard, yet it never amounted to wilful arrogance. He reposed the utmost confidence in his ship, knowing that everything within his remit was impeccably kept and nurtured.

A man who worked with his hands had to be practical, but Richard's credentials were not limited to an innate ability to arrest a fault and remedy it before a disastrous stoppage at sea imposed itself, nor was it to lead and maintain morale amongst a diverse group of tough men under him. Having developed a hunger for good books, he also prided himself on being well-read, whetting an active imagination that searched for more wherever he could get it. His upbringing was one that kept him in touch with politics and world events. So when it came to any country, including Japan, he could speak with a degree of both knowledge and insight.

It suited him that most ships had a tolerably good library. The young engineer became renowned for preferring to tuck in with a good book than quaff inexpensive duty-free alcohol, such that he earned the nickname 'professor'. Yet he was not given to airing knowledge and refrained from voicing an opinion unless it was specifically sought. Shying away from any temptation to importune others to his way of thinking, he preferred to keep his own counsel. This characteristic earned him respect.

The ascension to power of the Nazis in Germany and the declaration of hostilities with Britain and the Allies increased his search for knowledge. Japan, though behaving in a strident fashion, didn't seem to have the capacity to wage a wider war beyond its aggression in China. However, he was ready to concede that this fervent nation still remained an unknown quantity in the longer term. His view continued to prevail despite some scepticism at the Japanese ambassador to Washington appearing to take the country into a peaceful sphere in diplomatic negotiations with the United States. Whatever the outcome, Richard didn't imagine a nondescript ship like the *Erakai* lifting innocuous goods would excite too much interest.

World events aside, issues nearer to hand needed consideration, namely scheduled work while in port. Cargo movements could take up to a week and that meant more than adequate time to carry out routine maintenance on the main engine. The ship would be tied up at about 1100 hours and in the afternoon see a piston removed, with the bulk of the unit being completed in a further half day.

Other than the allotted duty engineer, unless it was absolutely necessary the men ceased work Saturday at noon and Sundays were free when the vessel was in port. The current maintenance schedule didn't require any departure from the usual hours and would thereby allow officers and crew alike opportunities to go ashore.

Richard had become well acquainted with nearby Kuala Lumpur. Shore leave there had always been singularly pleasurable. But this time, for reasons that challenged his ordinary routine, he was more than a little anxious about what it might hold for him.

*****

Lieutenant Tohiro Osaji, indifferent to the *Erakai* far below, had dreamed of this moment since he left the Japanese Imperial Air Force Academy a fully-fledged pilot in 1936. As a religious and deeply patriotic man, the Asianisation of the Malayan peninsula was the paramount object in his mind, the ultimate prize being the capture and liberation of Singapore. At the controls of the superior Japanese medium-range bomber, he was less than a hundred miles from that very destination in company with twenty other pilots passing over the Straits of Malacca before beginning the first air assault.

Meanwhile, the Japanese army had commenced hostilities with landings at Kota Bharu on the north-west coast of Malaya not far from the border with Siam. The officer commanding these operations, Lieutenant-General Tomoyuki Yamashita, was satisfied. Contained by nature, he digested enormous pride as reports reached him of success at Pearl Harbour.

Despite heavy resistance, the invaders had established a significant beachhead and, as the morning wore on, bombing and strafing of the airport led the defenders to abandon their posts, fearing annihilation. By day's end, the airport was in Japanese hands and Yamashita had taken his first steps on Malayan soil.

Chapter 2

Li Chin Ming

Port Swettenham rose from a reclaimed malaria-infested swamp. Thousands of ships, small and large, discharged general cargo and loaded tin, rubber and timber destined for processing all over the world. Servicing Malaya's busiest port, a town had expanded over the previous forty years. Ships' chandlers, godowns, shops, hotels, eating-places and clammy offices fronted rows of fetid streets and rat-infested drains. In these elongated spittoons, all manner of unspeakable refuse would routinely find its berth and liquify offensively for months before the cleansing monsoon arrived.

The town area burst with a mix of gusto and barter, replicating the Singaporean combination of Little India and Chinatown. Essentially a sailors' repast, crews were enticed to spend their money on gambling and cheap grog. Missing female companionship, eager seamen looked forward to leisure time, and Swettenham was convivial. Common vices were on hand in the various bars that transformed from mucky, streaked and smeared shopfronts during daylight to gaudy red-light inns on nightfall. Other more subtle traders in voluptuary entertainment, the chief commodity marketed as the sun fell, operated behind the façade of hairdressing salons. Many a young sailor who innocently entered to seek a trim or shave, left some considerable time later shorn of much more than its price.

The port's great advantage was its juxtaposition to the capital city of Malaya, less than an hour away by road or rail transport. Kuala Lumpur was a large, teeming sweatpot of a place where poverty and affluence co-existed uneasily, and a seafarer could go about with greater anonymity than if he kept near to his ship. Thrown into a complex mix of Asiatic and subcontinental colour, a lone white face didn't escape curious and envious eyes. Being European guaranteed a degree of prestige in quarters where attention was lavished and bargains could be gained. Conversely, there were some areas where a white person would not wittingly care to venture alone after a certain time of night. Muggings and unexplained disappearances driven by robbery or blackmail were not uncommon.

For Richard Kirnst, the city had all of the positives, and he refused to contemplate any negatives. It was one of his favourite places in the Far East. On his last visit and contrary to his disposition, he had become enamoured with a beautiful young Chinese woman. He first noticed her when she took his lunch order in a café next to a joss house on the city fringes.

She appeared enthralled to find a person of his quality patronising the establishment and assumed he was of British stock. Yet, she was even more pleased that there was neither arrogance nor any hint of the toff about him. Rather, she perceived something self-effacing, even earthy, belying his neat demeanour.

He mentioned that his presence was accidental. He liked walking around, especially away from the main hub. "Often these sorts of places have the best food, and you haven't disappointed me," the spark in his eye suggestive of his having found her more than mere passive company.

On learning he was an Australian ship's officer, a precautionary restraint dissolved. Richard was flattered by an eagerness to engage him in conversation and her rapid transformation from detachment to intimacy in speech and proximity. More than once her body contacted his as she walked between tables attending to increasing numbers of customers while the afternoon advanced.

The longer he stayed, talked to and watched her, the less desirous he was to leave.

She was taller than most women of Chinese ethnicity, slender with shiny, honey-coloured skin that provided a fitting contrast with wavy, shoulder-length black hair. Her figure tapered from narrow shoulder blades to a trim waistline. Hands and feet were small and well-manicured. She wore a full-length silk cheongsam cut on one side just high enough to reveal a shapely calf and delicate ankle. The only imperfection was to be found in the premature appearance of faint lines tracing out a tributary pattern from either side of her bottom lip, a suggestion of harshness that made him curious as to its aetiology.

He was entranced by the fluency of her English. Educated and intelligent, her name was Li Chin Ming and she called herself 'Eva'. Recounting earlier times, Eva told him all but two family members had lost their lives during the Japanese occupation of Nanking. Along with an older brother, she had escaped through Indo-China, settling in Malaya.

At this, tears compressed her eyes and she piloted the conversation towards things concerning Australia: *how do the women dress, wear their hair?* With a degree of familiarity, she began to tease him about his sheepish plea of ignorance respecting hometown female deportment.

He spoke of life in south-east Queensland, and the manner of her smile was as sweet as any he had ever felt. Whether it was the early evening or several infusions of beer too many, when he blurted out "You should come to my country sometime; it's the best place to live on God's earth," she seemed to interpret this as an offer with the evocative reply, "I would love to." This sobered him somewhat, producing an embarrassing silence. She was too astute not to notice his unease. Fortuitously, a rapid exchange in a foreign tongue from a nearby table saw her committing to the needs of other patrons. And then she vanished.

Richard finished his drink, remaining for a while before settling the account with a wizened old woman who had materialised as he approached the counter. His attempts to convey that the tip was for the waitress fell flat, as did eliciting from the hag Eva's whereabouts. He left disconcerted. Perhaps he'd misconstrued the signs and the attraction had been entirely one-sided. He wasn't intoxicated, but alcohol played a little with the mind as well as the body, a factor more appreciated with each step away from the café.

Disordered notions evaporated when he heard her voice. "Richard, will you come again to see me?" Eva was standing in the doorway.

He dashed back and she was in his arms. Yielding to his embrace, in which the presence of a generous bosom didn't go unnoticed, he kissed her on the mouth, thrilled by her receptive lips. "I'll be here same time tomorrow," he said as soft fingertips cupped his face, stroking his cheeks, before a sharp call sent her inside.

The following day, Sunday, saw some unscheduled work arise. The job should have been finished by lunchtime, but late afternoon arrived before the errant pump was back in working order. Richard excused himself from the evening meal, cleaned up and took the train to Kuala Lumpur.

Arriving at the café just after seven o'clock, he was met by a less than amiable individual, gelatinous of body and suspicious of mien. He announced himself as Eva's brother, Nu, and said she had gone home. Short, sweaty and pudgy, his attitude evinced a hint of truculence and barely hidden displeasure, Richard assumed, at his sister's consorting with a foreigner. He was nothing like Eva in any respect.

"Where does she live? I was supposed to be here earlier but had to work, and it took all day. Is there any message for me?" Richard asked, endeavouring to overlook the man's obvious disdain.

Pointedly ignoring the enquiry, Nu replied, "She working at other restaurant in city."

"So, where's that?" he queried innocently, wondering at the contradiction.

"I, I don't know," his face a panoply of evasion. "She left this note for you."

The shifty-eyed man flicked across a piece of paper. It read: *I'm sorry I did miss you today. Can you see me tomorrow at 6 o'clock at the café? Eva.*

Richard was relieved, but questions nettled as he trudged away, contemplating the fruitless journey and feeling frustrated, but this was overtaken by recollections of how much he enjoyed her company, their impulsive kiss and the promise of more.

The following day saw her there as promised. She seemed happy, her eyes shining as if only just releasing him from their previous embrace. Other than some discreet touching of hands, she maintained physical detachment. Richard sensed reticence and wondered if her sibling was watching. He would have preferred to go elsewhere but, as the cafe was quiet, they sat at a table in the far corner sharing tea.

Detecting unease on Richard's part as he informed her of the exchange with her brother, Eva volunteered that Nu was like a 'guardian angel' shielding her during the darkest days and nights of their flight from China. With some money they'd saved, he set up the café. Eva told him about her living quarters above the very place where they now sat. She explained that Nu spent most of his time working in the business and, apart from occasional trips to replenish provisions, was rarely absent. This evening was her only night off.

"I'm working in another job. Didn't Nu tell you?"

"Yes, he did, but I was surprised you hadn't mentioned it," he offered tentatively, seeing no acceptance of reproof as she studied his eyes.

"I did, remember? I think you had a little too much to drink," she responded, her voice quavering with a gently sardonic merriment that absorbed him. He was sure she hadn't but didn't press the point.

"I am waitressing in a restaurant in central Kuala Lumpur." Because of her fluency with English, she told him and the patrons predominantly so, her wages were far above the average Malayan rate. Eva glowed with a convincing pride when adding that she was one of the most popular members of the staff among the clientele. "Sometimes I earn more in a night's tips than in two months' salary."

As the evening lingered, Richard felt himself becoming more enchanted. At times he simply gazed, and she met his eyes beguilingly while her foot found the inside of his trouser cuff under the table. A not unattractive meal, of which they partook very little, came and went and, at her suggestion, they stepped outside, walking casually down the street. His movement to clasp her hand found an arm encircling his waist, her fingers pinching him provocatively.

He wondered how much he would see of her before sailing. She appeared to read his thoughts. "I might be able to get all of Saturday off if you can drag yourself away from that silly ship," she said, nibbling at his neck.

The saucy invitation prompted an effusive acceptance. "Yes, of course I'll be free." He embraced her eagerly. "I'd really love to see you. We can hire a car and drive about a bit, maybe spend time in the countryside." His diffident manner was a quality to which Eva was unaccustomed.

With the arrangement finalised, she called time. Leaning over to him, their lips touched, and she apologised for the sudden curtailment, while adding that she was looking forward to their outing.

In the ensuing days, work was superintended at a pace that shook Richard's junior engineers. He was missing Eva and counting down the hours until they would next meet. After a nod from the chief engineer, who had been delighted that maintenance was up to date, Richard told the engine room crew they could sleep in on Saturday.

None of his frenzied activity and unassigned movements ashore had been lost on Willie O'Connell. Suspecting something was afoot, he chided Richard about 'going missing a bit lately', asking what 'she' was like. Richard's eyes grew darker and his cheeks reddened, earning him a flippant rebuke. "Come on, prof, keep yer 'air on."

Richard regained his equanimity. "Listen, Willie," he said jovially, "you stick your nose in the direction of the loading, keep your specs glued to the charts and the next weather pattern on the horizon and we'll be a happy little ship. Okay, old mate?"

Saturday morning saw Eva waiting when he pulled up. She made a becoming sight, wearing a summer dress that was yellow in colour, sprinkled with white polka dots and pulled in at the waist by a gold-and-blue belt embossed with Chinese characters. She was holding a white hat and handbag. On her feet were elegant, strappy, high-heeled sandals. The contrast between her crisp, clean bearing and the dingy dwellings and potholed alleyway was striking.

He bounded out of the car to help her across the
open drain. As she stepped over to the door, he noticed
abundant makeup—crimson lipstick dabbed liberally,
rouge highlighting cheekbones, dark eye shadow and ruby
nail polish. They started off and, fingers imprinting his
arm, she leaned over to bestow an impromptu kiss.

"You're so pretty," he couldn't help saying. She laid her
hand squarely on his leg, stroking his outer thigh with her
nails, and smiled. Her teeth were even behind luscious,
moist lips.

The day emerged as perfect a dream accompaniment as
he could have conjured. Beside Richard was a beautiful and
sensuous woman, around whom there was a worldliness
he found captivating. Eva was very different to how she'd
presented at their first meeting, inviting touch and oozing
sex appeal. Time in her company seemed to evaporate as
easily as mist from the sun's consumption of damp patches
on the road. Effervescent talk and laughter swallowed up
their journey. Her hand now traced a more thrilling path,
drawing circles on the inside of his thigh, creating an
anticipation of intimacy so intense that he began to think
she was setting out to seduce him.

Arriving at the coast, they took a ferry to Penang,
followed by a leisurely stroll around the markets. No
amount of cajoling could persuade her to accept his offer
of a gift or trinket from insistent traders peddling a variety
of merchandise.

"Richard, have you ever been to the Eastern and Oriental
Hotel," she asked unexpectedly. He shook his head. "Come
on then. I want to show you."

She led him past several stately homes towards a high,
white-washed wall. When the road straightened, they came
to an imperial entrance. The E & O had been built and
operated for many years by the same Armenian brothers
who had created Raffles Hotel in Singapore. In no measure
as large as its more famous cousin, the design was similar.
Marble floors, magnificent sweeping staircases, elaborate
porticoes; teak, cedar and English oak in abundance,
this was consummate architecture. Richard had not
experienced its like before. They lunched on lobster and

champagne from the vantage of a table away from the main diners and adjacent to the water's edge.

It became an afternoon that he didn't wish to end. He ventured to ask if Eva might be disposed to remain for the night and return to the mainland in the morning. Immediately thereafter, he considered the request ambitious and was certain she would reject it out of hand. So he began to equivocate, giving her no chance to reply, making excuses about the car—it was all too much trouble, he had left it at a garage and would have to try to telephone the caretaker to ensure the vehicle was safely stored for the night—before finally adding nervously, "Anyway, we haven't got a change of clothes."

She had let him run this long-winded line of retreat with a rakish elevation of her eyebrows. "I haven't said 'no', have I, Richard?" she offered with a most tempting smile.

A large, sandy-haired man standing about ten paces away, looking quizzically in their direction stymied his reaction. Eva followed Richard's gaze and the colour was despatched from her face.

"You're right," she offered brusquely. "I don't know what came over me. My brother would never understand. We should really get going soon and—"

"Carrie, is that you?" The observer walked unsteadily towards their table.

Appearing not to have heard the question, she stood up and excused herself.

"Sorry to blunder in, old man. Edward's the name, but most of my friends—well, the few I have," he laughed gregariously, "call me Ted. I could have sworn that was Carrie, but they all look alike, these ones, I guess, don't they? The girl's an acquaintance?"

"A friend," Richard said, rising in his place. "Her name isn't Carrie and, if you wouldn't mind, we're about to leave," he said coolly, assessing the middle-aged intruder as abundant in drink.

The man stood aside a little and laughed again. "Whatever you say, old man. No offence intended and none taken. You know, after half a dozen whisky and sodas, I find," repeating himself, "they all look the same, as no doubt you do. Do you?" He didn't wait for any response, adding, "You're from down under, am I right?"

Although somewhat peeved by the disruption, Richard perceived that the stranger wasn't being deliberately rude. An even-tempered individual, he put aside his irritation by concluding the man was just a convivial drunk caught in a blurry moment of mistaken identity.

"Yes, from Queensland, but I don't work in this country. I'm the second engineer on a ship in port, the *Erakai*. We—"

"Ah, I know that one, old chap. I own rubber plantations all over Malaya and we've some cargo being loaded on your ship right at this moment, if I'm not wrong. She'd be tied up in Port Swettenham?"

Richard nodded, recognising that a planter enlisting the services of a ship on which he served to move his cargo couldn't be fobbed off indelicately, no matter his state of sobriety.

"I thought so. I keep a close eye on everything I export. I know most of the ships, too. Anyway, remember, it's Edward Faircrossman, Ted to you, a kindred spirit. And you're?" he asked, extending his hand.

"Kirnst, Richard Kirnst," the reply hesitant and effecting the impression that the interruption was ill-timed. He had wanted to keep his assignation with Eva private. "It's, ah, good to meet you."

"Oh, don't you worry, mate, as you Aussies say." Faircrossman presumed to read his mind and pointed to himself, "I'm the very model of discretion. I'll probably see you sometime. You're on the Far East run a bit, are you?" to which Richard assented. "Well, apologise to—what did you say her name was?"

"I didn't, but it's Eva."

Richard habitually adopted a courteous and reserved disposition when meeting someone for the first time. Being on the engineering side, he didn't have the contact that would inevitably occur between shippers and deck officers. If Faircrossman was who he said, and there was no real reason to dispute it, then he'd no doubt that this man would probably be well-known to the captain.

"Such a coincidence, an Aussie here! And that girl, so like the one I helped out in a bar somewhere." Richard bridled at the connotation, but there was no repressing his unsolicited companion. "Bizarre spithole, too, ah, 'Sitosa Samootin'. Can you imagine that? Anyway, just one celebratory drink before we beat our separate paths. Take a seat. You'll have a beer? All Aussies love the stuff," Faircrossman said, posing as an unimpeachable authority on everything.

Pulling over a nearby chair, they sat down together. A quick signal brought an immaculately attired waiter with whom he seemed familiar.

"Yes, okay, I guess, but just the one as I must be getting back. The ship's sailing early Monday and we've a long way to drive as we, ah, have to be at Kuala Lumpur by early this evening."

His discomfort abated as they spoke further. Richard became content to listen. Faircrossman talked of his love of Malaya and the way of life as being infinitely superior to the one he'd left in England, where he had worked as a solicitor. He spoke fondly of his son, doctor wife and home. "Next time you're in port we'll have to get together. I don't think Mrs Faircrossman has ever met an Aussie before, although her sister lives in Sydney. We'll make sure you're most welcome."

He avoided any further reference to Eva and, even when she returned to the table after a protracted absence, no conversation of any moment was steered in her direction. She circumvented eye contact by busying herself with objects in her handbag and stayed silent, apart from politely declining Faircrossman's offer of a drink.

"Just look at the time." Richard sensed her disquiet. "I'm afraid we'll have to go."

The two men shook hands.

"I'll be seeing you sometime, old boy. Ah, now, Eva? Well, goodbye. Have a lovely trip back. We'll definitely be in touch. Be sure to remember me to your captain."

"Yes, I will. We'll be back over here in a couple of months or so."

The return ferry ride became her haven, chin on upturned thumb in a pensive display. Once off, Eva walked to the car briskly. Her manner left him in no doubt that she was thankful to be leaving. There was no continuance of earlier affections; the interlude with the Englishman seeming to pervade the atmosphere and inhibiting the free-flowing conversation previously enjoyed. Finally, he asked if anything was wrong. She dismissed his enquiry and sighed. He deduced this might be symptomatic of a general let-down feeling, the product of her realisation that he would soon be gone and they'd be separated for some time. Then she transformed, slipping her head across into his lap.

It was late evening when they arrived at the ramshackle tenement that housed the café. Eva's tears as she threw her arms around him were genuine. They promised to write to each other. He insisted that she take some money and was impressed by her firm resistance to the idea, even to the extent of telling him not to ever think her friendship was about reward. Theirs would be no lingering parting as she pronounced, "Goodbye."

Once upstairs, she hardly had time to undo her hair before the door was opened without ceremony by the clearly put-out Nu. "Where have you been, Eva? You were supposed to be working tonight. We're so busy here. I'm very unhappy with your behaviour."

"You told me I can be with the foreigners. I'm just doing what you say for me to do. I've not slept with—"

"Now, Eva, I know you've seen the Australian sailor. I told you before, I don't like him. You said he works on a ship and I know everything about that ship and about him. You mustn't go further with this man. I have a very bad feeling he could be trouble for us."

"I'm not involved. He's just a friend and—"

"Eva, when we leave China, our whole family and our future depends on what we do here. You're to work where and when I tell you. If you want to see our mother and uncle killed, go your own way."

"You say this to me, Nu, and you know I'm not happy. But you say it so I'm under your control."

"Eva, I do it because I want to protect you from yourself. We keep our lives together and those of what are left of our family. Do you care for me and for them?" She sat down on the bed, head lowered. "I leave now, Eva, and in the future I expect you to obey me in all things."

She agreed not to see Richard again, but fortitude deserted her with his first communication, which she hid from Nu. Over more than six months they exchanged dozens of letters. When he read the one enclosing her photo with the inscription on its reverse side, *I love you. Always yours, forever, Eva*, he immediately reciprocated the sentiment.

A hitherto steadfast aim of attaining appointment as chief engineer was weakening as the predominant motivation in his life. Lonely nights and the vast, endless sea were taxing his reasoning. Years of ambition were being displaced by quick-fire infatuation. Yet to speak of it to shipmates would reveal a chink in his oft-made declarations of stoic resistance to feminine allure.

After the humdrum trip home and discharge of cargo in east-coast Australian capitals, there followed several voyages to New Zealand. Finally, he was on his way back to the Far East. The ship was expected in Port Swettenham about a week ahead of schedule. Richard deliberated as to whether he would let Eva know in advance of his earlier arrival.

For her, the letters had been an emollient diversion. She wanted the fantasy to continue and devised an elaborate scheme to prevent Nu detecting the letter-writing escapades. Then one fell into his custody after she had become careless. A frenetic search of her room and the café produced nothing. It didn't cross her mind that the misplaced item had anything to do with Nu's newly found munificence towards her.

*****

Captain Treacy was anxiously pacing his suite as Richard entered with the chief engineer, mate and second mate. A distinguished man with a full head of unparted wavy, grey hair, he was a master of conservative disposition who enjoyed unquestionable status among officers and crew alike. Richard had sailed with Treacy on several ships and his respect for him was limitless.

Appearing drawn, he motioned for the group to be seated. "The Japanese bombed Singapore early this morning and last night invaded north-eastern Malaya at Kota Bharu. Simultaneously, a large force hit the naval base at Pearl Harbour. This equates to war, gentlemen." He continued briskly. "The good news is that there'll be a substantial counterattack by British forces on the peninsula. The Japs aren't expected to get much of a toehold."

"What about commercial shipping," asked the chief engineer.

"Our agents instruct us to proceed with the current arrangements, but I'm hoping we'll be gone from here in seven days." Turning to the mate, he continued, "I'm assured that twelve-hour shifts are available, but we might do better. All of the ships will be vying for labour. It may be a while before round-the-clock shore gangs can be found. The situation will be monitored daily. Henceforth, *Erakai* has to be ready for sea on four hours' notice or shorter." Treacy was now directing his remarks to the chief and second engineer. "I know I can rely on the engineer officers to be in standby mode." They nodded. "Good."

Addressing the group generally, he advised, "This means unlimited discretionary excursions are curtailed. There'll be no exceptions. No person may absent himself for more than three hours and any breach of that rule will lead to all shore outings being cancelled. The mate and the second engineer will superintend leave."

In a voice heavy with augury, he added, "Gentlemen, this is a serious business. Lest there be any misunderstanding, if the ship has to sail, anyone breaching the curfew will be left behind and shouldn't expect sympathy for his folly. Are there any questions?"

"I have just one, Captain," said the second mate. "What if there's an air attack on the port and half a dozen men are ashore? Will we just put to sea immediately or wait for everyone to get back?"

"The primary targets are military ones, Willie, but all need to be aware of the risks entailed in straying too far from the ship."

Seeming to relax, Treacy continued. "The safety of the *Erakai* and its cargo are my prime concerns. Remaining in the port precinct guarantees every man will be back on board at the first sign of trouble. Three blasts of the horn will serve as a signal that we will put to sea within half an hour of its sounding."

An apprehensive silence followed as each looked to the others. The captain sensed the mood. "You're shocked? Well, stay shocked, though it's important to convey to the crew a sense of calm and conduct ourselves appropriately. All of you will be anxious to get back to Australia. Right," he said, rising to preclude further debate, "back to work and we'll meet again at this time tomorrow."

"That's laying it on the line," Richard observed as they walked down the stairway.

"What about your girl in KL? Won't you want to catch up?" asked O'Connell quietly.

Richard was not surprised by the question. Ribbed by the other for his secretive behaviour in going off to read his mail in private, he finally opened up as the two men entered his cabin. "I can't tell you how much I was looking forward to seeing her again. You'll keep it to yourself, won't you, mate?"

"Course I will, you silly bastard."

"The last letter from my end was when I told her I'd be back in a few weeks. I haven't heard anything since and there's no other way of contacting her. She'll be expecting me soon. I was going to make it a surprise."

"You can still do that. The old man said shore leave was restricted to three hours, so you'd have time to bring her back and put her up somewhere. Otherwise, there wouldn't be much more than a 'hello' and 'goodbye' and a smooch or two."

Richard sighed. "Little chance of getting her down here, I think. Just seeing her for half an hour would be a start."

"Well, prof, you know I'll cover for you and, either way, you've a bit of rank to pull on the rest of the engine room."

"I wouldn't do it. We're all in this together. The old man said the rules apply to officers and crew alike, but I appreciate the offer."

"Whatever, mate. Just thinking aloud." O'Connell rose to leave.

"As I say, Willie, if you can keep this thing between us. I'm a bit torn up, I hate to admit. She's unique, sort of thing, bright, mysterious, sexy. I'm hooked, I think. Whole new territory for me."

"Oh, come off it, she's Chinese, isn't she?"

The dismissive remark grated. "Is that a problem?"

O'Connell softened his tone. "Of course not, but can you trust her? Don't get me wrong, but some of these birds are convincing and turn out to be on the game. If you've doubts about anything now—"

Richard cut the other man short. "Thanks for the warning, Willie, but I'm a big boy and she's—well, I believe this one's kosher. Yeah, I do trust her."

"That's good, and I'm happy for you." O'Connell shook his head ruefully. "You're a bloody closed book for months and then it all tumbles out. 'Course you can rely on the old Paddy here. Bloody hell, a real seachange if ever there was one." A familiar voice boomed out. "There's the mate. I expect we're going to give the crew the good news and you'll want to do the same."

"Okay. See you after dinner."

Richard descended to the engine room, where he called the men together to inform them of the new regime. There were no whispers of disapproval at the limits on shore leave, the atmosphere more one of resignation. The fourth engineer, a twenty-year-old from Southampton, echoed the unspoken thoughts of some when he wished they were going home. The septuagenarian, Sid Coils, scowled at him. As senior greaser and oldest man aboard, he was accorded a reverence rarely seen among sailors. Longevity bred acceptance as well as considerable independence and, though respectful to a fault with Richard, he did not suffer junior engineers without haughty disdain.

The meeting broke up and Richard remained detached throughout the day's work. He'd hoped to have heard something from Eva. When no letter had come just prior to leaving Australia he'd been surprised, but when still nothing was waiting for him in Singapore, he was frustrated and disappointed. She had been a reliable and regular correspondent, and he had kept her apprised of the ship's ongoing destinations. After work finished for the day, he approved the list of personnel going ashore. He reminded those crew members of the captain's orders and the consequences of their breach. As evening came, there was still no word from her.

That night his mind was inundated, weighing the risks in courting a shoreside venture. He wondered if dangers would be posed to Eva in the event of Kuala Lumpur being overrun, recalling her cryptic references to the invasion of Nanking. She'd been vague in discussing the background of her flight from China. *Was there much more to it?* These issues he pondered, as midnight moved to one, two and, finally, three o'clock, with an elusive search for slumber. There had hardly been a breath of air in his cabin, where the fan had done little except keep the mosquitoes at bay. Able to stand it no longer, he rose and dressed, filled a pannikin and ascended to the bridge deck.

Save for the intermittent clanging of a turnbuckle against the foremast, it was eerily quiet since the cessation of cargo movements. Strong tea repaired his ragged nerves and the cool, slight breeze reinvigorated him. He paced the deck relentlessly, trying to determine what to do. He had arrived at a point where it was not simply about whether he would try to see Eva but when he should go.

Returning to his cabin, he found a note confirming the arrival of a dozen stevedores from Penang in two days. That would halve the loading time. He was unable to contemplate not seeing her on this trip and began to imagine that if the invasion toppled Kuala Lumpur they might never meet again. As a fragment of dawn peeped through his porthole, he could vacillate no longer. Saturday would be his last chance. Having resolved the predicament, his anxiety eased, and he turned in.

Three hours remained until his routine call. And as his head embraced the pillow, there Eva was, rapturous at his surprise appearance outside the café, evincing no limits upon her affection until a vulgar perturbation severed Richard's lifeline. It coincided with a familiar loud rap on his cabin door and the gravelly announcement from his number one greaser, Sid Coils, "Second Engineer, 0700."

Chapter 3

Horror in Nanking

Li Chin Ming's life changed forever when the Japanese Imperial Army fell on Nanking. Hers had been a childhood surrounded by a loving family. She had enjoyed a disciplined upbringing and, until the Emperor's soldiers went on an indiscriminate rampage and killing spree, could have expected to achieve almost anything.

Her parents ran a thriving produce and hardware enterprise in the commercial sector of the Chinese capital. Li Ming, her formidable father, was the innovative force who had reared the business since its inception. He started off travelling about on foot, pulling a large crate resembling a box trailer, the component parts of his mobile store acquired from the civic dump.

Within the space of three years, he was able to purchase a dilapidated shop in the heart of the city. At its rear, he fashioned a three-roomed residence where his young family lived and traded every day. The enterprise prospered. He acquired other business interests and achieved an important status in Nanking.

He raised two sons and Eva. The second son took after his father and fitted as his natural successor, but the eldest, Nu, was a great disappointment. Li could not abide stealing, and he agonised over how it was that Nu, not just once, had been caught abstracting money from the cash box.

Li's contact with English people and a quick wit had afforded him a jaunty conversance with their tongue. He and his wife, Wang, became acquainted with local British families. Friendships also formed between his children and theirs. They attended the same schools, where the teaching of English was mandatory. Being anxious to learn, by the age of sixteen his daughter had become fluent in that language. She delighted in reading passages out of classic novels to her parents. Eva was the child he cherished. Shy and dutiful, she worked for her parents from a very early age, yet managed to excel as a conscientious student now in her final year of high school.

By December 1937, the Japanese were encamped at the gates of Nanking. Amidst a furious bombardment, Li appreciated that nothing could withstand the onslaught. Some members of the European contingent, including German, American and English families, had assembled in a safety zone in the centre of the city established around factories owned by John Rabe, a German businessman with strong connections to the Japanese embassy and the Nazi Party. Through his offices, barrages, preparatory incursions and raids had deliberately avoided that area.

Rabe and his children had become known to Li and his family. As Li's stature grew, they sat together as members of the Nanking Chamber of Commerce. After Li consulted with Rabe, he made the decision to leave, opting for transport by boat up the Yangtze River to the relative safety of Chongqing, where he had family ties.

The twelfth of December saw pandemonium descend on Nanking. Roads were clogged and access to embarkation points problematic. Within the city's ancient walls, panic was ubiquitous. Many rushed towards the river with whatever they could carry, expectations high that boats would materialise to spirit them away.

The remnants of the Chinese army had disintegrated except for a few stray pockets of disciplined men. Others, boy soldiers barely fifteen, tore off their uniforms.

Wang, Eva and her brothers listened intently as Li said that evacuation was their only hope. He gave a small portion of money to his wife, lest they should be separated. On entering the street in the late afternoon, the family was swept up in a vast crowd. Arriving at the banks of the river, they joined thousands of others compressed into an area that would comfortably have held a few hundred. In that milieu, young children were separated from their parents and the old trampled underfoot.

Forcing their way along a narrow wharf, Li sought the vessel *Chung Wu*. He had sent on one of his servants earlier, possessed of the wherewithal to bribe the captain and thus ensure their priority in getting aboard. With a first-hand assessment of the chaos, Li concluded that his emissary was unlikely to have been able to undertake this task. Despite peering intently at every vessel, he could not find the *Chung Wu*. He scrambled towards anything that looked seaworthy, but no sooner was a junk moored alongside than it was overloaded.

Their position was increasingly untenable. Li was screaming to skippers that he would give anything to get passage, but his voice was lost amidst scores of others. In a normal situation, gold might have resonated, but now placement and luck were everything. Boats were cast off without being tied up. Men, women and children succumbed to the freezing water as leaky craft foundered.

Rifle shots cracked out at regular intervals and echoing in the distance was the roar of artillery. Above the din, the earsplitting engines of planes streaked overhead. Bombs began falling. Canon fire was smashing its way into metal and timber.

Li cried out to his family that it was no use; that they must get back to the shop to collect provisions and then go to the safety zone. As the group set off, bombing became intense. The crowd surged like waves in a confused sea driven by capricious gusts of wind, first one way and then the other.

An indiscriminate shoulder charge saw Eva parted from the family. She was stampeded in the opposite direction. Twisting from side-to-side, she tried to find them. Futilely screaming out their names and barely able to hear herself, she was hit by shockwaves from a tremendous explosion, throwing her several yards where she landed among concrete rubble as the strafing continued. What remained of the fleet motored upstream. Fires were consuming anything left afloat. Of the many who had been in the docks area when the bomb landed, she was one of the few alive.

Eva revived to the sound of salvos all around her. With natural light departing, as her eyes adjusted, the flashes from gun and mortar fire became more pronounced. Her head was throbbing and instinctively she began to rub her hands over her body in a search for injuries. Tracing with her forefinger a mass of congealed blood above the hairline, she felt a large oozing cut, surprised that it seemed numb rather than sore. A small piece of shrapnel had embedded itself in her scalp and she worked the fragment loose until it dropped out.

She could move her arms and legs and taking deep breaths was restorative. Eva stood up and walked a few paces, stooping and then crouching in fear. A spattering of shots sounding ever closer caused her to lie flat on the ground momentarily but, as wits took command, she became aware of her situation. A surrealistic montage surrounded her, with dead and broken bodies strewn about like refuse.

The bombardment had wrought devastation everywhere she looked. Gaping holes and shattered beams replaced the wharf decking. All that remained intact were the concrete pylons sunk into the mud at the edge of the river. A number of stout wooden bearers were also evident, a few lengths hanging precariously at acute angles. Perhaps her family would materialise if she wished it for long enough. As the minutes passed with eyes closed, nothing happened. Daring to blink, she realised the prospects of finding them were remote.

Recovering her senses further and assembling what strength endured, she made for a large warehouse. Most of the structure had been obliterated, but the flooring was secure, and she managed to find a water tank that had several bullet holes around its circumference. She lay on her back, mouth open, and swallowed the cool liquid as it cascaded across her face and head.

Tearing a piece of fabric from the hem of her dress and allowing it to become soaked. Eva dabbed at the cut, erasing the dried blood and trembling as she did so. She held the cloth to her head for some time, rinsing it at intervals, until the wound sealed itself. Fashioning a makeshift bandage by tying it under her chin and around the top of her head, she presented a pitiful appearance. With a sedulous application of water and blind swishing, she managed to clean herself up. The whole process took about twenty minutes, time well spent as it made a considerable difference to her spirits. The throbbing in her head had eased, strength was returning, and her mind was able to plan a course of action. Eva remembered what her father had said about getting to the Rabe safety zone. That refuge was several miles away.

Gunfire persisted and mortars exploded sporadically. There were no signs of life, other than a cat howling nearby. It came closer and began to lick at the water on the ground. She held it to her and whispered girlishly as her thoughts returned to finding her parents and brothers. Footsteps and gruff voices in a strange tongue closed, spooking the cat. It wriggled free, screeched and darted off, enlivening Eva's instincts for survival. There were few places to hide.

She crept towards the intact rear of the warehouse, searching for a way out. The windows were too high and there was nothing on which to stand. In a far corner she spied a door slightly ajar. This offered the only chance of escape. Embarking on a run, she heard shouts but ignored them, wrenching at the door and just making it through. A Japanese officer sprang, catching her around the neck and rendering her immobile. She was dragged back into the warehouse where two other soldiers seized her.

With one on each side holding her arms and the officer thrusting a gun into her back, Eva was frogmarched towards a wooden pallet. Roughly wheeled around, she was pushed backwards onto it, arms held beside her body, wrists tied down and underpants ripped off. Each leg was spread and lashed at the ankles. Her terror was now palpable as she pleaded to be spared.

Rank claimed precedence. Piercing screams followed the splitting of each adjacent orifice. "Chinese slut, we cut off your head."

Her ankles were untied for the next in line. She was punched in the face to quell further resistance and knees were forced onto her chest. Excruciating pain followed another variant of the defilement. At completion and laughing hideously, he yelled, "Banzai". One of the cords securing a wrist had worked loose and intuitively she slid her hand down to feel a sticky substance oozing from the inside of her buttocks. There would be no respite as Eva was set upon again. Cries were extinguished by a second blow, her body inert to the third soldier. After he had finished, the officer used a splintered broom-handle to symbolise the consequences attending resistance.

It was the early hours of the morning when Eva woke. Her head was battered and swollen, one eye almost closed over. She could just open her mouth. There were lacerations and bruises all over her body, but she sensed that no soul was near her. Perceiving a bright sliver of moon, she began the quest for recovery by imagining a shell had blown a hole in the roof, scattering debris on top of her and leading to a raft of injuries. She could wriggle her toes. Each finger was flexed, and Eva could turn her head from side-to-side. *Thank God*, she thought, *I'm not paralysed.*

When she tried to move her legs, a searing pain rose from her groin. She dared not twist again and recalled an inferno of piercing engines, blasts, bodies, a shrieking cat, running and then loud groans. Although one hand was free, she could not move the other. It was when she felt it secured by rope that a terrible dread enveloped her. *Bombs had not fashioned knots.* She determined to purge any further recollections.

Untying the rope earned another excruciating spasm. She detected an object protruding from her lower body. Each time she tried to sit up, the pain forced her down. Somehow the thing had to be removed. Incrementally, she inched up onto her elbows and lifted one leg so the back of her heel rested on the handle. With her foot pressing downward, she pushed. At the same time, she moved her pelvis so as to detach herself from it and almost passed out. She was determined not to make a sound, tearing at the remnants of the blouse until her lips were bleached.

Blood was splattered on her dress and smeared all over her legs. An indomitable will to live inoculated Eva as she mentally retraced her steps prior to slaking her thirst. Reuniting with her parents became a priority and she prayed they had escaped from this befouled precinct.

Adjusting her tattered clothing, Eva eased off the pallet, grimacing with every action. Amongst the rubble, she had located a stout piece of steel rod with one end bent. It was long enough to hold and maintain her balance. Gradually she attempted to stand, resting halfway and then trying to straighten her knees. With consummate effort she assumed her feet and began to shuffle along, one foot at a time. In the hour that followed, the miracle was that she had taken herself beyond sight of where she had lain. She persisted for another hundred yards, but knew she had to go faster if there was any prospect of making it to town before daylight.

At this point Eva reasoned that the chances of survival might be increased if both in appearance and odour she became so repulsive as would deter any interest in her. Scraping some evil-smelling slime from the gutter, she rubbed it over much of her body using the ragged bandage and then retied it leaving one eye visible.

Thereafter she advanced gingerly. Isolated raindrops were the prelude to a steady downpour. It was the first moisture in her mouth since she had regained consciousness and the drenching with its bitter coldness anaesthetised the pain. Inexorably, traction was gained by putting all adversity out of mind, her body responding better as she closed on the centre of the city.

The few shadows flirting with the backstreets moved around in a plethora of directions. She was oblivious. Arriving opposite her father's store, she rested no more than a minute before angling her way across the road to the open front doors. Even in the darkness, the surroundings were familiar to her, save the emptiness of the place. Almost everything, including the fittings, had been looted. She found her way to an area at the rear above the basement and called out in a pleading voice. Silence was the only return.

Needing to relieve herself, she squatted down, but the agony spearing up from between her legs caused her to overbalance. By immense self-control, she stopped herself from screaming. She needed help and there was none here. The Rabe compound was the last chance she had.

*****

Eva's mother and Nu had managed to escape the inferno by the river with minor injuries. Wang sobbed when she was informed that they were the only members of the family to have arrived. She recounted to Rabe that her husband, other son and daughter were separated in the crush and carnage within the dockyards. Her sobs moved Rabe to place his arm around her shoulders and promote some hope.

"I'll check on this personally. The moment I hear anything you'll be advised, Madam Wang. People are streaming in all the time. My staff and I will look out for them."

"Eva taken before bombing properly. She come here soon, Mr Rabe?"

"I know her, Madam. Do not despair," he said.

Though fully occupied in its management as the safety zone's director, Rabe took time to do all he could to establish the whereabouts of his friend and colleague. He went throughout the compound and walked the perimeter, but the search proved fruitless. Then he ventured further in his black Mercedes-Benz flying the swastika. His was a distinctive presence.

Realising the task was beyond him, Rabe returned disconsolate and readied himself to deliver the bad news. Near to his gate, he observed a number of soldiers involved in a fracas reminiscent of many others he had seen. He could see a young woman, illuminated by the lights of an army truck. She had been cornered and was the subject of much sport. He stopped the car and pulled out his pistol, discharging three volleys skywards.

The group recognised the vehicle and dispersed. The girl was lying on the ground, her lower body uncovered, the upper barely so. As Rabe knelt to raise her, he heard a faint cry, but the battered face he held was far removed from the one he had seen not more than a week ago. "Eva Li, is it you?" His voice was replete with apprehension.

"Yes, Mr Rabe," she whispered, before passing out.

She had the best of medical care and recovered remarkably well. In the first few weeks of her confinement after discharge from the infirmary, when trying to get her mind back into some sort of order, she began thinking of the remnants of her family and of its prospects. Their father gone, along with the disintegration of his business, the future was perilous.

Hitherto, Eva's own ambitions had never been confined to China. Through sheer application and hard work, with encouragement from Li, she had been looking to study history and the classics in either America or England. Li had received favourable responses to enquiries about overseas education and was pleased to fund advanced studies without hesitation.

Her preference was Oxford University, where she longed for tutelage with C. S. Lewis. One of the greatest thrills of her life was receiving his letter. She had written in a moment of impulsivity after reading *The Allegory of Love*. Not only favoured with a polite response, she had been asked about her homeland and encouraged to read selected works of his recommendation. This advice was followed enthusiastically. She loved the Brontë sisters, Thackeray, Dickens and G. K. Chesterton, consuming every jotting of theirs that she could find.

A romantic attachment to the character of Mr Rochester had led her to fantasise that one day, after securing a higher degree, she might meet an older, landed gentleman and marry much later in life than all of her friends, have children—at least one—and become an English country lady who would tutor the boys and girls of rich parents. Now these notions had vanished, leaving besmirched memories.

She had become not just damaged goods, but barren. A doctor, called to perform a curette when she miscarried some months after arriving at the safety zone, told her that any notion of having children was now gone. Unable to speak the truth of what had occurred to her disaffected mother, she invented a boyfriend. Horrified by this revelation, Wang never ceased reminding her of the shame she had occasioned the family. In her mother's eyes, unchaste activities meant relations between them would never be the same. Eva was told that if her father had known she would have been disowned. The chances of finding a husband were ruined. No young man would want a woman who could not bear children, especially if the cause was carnality.

Though unable to let go of a faint hope that her father and other brother might have survived, she did have Nu and her uncle. Eva would devote herself to doing anything for the family in the plaintive belief that they might come to love her again.

Deep down she felt a profound sense of loss without her father's emotional support and wise counsel. He had always been there to listen. She would have told him everything and he could have helped her recover. Now little teasing voices inside made mischief and had opened her to perverse thoughts. She became indifferent to the clandestine activities and deviousness in which Nu, as the wayward sibling, was very much a willing participant.

He had begun to provide scraps of information to the Japanese about some of the matters that were occurring inside the safety zone in return for modest consideration. It was a man called Devis who formally recruited Nu and offered what he thought would be the perfect solution to the present impasse confronting the family. The proposal was that he would provide Nu with enough money to buy a shop in Kuala Lumpur. This would also be good cover for information-gathering.

Nu introduced Eva to Devis. With her cooperation, he could continue to assist the family in relocating from Nanking to Shanghai. Devis was most taken with this young woman, intuiting her usefulness. With subtle grooming, Eva could be eased into furthering their nefarious activities. She must do the bidding of her eldest male sibling. Devis had been assured by Nu that compliance was guaranteed—a younger sister could never question the first-born brother.

This was a desirable outcome. The family would be protected, and Shanghai was seen as safe. For Eva, leaving the Nanking horror behind loomed as the only means of retaining a semblance of purpose in her life.

Chapter 4

Britisher in khaki

Sleep had overtaken the gargantuan figure sprawled on the bed beside her. Experience of the last nine months had demonstrated that liquor and sex usually, though not without exception in that order, transformed the bullet-headed, pugnacious temper into a snoring heap.

She surveyed him with a mixture of resignation and contempt but reserved a filtrate of fear that contained any outward show for the British army captain in case he was feigning sleep. Unpredictable, he could suddenly emerge from an apparent alcoholic stupor and rain slaps on her. "Sorry" invariably followed, but the cycle never altered. It was his psychosis after all. Eva would let it go and forgive him.

How, she often asked herself, could it be that the likes of this individual had ever found his way into her life? Had she fallen so low that nothing perturbed her when it came to matters of self-worth? But Patrick Heenan was someone to whom she and Nu were in great debt. Nu had never left her in doubt that they owed their affluence to Devis, and now this man because of his connections. It did not stop there. The family needed ongoing sustenance and protection.

As Nu reminded her, "You must, for Mama's sake, show respect to Mister Heenan."

A once enquiring, active intellect had given way to resignation. Duty to her family was the last pillar of honour she possessed.

Eva had known Heenan for about a year since meeting him one day at the café where she lived and worked. There was something dashing about him—a British officer, the uniform, the rank, his bearing—that exuded singular confidence and disguised all other shortcomings. Her brother's intimate acquaintanceship with him had rapidly progressed to a combination of the bizarre and the stealthy. Heenan could show up at the oddest times. He and Nu would go into a room where the door would be shut for hours. Just what they talked about, Eva could only surmise.

Initially she felt Heenan viewed her with suspicion, gesturing to Nu that he didn't want her about when matters demanded immediate attention. Her role was to ensure hot food and drink was laid on before she was contemptuously dismissed. Yet, she mistook the seedy eyes that followed her, much as a serpent sizes up its prey, as nothing more than mere curiosity and was flattered.

Nu regarded this relationship and its outcomes as one of especial economic significance. On every occasion after these visits, he was infused with a spirit of fiscal liberality. His gifts to her were accompanied by the excuse that he and 'Pat' appreciated the efforts she took in making him feel comfortable. Eva accepted Nu's rationale.

One night there was an incident that irrevocably altered relations between them. Nu informed her that the captain would be coming to the restaurant for a special meeting and she must be discreet about it taking place. He arrived later than expected, after Eva had retired. She awoke to the sounds of raised voices in the street. In an instant, Nu was in her room, a flushed and agitated Heenan behind him, pistol in hand pointing directly at her sibling's back.

"What are you doing here? Nu, you must get out and—" Eva broke off as she caught a glimpse of the weapon.

"Shut up, Eva," said Heenan. "You'll do as I say, or you won't live to see sunlight. Take your clothes off and get back into bed." She froze before he roared, "Do it now or he'll be shot!"

The noise outside grew louder and there were shouts. Nu went over to the window and confirmed the presence of half a dozen soldiers. A series of raps on the front door followed.

"Now listen. I've been here all night, as your brother will confirm. You are my fiancée, Eva, and that's why I visit.

We're in love and are to be married. Nu wants you to say that, don't you, Nu?"

Eva's eyes fixed on her brother and there was no dissent. "You see, we have this understanding. I'll tell you all about it after these bastards come up and are satisfied. Now, move over and put your arms around me. Nu, go and see to all that knocking, damn you. There might be enough time to offer proof of what will become a nice little thing between us."

Like a rock spider, Heenan enveloped her in his immense frame. Eva's eyes flashed in despair at Nu, who turned away and attended to the incessant commotion. Heenan easily overcame her uncertain efforts at resistance. On cue, several military police burst into the room with torches and revolvers drawn, with one officer shining a flashlight.

"What the bloody hell's going on here?" thundered the captain, rolling off Eva and regaining his feet with enterprising agility. His penis left no doubt as to its recent disposition. She covered herself with a sheet.

"I would like you to get dressed, ah, um, sir, immediately. Colonel Moore wants to speak with you," an agitated lieutenant stumbled.

The request was ignored. "I repeat; what in god's name are you doing here? You've no right to barge in like this? Do you know who I am? Heenan's the name, Captain Heenan, and this is my fiancée. I'm not AWOL. Do I need to account for my every move, even this one, or am I able to see the woman I love when I can in my own time?" he demanded.

"Sir, I have my orders. The owner of this place has been under surveillance. And your coming here—"

"Of course I've been coming here. Haven't I, Eva?"

She acquiesced with a nod and a steady glance at the young officer.

"This is absolute nonsense. Tell them, Eva, tell them where we stand."

She adopted a deliberate simplicity of language. "It true, sir. Captain Patrick come here see me. We love together. My brother good man and us hate Japanese. They kill my father and we escape Nanking to Malaya. Patrick, he help my brother and me. Are you saying we bad traitors?"

Her manner was convincing, and it was clear from the officer's demeanour that it resonated with him. "Miss, I didn't mention the Japanese though I'm appreciative you did. It's not for me to debate with you what should be happening. This is a matter for headquarters to determine and, in the meantime, I will probably have to take you, along with your brother, into custody."

Heenan sensed the officer's resolve was waning. Knowing that an individual interrogation of Eva and Nu could be his undoing, he opted for bravado.

"I'll go anywhere you like, Lieutenant. They won't be. You've got your bloody wires crossed somehow, but I cannot allow you to draw these innocent Chinese people into any of your fantastic games. You know they despise the Japanese. Have you any understanding of the bloody rape of Nanking? And what of it that I've been coming here? The perfectly reasonable and proper explanation for my presence you've heard. Take me back and I'll front the colonel right now. These people shall remain. You can see what sort of a business this is. Barely making ends meet. I give you my word they'll stay put and, after I've met the colonel, I'm sure that's where you'll leave them, unhindered by this arrant nonsense."

The lieutenant cleared his throat. Encouraged to conclude he had gained the ascendancy, Heenan quickly dressed. Towering over the younger man and outranking him, he leaned uncomfortably close to the lieutenant's face. His dictates weren't going to be countermanded at that juncture.

"We'll see the colonel, sir. I would ask you to tell your, ah, fiancée here that if she and her brother attempt to leave the café, they'll be arrested. Two of my men are being detailed to remain on guard. Goodnight, Miss."

Heenan made an ostentatious display of farewelling Eva with much kissing and soothing. Acting like a ringmaster taking in thundering applause from a sellout crowd at a circus he mused, *The colonel will be a cinch after this dolt.*

Eva digested the import of the evening's events without the need to interrogate her sibling. She had suspected all along that Nu and the British officer had more in common than the affairs of ordinary trading and bartering or a regular session of mahjong. To have enquired further might have risked her brother's displeasure.

Following the visit by the military police, the picture was clear. Their increased liquidity wasn't accidental. The cafe had achieved an appreciable growth in patronage, but a greater number of questionable characters lacking even a transient interest in the menu now often habituated the premises. Their visit was accommodated by the exchange of furtive conversation and items in crumpled envelopes.

It was these thoughts that predominated rather than her surrender after a self-imposed troth never to allow any man to go near her again. Her action was made easier because Heenan was English became the rationalisation. When they met, Heenan was surly but not unkind. Eva developed a mild infatuation from afar in a dreamy fashion when she perceived that he had begun to take notice of her.

After calm had returned, she met Nu in his room. His agitation was palpable, as he stubbed out his fourth cigarette in not many more minutes since Heenan's departure.

"Eva," he whispered in Mandarin, "whatever you do, speak nothing about this. You and the captain are here because he's your fiancé. I only see him because he knows you. Do you understand?"

"Yes, but what is—"

"Don't ask questions. This is a matter of my life. If anything comes out, I'll be killed. He's been very good to me—to us. Do you think all of these things have come here in the last twelve months by accident?"

"Nu, you're my brother and I trust you. But I'm worried about your safety. Are you in danger from someone else?"

"I'm telling you what we've got with the captain is okay, provided we keep it to ourselves. The moment we start talking, there will be serious trouble," he replied.

"But what *are* you doing and why are you meeting with him? The authorities suspect something is wrong and that's the reason they came."

"We must obey Pat and stay here until he contacts us. That's what we do."

"But, Nu, you're not yourself, looking so worried. I've never seen you like this since we left Nanking."

Nu fumbled for another cigarette, poured a liberal quantity of whisky and downed it neat. He motioned for her to sit on the bed and pulled a chair from the table on the other side of the simply furnished room. He leant close to her and whispered, "He pays me for things," placing his forefinger across her lips as she was about to ask him the nature of the dealings. "It doesn't matter what, but it's all secret for his job. He pays me well and is a friend of Devis."

"So all the people who have been coming and going, who are they?"

"Eva, don't. They're friends, and the more I give Pat, the more comes to me. Understand? You must trust me as your older brother and keep being friendly to the captain. He likes you and has told me so and wants to marry you. An English husband's good. Now go back to bed and get some sleep. I think he'll be back here to see us soon."

"How can you just push this aside knowing I was forced to give myself to the first man I've ever known?"

"You and I know that's untrue, Eva. You've been a wicked girl and shamed the family. We couldn't have stayed in Nanking because all the people say it was wrong about what you did."

She began to cry and wanted to tell him it was all made up. But it was too late. He would never believe her. Eva had become enmeshed in their underhanded dealings, and as a beneficiary too. As regards the Englishman, they would surely marry after what had happened in that bed. At this point, she rationalised that Heenan was the only chance of a life that could expunge all that had gone before, provide for a fractured family and afford her security.

*****

Patrick Heenan, solid, well-built, handsome and of slightly dark complexion, was commissioned in 1935 as a second lieutenant and placed on the unattached list of the Indian Army, whose officers were predominantly British. Here was a man who courted trouble from the beginning of his service. Shunned by most who encountered him, he was aggressive, a sponger, a womaniser, a bully and sometimes an outright public drunk. If he had a redeeming characteristic, it was an indomitable commitment to protecting the underdog, earning him popularity among the Indian ranks.

One reason for his ostracisation was a feeling among his contemporaries that he had a touch of the 'tar-brush', which held him up to whisperings of the basest kind. There may have been an element of truth in that perception, but his thuggish behaviour was deserving of condign censure.

It was in India that Ashton Ali Devis recruited Heenan after an attenuated watching brief. His mission was to identify and ingratiate himself with susceptible army personnel who could become useful to Japanese expansionist goals. Devis would be the link between his masters and Heenan. In the former lawyer and moneylender of sharp and usurious practice lurked a feverish manipulator belying a spindly frame and tepid appearance.

All of these characteristics were utilised in his target's case to avert Heenan's dishonourable discharge following a fracas in which a street vendor died. Witnesses vanished without trace. Police interest in locating them abated. Disbursement of consideration to pervert the course of justice was suspected but could not be verified. Heenan owed him and was not allowed to forget the ransom that was paid, nor the risks incurred. And just often enough to alert a big-noter like Heenan to the power his handler could exercise, a switch would flick and a hint emerge of something diabolical occurring to any soul who might contemplate crossing him.

Devis was the only person who commanded Heenan's respect. His nationality, Heenan couldn't discern. Outwardly he appeared a combination of Asiatic, Indian and European. His speech was accented in the subcontinental brogue, but his range of vocabulary stamped him as someone accomplished in English.

Past favours aside, by playing on Heenan's displeasure with the army, his giant ego and making liberal offers of money—'untied grants' as he preferred to call them—Devis had found a man who would be very useful. To transform almost overnight from disaffected officer to traitor was not the leap Devis had anticipated. Thereafter Heenan was managed skillfully, cradled at times, then shaken roughly as if a sudden regression into infancy needed exorcising.

Under watchful tutelage, Heenan grew into the job, a sinecure he came to relish, fulfilling a latent desire to be treated as important and integral to a military power. He took to the clandestine operations, the extra money and prestige that went with it, all of which were necessary to augment a profligate lifestyle.

*****

Heenan's meeting with Colonel Moore that night was a civilised affair after explanations were proffered. Moore was of the cut more at home at gin and tonic time than in dealing with matters of this kind. He had also become aware of several unauthorised trips by Heenan into Thailand but overlooked them, deciding that the best way of dealing with the problem was to shift him sideways. He was made an intelligence staff officer and posted to a secret unit that liaised between the Army and the RAF. The new position was based at Alor Star in northern Malaya, but there would be a period of training involved before he took up the posting.

Six hours after placating Moore and enduring a further de-briefing, Heenan arrived back at the café. Over the next ninety minutes he was bolted up in Nu's room. As they emerged, he took a late breakfast downstairs and contemplated a nervous-looking Eva as she waited on them.

After he left, Eva's anxiety did not abate. "What's going to happen now, Nu?"

"We'll continue to work with the captain and, because you must help me, too, the rewards will be much greater."

"But what does he want me to do, my brother? Who's it for? The Japanese or who else? I need to know."

"The less we speak of things the better. You're lucky he wants you to be his fiancée. I said you'd agree. So be nice to him and keep it all inside. There's information associated with the work he does for the army. Movements of ships and what cargoes they carry are important to find out. Your English will help you get to know local British people. The more we give him, the better our reward, and we can send money to the family. But we cannot be caught, for the penalty could be death."

"You mean he's a spy? That's treason. We cannot do it. We mustn't. I won't." She became hysterical, shaking her head and waving her arms around.

Nu seized her. "For the love of me and your mother, you will do it without question. Anyway, you're now seen to be involved. Police might still be watching this place even though those two have now gone. Pat will not meet with us here again. He wants you to work in a club in Kuala Lumpur where you can see each other at least once a week. You must," he paused insinuatingly, "get on with European men at the club. I will give you a sealed packet for him. What he gives back, you'll deliver to me. You're not to look at anything. You know what I've done for you and how I saved the family. It's your turn now to obey your older brother, as our mother said when we left her and uncle in China."

She recalled her mother's words and how she elevated Nu over the others when they were young, forgiving his indiscretions and saving him from Li's discipline. What had been sown by these felicitations towards her favoured son was a sibling without a skerrick of conscience and, absent his father, was unrestrained.

*****

The first three days of the Japanese invasion confirmed the worst fears that the British government held but didn't openly acknowledge. Singapore and Malaya were facing potential disaster. Ceding the airfield at Kota Bharu proved to be an enormous fillip to the campaign, already ahead of schedule and exceeding preliminary forecasts.

Soon after hostilities commenced, the British Navy intended a bold response amassing a naval flotilla titled, "Force Z". Accompanied by three destroyers, the almost-new *Prince of Wales* and recently modernised *Repulse* sailed from Singapore. Farewelled amid huge fanfare and general acclaim, it became a demonstration to the world that Britain would not stand idly by and watch its Far Eastern empire plundered. Devoid of any strategic objective, the convoy proceeded up the eastern coast of Malaya until advised the Japanese fleet was closing. Orders were despatched to oppose the enemy's progress and destroy their ships. Remote from that goal, just after midday on the tenth of December, Japanese aircraft attacked. Lacking any cover, within an hour both battleships and one of the destroyers lay on the sea bed.

Chapter 5

Duties and machinations

T he fate of the British battleships soon found its way
to the officer's saloon on the *Erakai*. In a domain
where rumour thrived, initial disbelief turned to
a quiet prayer for the hundreds of sailors who perished.
Some put the loss down to poor strategic planning, often
the concomitant of naval disasters. Others, more perceptively, wondered how ships of that size and disposition
could have been sunk by forces regarded as inferior.

Meanwhile, cargo movements were dragging on
interminably. When the labourers from Penang did not
materialise, deck and engine room crew volunteered to
work on the gantries. In considering the gesture, Captain
Treacy was circumspect.

"This could serve to alienate the existing wharf workers
and we don't want that." The offer was politely sidestepped,
albeit with gratitude.

As each idle hour passed, so the desire to get the ship
loaded and at sea pervaded the atmosphere of the smoke-
room where the full complement of officers had assembled
to meet with the captain. It was soon apparent that there
were no further updates from the ship's agents.

"We need to sit tight for the moment, I regret to say,"
offered the master. "They have been informed that there's
no reason to think an attack will be launched against
merchant shipping here, and Penang remains untouched.
Of course, that could change. Is there anything further on
the labour situation?"

"Yes, there is," spoke the mate. "On the thirteenth another
gang will start and we'll be able to work the gear from six

until two in the morning. That gives an estimated time of departure on the sixteenth or seventeeth at the latest."

Treacy looked at Richard. "And maintenance is so up to date even the engineer officers have taken to polishing brass, Richard?" chirped the captain with a roguish smile.

"Not quite, sir. There'll be a revolution if anyone stepped into Siddie Coils territory. He spurns every negative report doing the rounds as 'old hens' gossip', referring *ad infinitem* to his Great War exploits in a lifeboat. We never tire of it."

"That man's one of those rare treasures the sea throws up. I've lost count of the number of times we've sailed together. He once fixed me with a cockatoo eye when I asked him not to call me 'sir' and delivered a lecture about the pecking order. Alright then, we've less than a week to go. Keep your spirits up. The sooner the *Erakai's* hatches are battened down and we're on our way to Australia, the better."

Saturday was Richard's opportunity. He planned to take the six-thirty evening train to Kuala Lumpur and return on the eight forty-five. A voice telling him to state his case to the captain seeking tacit approval for his absence was resisted. Fearing a rejection and determined to make contact with Eva, he banished every competing consideration.

O'Connell wouldn't be acquainted with his intentions either. When he made up his mind, Richard was imbued with a myopic drive to follow a decision through.

His powers of reasoning weren't assisted by the puzzling absence of contact from Eva, which had him bordering on fantasy. He began indulging images of appearing at her window just in time to prevent some calamity, whereupon she would fall into his arms like a breathless damsel craving her Prince.

The day of his departure arrived with Coils sensing that something was amiss when Richard remained below after the men had finished. An offer to assist was met with an offhand response.

"I don't expect any of my men to work beyond twelve o'clock, Number One."

"Right you are, Second," Coils replied, cocking an upward eye. Too weathered a man to mistake his station, he left him bent over with a torch examining the bilges.

*****

For the first time in her life, Eva had been treated like a lady, and she began to believe that some men were capable of bestowing unconditional love rather than simply viewing her as flesh to use and discard.

Hardening during her time in Malaya, she could switch to playing the innocent girl without demur. Eva had acquired sexual guile. Richard was a novice and she had no qualms about exploiting the ascendancy. His letters evinced naivety in elevating her as a project. He could *help, encourage and make my Eva happy forever*, his impassioned hand wrote, and Richard wanted to take her *out of the lot* into which she'd been dumped. In an ironic way, it was bitterly amusing. When conscience pricked her, this opportunistic trait was the one she least embraced, yet an instinct for survival had become finely honed.

Eva assumed an entitlement to a relationship with Richard, though she would adhere to all filial requirements for just a little longer. Over time the situation would change, as everything did, leaving her free to pursue a future as near to the one she envisaged being rightly hers.

Penang propelled her back to reality, as did Nu's reprimands, recalling the duties she had promised to undertake. Edward Faircrossman's blundering into these artifices shook her. But with Richard's gullibility and the Englishman's intoxication, she retained a hope that not all had been lost. The subsequent stream of correspondence bore out her conclusion that things between them had not merely been unaffected but strengthened.

Byzantine imaginings led to a belief that Heenan was tiring of their relationship. He had always played the field if it suited him. When she heard about his liaison with an expatriate white woman, Eva wasn't perturbed, yet remained cognisant of the standard for the gander being different from that of its playmate. She daren't admit any serious involvement with another man should Heenan tax her.

His distractions afforded her more scope to focus on the prospect of life with a man she could really care about and who might take her away from a succession of dissolute encounters, reprieve from which had seemed a forlorn hope. And Richard would never know of that life, made easier by the fact that he was at sea so much.

Underhanded this was, but her existence and that of the Li family remained at stake. Eva thought back to six months earlier when she and Richard journeyed to Georgetown and their encounter with the planter and how she had then teetered on exposure. If Richard truly discovered her duplicity it would be disheartening, but basic survival instincts would re-engage, and life couldn't be much worse than it was under her brother's roof.

And, if the truth should emerge, what of Richard's feelings? She didn't deign to spend much time thinking about it. He had everything in front of him and aspired to greater heights. A seaman after all, she knew that breed, too. He would toughen up from the experience, not that she wished him any ill will. Eva wanted to believe she could offer Richard experiences he had never previously found.

Then the letters stopped. She wondered whether something was wrong. The answer came the day after the *Erakai* had sailed from Singapore. The eagerly awaited article flapped airily from the tips of her fingers, so unlike the bulky thickness to which she was accustomed from prior correspondence. Resignation swept over her as she waited a moment before tearing it open. There was one line on a scrap of paper smeared with grease saying Richard could no longer see her. Disavowal of unfailing love returned with neither reasons nor regret. It prompted her to make the link between the Faircrossman affair and a more considered assessment of her domestic circumstances. That he couldn't even take a moment to clean his hands before he wrote spoke much of his real feelings.

Out of view, Nu surveyed his sister as she took in the contents. The forger's work deserved a bonus.

*****

The *Erakai's* bow pointed seaward from the narrow stretch of the river harbouring the ships berthed at Port Swettenham. In his cabin, Richard, having foregone dinner, dressed for his trip ashore and paused to look through the porthole. Vestiges of light formed a sharp line of quicksilver circumnavigating a vast inky bank of cloud threading its way to join with an equally dark mass gathering from the north-east, now sparking with ominous flashes of lightning.

Like a schoolboy playing truant after the lunch break, Richard made a furtive departure. Even if he had been seen by the captain, no order to halt and explain himself would issue. But in adopting such stealth, the belief that he had become the sinner tore at his conscience.

The rain lightened soon after he exited the gates. The railway station was a good ten-minute walk away. He didn't dawdle, believing rightly, as he found his way to the only seat, that the evening train to Kuala Lumpur would be crowded with workers going home after their shift. A deep sigh was more an expression of relief that he had parted from the ship without detection. Fatigue from working all day was supplanted by expectation. He could only envisage the supple body, her lips warmly engaging his, and the joy of a surprise reunion after so long apart. Time was against very much more unless he could persuade Eva to come back to Swettenham, perhaps even sneak her on board. Bolstered by his recent escapade, the chance of its unobserved accomplishment grew stronger the further he travelled. *Why not give it a go?* he thought.

When he arrived outside, there were red and blue lights flashing the words 'Nu's Café' above the entrance. A few expectant rickshaw and pedicab vendors lounged about, and more materialsed, as he paid off the taxi. Prosperity abounded, an altogether different scene from when he was last there.

Inside was busy, too. The old woman who guarded the cash register was nowhere in sight, nor was Eva. Some time elapsed before a teenage waitress found him a table. There were few places in the noisy, crowded area, and his was the only spare table. It was long, and a quartet of

Asian and Malay men occupied its far end, conversing in a cocktail of languages.

Taking in the surroundings seemed to accentuate the disappointment he felt by Eva's apparent absence. The waitress returned, inviting an order for a meal, but he declined. He asked for a soda water and enquired if Eva was around. The girl seemed to hesitate, and he repeated, "Eva, you know her?" She nodded. "Is she working here tonight, in the café?"

"Not working café here, Eva at Sitosa Samootin club. Eva has—"

She whirred around to a reproving call and disappeared.

Richard sourced the voice and his eyes met Nu's, who was in no mood to return the gesture of greeting. This didn't deter the upbeat manner of Richard's approach.

"Hello, Nu. I trust you're well." His geniality made no impression. "I've only a little time and was hoping to speak to Eva."

Nu's surprise was evident. His face turned ugly and he fidgeted with a water jug. Richard remembered Nu was not a nimble thinker. He began with a rush of words. "She not here tonight, gone other job and too late finish. Cannot see. I tell her tomorrow."

Richard's expression remained inscrutable. "What do you mean, Nu?" He said the name in a brusque tone. "She'll not be back at all? You won't be picking her up?"

"Ah, no," Nu replied hesitantly. "She come by taxi herself. Café too busy for me." *Transparent fudging*, Richard thought, but he stymied his irritation. "I'm sure she won't mind if I drop in at the other place to say hello. I haven't seen her for quite a while and my ship isn't long in port. If you can just tell me where she's working—"

"Ah, no good. Eva not want see you anymore. Has boyfriend now and married very soon, very sorry. You leave note and I take to her." The abrupt reply signalled the intention to break off further discussion.

The twisting and turning had come full circle, but there was no point in bandying words. Richard nodded and parted from his erstwhile host, conscious of Nu's eyes boring into his back as he paid his bill. He shrugged aside the offers of conveyance from the drivers still idling nearby and stepped off at a contemplative pace.

Another alighted from his taxi as Richard passed and began to tail him. "You want girl, you handsome man, take to girl bar, have car. You keep dry. Two US dollar can take you everywhere, many bars, many girls."

"Nah, thanks, mate, but no. It's okay. I'm not going anywhere. Good marks for trying. Here's a couple of bob for your trouble. You should be able to change it."

He examined the coins before pocketing them. "Ah, Aussie, yes, can change, sir."

If Richard thought the gratuity might shake off this persistent entrepreneur, he was mistaken. It emboldened further inducements. "Take to nice girl, very pretty, very cheap, plenty girl. For you cheaper, you Australie, special Aussie just one dollar."

"Thanks, no."

He had some American currency in his pocket and wondered at just how base bartering for human flesh had become, then suddenly recalled a correlation between the name mentioned by the waitress and that club spoken of by the Englishman in Georgetown. "Yes, you, hello." He called back to the taxi operator. "Do you know a place called 'tosa smootin' or something?"

"Yes, yes. Sitosa Samootin Club, can take. Very good girl, beautiful, close here."

"It's a girlie-bar?"

"Sure, yes, good drink and very good yum cha. And the girls, mmm." The man traced a shapely figure with both hands. "Me Kinni. Wait, I bring cab to you."

The trip took him back in a similar direction from which he had come after leaving the station, but this time they drove past a number of the better hotels in the city before turning into a series of narrow streets, ending in a part of town with which he was unfamiliar. There was a steady movement of people entering the premises, European and Chinese men dominating the numbers.

"This Sitosa Samootin, sir. You look for me when leave, I take you anywhere."

"Yes. Thanks, Kinni."

Richard was greeted by two becoming hostesses, one of whom escorted him inside to a large open restaurant. Providing seating for at least a hundred people, it was three-quarters full. Tastefully attired waitresses scurried between tables, bringing meals and serving drinks. Their every activity was overseen by a sphinx-like Chinese maître d' immaculately configured in black tie, white silk shirt, white tails, black trousers and a ludicrous top hat. Obsequious when customers caught his eye, he became imperious if there was any misstep by the girls in the performance of their duties.

"Sir, my name Lily. You can eat first or have drink with me. I show you bar," said the petite hostess in a passable accent, inching closer to exhibit a showy perfume.

"Ah, alright," said Richard, cautiously. "If you like. I'll just have a look."

She took him along a narrow corridor that led into a bar modelled on English design. "What beer would you like, sir? We've all sorts. Tiger, the popular one, or the German or—"

"Anything." He passed over more than enough money for the local brew. It was noisy, giggling girls outnumbering patrons. At the far end he noticed a lavish staircase with mahogany banisters. On either side were carved two lions whose tails evolved into slithering serpents, their grotesque heads poised as if to strike, beckoning the eye upwards. From the first landing rose a vast tapestry depicting a dominant, nubile young woman surrounded by reclining female forms in various stages of undress.

At the foot of the stairs stood a Eurasian hostess, wearing a tiara, long white gloves and figure-hugging gown. She smiled invitingly when any man cast a glance her way, bowing just enough to present bountiful cleavage, and then depositing a kiss on the cheek of those who ascended.

"What's up there, Lily?"

"Special private club for those who wish to gamble. Also, more friendly and comfortable, and another small bar. You wish to see?"

"Not just yet. I'll go back to the restaurant now."

She whispered to one of the waitresses. He was placed at a far table that sat two.

"Are you going to be around while I'm here?"

"Can be if you tip me to stay."

He was unsure what reply to give but settled on a conservative one. "I'll have something to eat. Come back when I finish."

"Yes, sir. Thank you so very much."

After half an hour and an entrée tinkered with, he had still not sighted Eva. Richard left his table for the bar, sensing the eyes of the tuxedoed man rooted to his tracks.

Lily soon appeared. "What's your name, sir?"

"It's, ah, Dick," he said, choosing the abbreviation, turning his shoulders inward as she pressed against him and took his hand.

"You want go upstairs now?" she asked, stroking his arm and leg at the same time.

There was no doubting the insinuation. "I'd like some time with you, Lily. Not upstairs," he fumbled. "Is ten dollars enough?" He produced a crisp bill.

"You can spend three hours with me for that, plus two drinks. I back in a minute."

He watched as the money was handed over at the bar. She returned with beer and sipped coloured water. He wanted to ask if she knew Eva without appearing too earnest, designing a discussion to win her confidence. Lily was from Singapore and had been at the restaurant for two years. She worked hard at English and was proud of her proficiency, having been unable to utter a syllable at the start. He complimented her, proffering advice on how to acquire a broader vocabulary.

"I like you, Dick, nice man." She kissed him lightly and tickled his forearm.

He fidgeted a little, trying to think of something to say, when he heard a grandfather clock chiming a disconcerting number. "Lily, I need to know about a person who works here. I'll pay you more money if you can tell me about her."

"I try, sir. But sad you want this girl and not me," she offered intuitively.

"No, you take me the wrong way. I've a friend in Australia who met her when he was visiting here. He wanted me to give a message. The name's Eva. Do you know her?"

She tilted her head and frowned perplexedly. "Is she hostess, sir?"

"Maybe a waitress."

"Sometimes people start here waitress then become hostess. It depends—"

"She speaks good English, even better than you. She's from Nanking in China."

Recognition was immediate. "Oh, yes. I do know one girl from there. English like you say, very beautiful, but not Eva. Her name Carrie."

Richard sculled his beer. "And what does she look like, Lily?" he asked with a tremble in his voice. The description matched perfectly. "Never mind." He shook his head. "Maybe another place."

Lily searched his eyes, drawing out a foot fault.

"Is Carrie, here tonight?" he asked, reaching into his pocket and striving to effect disinterest.

Lily had other ideas, stroking his thigh. "She working today, but finish and go with gentleman."

"Her brother? My friend told me of him."

"No, with Englishman. Cannot take money when I not give the service."

"Lily, I insist you have it," he said, two single dollar bills secreted to ensure the house would not exact its levy. "Now I must get back to my ship." He rose to leave.

"You mean no longer want me? You paid, and we go upstairs. That what I am: hostess, Dick."

"Lily, really," his smile broadening to satisfy the grave top-hatted Mandarin, perturbed at the apparent cessation of relations. "I do like you, but I can't treat you just as something I've bought at a shop." He kissed her forehead.

"Will you come back and see me next time you here?"

"I'd like to. You can do better than this job. More work on your English and you could be a teacher."

"Thank you, Dick. Give me chance get better. Go back way? I show."

Richard briefly entertained the thought of abandoning his notion to take it further, but he'd come this far and wanted to see Eva for one last time. Perhaps he would be favoured with some attempt at justification or receive an impassioned denial. Beyond that, there was nothing left but to return and confess to O'Connell over copious drink his salutary lesson and emerge a little wiser.

There was no sign of the taxi that had conveyed him to the club, so he engaged another, still with just enough time to accost Eva and then catch the train. If she was not to be found, that might be the best signal Providence could provide.

He positioned himself opposite Nu's Café before the arrival of Kinni's taxi alerted him. A light came on inside, and Richard could clearly see a couple embracing. The driver was then visited with a barrage of expletives that culminated in the voice declaring he could sing for his fare. Kinni stepped out of the taxi and became very animated, shouting and gesticulating so much that it drew a gaggle of spectators anticipating an explosive fracas. Now on the scene, Nu was anxious to placate the ire of one of the passengers, while at the same time minimising any commotion.

Never one to suffer idle parley, the man struck at the hapless driver sending him to the pavement. Still far from content, he delivered a vicious kick leaving him prone.

Richard called out in a firm voice, "Let him be, the poor devil's had enough!"

The assailant turned to face the intervener positioned a few yards away. "And who the bloody hell might you be to butt into other people's business?"

"Don't concern yourself with who I am," Richard replied, in the instant taking a serious dislike to everything about the assailant. "Where I come from, mate, men fight fair, face-to-face and for good reason. And you're damn well twice his build."

"You sound like one of those convict bastards, the mouths from the south." Heenan guffawed at the rhyme. "Big-arsed on talk, but weak as piss on action."

Ignoring the jibe, Richard regarded the injured Kinni. Nu knelt down, swabbing his face. Several banknotes from the same source amounting to a tenfold bonus above the fare convinced Kinni that leaving with his taxi intact would be propitious.

Not for a moment taking his eyes off the towering form sizing him up, out of the corner of his eye Richard saw the woman. She was wearing a gaudy purple dress split two-thirds of the way up her leg. Unsteadily, she moved from the rear of the taxi towards Heenan. Her form appeared familiar but, focused on the truculent Heenan, he did not stop to consider identity. Pulling at her companion's shirt, then his arm, she attempted to drag him inside. She stumbled forward, lost a shoe and almost her footing when he resisted her efforts.

Heenan's temper, far from abating, took on a ferocity that defied Nu's entreaties. Once riled, he acted without restraint and countenanced no interference. Possessed of unassailable cockiness when an opponent matched him in size, he was ready to taste blood again. The man opposite him showed no fear. Slightly shorter in height but more broad-shouldered, he loomed as a far greater challenge than any scrawny, middle-aged taxi driver. Spoiling for a fight where his pugilistic skills might receive a testing, Heenan was not going to take this upstart's rebuke lightly.

There was something about the interloper that aggravated him, yet, at the same time, exerted restraint on his actions. Preternaturally indisposed to Australians, it was the voice that irritated him most. The accent was plain to hear, but there was an unusual sophistication of language that Heenan interpreted as a bloated confidence in bearing and demeanour.

He divined that Richard would not stay idle to be insulted and abused but didn't want to throw the first punch. Goading might just work. This had some perverse attraction, for he was entitled to protect himself if attacked, and his response need not be measured once a flurry of action commenced. But for all his quick-fire prognostications, old habits lurked deep within him. The chance of a first strike, if it arose, proved too good to pass up.

His female companion reappeared, sounding like a raucous termagant, demanding his company inside. "What're you doing with that c—"

Richard saw clothes that were certainly not her normal attire and recognised a face that bore the signs of a woman who had had more to drink than was becoming. Their eyes met.

The fist felled him. As she advanced, Heenan pushed Eva in the chest with the palm of his other hand, sending her careering through the open doors into the café, where she fell and remained.

Richard was down but not insensible. He blocked an oversize shoe in mid-flight, twisted the foot and sent Heenan toppling sideways, swearing as he landed. On wobbly feet, Richard managed to land a left jab, an action more instinctive than measured. It opened him up to a destructive right cross that floored him, and this time the boot found its unerring mark.

Chapter 6

Husband and wife

S wift had become their conjugality. Malayan domesticity followed in the vast estate the planter named
Melmingreda Kediaman in honour of his new bride.
It had undergone a complete renovation prior to her arrival. Climate, culture and surroundings were illimitably
different from anything the refined Mrs Faircrossman
had experienced. Coping with her husband's exuberant
personality provided an immediate test, but she was a redoubtable young woman who relished the challenge. So
began an existence that many of her penfriends and acquaintances regarded with considerable envy. Their only
child, Jonathon, was born three summers later. With a
houseful of servants, no home duties arose to trouble her,
and she was always supported by a nanny.

Almost two decades earlier, when Edward Faircrossman
proclaimed his rubber-planting sortie, there was little
debate amongst sniffily-disposed legal contemporaries
about him being an ambitious dreamer. Swashbuckling
and full of bluster, they posited that he would go to Malaya,
probably make a 'good show' of it, upset the established
order and, within relatively few years, end up with some
tropical malady. He would return a filament of his former
self, if he came back at all.

True, he had always garnered attention and was uncon-
ventional. As well as being an adventurer and raconteur,
he had been an accomplished all-round sportsman. Winning a Blue for rowing was a fine attainment, but it didn't
stop there. A regular member of the second eleven for his
county, he was a stylish left-hand opening batsman and

superb cover fielder with an unerring aim. In winter, he had strapped on rugby boots for five consecutive seasons as a rambunctious number eight, revelling in taking punishment and never flinching.

A beefy figure standing six foot three inches and over fifteen stone in his playing days, Faircrossman was craggily good-looking. His face bore the imprints of a broken nose and ears, embossed with the insignia of scrummaging, giving him more the appearance of a wrestler than an educated gentleman. During his time at Cambridge, he was not to be ignored either on or off the pitch.

He had a jaunty sense of humour and could laugh at himself, though was at his most boisterous when regaling an audience with his own storytelling. Liked and disliked in roughly equal measure by those who met him, many in the 'dislike' category thought him arrogant, chauvinistic, pompous and an autocrat. But even among them there was muted respect mingled with covetousness. Those who appreciated the man saw him as honest and a straight-shooter, always ready to help someone deserted by fortune.

Despite an expanding legal practice that had him elevated to a junior partnership in a prestigious London law firm, Faircrossman threw it aside and invested the equity remnants in what seemed a dubious, rundown rubber enterprise. Presaging this event, he had been bequeathed a modest legacy from the estate of his mordantly eccentric, feminist aunt. She had spiked an interest in Malaya and Singapore with unabridged tales of colourful and intriguing shenanigans in the Far East.

Possessing an uncanny knack for sighting a bargain, Faircrossman's first decade on the peninsula saw him acquire four more plantations. A go-getter, frenetically brokering deals and ever advancing his business interests, he was that kind of entrepreneur who brooked no opposition. Some of the doubters who railed against his plans had since come on board, without any rancour on his part other than occasional good-natured reminders of their misconceived prognostications. His estates produced nearly one-quarter of all rubber exported from the Malayan peninsula and made Faircrossman seriously rich.

During the acquisitive phase, he had laboured unflaggingly, though still managing to find time and opportunity to play the irrepressible dashing bachelor. The shortage of single European females saw him stray beyond proprietorial boundaries. Liaisons with married women sometimes developed perilous complications when husbands took umbrage.

Those peripatetic activities ended in 1929 on a return visit to England when he met Melmingreda Adamson. Faircrossman was a stone heavier, but no less presentable for it. He arranged a social outing with her father, a London King's Counsel who he used to brief. Without forewarning, Adamson secured his daughter's presence for the occasion. Having completed her internship, she worked as a registrar at a London hospital.

'Greda', as Adamson fondly called her, was his only child. Curious, unattached and free-spirited, she had heard much about this man from her father. At twenty-three, Greda was coal-haired, ivory-toned and statuesque, possessing the classic discernments of an English rose. The sixteen-year disparity in ages aside, the rubber tycoon was one of the most eligible bachelors around.

He had originally intended to stay in London for a month, but Faircrossman was smitten at first glimpse and kept postponing his departure in a relentless pursuit of her. Not so enamoured with him, Greda still remained gracious. Her experience with men was limited and, when words eluded her, the flush of colour coursing through elevated cheekbones proved irresistible to him. And she had never met one as irrepressible as he.

Even during that feverish courtship in London, some of their acquaintance would say the couple was complete opposites, yet they blended as a striking unit, he, holding his years with tanned and weather-etched face, contrasted with her subtle freshness and studied outlook.

Perhaps she might have been swept along, seeing most of her female friends had young families. Early twenties was still remote from spinsterhood and Adamson's only mention of her status came after graduation when he had observed to her at a society wedding that marriage was an 'honourable estate'. After the efforts taken to encourage her studies, she found the remark pointed.

Holy matrimony was solemnised within eight weeks. Greda understood what being Edward's wife entailed and drank in his overt candour from the outset. He made it plain that he wanted a son and heir. Not without a streak of adventurism herself, she relished her new status, albeit with some trepidation given the dramatic change in circumstances that ensued in making Malaya home.

Her husband marked himself out as a man of indefatigable enterprise. He visited plantations, oversaw storage facilities and met importers and shipowners at the ports of Swettenham, Penang, Malacca and Singapore itself. Business dominated his existence. But he was a devoted and loving father to his son, whose birth was, in remarking to anyone he met, the most important event in his life.

Edward's regular and prolonged absences were the part of Greda's being she found most difficult to accept. She grew accustomed to routine in the tropics, this one least of all for a time. And as her own interests widened, so did the emotional distance between husband and wife. Thus began a journey that engraved quite separate and independent lives.

Greda was well-liked by the Malays. Her proficiency as a casual clinician proved to be of considerable assistance, not only to the household servants and plantation labourers, but also to a wider cohort. It led to the local medical officer, Dr Maganly, inviting her to act as a locum for his practice. This would occupy one to two days a fortnight of her time.

Excitedly informing her husband of the offer, she was stunned by his outright antagonism. He refused to entertain the idea, citing that undertaking the position would imperil Greda's capacity to look after their son and manage the plantation in his absences. Eventually, an incommodious compromise was reached, whereby he conceded to her treating employees and their immediate families from the estate for minor ailments. And she could step in for a few hours if an emergency arose and Maganly was unavailable.

Greda was baffled by his attitude. In retrospect, this was the point within the marriage where the frustrations of her confined existence were beginning to tell on the integrity of their relationship. Notwithstanding his domestic decree, Greda decided to maintain continuity with Dr Maganly. She furthered an unobtrusive association in order to avoid any discord within the home.

The subterfuge could not remain undiscovered forever. With a growing reputation, demand for her services increased. She suspected that it was only a matter of time before something occurred to undermine the truce they had brokered. It happened somewhat later than sooner when Faircrossman, usually an astringent keeper to an announced schedule, returned early from a business meeting in Singapore. Fully expecting to find Greda at home, he was surprised to see the new maid occupied with the household chores and his wife nowhere in sight.

"Mistress, she work for Doctor today," was the innocent response to the master's enquiry as to her whereabouts.

"Oh, Hannah, madam is busy today in this terrible weather?"

"Yes, sir, go every day. She important doctor and everyone love her."

This disclosure irritated Faircrossman more than it angered him. The rain that followed his return to the plantation became heavier. Little could be done until it eased, and he ordered Hannah to keep the gin and tonic within reach. The liquor ameliorated his irascibility for a period. But as the afternoon wore away and squalls blanketed the luxurious gardens fronting the study, his mood turned morbid. Although not a violent man, he was quick to take exception if he felt countermanded.

The back door was unlatched. Spreadeagled on a lounge-chair with drink in hand, Faircrossman, eyeing his wife as she entered, was preparing his ire for an opening. She dallied in unbuttoning her coat and replacing the umbrella in its stand. He rose and walked unsteadily toward her, face streaked with crimson, while she conjured a way to disarm him.

Opting for blandness, Greda announced, "Oh, you're home early. Well, thank goodness. This weather's awful, isn't it? I expected you to be rained out somewhere between here and Singapore."

He surveyed her for some moments, offering a sneering smile. "My dear compliant wife, have you been out in it? Surely not playing tennis, and it isn't the sort of day for a long luncheon with the other wives."

"Edward." She said his name through a set jaw, realising that he was beyond propitiation, her eyes flashing. "I have looked after this place for a dozen years. At least three-quarters of that time you have been away on business. The paperwork is always up to date. I've made sure the estate functions efficiently and I remained here for Jonathon before he went to boarding school. I have—"

"I, I, I. It's always the same monologue we're hearing."

She prickled at his words and their import, recalling having never put *I* before *he* at any stage of their marriage. It had all been about pleasing him, serving his enterprise, tending to her child before reposing any emphasis elsewhere.

He kept at her. "Contrary to my wishes, you've been working. You don't need to, Greda, and *you* know it. Your place is here. That arrangement was struck when we were married and in the spring of love's first bloom." He gesticulated extravagantly towards her and, in a voice laden with irony, added, "You had no trouble accepting it. Now you've chosen to do as you please but, even worse than that, you've practised outright bloody deception upon me. I know you're locuming for Maganly and—"

Eyes ablaze and arms locked across her chest, body unflinching, she cut him short audaciously. "And why shouldn't that be, Edward? It's my professional training. These people need me. The local doctor is overwhelmed. You say one thing I have not done around here, one task I've neglected to do on your behalf or for Jon. Name one instance of estate management being compromised, one occasion when this wife has not been at your beck and call, jumping to attention like your whistle-boy!"

His voice speared at her through pursed lips. "I will say this just once to you. Don't *ever* deceive me again."

"Deceive, deception? Damn you for making that charge!" Greda shot back with equal intensity. "What do you think I am, some sort of child? You're not my keeper! Am I merely your possession?" She sped on to forestall argument from his side. "And furthermore, don't come the bounce when you've been drinking. Be the man I once thought I'd married without summoning Dutch courage to attack me in such a puerile manner!"

Back to him, Greda's command of the stairs jolted her husband into a modicum of sobriety. Edward had not experienced such insubordination before and was incredulous at its stridency. Shaking his head, he followed her assertive exit, perceiving not even a tremor of tearful breakdown or shaken disposition. Reflecting on the implications of what she had just said, he sniggered, poured another drink and retreated to a couch in his study.

Chapter 7

A fork in the road

Against the threat posed by the Japanese landings in Malaya, prominent ex-patriot businessmen were raising questions about their future. Convened in Kuala Lumpur by Edward Faircrossman with the British authorities, the unofficial Planters' Conference had sought explanations as to how their assets were going to be protected. The loss of the *Prince of Wales* and the *Repulse* overshadowed the meeting.

General Percival had been visiting the northern army headquarters and met with the group to address their concerns.

Faircrossman's impressions were not flattering. He perceived in the general many contradictions; an uninspiring, emotionless individual and a robust sense of self-belief sitting astride ineffectual presentation, accentuating the quandary. Clearly, he had been shaken by the events at Kota Bharu. No one listening to him would deny that the naval catastrophe must have had as profound an impact as it did upon a stunned House of Commons after it heard Churchill's announcement, but Percival's homily evaded the seriousness that the Japanese incursion now posed, and this left Faircrossman more than perturbed. There seemed no urgency to the man, and he detected a trace of bewilderment. Had there been any outward sign that the Japanese loomed as the greatest threat to the Empire in the Far East, he might have felt better. Rather, it was a case of the general giving every appearance of saying, *Now that the ships are gone, we can move on to the next phase where victory is assured.*

Edward Faircrossman was not an easy man to impress, but his wife, also present at the meeting and usually circumspect when called on to give first impressions, was less than sanguine about any imminent chances of repelling the invasion.

"Sorry, but this fellow is an oddity," she whispered with uncharacteristic bluntness to her husband halfway through the dissertation.

The planters had been told to carry on business as before, that the situation was contained, and that their safety and assets would be protected. For many, the reassurances were enough. However, Faircrossman was sceptical of what he termed 'soft soap' and, as they took supper on the veranda afterwards, could not forebear from giving vent to his contemplations.

"I wish I could really see inside that chap's head," he remarked to Ernest Habbersfield, a planter from a neighbouring estate. "He'd be my last choice to captain a third eleven of a minor county."

"Doesn't look like he's been to bed for a while. Anyway, what would you expect after setbacks like that so soon after it started," replied Habbersfield.

"Perhaps you're right," Faircrossman said, yawning dubiously as he was joined by Greda and Joy Habbersfield.

"Sure I'm right. You heard what he said about the army. We're more than a match for those trumped-up, poser-emperors. Our forces are trained to fight in this jungle."

"But do you feel the general is on top of it all?" offered Greda, charily this time. "He didn't capture the mood in the room or, perhaps, preferred to ignore it."

"My very point, dear," Faircrossman observed haughtily. "However, if we cannot accept his statements about the security situation, we'd all better clear out fast."

"Agreed," said his wife, directing a strand of hair over her ear. "Aside from what the general had to say, there are decisions for all of us here concerning our children. Jonathon is at school in the Camerons and you have a son there, as well as little ones at home, Joy. It's worrying with Jonathon away, Edward."

"Jon's safe at the moment," put in Faircrossman peremptorily. "If we have to get him, he's within easy reach. It won't be long until all the children are back for Christmas."

Talk among the men turned to their exports and any potential disruption to merchant shipping consequent upon the Royal Navy's losses. By midnight, conviviality waned and the planters separated.

*****

Muddy water lapping the corner of Richard's swollen mouth siphoned into his lungs. A paroxysm of coughing followed clearing his airways, but excruciating chest pain engulfed him. A torrential Malayan downpour hammered his body like pellets from an air rifle. A minute more and he would have drowned.

As the agony subsided, he sat up in a drainage ditch. To one side a narrow, unsealed road wove ahead. To the other, a row of trees. He swivelled onto all fours and tried to push himself up but slumped down again as a wave of nausea overtook him. It was as if a bolt of lightning had struck, befuddling his capacity to reason and gnawing at his head.

He had no idea where he was except that he was exposed to a cloudburst. For a chilling moment, an illusion enshrouded him where some phantasmagoric director, intent on mayhem rather than filming a scene, had ratcheted up the rainmaking jets to unendurable pressure in order to capture an actor in his death throes.

Then the rain began to ease, and wits returned. He felt the striations of several cuts and lumps as recollection of the conflagration gradually formed on him. Richard Kirnst had been pole-axed. Skin flaps on the prominent knuckles of his left hand implied that he must have reacted instinctively. The thought gave him a grim feeling of accomplishment, for he hated to concede that, notwithstanding having been bettered in the affray, the assailant had avoided being tagged.

Anger welled within and a wild desire to seek redress for the iniquity of the incident overcame inertia as he staggered to his feet. Severe discomfort continued to wrack his chest, lower back and ribs, leading him to remember the denouement as the repetitive application of a heavy boot.

As Richard staggered out of the bog, the garish image persisted. He could not bring himself to think of her by name. After all, which one? Eva, Carrie and Chin Ming, could be plucked from the veritable store on offer. That alone galled him. There she was, openly cavorting with the man responsible for his current predicament. He stopped short at contemplating the duration of their liaison. As he tried taking deeper breaths, the repugnance he experienced outdid any feelings of rage towards the miserable characteristics of her partner.

No matter how Richard laboured on about her duplicity, none of this was going to solve the immediate problem. What was he going to do? His skull felt as if it had been raked with a claw hammer and squeezed in a vice. Every time he moved his chest tried to leap from his body. Breathing was difficult, as each intake of air attested.

The road was of sufficient width to accommodate a lorry. On the side opposite to the cultivated trees grew thick jungle. There were no lights around, but in the distance he could hear the rumble of road traffic. He looked at his luminous watch and saw that it had gone midnight.

Panic swept over him. He had intended to be back on board before the curfew. He staggered off towards the sound, following wheel impressions. Every pace proved far more difficult than he had anticipated. Richard made twenty yards before leaning against a tree, gasping for air and grimacing. Refusing to allow himself to linger, he began again, counting the steps and hoping each interval would increase to prove to himself that his body was becoming more proficient. With every forward movement Richard was more desperate to make it back to Port Swettenham before daylight.

Checking the time again, he saw it was after one o'clock, and the reverberations in the distance were no closer. Resting only prolonged the agony of the restart, so he pressed on. But, having no realisation of how badly beaten he was, his lungs refused to provide the sustenance required to maintain greater than inept movement.

On such occasions, when the human instinct somehow produces additional physical strength, mental acuity begins to shut down. Richard failed to pick up the vehicle's approach until it was almost upon him. By then he was beyond dreading the consequences of his enemy's return, blank to all cognition except for the sound of a woman's voice.

*****

Faircrossman opted to take a shorter, less-travelled route for their return drive. In private confines, their ongoing relationship tensions were in sharp contrast to the displays of equanimity he manifested in front of his friends. The meeting had been an expedient diversion and the socialising welcome, yet a tentative hope for an embryonic thaw was soon dispelled.

Not given to skirting any topic on his mind, Faircrossman moved to the source of most conflict as delicately as if he was trying to lance a boil. "No doubt we'll need to be more vigilant from now on as far as the plantation is concerned."

"You mean with the expanded tapping and export demands?" Greda enquired disingenuously.

"All of that, of course." He hesitated, sensing trouble. "I think you should, ah, try to, with these developments, keep focusing pretty much on the home front and Jonathon."

"Meaning that I cease working," unable to resist the pointed response.

He tried to sound relaxed. "Well, until we know more, you're at risk getting about."

She wasn't so diplomatic. "Just as you are, Edward? So, you'll stop touring the countryside? Your son just might need his father, too."

Sarcasm infuriated him. There was a pause which afforded her all the more incentive to employ the advantage she'd gained. "You were saying?"

After a silence, he snorted imperiously. "Greda, I wish you'd understand one thing. Whatever you do is discretionary. I don't *have* a choice. The entire outfit depends on me. It demands travel, sourcing labourers, checking the mine, getting contracts signed, sealed and delivered and ensuring my exports are loaded onto ships. My point is, your place is at home."

"My pla—"

He overrode the attempt to speak by bracing his forearm across her chest. Greda arched her body forward in an effort to push him away. "What's come over you? Shut up and listen, damn it," his voice plagued with fury, "None of this can be done by me idling away at home hoping all will somehow—"

"Look out!" she screamed as a silhouette loomed before their headlights. Stooped and apparently insensible to the vehicle's presence, it lurched forward. Faircrossman seized the steering wheel with both hands swinging it hard to the left before bringing the car to a halt.

"Lord, did I hit him?" he asked, unaware that his passenger had decamped.

Greda was kneeling beside the man. "It's alright, you're okay," she whispered, placing one hand on his wrist while her arm slid under his head. Edward was almost out of the vehicle when she called, "Bring my medical bag and the flashlight, and be quick about it." She felt a strong pulse. While her husband held the light, she retrieved a pencil torch from the bag and made an instinctive pronouncement as to his wellbeing.

"Is he," Faircrossman cleared his throat, "going to be—"

"He has a number of facial injuries, possibly some concussion, and his laboured breathing is troubling. We must get him home as quickly as possible. Fetch the car, will you?"

Faircrossman reversed the vehicle until the rear door was in line with the prone figure.

"We need to handle him carefully in case his ribs are broken." Between them, they eased him onto the back seat. Greda slid in from the other side, cradling his head.

Her husband's voice was elevated as he started off. "I'm positive I didn't hit him," he said, seeking some reassurance from her. None was forthcoming. After a lengthy pause he added, "Ah, won't do to go too fast if he has chest injuries. How's he doing back there now?"

"Something of a mess, but I'm hoping it's a case of seeming much worse than it really is. When we get back, I'll assess whether he needs hospitalisation," she said coolly.

Upon arrival at the estate, Faircrossman roused the servants. They brought a stretcher. He was carried to one of the guest rooms and placed on a bed. Under Greda's supervision, his clothes were removed, and she applied warm, soapy water from a basin before looking more closely at his injuries.

The picture under the electric lamps made him appear more like a boxer after five rounds of unrelenting punishment. His left eye was blackening and there was a cut above his eyebrow. His face was swollen. There were contusions around his ribs and on his back. Greda noticed a gash at the back of his head. She applied a sterilised pad before inserting several stitches. Apart from a maidservant holding the basin, she was alone in her ministrations. Faircrossman had been summoned to the telephone.

Having attended to her charge, she rejoined her husband in the living room.

"That was Habbersfield. The Japanese have bombed Swettenham and there's been quite a lot of damage. Just like Percival said, 'It's all under control'—bloody rot. How's our man?"

"He's more comfortable. I don't think he has broken ribs, and his lungs seem to be functioning pretty well."

"Has he said much?"

"Nothing coherent, I gave him pain relief and a sedative. He's sleeping peacefully. There's not much more I can do for the moment."

"I wonder who he is. The state of his face would have made him unrecognisable even to his own mother." No flippancy resided in his tone.

"He's cleaned up quite well. Nothing on him, no papers or identification, just a watch and he's quite smartly dressed. When we took his shoes off, I noticed they were made in Australia. The shirt and pants had labels marked 'Scarfs, Outfitters to Seafarers, Sydney'."

"Well, he may be from one of the ships in port. I know there was one tied up"—Faircrossman was unsettled by an infelicitous recollection and lingered before resuming—"ah, taking on some of my produce at the moment. But I wonder why he was such a long way from there?"

Greda poured tea with formality and elaborated on the injured man.

"I've left Sonia to keep watch, with instructions to call me if there's any change in his condition. I think rest will do him good. He's a pretty robust-looking fellow. I wouldn't be surprised if he's up and about fairly quickly, but we shall see."

"Ah, then looks as if he'll be right. I have to leave early tomorrow." Faircrossman waited for any word of dissent.

"I expected you would," was her perfunctory response.

"And there are some matters requiring my attendance for a day or two." He waited on her, desiring some reaction.

Sensing this, she avoided direct engagement, shrugging her shoulders. "Everything here will be looked after in the usual way."

There was an element of derision in her voice. She was aware of the annoyance it gave him and its alienating effect on their relations but had ceased to be concerned, save for some reflective moments when she wished that things could be different.

Faircrossman had found her attitude dissonant, exacerbated by her verbal ascendency over him, subtle with acerbity but never so pointed as to prompt unseemly rowing. Amid this disharmony, he chose to tell his wife just enough to make his various excursions seem credible. Not that he thought Greda remotely suspected him of cribbing additional periods away for extra-marital perambulations.

Denying unfaithfulness, he resorted to legal sophistry whereby the mental element, namely, the intention to betray his marital vows, was absent. Thus, he could remain unflinching in a denial of adultery.

In his mind, he revisited the erotic casual dalliance in Kuala Lumpur. Recalling their first tryst, he'd enjoyed good wine with some other planters after a meeting and, on his way back to the hotel, heard a shriek from inside one of the bars nearby. He ran in to see a sleazy and corpulent Latino trying to usher a striking Chinese woman towards a stairway. She was resisting his attempts to do so and Edward, an ever-chivalrous individual irrespective of his state of sobriety, promptly intervened. He broke the malefactor's grasp on her and dispatched him through the door and into the street.

Though he assumed she was a resident bar girl, by her looks and command of English, she was no ordinary bearer of that title. Alluring and confident, she carried conversation well beyond the platitudinous and was earnest in her gratitude for his intervention. This was endearing, as it pandered to his solipsistic disposition. Beyond their conversation, an intimate embrace led to a tempting kiss as they parted. She need not have asked if he would return.

He had acquired a sensuous companion. The taste had stayed with him until the following evening, when she became far more accommodating. There followed several subsequent encounters as he tarried a few days. No money changed hands, sealing a pact within himself that made securing her favours the more attractive. He insisted on buying her some fine clothes and jewellery. That she was a good listener, perceptively focused on what he was doing with his various businesses, he found satisfying, as if compensating for his wife's indifference, but the primary purpose of his contact with her remained sexual gratification.

Pleasurable memories lingered, but their connection became little more than an itinerant sequence of convenient interludes, until that chance meeting six months earlier in Georgetown. Seeing her at close range, and being a party to her insipid disavowal of ever having met him, had greatly renewed his interest. Yes, she was having her fun, as Carrie always would, and that was unsurprising, but he could do more for her materially than any lowly young ship's engineer.

Faircrossman glanced towards his wife, somewhat remorseful. Greda wasn't cognisant of the attention and his penitence evaporated. Her thoughts were centred on the injured man. She went to the stairway, saying she would check on him.

He used her absence to access a safe. Returning with his wallet, he took out a photograph of the comely Asian woman. It was a sight so salacious that he missed the light step. Having scarcely concealed the item as Greda passed nearby, he retreated to his office. She came to the door, surveying him as the wallet was replaced.

"Well, how's he going?" he asked sheepishly. There was an elongated pause as he avoided her eyes. "I, ah, suppose that's that then."

She prolonged the silence. "Not quite. Don't you ever lay a hand on me again!"

Chapter 8

The Australian patient

A primeval sun, having assumed early mastery of the day, bathed the large bay window whose shutters had been unfastened to accommodate its penetrative glory. Chintz curtains, one on either side, were drawn in by fluffy ties fixed to hooks. The interior décor in every respect replicated the guestroom of a tasteful Surrey manor house.

Though enervating outside, for Richard, the effect produced a restorative balm that persisted until he tried to move. Stymied in this small attempt, he smoothed one hand over a head that felt tender from crown to jawbone. There was tightness in his chest on aspiration. As his eyes adjusted, it was some time before he began to greet the surroundings. He determined that it was neither his cranium nor the room spinning but rather an overhead fan flicking the voyeur light like a carousel.

Almost imperceptible footsteps alerted him to the presence of a petite woman bearing a tray that supported a silver teapot, a bowl and a delicate cup and saucer. At first, she appeared to float around him, the starched bows of her apron appended like angels' wings. A few blinks of his eyelids positioned her some distance away setting the items on a mobile table.

He started to murmur some words of thanks when a voice wafted over his.

"Good morning. How are you?" The lissome figure at the door had eluded his cognisance. "Thank you, Fanny; I'll take over."

The English accent solaced him even if the source of that mellifluous sound was not instantly apparent. She spoke again, and yet a third time, before Richard appreciated he was being addressed.

"Surely we might be entitled to hear who you are?" her inflections leavening the question. "What is your name?"

Habitually active from first light, this was a second visit. Always a picture of studied elegance however she chose her apparel—which was never finalised without the utmost attention to detail—today she had dressed in a calf-length blue skirt with a sleeveless soft-pink blouse. Apricot sandals completed the ensemble.

Richard attempted to slide up onto his elbows, embarrassed to find himself at a combined disadvantage in the presence of a stranger and unfamiliar ambiances. He groaned and she was beside him, having procured the chair occupied during the night by one of his attendants.

She laid her hand on his forearm delivering a mild chastisement. "That wasn't wise. You must relax."

Compliant, he sank back on several pillows, wondering whether he was dreaming. Trusting that instinct, Richard was desirous of prolonging its sustenance.

The earlier question earned a belated reply. "I'm alright, thanks. Where am I? How did I get here?" He wanted to add that he was hungry.

Greda followed his eyes regarding the twisting string of steam. "At least you retain some sensory intuitions," she offered spryly. "I suppose you're also wondering who this odd female is. I'm a doctor and you're at our bungalow. I live here with my husband. Our son is at boarding school. Last night we found you at the side of the road, south of Kuala Lumpur. Can you remember what happened?" she enquired. "Take a moment, no rush."

Leaning over him, her fingers pressed his wrist while her eyes studied a timepiece. Satisfied, she wheeled the tray to his bed and poured tea. "I hope you take it with milk. I've ensured it's not too hot. You must be famished. Are you alright to help yourself?" she asked, motioning with an open hand.

He nodded. She adjusted the pillows with assistance from the maid and they gently repositioned him.

"Now, how's that?" she enquired, facing him.

What he saw so mesmerised Richard that it necessitated redistribution of the remnants of his energy to restrain an exposé of awe. An arresting woman, five foot nine inches tall, perhaps more, her legs rising idyllically from calves embellished by the pleasing fabric. Slender ankles captured feet that arched and tapered, complemented by toes finished with subtle nail polish. A wide brown belt accentuated her trim waist where blouse and skirt united.

He followed every motion, the turning away and back again, busying herself about the room, collecting a cloth that she tucked into his nightshirt. Her hands and fine, delicate fingers were artistic in symmetry and dexterity, a plain, narrow, gold wedding band the only jewellery. Long, lean arms bearing a pale dusting of freckles met proportionate shoulders. When she reached across to improve the position of his supports, their proximity was such that he sampled the sensuous attar, gifted like a slipstream coursing through a tight copse of Cootamundra wattle trees.

Femininity crowned this creature blessed with natural beauty, evincing health and vitality, yet earthiness persisted. Something told she wouldn't shrink from having her hands deployed wherever they might be required. Ears clasped their stem like rosebuds in early spring and rich, black, wavy hair, fastened with a gold braid, spilled down her back. When she turned around, the cut of her blouse invited a glimpse of a perfect cervical spine overlaid with unblemished skin. He estimated her age in the late-twenties to early-thirties range and large, languid, grey eyes revealed a shade of fragility that evoked curiosity. For a split second, the thought arose that she was intent on signalling, even at this inopportune moment, an unmet emotional need. Brittleness impelled him to contemplate her thus.

Wanting to be sure there was substance to her form, he reached out. Moving to his side, she met this gesture and supported his upper body as he tried to inch into a more upright position, shaking him free of her distracting features.

"Just a little confused at the moment," he said, speaking slowly. "Richard Kirnst. I'm a marine engineer and—" the precariousness of his position descended. "Hell, I, I must get back to my ship at Swettenham. What day's this? And wha—"

The working of his jaw pained him.

"Richard, steady on." Her instant adoption of his Christian name engaged him. "I'll need to write all of your questions down to remember them. It's Sunday morning. You've been here since we found you on the road. The Japanese bombed the port last night. I'd be surprised if your ship is still there, but I can find out by making a call on our two-way wireless. What's her name?"

He inhaled slowly taking a moment before responding, "*Erakai*, and I'm the second engineer. I can't imagine her leaving without me. Must've been some sort of altercation or trying to defend myself, but there was some trouble. I wasn't drunk or anything, I—"

He began to recall more as he spoke, but shame at having to acknowledge to a woman of her breeding an act of street brawling precluded further elaboration. "It's, ah, hard to remember and—"

She rescued him. "Would I be correct in thinking you're Australian?"

"Yes," he answered, realising his personal effects weren't within reach. "My clothes, you have them, I guess. How did you know my nationality? From my wallet?"

"No wallet, unfortunately. It was probably stolen when you were attacked. I recognised your accent. Yesterday my husband and I and some other Brits were in Kuala Lumpur at a meeting with army personnel, and we met an Australian officer."

She noticed his glance towards the food and indicated for him to partake. Richard consumed several mouthfuls under her watchful eye. The delicious mix of coconut milk, Penang curry and noodles was a placid companion to his tender jaw.

"My husband liaises closely with ships carrying rubber, because he owns several estates." Richard's querying frown attracted a solicitation. "Are you alright?"

"Ah, it's nothing. Go on."

"Yes. Well, the export trade's integral to his business. Oh, pardon me, I'm Greda," she said, extending her hand and retaining his. "You're still hungry? That's a good sign. You'll have another bowl." Before he could say anything, she gave the instruction. "Strength will return once you've eaten properly. Your first decent meal for a while, I imagine?"

"Oh, I'm doing alright, thanks. Sorry for the inconvenience."

She warmed to his reserved manner. "No trouble at all. We're here to make you well."

"I'd like to enquire about my ship. You mentioned a two-way. Do you have a phone? I could call the agents in Singapore. They'd know if she's sailed."

She nodded. "Yes, we have a telephone. May take a while getting through."

Despite her remonstrations, Richard couldn't be dissuaded from rising. His ribs stalled him. He took the initial steps around the room grimly, but this made him more determined to keep going. He moved to the door, winking at her amiably. She did not protest further and assisted him downstairs, pointing to the telephone in her husband's office and ensuring he was comfortable.

Over the next hour he spoke to several operators, seeking to be put through to Caswell & Sons. Each time someone promised to call back. When he asked why there had been such a delay, blame was attributed to an air raid. The last telephonist assured him that he would be put through 'shortly'.

He shook his head at Greda's enquiry into whether a connection had been secured. She insisted he lie down on a chaise longue, where the maid had gathered cushions and pillows, and asked if he liked to read.

"Yes, I do, as a matter of fact." The question surprised him.

"You'll find something in the library cabinet. Anything in particular I can grab?"

"I like the odd Zane Grey, and Edgar Wallace for some escapism."

"Here, how about you start with the *Straits Times*?" She passed over the Saturday edition. "Make sure you rest.

I have some work at the hospital, a place you only just avoided."

He smiled. "On Sundays?"

"Health does not recognise the sabbath. I shan't be away for long."

Right on three o'clock in the afternoon he stirred, and the maid offered iced lemon squash. His clothes had been washed, pressed and were neatly folded on the chair beside him. He asked her whether any personal effects had been found with the garments.

"Passport. *Passeport*?" he repeated.

She disappeared for a few minutes, returning empty-handed, and he registered a sigh. He felt considerably better in body at least, but with neither passport nor money, it was impossible to do very much.

As he rose, the phone rang. He could hear the maid talking and she announced that somebody was asking for him. A voice identified herself as the secretary for Mr Clive Oram, a functionary who sometimes handled the *Erakai*'s affairs. Richard remembered him as a flabby Yorkshireman, surly, disagreeable, taciturn, and always grossly put out when a request was made for his services. Apprehensive, he waited for the grating accent.

"Ah, you, is it, Kirnst?"

"Mr Oram," he began respectfully, "I'm urgently in need of your help. Can you—"

"'ave bun fully briefed on ya behavya, Mr Kirnst," Oram cut in abruptly. "Ther're many urgint mattas t'attend where 'onourable and loyal employees, unlick the leeks of ya, find themselves in truble through na fault of their own. Ya missed ya ship and 'ave cost the cump'ny muney. Ya disobeyed ordas by the Cap'n when ya went to Kuala Lumpur chasin' some Asian floozy. Am I rit, Kirnst?"

The accusations, laced in a sneering tone, were calculated to stir him to a fury. An inclination to oblige was only curtailed by Richard's predicament.

"Sir, I'll explain what's occurred to the master, but at the moment all I want to do is get back to my ship. Can you tell me if the vessel's left Port Swettenham? She'd only be half-loaded and presumably picking up more cargo in Singapore. I'll get—"

"Presume be damned. Shu's on 'er way ta Oostralya. So ya've missed the boat and good riddance, I say to ya," Oram said, chuckling and breaking out in a series of consumptive coughs.

Richard ignored the barbs. "Well, I'm somewhere near Kuala Lumpur, staying with a plantation owner and his wife. They'll do what they can to help me. I don't have a passport or money, but there are wages due and I can probably come to see you. If you could just find a position for me on another vessel, I can work my way back to Australia."

Oram sniffed raucously before beginning, "I'm afraeed it'sanot t'at simple. Ya had na business takin' off t' way ya did. Absent widdout permissin. Ya're in breach of cump'ny policy and the articles ya signed on ta respect, senior offica at t'at. Ya shoulda known betta. The *Erakai*'s put to sea short-handed because of ya reckless an' dilatchry behavya." His voice went off into an air of high dudgeon, as he repeated a torrent of misdemeanors committed by this 'flagrantly errant' second engineer.

Richard seethed, but hoped the vituperation had reached its zenith and a path taking him back to sea might be found.

But Oram was far from spent. "'nfact, wit' t'war and everythin' else t'at's occu'd, I'm afraid t'at ya surplus to cump'ny requirements. We've 'ad t' let ya go, and t'ose instrucshoons 'ave cum from t'ownas, ya employers. Ya sev'rance cheque will be 'ere for ya when ya care t' drop in t' pick it up. Bin suitably docked against the extra wages t'cump'ny must pay to t'other engineers who a'doin' ya duties, so ya might not think it worth ya botha."

"But this is unfair. I've been with them eight years. I demand to speak to your manager."

"T'at will be somewhut diff'cult. My managa and his assistant were killed yestidee in the bombin'. Ai'm in charge and me instrucshoons from t'ownas are very clear. O' course thay wa grateful for me rec'mendashoons." He laughed until the coughing resumed. "Ya'r finished, Kirnst, finished with tha cump'ny and with t' sea."

"But I do have mitigating—"

"Ya've shit in ya own nest and abandoned ya post. Ya've torn up ya articles and I 'ave no time t'waste wit' the likes of ya. There's a war and me priorities are elsewhere occupied tryin t'assist decen' people. Good afternun."

"What the devil? Hello, hello?" But the line had gone dead.

Richard was incredulous at the posturing contempt shown but fearful of the repercussions. Reflecting on his position, he retreated to the chaise, head in hands, ruefully concluding that his ructions with Oram in the past had come back to afflict him now. Aside from his ruined reputation in the company and the seafaring fraternity, he was marooned in Malaya. While the food and rest had made him feel tolerably better, he was in no condition to embark on a trek to Singapore, over a hundred miles away.

Richard was forced to confront an uncomfortable truth among Oram's venomous accusations. He had disobeyed the captain, albeit never intending to be away more than the allotted time, and so placed himself in a situation where personal interests had prevailed over his vessel and shipmates.

There was no simple way out of this mess. By staying where he was, the situation became a problem for those under whose roof he lay. Of necessity, and out of decency for their kindness in taking him in, he would have to explain in greater detail what had happened. The plea of short-term memory loss through concussion wouldn't assist him forever with the doctor sure to deduce that he had something to hide.

Borrowing a small amount of money might get him to Singapore by train, where he could at least obtain the remainder of his discharge pay and perhaps employment with another shipping line. Commuting would not be easy, but once underway he would improve. His headache had eased, and the supply of aspirin left for him would be useful.

Returning to the guestroom, he changed into his clothes. The sun and relentless humidity throughout the afternoon succumbed to a brooding atmosphere punctuated by approaching thunder. Before long, the heavens released a thudding, evanescent storm dumping inches of rain. From the window, Richard watched torrents of water cascading down slopes and into creeks. Only then did he appreciate the vast size of the estate and its endless lines of rubber trees extending upwards and outwards. The bungalow was situated on an elevated spur of land spanning two gullies. Next to the dwelling, there were large vegetable and flower gardens.

At last, diminishing light peeped through the clouds. A man and woman emerged from a large shed at the rear of the house with hoes and buckets. They set to planting seedlings of Chinese cabbage and English spinach in a manner so rapid as to convince him that the task had to be completed before dark. Nestled in half an acre, the market garden was filled with silverbeet, ginger, miniature tomatoes and a variety of exotic greens and vegetables at various stages of maturity. It made him think of home.

He returned to lie down and review his position, but when his head met the softness of the pillow his analysis disbanded.

*****

The ire of a wild boar broadsided by grapeshot would have been less fearsome than the fury of Captain Heenan after his orgy of assault and battery. That he hadn't emerged unscathed from the encounter with the bulky Australian was a major source of his outrage.

"I should have personally murdered that bastard," he muttered, cursing the intervention of others who had held him back. A lump half the size of a plum and of similar colour decorated his right cheekbone and his joints were stiff.

He took his leave of Eva, growling at the hour to which she had let him slumber, and dismissing her breakfast preparations with a scowl.

"What's wrong with you? Cat's got your tongue? Oh, it's your mouth," he said, when the puffiness of her upper lip became evident.

A taxi was waiting for him. He sat up suddenly when the omnipresent Devis, reclining in the rear seat, countermanded the order to return to barracks. He suspected trouble. "We'll just take a little detour first, good sir. Thank you, Jamal."

Over the years, the secular oracle had bathed in the pleasure of seeing his pupil grow into a special body of work. Heenan still carried many grudges against the army establishment. Devis was never slow to massage an ego that nurtured those grievances and kept him ensnared, provided he delivered.

Rarely did Heenan disappoint. They shared a skin colour—even if Heenan's was marginally darker. Devis extolled Heenan's fortitude in living with this 'sad handicap', which engendered camaraderie and maintained Heenan's resentment about how he was perceived by the other officers. When Devis moved his base to Malaya, Heenan followed, and the disgruntled soldier relished his well-renumerated role. His intellect worked so aberrantly that he did not even regard the activity as traitorous. Deriving solace from Devis's prognosis, he justified what he did by drawing on the theory that the Asian people were being racially exploited and deserved to be liberated from the vile yoke of their colonial oppressors. He learnt that this philosophy resonated with disaffected provincials.

They had much history together. Heenan had surreptitiously journeyed to Japan accompanied by Devis. He was treated to the comforts afforded a visiting dignitary. First-class accommodation, alcohol, women on demand and lavish spending money combined to satiate the dissipations firmly within his repertoire. Heenan's excesses were a prominent weakness that worried his masters, and more than once Devis had to exert the necessary restraint to appease them. However, his value as an insider operative outweighed any shortcomings.

While in Tokyo, Devis introduced him to Nu. A productive relationship between the two was critical to the establishment of an effective spying organisation in Malaya. The café business in Kuala Lumpur would become a clearing-house for information. Somewhat surprisingly to Devis, they seemed to develop an instant rapport. Heenan was pliable when he demanded respect, and Nu obliged. Devis accepted the relationship between Heenan and Eva, for a time ignorant of the military police's visit.

But it suited Devis that Eva had become entangled in the seedy world created by Nu and was effective as a cipher. He had no cause to doubt her loyalty.

Through his assistant, one Jamal Viranhi, Devis had also acquired knowledge of her involvement with the Australian engineer. That liaison had no real intelligence value and was to be discouraged, unlike her dalliance with the influential rubber baron. As the Japanese were very keen to find out the disposition of the planters towards them, maintaining associations with Britishers became useful. Information about relations between the planters and the military establishment was also significant. Eva was enjoined to find out more about the planters' attitudes, and she did.

But now Heenan's instability was worrying. The previous evening's imbroglio was another manifestation of how he could pose a threat to the covert activities of the cell. His volatility was assuming serious proportions. Nu had disposed of the matter without revealing the identity of the victim, fearing repercussions from Devis.

But much more troubled Devis. Non-compliance with set timeframes for the delivery of information had brought about this unscheduled meeting, Heenan having missed a critical deadline respecting allied troop numbers and movements.

In the close confines of the taxi, Devis commenced with his trademark insinuating sneer, which became contorted with an upward stare at his charge's bruised face. "I see someone has been picking on you again. It's always the way with these pesky irritants. And what happened this time, a coolie failed to bow as you passed?"

"I can honestly say—"

"Spare me the exculpation." An interruption like this would, if it had been delivered by anyone else, have brooked a severe rebuke, but Heenan's shoulders slumped. "You know, sir, the bargain. What is expected and was not delivered? And time is, well, the essence. The core of things, as you British say. Now, there's no need to panic, for you have until three o'clock today to deliver the package."

"That's bloody impossible!" Heenan's features were mapped with dismay. "I have to explain this," pointing to his face, "to the CO and I'll be under pressure to—"

"Not, my dear, gallant sir, the sort of unpleasant pressure that our mutual friends, not very far from here, are capable of bringing to bear before this day is out. So you will accommodate. We all remember how important you've been. Comfortable futures are very much in our own hands."

Heenan remained sullen.

"Just pull up here, Jamal," said Devis. "Thank you and goodbye, my friend. We all need to please each other to survive for our many years."

Heenan could not mistake the parting glance. A late delivery had been overlooked before. This time Devis was acting at an entirely different level. No matter what happened at headquarters—and his commanding officer was especially tolerant of his many peccadilloes—he needed to expedite copying of the classified material.

With insulating himself in mind, Devis had already spawned a theory that Heenan might be a double agent collaborating with the enemy. When the deadline was not met, incautiously, he informed Jamal, his ambitious and avaricious lieutenant, that Heenan's future usefulness was outweighed by the dangers he posed.

However, Jamal had other ideas. He inveigled the commander of the cell to believe that the suggestion was an elaborate strategy by Devis where he would roll over to the enemy and take Heenan with him. It was the precursor to Jamal's succession to the position he had long coveted.

An ineffectual command structure protected Heenan against removal or a reprimand. Until evidence of his treachery proved overwhelming, he was not in British sights. Rather, rowing, drunkenness and street brawling were his major crimes.

Devis's consequent liquidation saved the Britisher from similar despatch. In a twist of fate characteristic of the work undertaken by Heenan, his delay in procuring the secret documents had allowed him time to access more up-to-date material that the Japanese were desperate for, information relating not just to troop placements but to air capacities as well. His position was enhanced.

Thereafter, Heenan was given a large bonus and a wider remit to carry on his nefarious undertakings, consistent with the progress of the invasion.

*****

The week following the landing at Kota Bharu had been marked by stunning success for the Japanese forces and chronic failure by the British. The Jitra line in the north was smashed, the strategic town of Alor Star had fallen, and, by the nineteenth of December, Penang was captured.

On the defenders' side, lines continually altered. Fuel dumps, ammunition, vehicles and enormous quantities of stores had been gifted to the invaders. Bewildered Malays were waving to Japanese soldiers cycling unhindered along main roads. Such was the footloose, Allied command that tactical advantages secured by any partly successful resistance were quickly dissipated by haphazard orders to withdraw.

The Japanese held total air superiority. Yamashita, inspirational, brimming with physical and mental toughness and an uncompromising attitude to discipline, was a textbook field general. There were thirty thousand soldiers under his control as part of the strike force, backed by a further thirty-five thousand troops and conscripted labour responsible for maintaining supply lines throughout the Malayan campaign. He had several hundred tanks and aircraft.

General Percival grossly overestimated the actual fighting force making its way down the peninsula, believing his troops were confronting more than one hundred thousand men. Defences were spread thinly, weapons and equipment woefully inadequate.

But none of this was known to the planters and their families, scattered all the way down the peninsula in this vulnerable region. Most still trusted implicitly in the army.

Chapter 9

Renewing an acquaintance

Approaching the third evening of Richard's convalescence, a brackish torpor surrounded him. There was nothing he could change about his missing the *Erakai's* enforced departure, yet he imagined fanciful scenarios in which the misdemeanor might be redressed and redemption conferred. He would make for Singapore, speak directly to Oram and offer to sail on any ship in a lowly capacity without wages for a year, then radio Treacy, apologise and raise mitigating factors. Writing to the company's managing director in London might just work. His lengthy service counted for something and he could plead the case as being an unwitting victim of a vicious, unprovoked attack. A medical report fortifying the entreaty for re-engagement was a simple request away. As each hour passed, these theories sank into a miasma of despair.

Outside, the sounds of impending nightfall were subsumed. A tropical downpour smashing above his head was trivially muffled by the slatted, wooden ceiling. The storm reminded him of the dismissive finality in the Oram diatribe. This reinforced a perception of psychological weakness within his make-up, a debilitating malaise, and, under the unfamiliar roof, his anxieties multiplied.

Before leaving for the hospital, the prescient Greda had assured Richard he must not concern himself about the future, and that her husband would be able to help. He knew she was unconvinced by his protestations of indifference. Continued presence in that house carried powerlessness, dependence and was a reminder of failure. He may as well have hung a board around his neck with the word 'Deserter' painted in bold letters and paraded himself in the streets like some Chinese miscreant found in the act of stealing.

Being decoupled from the calling he loved had induced a lackadaisical presentiment, and neglecting to shave became a potent illustration of his disinhibited state. It was something he had done every morning since receiving a safety razor on his seventeenth birthday. He rushed to rectify the oversight before husband and wife returned. A glabrous face revived him.

In easing rain, the screeching brakes of a heavy vehicle pulling up caused Richard to move to the veranda. He didn't hear Greda's coincidental arrival. Carrying a leather medical bag in one hand, she waved and was met by one of the house-servants shielding her with an umbrella. No such acknowledgement was made towards the heavyset man emerging from the truck. That individual issued instructions to the head foreman and dismissed him. Before long, he strolled towards his domain. The man of the house, for no one exercising that degree of authority could be anything else, appeared familiar to Richard in voice and even more so in physical appearance as he closed the distance between them. The sight produced a bead of sweat on his forehead and threw him into a panic. For a moment he contemplated a side egress from the veranda as the closest means of avoiding the inevitable confrontation. Escape was quashed when a resurgent rain squall thrashed the bungalow with such ferocity that the roof strained to part from its battens.

Richard just had time to wipe his brow when the office door was flung open. He hoped the thumping in his chest wasn't evident.

"Well, how's the gay wanderer?" Faircrossman asked, without the slightest betrayal of recognition. The irony was not lost on Richard, as the older man plunged forward to grip his hand, tempered by anomalous jocularity. "Edward. Call me Ted if you wish, or just plain bulldust, to which you Australians are used."

A poignant slip perhaps, Richard considered, for he was still speechless.

"Say, you seem familiar. I see quite a few Aussies from time to time. Never mind. Are you well? You certainly look a hundred per cent on what we lifted from the side of the road a few nights ago," the brash planter maintaining his stance of incognisance.

"Much better thank you, sir. Gidday, Richard Kirnst." He hung back with the faintest smile, unable to resist emphasis on his surname. *A cool customer, and shrewd too.* In search of a narrative, the guest regarded several oil paintings. "Ah, I'm indebted to you and your wife." Trying to recover his equanimity, he added, "I realise I can't stay too much longer and impose—"

"Nonsense! No imposition whatsoever. You'll have a drink? Hannah, a gin and tonic. And for you?"

"Just a glass of water would be terrific."

"Hannah, attend if you please. Greda will be down soon. We take dinner in the dining room, if you can manage." Faircrossman did not wait for a reply. "Now, you must tell me what happened, mate," issuing another quixotic reminder of Georgetown.

Richard recounted the events in Kuala Lumpur with a studied editing of the background. Were he not lodging in the other man's house, he might have been tempted to mention Carrie as a tantalising riposte to Faircrossman's avoidance, but the thought had no sooner arrived than departed. The planter blithely sank his liquor and called for another. At times, he interrupted to shake his head and observe that this type of thuggery was pretty rare. He dismissed Richard's concerns about impecuniosity.

"They seemed to have missed the few coins in change sitting in my fob pocket," Richard joked.

But Faircrossman was not a man given to dwell on another's attempt at levity if it abstracted him from the limelight. "I must've seen you down on the docks at Swettenham," he offered tangentially and with considerable aplomb, as if tacitly assuaging his conscience. "Some of my rubber was lifted on the *Erakai* before it put to sea, and we had to compete with other ships for stevedores. The confounded Japs have made the situation even more acute with those weaklings heading for the hills. I don't trust the coolies. They'll swing with whoever looks after them. Agitators at best, collaborators and cut-throats at worst. Wouldn't surprise me if they'd passed word down to their cohorts, or followed you or something, not just for the money, but to delay the ship and work in with the Japs."

Richard nodded with unction, perplexed by the convoluted linkages.

"The *Erakai's* long gone, leaving you high, dry and stateless now, I gather. No pun intended, of course."

Richard remembered the quizzical feelings he had derived from their previous meeting, the hail-fellow-well-met rowdiness and desire to be everyone's favourite. "Yes, I suppose that's a reasonable way to sum it up," he replied cautiously, considering what his best approach to dealing with Faircrossman should be. Opting to continue, he added, "It illustrates the second part of my dilemma. I spoke to the agent in Singapore hoping to rejoin my ship or get another berth."

"There was never any chance of that, since the vessel's steaming to Australia. Go on."

Faircrossman knew a good deal more about the *Erakai* than he'd expected.

"If I may be blunt, sir," he could not bring himself to use a less formal mode of address notwithstanding their clandestine commonality. "I'm effectively *persona non grata*, sacked by the company. No documents, no passport and no—"

"You can stay here as long as you like and work for me," Faircrossman declared unblinkingly. "I said you're looking better, and the more I observe and hear, the greater I'm convinced you'll be right. Look, come on, enough of the 'sir' business. Ted will do."

"I'm feeling pretty good now," Richard said phlegmatically.

"Well, there you are then, old chap, and I've just the answer. You're a marine engineer, but I know that covers a multitude of skills and peccadilloes, too," the planter laughed with undisguised hilarity.

Richard wondered whether Faircrossman might know something more of what had happened in Kuala Lumpur and was trying to elicit mis-speech. "Well, um—"

"No need to comment," Faircrossman intervened. "I can tell you it's a blasted battle keeping our plant functioning. Machinery is home for you. I'll pay a decent wage. We can arrange for a passport and, in the interim, while these little short-sighted animals are pitched back into the sea, come up with something to appease the company. Look after me and I guarantee that bloody favour will be returned."

The offer astonished him. "What can I say?" He paused. "You've got yourself an engineer. It's a huge relief to be useful somewhere."

"Don't worry about that, you'll earn your keep," Faircrossman quipped. A roguish charm resided in the man. He continued, "I just want the machinery running and my workers happy."

"As to speaking on my behalf, I doubt whether that'll cut any ice with the cretinous little agent who let me know my seagoing days are over. I—"

Straightaway he regretted so describing Oram and was relieved that neither Faircrossman's bearing nor predilection to interrupt remained unaffected.

"Never mind about flunkeys like that. I'll go straight to the top in London. Been shipping with them for years." The planter yawned unconcernedly.

"I couldn't let you do that, although I'm appreciative of the offer," said Richard, surveying him again.

He did not want to feel wholly in anyone's debt, but no ulterior motive seemed to mark Faircrossman's generosity. He began to repent of his doubts. Was the man's private life any of his business? On the strength of what had happened to him, he had little doubt that Faircrossman was another of Eva's casual liaisons. That history needed to be archived. O'Connell would have ribbed him good-naturedly about it. Therapeutically, Richard chose to mock himself. *A novel situation,* he imagined.

"You won't regret this. I can't thank you—"

The French doors parted behind him and he heard Greda's voice. "Hello."

"Ah, here's my wife now. Have you had a chance to get acquainted? Probably not. She's so busy." A cool stare marked him out. "Here's a lark, my dear. Our guest has just inveigled his way into my confidence and persuaded me to create a job for him," Faircrossman chuckled. Seeing embarrassment manifested in Richard, he qualified the statement. "No. Actually, he's a fine fellow and in a bit of a bind."

Declining his offer of alcohol, Greda requested that tea be fetched after ascertaining that such was also Richard's preference. "You've disobeyed your doctor's orders to take it easy," she chided, "but you *are* looking well." She took his arm and placed her other hand lightly on his shoulder, leading Richard to an expansive wicker chair festooned with cushions. "There, you should be resting up comfortably. How are the ribs? Still a little tender, I see," she said, noticing a grimace as he sat.

"They're actually pretty good. Everything's coming back to normal."

"And with more time healing will be complete," she added swiftly.

"I've always been a quick healer. I'm up for the job as a maintenance man around here for a bit, though I'd still like to sort out my long-term situation."

"As I said, mate, anything's possible. We need the help," Faircrossman affirmed, his gaze alternating between her and Richard. "Since we lost our best mechanic nothing's gone well, particularly that infernal generator, which my new employee promises to get running sweetly tomorrow."

"I don't know that he should be doing any heavy manual work yet," she remarked, irritating her husband. "He needs another week."

"If he wants a week he can have one, or more for that matter, as long as he gets there at some stage."

"Mr and Mrs Faircrossman, there's no problem with me," Richard insisted, taking the initiative. "I'm determined to make myself useful, and tomorrow I'll be right to at least have a preliminary look. If the issue's not too complex, I'll try to have the engine on load by lunchtime."

"Well, all the help you need is here. I'm going out to clear it with Ah Fut, who's managed so far to keep the other stuff just serviceable, but this problem's got him baffled. Help yourself to a gin if you tire of tepidity." Turning his head towards his wife he added, "Greda, we'll have dinner in about an hour."

Faircrossman finished his drink in one unceremonious gulp. He walked outside to the workers' quarters while Greda moved off to finalise preparations for dinner.

Passing Richard, the tips of her fingers glided over his shoulder. "Sit easy, and please be comfortable. Feet up is fine."

Within twenty minutes, Faircrossman, resplendent in white dinner jacket and glass replenished, ensured Richard's cup had been refreshed before sitting down. Greda soon rejoined them, having changed into a full-length blue-and-white embroidered gown.

She addressed Richard as if her husband wasn't present. "You seem surprised at my bustling around in there. I've no qualms about donning an apron. Our dear old chef has been with us for years and is getting on a bit, so I help out sometimes."

"My wife's selling herself short. It's really the other way around these days. Greda's an excellent cook, when she has time to acquaint herself with the kitchen that is. She leads quite a busy life, mostly down at the hospital."

Greda bristled reprovingly. Richard cleared his throat, trying not to look at either of them, the hiatus disconcerting. Her spouse, exhausting half of his drink, continued indifferently.

"So, tell us about your life down under."

"Nothing much of interest, really, I was brought up on a farm called Oakleigh Ridge. It was a two thousand-acre cattle and wheat property on the Darling Downs, about four hours from Brisbane and just over an hour and a half west of—"

"Names mean nothing to us, old chap, so come again, name a decent nearby town," Faircrossman butted in gratuitously.

"Brisbane's about—"

"Yes, went there once, bloody backward, hick place."

Greda squirmed despairingly at her husband's interventions. Determined to prevent any recurrence, she urged him on with a steely, "Go on, Richard."

"Went to a little one-teacher primary school close by, then boarded at Toowoomba Grammar and—"

"Bloody hell, a grammar school. Sounds fancy, up yours—"

"Edward, please."

"Sorry. She's on the warpath. Continue."

"Had to leave and get a job, as there was an endless drought and my parents couldn't afford to keep me. Did a trade in the foundry and ended up going to sea as an engineer. Undertook some more study and, well, here I am. Or at least, there I was," Richard corrected himself, realising the overstatement, "until you found me, and now just footloose and somewhat of a nuisance, I've no doubt."

"Enough bloody guff and nonsense; you're anything but that, old fellow. And you won't be footloose or stateless either for too long, when I have my way."

"I'm very thankful for everything you've both done for me, and I promise you'll be satisfied, and the work—"

"No need to keep banging on, old boy, or I'll wonder whether that crack on the head has dislodged some of your screws."

"Do you have family, Richard?" she interposed testily.

"Yes, I have an older sister, Ruth, who's married with two boys, but my parents passed on. They lost the farm when the bank foreclosed. Dad died of a heart attack and within another year Mum was gone. Ruth lives in Toowoomba. Her sons also go to Grammar. They have some of the best schools in Australia there," he couldn't help pointedly mentioning. "We're very close, my sister and me."

"You look like you played some sport. Cricket, rugby?" his host preferring a course close to himself.

"Ah, yes. I played both of those. Not so great at rugby— well, rugby league. That's a bit different, but—"

"I know it. Uncouth version played in that frightful north of England." This time his wife's expression did not go unnoticed and his refuge involved urging elaboration.

"I bowled the odd bumper in cricket and opened the batting in the A-grade side."

"You enjoy your vocation, do you, Richard, as a ship's engineer?" enquired Greda, determined to inject herself into the dialogue.

"Yes, I do, actually, and like the life—well, did," he said, admonishing himself.

Faircrossman intervened again, louder than ever. "Oh, bugger me dead, stop worrying about it. So, what are the advantages?"

"Well, the solitude, pay's reasonable and you get to visit a lot of new places. Mostly you see the sea, as the song goes."

"Ah, and see the girls, hey, old fellow? You like the Asian ones, I vow," Faircrossman's smirk introducing an uglier side to his inebriation.

Exhausted by these insinuations, Greda glowered at him before shepherding Richard to the dinner table.

Faircrossman apologised ineffectually, saying his wife lacked a sense of humour. "Don't mind me, old chap. Out again," he called, holding the glass at arm's length towards the light as he followed them. "A few of these liberates the tongue and beckons the risqué in me."

A one-dimensional table-talk exposé followed in which Faircrossman expatiated about jettisoning his estimable prospects as a solicitor, "Equity was my forté," to descend on Malaya in the early twenties. At his most effusive in alluding to Jonathon, he added that his son had grown into a 'fine lad'. Producing a photograph, he boasted with unbridled conviction. "Takes after me—into sport, born cricketer, very practical."

Faircrossman favoured red wine at dinner. An Indian boy stood by tasked with the duty of ensuring his receptacle was never wanting. Greda, of abstemious disposition, toyed with a second burgundy for the balance of the meal. Her husband's drinking was an obvious font of dissension between them. On more than one occasion, a surreptitious movement stayed the boy's hand when Faircrossman sought a top-up. Greda's unease was especially noticeable when he strayed into areas that touched on his wife's independence, dressing this up in a societal context to illustrate a dismissive view of modernity where women were 'on the ascendency'.

Although not spelt out, Richard estimated that their marriage had subsisted just over twelve years. Most apparent was the absence of chemistry between them. If he hadn't been present, Richard imagined that salt and pepper shakers would be passed between them with more ceremony than a fatality in his tin concession.

In the course of her husband's various soliloquies and taking in the few exchanges between them, he reflected that Greda appeared a disconnected listener though not wholly content to let him do most of the talking. When she managed an utterance, he retook the conversation and moved onto another topic, jarring to the point of rebellion between them.

As dinner drew to a close, Faircrossman declared that he would be departing next morning on what could be protracted business. "Always got to guard against those who'd unjustly use me, as the Good Book reminds us," he burbled.

Richard felt loathe to absent himself from their company. Sensing discomposure, Greda forced the issue by suggesting that their guest could do with some respite when he declined his host's offer of after-dinner port. Nodding towards them on rising, he concluded that if a debriefing session followed his excusal, judging by the desultory exchanges between husband and wife, it wouldn't be much less clipped.

His assumption was correct. The bedside lamp was still shining as his head reposed briefly on the pillow before a gentle knocking presaged a hushed voice. The latch's click saw him adjust to a sitting position as Greda entered the room.

"Not a habit of mine to intrude on a male visitor's bedroom late at night," she offered, with a winking humour. "I saw the light and thought you might be reading."

He brandished the unopened book beside him.

"Not quite yet, I see." She asked whether he would like some chamomile tea. "It's a relaxant, you know." Her eyebrows arched enchantingly before she added, "And very good for you, too."

"Thanks, but please, I can go and make it, and your husband's downstairs."

"Oh, he's long departed us." She sounded relieved. "Blissfully awash. Argues he needs it to relax at the end of a long day," her voice suggestive of thinly disguised scepticism at the justification Faircrossman resorted to if queried whether he might prefer something soft to drink. "There won't be a stir until first thing tomorrow. But he has an indomitable constitution, quite remarkable, really. I'll be back soon."

She returned carrying a decorative kettle and two fine bone china cups. "Hope you don't mind me joining you," she said, positioning herself at the foot of the bed. "I decided to have another myself. A glass or two of wine and I'm in need of a cleansing. You said you liked reading, so I left that book." It was a well-leafed copy of *Pride and Prejudice*. "Somewhat romantic and may not suit your taste. But you told me how you liked language, and it's beautifully written."

"Yes, I've heard that. Your recommendation's enough for me." He opened the cover and saw her name inscribed inside. "Yours, too."

"Richard, you can make a start on it in the morning and have at least one more solid day's rest before taking on heavy physical work."

"You really don't have to bother about me anymore. I'm getting stronger by the minute and tomorrow—well, it's just gone today now, I guess," he said, regarding the wall clock. "I'll then have a chance to return something for the consideration you've both shown me."

Greda nodded with resignation. He couldn't avoid her endless fingers tilting the cup that paused as it met her mouth. She drank barely a drop as he watched her lips part to touch the liquid. In turn, she was drawn to his eyes upon her. "I trust you managed to get something from the evening. Edward tends to go on a little at times," she offered apologetically. "He's basically a good man; different, but very hard-working."

Richard saved her from continuing. "Perfectly okay with me. I'm used to all types of personalities. The dinner, the company, was most enjoyable."

High-pitched cicadas replaced the softness of rain rippling on the leaves. The sound streaming into their space was evocative, prompting his reflection on campfires at night in the bush.

"The way you describe it, Toowoomba must be a lovely place. I've never been to Australia. My sister lives in Sydney. One day I'll visit her and perhaps allow myself time to see where you grew up."

"You might have to cross the McPherson Ranges to do so," he said teasingly.

"No trouble for me. And I'd have a guide, wouldn't I?" she shot back.

Touché, he thought. Greda's discernment fascinated him, not that she was an obligated listener. She returned his appreciative smile.

"It's very unlike this country, quite cold in winter, always picturesque. Picnic Point is perched above the escarpment, just a short distance from town, and the views are spectacular. As the name suggests, an ideal area for a basket lunch among the majestic gum trees. They sell tins of mountain air at the kiosk. It's a bit of a gimmick, but if there's fresher air around than that place can produce, I've yet to—"

When listing her head enquiringly, expressive eyes radiated a hypnotic beam, and Richard had detached from the pathway of his sentence.

"You were saying?" she asked, her nuance all-knowing and beguiling.

"Sorry. Where was I? These damn knocks on the head," he expostulated unconvincingly. "Anyway, I'm going on a bit," he was striving to recover his composure and wondered whether she was testing him.

"It's alright. I imagine you do get homesick. Would it help to be able to, well, talk about that?" Greda wanted to extend the discussion while hoping not to appear too transparent. She longed for an equitable conversation, broader in aspect and substance than the type to which she was accustomed.

"Yes, sometimes I do, and love seeing my sister and nephews, but I find that no sooner am I back home than I'm looking forward to my next ship. I miss the farm, of course. Nostalgia is all very well but, as one of my teachers at Marine College used to say, 'Metaphysics doesn't boil cabbages.' He wanted us to focus on the properties of steam, I suppose, rather than sentimental theories. What about you? I'm sure you miss England."

A perfect set of white teeth peeping between her lips indicated she was chuffed at the saying that she'd heard at university. "I did at first. I've had a few trips back there and we've been here for a long time. You get used to it. Edward's often away, and that was fine when Jonathon was young, but now he's at boarding school. I like to keep busy, so I've been practising medicine again, albeit with a few hurdles on the home front."

"No doubt these things get, sort of, worked through. You've, ah, skills people need in this area," he added, compacted with his clumsy response.

"Shall I take that as an endorsement?" She smiled appreciatively. "Well, you must be tiring of me prattling away. I shall leave the pot with you. Even at room temperature, it's refreshing, especially first thing in the morning. Good night, Richard." She offered an elegant hand and still her eyes refused to leave his, lengthening the time that he held it.

"Good night, and thanks," he said at last, as she nodded and closed the door.

In any other circumstance, sleep would have quickly overtaken him, but frangipani perfume hovered and he wasn't inclined to ignore the opportunity it presented to think of her.

A disagreeable air arrived contemporaneously with the last hint of fragrance, companioning an image of the slumbering figure below to whom he was both indebted and vicariously linked.

*****

Edward Faircrossman was as ingenious an individual in business as in life. *The more innovative the stratagem, the more abundant the dividends* was a frequently cited axiom. During nearly a quarter of a century in Malaya, ruthlessly applied, it had served to multiply wealth, demoralise opponents and magnetise admiration, all things the man craved.

Spending a night on his couch downstairs would have seen most men wake ill-tempered and sore, but not Faircrossman. He had an indefatigable zest to meet new challenges. *Hangovers were refuges for the indigent and dawn the jewel of day*, being another oft-repeated aphorism. If he could so punish himself and rise as refreshed as if he had slept on a feather mattress for twelve hours, he wouldn't countenance an excuse from anyone preferring duvets.

In the case of the Australian engineer he deigned to make an exception on that morning, conceding some admiration for a man energised to commence work so soon after a comprehensive flogging. Detecting movement through the shutters of his guest's window enlivened approval of the new employee. Kirnst was confirmed as another useful acquisition on his part.

As Faircrossman readied himself to leave, the efficacy of his false pretence at never having met Richard filled him with relish. *Gawd, but he was a card, carrying it off with impunity and the straightest of faces.* Wondering whether the other man had really come to believe in what was being said and acted out became unworthy of his time.

As for Greda, he gestated on the unusual degree of familiarity she displayed towards their handsome house guest. He was a husband of innumerable double standards. While he had no scruples about associating with the woman both men knew, Greda was not likewise untethered. Without irony at the proposition he conjured up, Faircrossman wondered how much Greda would recoil if she was informed of the type of woman with whom the much younger man was disporting: *If the doctor only knew where that little Dickie had been*, the pun titillating him with highbrow satisfaction.

Then he frowned. During her favourable regard towards the newcomer and their bilateral exchanges, he had felt sidelined at times. Greda's persistent curiosity respecting Richard's life in Australia went beyond a polite biographical pursuit. She was either attracted to the stranger or transparently setting out to get at him. The third possibility, that his bloviating debrided her patience, didn't cross his mind. Contemplating the absurdity of his sexless wife indulging in coquettish exploits loosened his mirth momentarily before he roared at the foreman's laxity in failing to have roused the crew for the day's tapping.

*****

Though he was up and alert with the knowledge that there was a job to be done, Richard was minded to recall his hosts from the previous evening. The overt brazenness and volubility of the husband contrasted with the understated grace of the wife. Greda's felicitous visit posed questions he constrained not to explore, content instead to act on her recommendation and finger the impression left on the rim of her empty cup.

He was fortunate to be in a place where recovery couldn't have been more efficacious. Even a clipped repose did nothing to diminish his physical reparation, which was much further advanced than at the same time yesterday.

When he heard the familiar bellowing, Richard accepted that, as just another employee, it included the commission he'd undertaken to perform. He watched the sleek, shiny Ford sedan drive off in a manner so furious as to give Richard cause to wonder whether a disgruntled rival wielding a shotgun was pursuing Faircrossman. Soon, the jungle swallowed it and quietude became the impetus to focus on mechanical engineering. Mixed light gave way as the sun pressed inexorably over the hill that rose behind the dwelling, showcasing a bowling-green carpet of manila grass, then becoming overlaid with uninterrupted rows of rubber trees.

Everything had been left for him—soap, warm water, a new razor and towel. He dressed in the navy-blue pants and shirt arrayed beside the bed. A pair of steel-capped boots fitted perfectly, socks sheathed his feet like cotton wool and even pigskin gaiters on hand to deter molten metal should cutting or welding be required. This was a gold-medal start to any new job. Whenever the body spoke as he dressed, his mind countermanded it. There was no circumstance in which another day would be spent idle.

A muffled, rhythmic sound emanated from an area about a hundred yards from the bungalow, where an imposing A-framed shed housed the estate's machinery. Inside, an agreeable surprise awaited him, a durable work bench on which was attached a large vice and a dual-wheeled electric grinder. Mounted within easy reach was a variety of tools arranged according to size and disposition on hooks. In a corner, at right angles to the bench, was a small but serviceable-looking lathe and a pedestal drill. The auxiliary machinery and the primary generator were partitioned off from the workshop.

Richard took little time to identify a deficiency within the fuel pump. It was not an original component. An hour later, it lay stripped down on the workbench. In another, it was rebuilt, much to the admiration of Ah Fut and his two assistants.

"Are you there?" It was a voice that made his heart skip. She had not seen him. Opening the frosted casement windows revealed the sunlight glazing her luxuriant hair. He took a moment before saying, "Yes, I'm here." Greasy hands rested on the sill as she approached.

"I thought you'd skipped without paying the bill." Her remark encouraged a contented grin. "Hannah told me you left the house very early and one of the boys said you were down here. You're ever the incorrigible chap, aren't you?"

"The job has to be done," he responded. "I heard your husband leave at dawn and, if he's up at that time, then why not me? Anyway, I've found the problem. There'll be more. The engine needs a spruce-up, so I'll be here all day."

"Richard, I've rung the breakfast bell. You'll find sand-soap and rags around the side, so get cleaned up and I'll see you soon."

Her tone obliged him not to dally and, fifteen minutes later, he was sitting down to a magnificent spread of thick, crusty bread, bacon, eggs, English spinach, tomatoes, coffee and freshly sliced star fruit.

Greda was buttering toast as he spoke. "Are you going to the hospital today?

"Yes, shortly. I've just heard from Edward. There's been a change of plans. He has to go up north again and won't be back for some days. The news from the front is not encouraging. It seems the Alor Star airfield has been overrun. Edward's trying to arrange transport of tin from a mine south of there. I'm dubious about that, but he's not to be dissuaded. That's him, I suppose," she sighed dreamily, as if talking to herself.

Richard was keen to avoid supplementing the implied criticism of her husband's activities. "Has he had any contact with the army?"

"At this stage they're saying the area remains secure. The ground won tells another story," she said without sarcasm.

"You've a son at boarding school?"

"In the Cameron Highlands, some distance north-east. With the front extending, counterattacks notwithstanding, I'm very troubled. His father and I discussed it with some other parents. Edward thinks Jonathon's alright where he is for the moment, but I'm not convinced. The whole situation needs to be reviewed. Perhaps it's serious enough to start questioning how long we should even remain here."

"Really? That'd be a huge decision to make," he said, downing his fork and knife, her tone removing any suggestion of flippancy.

"Just so," she lamented, before adding with a hint of reproach, "Edward regards me as being alarmist. Of course, he can't contemplate parting with his precious interests."

Richard began to wonder whether his sojourn at *Melmingreda Kediaman*, the name he noticed chiselled on a timber flitch at the entrance to the plantation when Ah Fut gave him a short tour, would be very long.

"Aren't the British forces numerically stronger? From what I've read, there are over a hundred thousand troops positioned between Singapore and the Japs."

Scepticism was evident in her response. "I didn't think it was that many. Rumours abound about the capacity of some of those men, along with the leadership qualities of their commanders."

"Tell me more. I mean, 'fortress Singapore' and all that's a figment?"

"Edward and I met some officers, including General Percival himself, in Kuala Lumpur the night we found you. He struggled to communicate and was awkward. Your General Gordon Bennett, apparently part of the team chosen to lead the defence, despises him, from what we're led to believe."

"Well, what I've read of Bennett reveals a cantankerous character. If the generals aren't paddling in unison, how can troops be welded together?"

Greda resumed her distracting propensity to fasten his eyes while inclining her head towards him when he spoke. At an intellectual level, this gave verisimilitude to the notion that she was interested in hearing what he had to say. From an altogether different perspective, the action invited an intimate dialogue.

Richard averted his gaze to the jackfruit tree outside the window. Laden with swaying edibles the size of watermelons, it provided an expedient diversion, permitting him to regain self-possession. He was determined to dispel any conviction he might unwittingly impose that the speaker, rather than the topic, was the focus of his attention.

Facing her again, he was unable to detect flirtation. Freed from Faircrossman's presence, Greda assumed a transformative persona; confident, relaxed and with speech punctuated by insightful observations. Even more magnetically, as they talked, she sought his opinions and dwelt on them. He harboured the desire to regard her interaction with him as driven by a freedom to find his company more stimulating than her husband's, but retreated to a refuge of belief that it was merely a manifestation of her Hippocratic Oath, winning and maintaining the confidence of anyone she had treated.

During Greda's time on the Malayan peninsula, there were many social occasions where expats had been captivated by her. Such charm and poise could never go unnoticed. Economical with commentary when choosing to air any, Greda was measured and only voiced an opinion if it was fitting. Universally acknowledged as gifted with stunning features, she was also liked and respected as a person.

In Richard, she had for the first time met a man whose traits offered something unique. She warmed to his old-fashioned nostalgia and love for his homeland. The glistening in his eyes when speaking of his sister hadn't escaped her. Misadventure had brought them together, as well as her innate vocation to care for a fellow human in need. His quiet, unassuming character, ready boyish smile, self-restraint and reserve of wisdom were other qualities to which Greda was unaccustomed. She couldn't help but notice those awkwardly shy moments when he tried to forfend his gaze from her, deriving pleasure from intuiting their genesis. This appreciation of his make-up was not traded on exploitatively but rather served to make him more likeable as a man of character. Greda felt she could both trust and relate to Richard without fear that her confidence would be compromised.

Even entertaining such instant thoughts forced her to contemplate where she stood, wondering whether marriage should offer more. There was her son, whom she cherished beyond anything. Greda also had professional satisfaction, and wanted for nothing materially, but there was something missing for which she could not account.

Marital discord was a topic that sometimes emerged in conversation with other wives at tennis parties. She listened, often inwardly scornful of their domestic complaints. Seen as a model wife and very settled, Greda was their ideal foil. Some told her that their needs found outlet in a discreet liaison, almost invariably with a similarly disaffected husband, occasionally one of their friends. "And are you really happy with Edward?" they would insinuate. "He's always galavanting about. Such men love making money, don't they? Surely you've been tempted?"

Such a question would irritate Greda, because marriage was one's own business, as were relations towards one's spouse. Ever the diplomat, she would dismiss the interlocutor with some flippant response about how clumsy it would be to embark on an affair. She and Edward were so close, he would read her eyes over their poached eggs and muffins. Her private doubts that he maintained the same steadfastness never became public nor were the subject of any interrogation.

Greda cast a pinched glance at Richard, content that he was gaining strength and thankful for his presence. That she felt drawn to him, she told herself, was primarily because he had needed help at the moment he was found. Now, in his recovery, the man had nowhere to go. As she regarded him, careful to avoid being seen doing so, a voice within her was speaking. But anything she felt beyond the existence of his predicament was something she should shunt quickly from consideration. To do otherwise was akin to behaving like a feckless teenager.

What troubled her, as the days with Richard extended, was the tendency for such thoughts to iterate, as absences from his immediate company beckoned her to seek it again. There was evolving, without its conscious appreciation, a sense of compulsion to be with him. This made Greda question her stability. Richard also seemed to enjoy their talks, even if his reserve betrayed an apparent insentience to her attraction to him, which she was being driven to concede.

An intuitive outsider witnessing their interactions might have proffered a laconic witticism. As neither wanted to acknowledge the existence of an internal struggle, each transmitted mixed and contradictory messages, the import of which was to disabuse the other of any interest beyond mere circumstance.

Practical countermeasures were also devised to take his and her mind off the other. Greda intensified commitments at the hospital. Likewise, Richard, finding nothing more to do in the workshop, scoured the estate for any leaky pipe. When he turned to eradicating weeds, Ah Fut was incredulous.

These artifices produced but an illusory reprieve for both.

Chapter 10

Edward and Carrie

Six days had elapsed since Edward Faircrossman had departed for his tin mine in Telok Anson and two rubber estates in Selangor. He had telephoned his wife from Kuala Lumpur to say he would collect Jonathon and be back in time for Christmas.

The largest air battle of the war had taken place on the morning of the twenty-second of December. Buffalo aircraft from the last fighter squadron based north of Singapore engaged a superior Japanese formation comprised mainly of the navy Zero. The British fighters had received a thorough drubbing. Low-flying, unhindered attacks on the Kuala Lumpur aerodrome ensued. Like many observers on the ground, Faircrossman witnessed the one-sided spectacle.

That night saw him in the company of other planters and some officers. Their gathering at the favoured and ludicrously titled expat watering hole, Blow-in Inn, in the northern capital was a subdued one. With stocks of English ale rationed, conviviality was not enhanced. They were cognisant of the decision to evacuate the airfield. Nobody spoke of defeat, but no longer could enemy attainments be regarded as transient aberrations. Radio bulletins suggesting the Buffaloes had shot down a large number of planes were treated with universal disdain, although not everyone was entirely pessimistic.

The group had just finished dinner when Faircrossman opted to leave. Farewelling his colleagues, he took a diversionary tour on foot through the red-light district. He found the nightclub Carrie usually frequented on a

Monday, but the barman said it had been some time since she'd worked there and directed him to the place where Richard had discovered her secret.

The Sitosa Samootin bar in the Chinese quarter was nearby. Faircrossman made an unobtrusive entrance, shaking off the attentions of the hostess who greeted him. Eva was in desultory conversation with a man, his greasy, globular hands bulging with chunky rings, and whose carelessness with foreign currency had attracted an expectant entourage. That Carrie was happy to gravitate towards such an individual was less than edifying and impelled the planter to adopt discretion.

It transpired that Mr Ling, as the maitre d' called him, was poised to leave with a bevy of youthful consorts. They, having assembled at the door with an older woman, were instructed to attend to all his needs. With much giggling, they led him to waiting transport.

Carrie did not even look up. Fixed on her barstool and drinking pink gin, she seemed detached, chain-smoking through a silver filter of extravagant length. As soon as she finished one drink, another replaced it. Two more waited courtesy of her recent benefactor, leaving Faircrossman in no doubt that the interval pending their consumption would not be lengthy.

"I didn't know you smoked," he said, slipping behind the tantalising form and pulling her slender waist towards his groin. She resisted, ever so slightly arching her pelvis away from him without total disengagement and expressed no surprise at his sudden appearance. "What is it now, a couple of months? More, I think, maybe six or so. Carrie, don't I even warrant a 'hello, how are you'?"

She drew on her cigarette and consumed a sizeable measure before a lazy reply. "I've always smoked. What do you want from me? We can go wherever and relieve your tension. It's of no consequence, as I want for nothing."

Crestfallen at being tossed off as easily as the retreating liquid, he leaned over her. Faircrossman had never considered Carrie a bar girl in the traditional sense, more a very classy and selective independent contractor. An affinity with alcohol and late nights had left its imprint—

dark shadows and hard lines prominent—yet something about her fascinated him.

"Carrie, I wonder why you think so little of us. There's a better way. You're drinking too much for a start and—"

"You can talk," she snapped back.

He ignored the retort. "Do you want to tell me what's troubling you? I do care. What's happened that I find you like this?"

"When did you get to town? No doubt you went to see if I was dancing tonight. I haven't been there for a while and won't be going back."

He was appreciative of even shallow exchanges. Her temperament was volatile and to press might lead to sudden disengagement. He spoke of his trip and the Japanese bombing of the airfield, which she took in languorously, avoiding his eyes. The conversation was petering out and he was constrained to order a drink on the casual acceptance of another for herself.

Exasperated, he asked, "Is it about the Australian, the one I saw you with at the E & O? Unfortunate business, that. My behaviour was appalling, I was boozed and—"

She spun around, tears forming in determined eyes, and steered him to a table in a quiet corner. "Richard's dead, and I know the man responsible," she stammered. "You have a lot of connections in the British Army, don't you?"

"What do you mean, Carrie, I—"

"You'd only need mention to someone high up that you knew an officer who was supplying information to the Japanese and it would instantly go to the proper people to be dealt with. Traitors get hanged like dogs, and the authorities trust you."

"Why yes," he said with some reserve. Taking in the disclosure, any vestiges of insobriety were erased. His reaction wasn't lost on her. "Carrie, if you're certain someone's betraying my country and you want to give me his name, I'll see it's done with the utmost discretion."

Her attitude softened and she pressed against him. "I'll give you a thorough account. Now we can go to a place I stay sometimes. Very private."

She led him to a semi-detached room situated at the rear of the building. Opening a bedside drawer, she removed a pencil and paper.

"You're sure you want to do this, and it's absolutely correct?" He was tempted to hint that the Australian might be alive as a means of testing her motives but, as her influence upon him rose, his willpower to do so waned.

"Of course it is, and that's why I need your help. The man's a vile, detestable individual. I'll write this down." Her hand was as fluent as her speech. "His name's Patrick Heenan, a captain in an intelligence unit here, and has been passing military secrets to the enemy for years. He's even been to Japan once. As recently as a week ago, he provided a layout of the aerodrome, including numbers of planes, fuel and ammunition hangars, and—"

"What! How do you know this? Did he admit it, a British officer?"

"Look at me. No one could invent such a monstrosity," Eva replied as surely as the fracture of a twig.

She told of a personal file Heenan had inadvertently overlooked after one of his visits. Having memorised the contents, hers was a comprehensive account, intricate in detail, disturbing of implication. That it was inspired by a conviction of Richard's demise was undoubted and this led Faircrossman to sideline the inference of her own internecine connection.

He would reveal these assertions to the authorities at the first opportunity, so vital were their import coinciding with the recent air battle. But what hindered him from telling her that Richard was alive? It proved a short-lived moral quandary. She caught his preferment and terminated the memoir. The unfastening of her dress, released deliciously ripe and provocative breasts that he had coveted for so long. His pants slid off. Over the Australian, there was dilemma no more.

"We can stay here, for a while."

Inches from his face, she removed her stockings, one leg perched on the bed, encouraging his assistance with her underclothing until she was completely naked.

A quickening of loins overtook his brain, now white-hot with the possibility of unforbidden exploration. The room was noiseless, their proximity irresistible, and damn the aftermath, which he knew would lack the sweetness and anticipation of the imminent connection.

A faint light announced the next day, leading to another amatory encounter. Afterwards, she watched him dress. "You'll always find me here on Monday evenings. I don't entertain anymore, if that was the reason for your wry smile just now, but I tend to drink with the customers—ah, encourage them to drink, in preparation for the younger— yes," she added scornfully, "I'm too old at twenty-three! And well past the more varietal entertainment on hand, as with Mr Ling," she soliloquised, before speaking directly to him. "Now, attend to your side of the bargain. It's Captain Patrick Heenan."

Faircrossman strode quickly out the door and took a circuitous route away. He wanted to put some distance between them. Continuing for nearly half a mile, he saw an idle pedicab and summoned the carrier. Having fallen asleep inside, the gummy septuagenarian was slow to answer the call. Faircrossman's face was freshened by a breeze as the pedaller picked up speed down the grey streets. It was a welcome distraction, sweeping aside his cold sweat. An audible stirring of the local population became more pronounced in the approach to military headquarters. He intended to hand her notes to a senior officer, a 'Blow-in' compatriot of last evening.

"No, it's confidential, and I can't return later," he told an enlisted man at the guardhouse who mentioned that the major was unavailable. Faircrossman waited half an hour and still no one had come to see him. Impetus to press for a personal meeting seeped away with the effluxion of time. He scribbled a note down and was assured that the matter would be passed on.

Edward Faircrossman cut a gloomy image as he returned to his hotel. The enormity of what he had just done seeped into his consciousness. The planter was unable to escape the perturbation that this action might ultimately rebound on him. Not ordinarily the sort of man to brood for long, this time he drew uncertain comfort from the sizeable gratuity he'd left on her dresser.

*****

No regrets, inquisitions for the irresolute and just get on with it
always worked for Faircrossman. Piloting the lean early
years in Malaya, he had sweated through sixteen-hour days
and cooled off under lamplight poring over paperwork for
two more before his head hit the pillow. Now there was an
additional dimension, as implosions not many miles away
riveted his mind to the future of his business interests.

Unless they were halted, the Japanese might command
the region within weeks. The mine was beyond practical
reach. However, if his best plantation was to be abandoned,
he required contingency preparations. Seven hundred
tons of latex could be salvaged. He had hired a dozen
trucks, along with their drivers, for its carriage to Port
Swettenham in convoy.

The journey to his estate took less time than anticipated.
He was surprised at the apparent inertia of army operations,
given the amount of traffic proceeding in the opposite
direction. The sprinkling of military vehicles travelling
north could suggest any number of things, but he would
not make any precipitate decisions until he spoke to Erik
France.

The manager of Edward Faircrossman's most northern
estate, a seasoned expatriate hailing from Bath in the south
of England, had just celebrated sixteen years in Malaya. Of
Anglo-Germanic heritage, France possessed a remarkable
physical strength that belied his compact frame.

Faircrossman had observed his prowess at an Indian
wrestling competition where large sums of money were
wagered on the outcomes. After beating all-comers on
four successive evenings, his notoriety had spread, and
the starting price climbed to almost unbackable odds. At
the fifth such outing, Faircrossman decided that France
couldn't lose and won five hundred dollars after risking six
times that amount. Congratulating the ebullient victor and
slipping him fifty dollars as a bonus, an instant friendship
was struck between the two men.

"Now, no more of this grunty garbage, the punters' loss
will be yours and my gain," he said, thumping the young
man on the back. "I'm going to make you a much better
long-term offer. We'll discuss it over dinner."

France's association with the planter began from that point. It never wavered, and a more devoted employee couldn't be found. Ten years after that fateful encounter, it culminated in his prize appointment as plantation manager.

Faircrossman arrived to find telephone communications down and, besides a cook, the housemaid, two old gardeners and a few labourers, the other workers had taken flight. Rumours that the Japanese would deal harshly with anyone helping British interests were greedily digested. There had been a false alarm that the enemy was already at a plantation several miles away. The heightened level of fear stimulated rushed judgments amongst Malays and their families. Yet, reliable updates weren't available, and no shellfire could be heard in the distance. The two-way radio had limited range but was sufficient should the necessity to evacuate arise.

After a meal, the men took time to review the short- and longer-term positions.

"Erik, we'll be loaded and underway late tomorrow. A good run should see us arriving at Swettenham in a couple of hours. There's at least a further hundred tons down at the warehouse."

France accepted another mug of cocoa from his boss. "Thanks."

"We'll try to ship all the stuff out. There won't be enough space to lift everything in one trip. The place has suffered one airstrike. I didn't have time to go down there so who knows what to expect? We'll see about getting a ship."

"We're trusting a bit to chance by heading there cold, but it's worth a try. You'd think the Japs would want the operations to remain productive," France remarked absentmindedly.

"We're not going to wait and ask them, and I'm damned if I'm giving it away!"

"Hell no. By the way, the women and the old fellows have asked that we take them to a nearby village where their families are. Hope they'll be right," remarked France as he lit another cigarette.

"They will be."

"Okay, we'll convoy down, unload and come back for the rest."

"My bloody word, but if things change, then that's it. How do you feel about going back with me to *Melmingreda Kediaman*?"

France puffed vigorously before replying. "It's hard to even contemplate leaving here—well, not just yet. There's so much to be done. Surely they're not going to get so far past Kuala Lumpur as to cut us off, at least not for a few months?"

"Who really knows, Erik? I'd like to think so."

"Well, to hell with it, I'll decide after we come back for the rest."

"It suits me if you could remain a bit longer, even with a skeleton outfit. Once it looks like we've abandoned it, you can imagine what will occur, Japs or no Japs."

"My ear's to the ground, boss."

"Speaking of holding on, I have an Australian chap helping us. He's an engineer from one of the ships we use. Was mixed up in a scrap and missed her sailing. Nice fellow and, if he doesn't return to seafaring, has a ton of potential."

"Sounds overqualified, but I could do with that sort of help here too. What's his plan?"

"Oh, he wants to get back to sea, of course. I'll do what I can there. For the minute he's pretty much marooned, tough bastard and keen to work. Forget his name, but I'll use him while he's around. I did him a favour and it delayed me getting here," he offered as a convenient afterthought.

If Faircrossman had one outstanding feature it was his ability to impress people who depended on him, like France. He was adept at projecting a dutiful, caring side, as if the aspiration that drove him most was intellectual philanthropy. While there was no doubting his generosity, it suited his profile to portray these characteristics.

The ascription of the delay to the new engineer seemed glib to France. This was not the first occasion in recent months that the boss had demonstrated a less than usual adherence to schedules.

By the following afternoon the trucks were loaded. Begrudging the lack of space, Faircrossman conceded that three hundred tons was their carrying capacity.

"Two of the hands are coming down to help us unload, Erik. I'll take the kitchen staff. The others can easily reach their villages on foot. That detour's an hour there and back to the turn-off where you'll wait for me. We'll be on our way proper soon."

"The convoy's ready to move now, boss," replied the manager intensely. "I'm in the lead vehicle and, after you drop the others off, I'll join you. Do you want the blunderbuss in the car?"

"No, you keep it. I've a rifle. I'm in two minds about the car if the going gets rough. She's capable of over eighty miles an hour, so I can step on it."

"Up to you. The drivers have received half their pay and are keen for the rest on arrival, so they won't muck around." France exuded confidence. They shook hands, the physicality reminding Faircrossman how well he had punted.

Returning to the waiting lorries after his detour, he was joined by France and led off. The road south had become clogged and progress snail-like. Every manner of vehicle, from wagons towed by weary oxen to tricycles pulling loads dwarfing the persons propelling them, dominated the traffic. Cars and heavy vehicles were clearly outnumbered by mopeds, pedal and animal power. Even water buffalo were moving anything from furniture to bags of rice piled high on diminutive carts, rocking precariously from side-to-side, looking every bit as likely to overbalance and crush anyone underneath.

The pace frustrated the impatient planter. Logjams formed at intersections where people were feeding in. Others had stopped. Loaded wagons were detached, their oxen grazing the road verges nearby. Just where they were going inspired him to ask several cart drivers. "Japanese, we go down." Assuming this to refer to Singapore, Faircrossman envisaged the chaos about to befall the island. Was it premature?

On arrival, he searched in vain for his warehouse. "Bloody evil bastards!" he cried. Where once it stood lay piles of bricks, timber fragmented to smithereens and crumpled sheets of corrugated iron.

He walked around with France to survey the scene more closely. Much of the wharf nearby and some other storehouses had also been severely damaged. Torchlight revealed a line of masts peeping above the water.

"So much for getting cargo off by ship, boss," said the manager, shaking his head. "What next?"

The other man swore before sitting down on a wooden block. "We're certainly not leaving it," he responded grimly. "I'd drive this lot into the bloody sea rather than let the enemy get their hands on it."

France strolled over to rest a hand on his shoulder. "Tomorrow I'll ask around. Someone will know if the channel's blocked."

"Good way to go, Erik," said Faircrossman, trying not to let his despair show through. "It's a sure bet most of the ships have gone." France stood beside him as he peered across the water towards the open sea. He never remained self-absorbed for long. "You're a seasoned bugger to have around. What's on your mind?" he asked, accepting a lighted cigarette, puffing once and then grinding every last ember underfoot.

Ignoring the compliment, France continued, "We may be able to shift it on a barge and get towed down the coast."

"You're probably right. There's little sense in hitting a clogged road for Malacca and not much we can do now anyway."

"If I was religious, I might be tempted to pray. Just kidding, Ted," he said good-humouredly.

"For once, go ahead. I'm off to make a telephone call. Greda will want to know what's going on. We've no chance of getting home before Christmas. Let's go and put up somewhere. The drivers will stay with the trucks."

They found rooms in the business district. The hotel clerk related an account of the air raid before securing a connection for Faircrossman on the house phone.

Greda's icy manner unsettled Faircrossman's mood. "I'm very worried about Jonathon. Apart from Christmas being almost upon us, you're nearest to him. I was counting on your promise to bring him down from school. What on earth are you up to? Why have you taken so long?"

"Only lost two warehouses and neither insured, but did that register?"

"I'm sorry, but you were saying about Jonathon?"

"That's unfortunate," Faircrossman answered evasively, reflecting on the time misspent on his dalliance with Carrie. "I've spoken to Griffith-Jones to say I can't get there," he lied, intending to call the Principal in the morning. "She assures me Jon will be alright. There are plenty of boarders and other parents in a similar predicament. I don't think you should do anything until we hear back. How's your new, young engineer going?" he enquired suggestively.

"The work is done and he's anxious to be away from here," she said, irritated by the snide digression. "But he'll not leave us here until you're back. We should get out. I'll collect Jonathon and meet up with you somewhere," she pressed him anxiously.

"Stop panicking. Bugger me, not just yet!" he snorted, becoming increasingly impatient. "We're not going to hang around unless we can get what we've hauled down here sent off. Tomorrow I'll ask about. Looks like no ships in port, but Erik says there may be a barge or two for charter. If all fails, well, that's it." Almost as an afterthought, he muttered, "There's so much latex lying around. I could get it for a fraction of the price."

Frustration was evident in her voice and, uncharacteristically, she began to raise it. "When are you likely to be back? I'm not going to leave Jon up there. And to repeat, where have you been?"

"I've a mess to fix and you're going on like this?"

"I'm asking about Jon."

His nerves were frayed. Capital losses loomed before his eyes in the thousands of pounds and she was infuriating him. "I've bloody-well told you he's alright and I'll get him as soon as this business is finished!"

"Are you at least able to say when you're coming back?" She, too, was exasperated by the tenor of the conversation.

"I've no idea, but it has to be soon. We'll see. And be damned patient for once and enjoy the companionship your guest seems to be providing."

"Edward—"

"If I have to, I'll abandon the pulp, but it's the last option and I'm not, repeat not, ready yet. I'll contact you first thing tomorrow when we know what's available."

Before she could say anymore, he crashed the receiver down.

*****

The two men were at the wharves early the following day, in time to witness a one hundred-foot barge being tied up. There was some minor damage to her snub nose above the waterline. Faircrossman was undeterred. A voyage to Malacca would ordinarily occupy several hours. The tow could take a deal longer.

After France verified that the channel could accommodate the barge, the charter was finalised. Temporary repairs were made to ensure the craft's seaworthiness. The full load would see her ride much lower in the water. Faircrossman did not mull over his losses for long, buying five hundred tons of latex on the spot at a fraction of its true worth.

"We stay with this lot to Malacca. I'll be able to sell it down there and get it shipped," he said breathlessly after securing the tug for two voyages. "The barge goes back to Swettenham, then for another run with the balance and chockfull, I hope, if there's any more around. Once the rest is loaded, we're out of it. Ah, I love doing this. Doors swing open, old boy, after you crash through the first one. Works for me every time."

"You always seem to make your own luck," he stammered.

"What are you worried about? Spit it out!"

"Well, you don't need me to tell you, boss, that we shouldn't get too smug. We've a way to go before it's done."

"Good lad, and wise words. That's what I want to hear from my managers. You never were a 'yessirecho', Erik," he replied, welcoming the brake on his enthusiasm.

Faircrossman's vehicle was the last load lifted. It was lashed on top of the cargo hold.

"We're getting underway shortly. Tell the drivers we'll double their money if they head back to the plantation and load up in time for when we return, which should be by this hour tomorrow."

Just after six in the evening, they were aboard the heavily-laden craft. Tow lines securely fastened, they strained on the barge's bollards, groaning and creaking as if the forces being imparted might prove too much for the ropes. Signalling the commencement of the southward voyage, the tug's propeller churned, boiling the water, dredging mud and debris to the surface and crawling them forward. Their achievements in the last twelve hours were toasted with warm beer as the two men rested on the hatches, watching the horizon swallowing the sun. Faircrossman estimated the cargo to be over eight hundred tons. *To hell with the overloading,* he thought. Its value was the equivalent of several months' supply and had cost him a pittance of the charterparty to Malacca.

The dishevelled barge contained rudimentary quarters. A cabin aft was attached to a covered shelter with just enough room for two hammocks, a narrow table fixed to the deck and a tiny combustion stove. It was here they repaired as daylight dimmed and kerosene lamps glowed brightly. Both had worked furiously to achieve their early evening start. The big Englishman could hardly contain himself, promising his manager a generous bonus.

France had always fancied himself a short-order cook. The pan sizzled as noses were drawn to the aroma of fresh fish and chipped potatoes being fried. The beer was like nectar. As the two men ate and drank, bellicosity imprinted itself in the planter's face. Yet again, against all odds and the strawmen naysayers his mind always conjured up, he had done it. Full-stomached and swigging from a bottle, he strutted around the barge owning it as a man impregnated with his own invincibility. Allowing for a speed of four knots, the majority of their sea travel would be under the blanket of darkness, well away from scrutiny.

Or so Faircrossman thought.

Chapter 11

Getting Jonathon

After dinner, having made a tranquil transition to the spacious living room, Greda and Richard talked well into the night. Throughout the evening her aromatic presence possessed him. Time was the least tangible element of his manifold appreciations. When the clock in the hallway emitted a single chime, it could have been three, as she discarded her shoes and flexed her toes distractingly. Any thought of the hour announcing prohibition evaporated when she decanted sherry for two.

An expressed doubt that Edward would ring now escaped his notice. Still shoeless and smoothing her hair, she asked whether he was tired.

"No, not at all. Do I look it?"

Greda was not thinking of fatigue. Her eyes gleamed as she spoke. What an imposing figure he made, chest hair tufting above the second button of a white shirt straining to accommodate his shoulders, biceps at one with sleeves. When his hands clenched and unclenched, the armrests of the cane chair made a sound that alerted her to workmanlike fingers.

They traversed many topics. Speaking of life as a medical student, she admitted with a faint blush to having been somewhat radical and free-wheeling.

His imagination worked merrily on her description.

"University must've been a grind. Years of study, then the practical?"

"I recall an occasion when the stethoscope was nearly maimed. But I persevered." She leaned towards him. "And you?"

"I've also hurled my share of tools around, as you tend to do."

Greda touched on politics, where she conceded admiration for Churchill.

"My father follows it more closely than I do."

He sought to know about her family's estate in Leatherhead and she obliged.

"To hear you describe the countryside in Surrey—so green and lush—I can't help being provincial. Three head to the acre, only needing to graze half a day and then too fat. That's a pipedream where I come from."

"Mmm, quaint the way you put things, Richard; provincial indeed."

He pocketed this as a mild rebuke. "I would like to have your, ah," he checked himself "and your husband's command of language."

Momentarily, the colour fled her cheeks. "No," she said after a thoughtful pause, "I wasn't being critical. I dare say there's much in your vernacular from which we could all learn."

Richard savoured the observation.

She gauged his reaction before continuing. "It's not always like that, you know. Lush, I mean. Our winters are interminable. In an instant the grass vanishes under a foot of snow and not a cow in sight."

"Yes, I overlooked those really bitter conditions. That's a challenge we never get."

Their eyes met long enough for him to experience their penetrating clarity. He was relieved, if not thankful, when the telephone rang.

"I'll be upstairs if there's—"

"No, that's alright, stay here. I won't be very long." She motioned for him to sit and hurried off.

Muffled frustration was redolent and though it wasn't Richard's predilection to eavesdrop, her voice carried nearer.

Coming back into view, Greda's chest heaved. Her head shook from side-to-side. She sat down, staring into space for some minutes, oblivious to his scrutiny from the veranda. "Hello," she called.

"I'm out here."

She rose as he rejoined her.

"Forgive me for being rude, but I just had the most extraordinary conversation. I'm flabbergasted. Our son was to come home from school for the holidays, and—"

She turned away, arms splaying carelessly, before swinging around to face him.

"Are you alright, Greda?"

She nodded, tensing her jaw. "Now Edward tells me he won't be back and, ergo, Jonathon need not be, he's decided. And I'm supposed to cool my heels, not fret about a young boy alone because the Principal has reassured his father?" She took a few paces, arms unfolding and refolding. "None of this was discussed before he left." Full of piquant anger, she swept away from him. "Excuse me, Richard, tell me to settle down." She paused, hoping he would speak before continuing. "Yes, I know everything's chaotic, but here he is doing deals, chasing money, off to Malacca, while his son just has to wait. Well, his mother won't stand for it. Are you up for a car ride? Fairly substantial, could use a co-driver," she stuttered.

To acquiesce would make him party to obvious conflict between those in whose home he was being treated with exceptional regard. Conversely, he was not inclined to have her go alone, as she seemed determined to do anyway.

"Yes, whatever you want. How long will it take to get there?"

"If we left early and had a good run, maybe four hours."

"There's just one thing, I'd be doing it because—"

She narrowed the distance between them. "Let me worry about Edward. I shall simply tell him that you were co-opted. Anyway, I have it firsthand that he wouldn't want me to travel unchaperoned."

"Oh, he told you that."

Her expression provided no answer and beckoned other questions before she frowned. "Do you think it's the right thing, Richard?" The hesitancy and her seeking his imprimatur magnified the contrasts in this perplexing woman. Risking Faircrossman's wrath was not a consideration.

"I'd want *my* son home with me at this time," he said.

Hands held his shoulders, the spontaneity checking any further movement. "I've made my decision. Thanks."

*****

Tremulous light had emerged to reveal wispy strands of fog as Richard checked over the 1940 green Plymouth sedan that would take them to the Cameron Highlands. He lifted the bonnet and shone a torch over the engine. Not a smear of grime was evident. It was in immaculate condition, with barely a thousand miles on the odometer. The vehicle's interior retained a factory odour, its paintwork gleaming.

Impatient for the promised call from her husband, Greda made a brusque announcement of her readiness to leave, and they started out. Their route took them through Kuala Lumpur and on the road north to Ipoh. She handled the machine with a pronounced measure of efficacy. From the corner of his eye, he saw a series of frowns corresponding with movements of her lips suggestive of an internal debate. The degree of intensity was such that forbade any attempt at conversation.

Greda's mind picked over the telephone call. The lack of particularity about his movements, his capriciousness in decision-making, unexplained delays and his discursive responses excited suspicion, but pushing aside his son at this time was completely out of character. There could be no definitive resolution as to the basis for his disingenuous behaviour, save that she felt a sinistrous event unrelated to their ongoing disharmony was behind it.

When Greda emerged from her absorbed space, her mood had faded. "Sorry, miles away. We'll stop here." She pulled over and exited snappily. "Well, that was pretty straightforward. From now on you've the hard section." He was mystified, remaining in his seat before she added, "Seriously, we can swap around on the way back, but it's your show from here."

"Right you are," he said, opening the door.

"We're not quite halfway. How about some tea before resuming? I had Fanny pack a flask and sandwiches."

"Yes, if you like," he said, grateful for some refreshment after a light breakfast.

"I suppose these distances are something you're used to in Australia?"

"Well almost nowhere's close. Anything other than gum trees was a fair old run from the farm. If we ever abandoned toil for five hour's fishing spanning either side of the low tide, there was no change left out of a day. Only remember two of those though since both times Dad got nothing but tangled lines and I bagged some nice flathead."

She nodded appreciatively. "You're a sentimental young fellow, Richard."

The age adjective wrongfooted him, but he welcomed the personable tone. "Ah, things always look better when you think back. Not often so as you live them."

"Perhaps for some, neither of those statements is true," she said wistfully, as if willing him to ask what she meant. "You speak fondly of the old, well, not so old way of life. The country and fishing. Were there other good memories?"

He chewed on a sprig of grass. "We have to move on, I suppose."

"Yes, I guess one does." Her elliptical observation intrigued him.

The clouds had been blasted asunder by the Malayan sun. As they sat on the side of the road, the air heavy with humidity, Greda saw beads of perspiration reaching his chin. Retrieving a cloth, she dipped it into the small ice chest and offered it to him.

"That's kind of you." He wiped his face and wrapped it around his neck. "And did the trick."

"Must look after the helmsman, as you sailors would say. Shall we get on or may I recharge your cup?"

"No thanks, let's go."

It was by far the most powerful car Richard had ever driven. His take-off, which thrust them back into the bench seat, produced an amusing rebuke as she steadied his forearm with mock apprehension.

"Is this how Aussies drive? No wonder you hear about them being accident-prone."

He frowned. "Do you think I'm—" She put the other hand to her mouth and pretended to look afraid, then relaxed. "Ah, you're having me on, I see." He slowed to a more sedate, even pace. "I have to get used to this one."

"Me or the car?"

Their levity merged.

"Never take too much notice of *this one*." She was wagging her forefinger. "You're doing well."

"I'm pleased you seem to be feeling better. After we set off, I wondered whether you might be entertaining second thoughts."

"Not about what we're doing," she replied, confounding him further.

He changed tack. "I take it you've been up here before? I mean, apart from enrolling your son, of course?"

"Yes. Edward and I once loved visiting here, three times a year, sometimes more."

Her use of the past tense fed speculation about whether it was meant to convey a change in their situation. "How long is it since you've been for, ah, a break?" he enquired.

"Over a year now, it's a place frequented by expats: beautiful climate, virtually no mosquitoes and, at nearly five thousand feet above sea level, quite brisk. At night it can be very chilly, you know. Many of the homes and guesthouses up there have fireplaces. Its highest point is the delightfully named Mount Gunang Batu Brinchang."

"How does that translate?"

"A very good question, Richard," she said, easing back in the seat, enjoying the repartee and winding her window up as the air freshened. "I don't know. You're quite the enquiring scholar, aren't you?"

He chuckled and probed some more. "And, ah, did you go for holidays or social get-togethers, or what?"

"Well, a bit of both. Planters would visit there for conferences—really events where almost everyone gets tight, and the wives would tag along of course, like appendages." A trace of cynicism was evident. She turned to gauge his reaction.

He merely said, "Go on."

"Some saw it as an opportunity to buy property and even diversify their businesses. We didn't. Jonathon's school was established by Anne Griffith-Jones seven years ago and these days boasts 150 pupils."

The numbers surprised him. "So mostly boarders; it sounds prestigious."

"Yes, I suppose you could say it's like your school in Toowoomba."

"Do continue," he added, as she detached sandals and extended her feet.

"Oh, with the influx of the armed forces, the Camerons became something of an R&R facility for officers wanting to while away their leave and I—well, maybe it's just me, but I found this took away some of the mystique." She darkened, recalling a flirtatious episode involving Edward. "This will be the first time I've seen Jonathon since September, so I'm really chuffed to be bringing him home. He's never been away before. I wonder if his father thought of that," she added caustically. When Richard's Adam's apple rose and fell, Greda regretted her remark. "Don't mind me. I'm a woman after all, but a mother first and foremost."

Deciding against a venture into the esoteric, he offered, "I suppose you'd know a good many people there. Is it fair to have the impression that Malaya's a close-knit community for the English?"

"Yes, it is. I've a number of friends here. One in particular, Gyda Robertson, is single and keen to find a husband, having not long entered the decade of portentous prohibition for women's marriageability, the terrible thirties." He laughed and shook his head. "Glad you liked that one. I'm able to joke about it."

"I promise not to ask any more."

"You'd better not. Anyway, where was I? Yes, Gyda's become very serious, if not incautious, about finding someone."

"You mean, she's a little out there?"

"I like that expression. Is it Australian?"

"No, I just made it up then. Yes, so—"

"Well, you could say she's good at projecting herself, with ample accoutrements that men seem to like." An upward flick of his eyebrows drew a modest concession. "Present company excepted, of course. Right now she's comporting herself with a rather disagreeable sort, an army officer. Charming he may be to her, but there's something about him I find off-putting."

"So do you reckon she's making a mistake being involved with him?"

"If she was prepared to be a little more patient, she'd do better. He's a brutish-looking fellow. She's highly strung. They row quite publicly—I saw it once—and then they seem to make up. I'm not certain he's all that she imagines."

"You mean he's an imposter or a bounder?"

"They're descriptive words." She reflected for a moment before continuing. "You may be close there. He has an unnerving disposition to run his eyes over women."

"And you've experienced that?"

She was appreciative of the question and answered with arching eyebrows. "Yes."

"Are you intending to visit her while you're here?"

"I hope we can fit in tea or something. Certainly, it would be nice to fill her in on all that's happened, and maybe you could meet her. Just a minute, what did I say? I'm not into match-making." She laughed. "While I like Pinka— that's her nickname—I think you can do better too. She's not your type, that's my decree," she added playfully. "But then, who *is* your type, hmm?"

It was more a statement than a question, but engagingly personal nonetheless.

Richard was struggling to understand Greda, certain that she appreciated this characteristic in him. Taking things to heart a little too readily was a flaw. He asked himself whether he read too much into what she said. Did he need to believe Greda had, in that moment, thought about him in a way too outrageous to even contemplate? He wanted to tell her she infused his imagination with a kaleidoscope of expression more than any other person he'd ever known, but to do so might derail an absorbing discussion. Such a compliment could always be misconstrued.

Finally, she chided him for taking her too seriously. "Come on, Richard, lighten up."

He settled for, "Aw, I've abandoned trying to work that one out."

Greda was interested in his life, and he wanted her to be, but just why that was magnified the dilemma. Paradoxically, a notion settled on him. Physically so close, inside her lay an enigmatic destination well beyond reach.

*****

Colonel Gregsdaile was spending the afternoon at the officers' mess when he received Heenan's note seeking a short leave of absence. Among the barrack-room gossip about the various indulgences in which his troublesome captain had been embroiled, the CO was aware of one of less moment. His subordinate was openly consorting with an attractive, eligible woman socialising within the officer fraternity and polite society in the Cameron Highlands. She was an estimably popular dinner guest and desirable companion.

Meeting with Gregsdaile to finalise the request and keen to embroider the report, Heenan boasted that she was a most delightful creature who found his charms irresistible, hinting that a more permanent liaison was in the offing.

"Why, Patrick, you're not thinking of getting married?" put the colonel in the fashion of a mock challenge.

"I'm pretty close to popping the question, and she'll certainly say 'yes'," he responded, oblivious to the dangled bait.

"How spiffing for you. A good woman's a great boon to a soldier's career. Every chap needs a companion in this god-forsaken place, and she comes with apposite credentials. I know the Robertson family, fine outfit, and she'd make a wonderful wife. But mustn't jump to conclusions and all that?"

"Not just yet, sir. You know how these things are. Your complete discretion as regards the family would be appreciated," Heenan responded with a modicum of deference.

"Of course, Patrick, goes without saying. Anyway, you have a couple of days free, so enjoy yourself, and I hope to be the first to know—at least, next after her father, knowing you'll follow the usual protocol."

There were two phone calls to the Robertson residence over the next hour. The first was Heenan's, alerting Pinka that he'd be visiting and reserving her company for dinner. The second was Gregsdaile's to her father, advising him that his captain was taking leave and warning that this fellow had to be treated with circumspection.

"Speaking personally, the chap is best kept at arm's-length. He's not much of a team player, rows a lot and can be terribly disruptive."

"Well, she's an adult and able to handle herself," grumbled Pinka's father. "And damn her at times with that cantankerous jabber! If I said anything, she'd take the contrary view and probably elope with him. My wife and I will just stay out of it."

*****

The Principal was waiting for Greda when she arrived at the school office.

"Good day Dr Faircrossman, it's a pleasure to see you again. We've packed your son's things. He's ready to go and has no idea you're coming for him. You'll find Jonathon on the oval."

"I'm very much obliged to you. His father's away on business and incommunicado, so if he manages to call you again, could you please let him know I have Jonathon?"

"Excuse me, Mr Faircrossman hasn't phoned."

Greda raised her eyes. "Oh, I see. Well, if he does then."

"Yes, I'll do that, Madam. Your arrival is timely. Holidays aside, we're at the point of suspending attendance until the military situation is clear."

The cricket ground was the larger of two fields situated at the rear of the school. Greda proudly pointed to the boy padded up at the non-striker's end. She struggled to refrain from calling out his name and broke out in clapping and cheering when his first shot was a boundary. The ball thudded into the tree where they were standing. Jonathon followed its line of flight, saw her and waved his bat back and forward, his face beaming.

Richard identified a promising batting technique on a pitch sporting an even layer of grass. The wicket had been created in the dead centre of an outfield that replicated any manicured village ground in England.

Jon retired at the end of three further overs, but not before he'd struck another two boundaries. Excitedly, he ran to his mother. She retained him in her embrace until he became embarrassed in front of the other boys and she gave way.

After an introduction, accompanied by some background as to Richard's presence, the lad engaged easily with him and asked for some practice in the nearby nets.

"Who showed you how to bat like that?" Richard's question eliciting a generous smile that mirrored his mother's.

"Dad did when I was a real small kid, and helped me a lot," Jon said without a hint of shyness. "Since I've been up here, we've had a county player coaching us. I love hooking fast bowlers," he said with pride, prompting Greda to urge him to slow down. It seemed to have little effect. "That kid bowling was older than me, too, and he didn't like those fours."

"No bowler enjoys being carted about, Jon," said Richard.

"Can you bowl a couple more to me at your full pace. You're not too fast, I hope?"

"It won't be that quick."

Greda warmed to their interaction. Richard began to increase his pace and let one go at a much faster speed.

Jonathon took the loss of his middle stump with a rueful, "Wow, I didn't even see that! Was it your fastest?"

"Not quite, but the way you bat, in a few years' time you'll probably say I was a slow bowler." *This is a promising kid,* he thought, *respectful, eager to learn, even asking what he had done wrong to get out.* "Don't you know what let you down?" Richard was testing his cricketing insight.

"I left a gap between my bat and pad?"

"You got it, young fella."

"Thank you for the hit. Next time you won't get me so easily."

Jon's eyes lit up when he noticed his suitcase on the back seat of the car.

"Yes, darling, you're coming home for Christmas," Greda said as they all climbed in and drove away. Directed by the Robertsons to try the hotel after making a courtesy call, they added in cautionary tones, "You may find her there with that captain."

Greda was very familiar with the resort, the finest establishment of its kind in the Cameron Highlands and a favourite venue with the expatriate fraternity. Visitors approaching the distinguished entrance were greeted by two enormous wooden pillars a yard square, twenty feet high and supporting a beam of similar dimensions on which was carved *Selamat Datang*, meaning 'Welcome'.

Richard took in a saturated jungle below, stretching into cleared sections in which neat symmetrical rows of low trees announced a number of new rubber plantations. Unlike anything he'd experienced previously in Malaya, a breeze coursing from the east carried a chill reminiscent of the Darling Downs in autumn.

The foyer was bustling with sound at that time of the afternoon. Seasoned pre-booked aficionados were arriving fashionably late, while those having finished luncheon were ambling out of the dining room. Others milled around in anticipation of gaining a table.

"Might just wait outside, Greda, and look around the place. You go and see your friend," Richard said unpretentiously.

Greda flushed at his indisposition. "Nonsense. You're coming in with us." She fastened onto his arm, fingers applying a pressure with which he became readily compliant. "We won't stay very long. I do want you to meet Pinka. She's good fun, a pal of sorts, and take no notice of my earlier repartee, alright?"

The concierge pointed the way.

"Oh my God, Greda, hello, darling, over here!" exclaimed Pinka, waving her arms expressively, luxuriating in the spectacle it had created. "What rum luck."

Richard couldn't avoid the imposing cleavage, well-ornamented courtesy of a long chain bearing a gold heart encrusted with diamonds, a gift presented that very morning. The cloying figure bestowed kisses and hugs as if she hadn't seen her friend in years. Greda's introduction of Richard as an Australian who'd been repairing their machinery encouraged more than an indifferent survey of him. The accurate description of Pinka amused him.

Her companion, seated with his back to them, rose in the manner of a thespian making a belated and affected entry on stage. Towards Greda he bowed ostentatiously, kissing her hand that wasn't so readily offerred. For the two men, mutual recognition was instantaneous. A stealthy rearrangement of Heenan's perfunctory smile to a sneering, gloating arrogance conveying a deprecatory, *So it's you, is it,* before he began to raise his right limb in the same supercilious fashion.

The arm was still not fully forward, but accepting it would be heresy. Richard opted for the only course he could devise in the instant.

Heenan's hand opened and the fingers extended.

"I'll be outside," was Richard's only concession to instinct. "If you ladies will please excuse me?" He deigned not so much as a second glance towards his nemesis.

It was Jon who relieved the perplexed onlookers when he asked, "Mum, can I go out, too? There's a big yard at the front where we can have a few more hits."

His mother responded evenly, "Certainly, Jonathon. Off you go, but just stay near and do exactly as you're told."

It was as well that Richard didn't look back. He would have seen triumphant scorn on Heenan's face, a display not lost on Greda.

Pinka shrugged her shoulders and sat down. "What was that?"

"A cantankerous, rude colonial is what, my dear. Bloody convicts the lot of them, with manners to match."

Greda wouldn't permit the sleight to pass undefended. "He's actually a very presentable gentleman," she said, emphasising the last word. "And even seemed to know you. Perhaps he mistook you for someone else, and then again, perhaps not."

*****

Christmas Eve had Richard and Jonathon looking for a suitable tree in the jungle abutting the perimeter of the rubber estate. The boy chose a young Casuarina, sturdy, luxuriant in foliage and nearly ten feet tall. He insisted on administering the last rites from a tomahawk before it toppled over. Fixed in the centre of the living room, mother, son and Richard set about decorating the tree with Greda humming a contented accompaniment to Carols being played on the radiogram.

"You've done this before?" Greda enquired.

He gave a benign nod before switching on the power for the coloured lights. They flickered for a few seconds, before the whole house fell into darkness.

"Looks like I've blown everything up. I'll be back."

"Never mind about that, I can light some candles," Greda said hurriedly.

Richard rejected the suggestion, saying Christmas Eve without lights was like an empty stocking when the kids woke up next morning. "I'll have a look at the fuses down in the workshop." In quick time he fixed the problem and, while there, added a few finishing touches to the gifts he had made for them.

Morning saw Jonathon under the tree to open his presents. There was a brand new *Stuart Surridge* bat, a ball and gloves that his father had purchased in Singapore, meticulously wrapped by Greda in a large box. She, in turn, had given him an Enid Blyton book called, *The Secret Island*. There was a gift for Richard of a wallet with fifty US dollars inside and a little card with writing penned by a graceful hand: *To dear Richard, Thanks for all you have done and happy Christmas, 25/12/41 P.S. Your first pay, you have certainly earned it! The Faircrossman family.*

He was not a little humbled to have been remembered in this way. "Thank you," he said, tensing his jaw and swallowing. "Now I've a surprise for Jon." Richard winked at the boy.

He led them downstairs. There on the lawn was the billy-cart he had welded and fashioned from scrap and timber in the workshop. Jon was ecstatic. Richard pushed him around in it for some minutes before delegating the task to Ah Fut.

"Hey, I think Father Christmas has something for you, too, Greda," Richard said, bearing a little package swathed in crumpled brown paper and tied with twine.

"So much for your gift-wrapping. What is it?" she speculated, fondling the item.

"No card, I'm afraid. Open it and see."

Richard had melted down a battered old pewter mug, then machined and shaped it into a candlestick leaving an immaculate, burnished appearance. Under its base, he'd scribed the words, *Leatherhead in Malaya.* "Bit rough, I'm afraid."

Speechless, her lips silently followed the inscription, and she only just managed to overcome an impulse to kiss him. "It's, well, just beautiful. My hometown in Surrey with a twist. How were you able to make it? Did you really?"

He lowered his head bashfully. "I figured you can take the girl out of Surrey, but you can't take Surrey out of the woman."

Greda warmed to the congruence of his words with the belief she held about her life. It moved her to an unsettling degree. Her name and the date were also there. Richard detected a distant tear. "That's the most personal gift I've ever received. I shall treasure it for as long as I live," she said, grasping his hands until Jon called out.

"Sir, can you bowl to me?"

After breakfast, they attended a moving service at the little Anglican Church. A young Chinese priest uttered a solemn prayer for the soldiers engaged in defending Malaya against the enemy and for the safety of all those caught up in the conflict.

"Do you think God will bring Dad home soon? He's never missed Christmas before," the boy asked Richard later.

"Well, I was always taught to believe and have faith in everything turning out."

"Oh, Jonathon," said Greda. "You know what your father's like. We must be patient and trust God to look after him."

Chapter 12

Found and lost

Sergeant Yhiri Inchikowa spat out blood and grime to the ground with the scornful air of a man who'd just tasted a rancid plug of tobacco. The deposit was the product of an unsuccessful attempt to remove a fragment of bullet from his colleague's damaged arm. Contentment wasn't a condition with which Inchikowa enjoyed familiarity, even accounting for the success that had delivered another fillip to his guerrilla activities.

The primary *modus operandi* of his specialist unit entailed capricious hit-and-run harassment calculated to sap the morale of planters and require the maximum diversion of resources against his five-man unit. So far, he and his band had eluded interdiction by vanishing into the jungle, living off the land and re-emerging to strike again remote from the last point of engagement. Swathed in inconspicuous garb, they went about unhindered in the countryside, sometimes disguised as peasant farmers pulling small carts loaded with produce on the surface but shielding their weapons underneath.

Bicycles were their preferred mode of transport, and supply stashes, placed by allies, were accessed as needed. It was dangerous to stay for too long in any one location, regardless of certainty that they hadn't been observed. Inchikowa was a resourceful operator whose survival thus far owed much to rigorous training and inflexible discipline.

On this exceptional occasion where the group became locked in a firefight with civilians, the allure of what seemed like a soft target in a remote area had presented Inchikowa with the chance of quartering booty he couldn't pass up. But entanglement with the two Europeans had proved anything but easy.

The driver and occupant of the powerful motor vehicle, having found positions amidst wooded cover after fleeing its confines, gave almost as much as they received. If not for his obstinacy following the loss of a man and the wounding of another, Inchikowa may have acceded to the preferences of his minions and withdrawn. A furious fusillade brought the encounter to an end. When the return fire fell silent, they assessed one of them as dead and were certain that the other had been hit, though there was no sign of him. A speedy withdrawal by the insurgents followed the vehicle's and their comrade's secretion. Inchikowa then notified the coordinates to his contact, Jamal Viranhi.

*****

"You're a reserved bloke, aren't you, Richard?" Greda remarked, resorting to the vernacular with an emphatic English pronunciation. The rolling of the 'o' absorbed him, eliciting the comment that her accent sounded a little 'posh'. It had been a sedate Boxing Day and Jonathon was spending the night with the nearby Habbersfields.

"'Reserved', you say?" he asked, angling his jaw into a casual grin. "No one's ever suggested that of me. After a couple of scotches too many, a genial Glaswegian deck officer once told me I was a contrary cuss with ants in my pants. Said I'd never settle down at anything bar reading books, let alone settle for love and a family life."

"That man didn't know you very well!"

An audacious response might have been, *Do you?* He was content to be blasé. "Perhaps not, but who truly knows anyone?"

"Indeed. Who does?" She waited, perusing the space between them. "Why do you think he said that? Have you ever actually been in love?"

Her question startled him, compelling a belief of having known her much longer than reality permitted and prompting a frank response.

"I thought I was once, um, not all that long ago, but she turned out to be something, well, how do you—"

"There I go. It's none of my business," she intervened, least wanting to be the reagent of his unease yet deriving companionable pleasure from Richard's disclosure.

He reached for the mariner's refuge. "Ah, not to worry. I've never been long enough in one place to *really* be in love or want to love anybody."

"Sad, in a way," she replied sympathetically.

"Not particularly. Most of the fellas I sailed with were either single or, if married, happier to be at sea rather than full-time at home implying that their wives might have preferred it, too." His candour induced Greda to regard her own life.

"I might know something of what that feels like. Edward's away more than he is home, like now. It took some getting used to at first. I was persuaded to forget the practice of medicine when we came out here, and—" She searched for a politic way of continuing.

"And then?" urged Richard.

"Well, I did what I was told then," she replied with not-so-delicate emphasis, "but soon found the days and nights alone so long I almost felt useless and started helping down at the hospital—at first nothing much, really. Edward was never entirely comfortable with it."

He nodded reflectively. "That doesn't seem all that different from the lot of the caring seaman's widow, as some ruefully regard themselves, but you must have missed the company." An impulse to add, *and did you get lonely,* was stayed by a thought that the conversation was encroaching upon marital privilege.

"Yes, and loneliness became a consideration," she shot back seeming to read his mind.

"That's a difficult place."

"Not really, I'm not the poor *moi* type. Life's just like that, often defying the pattern everyone forecasts. The frustration I felt at being unable to fill an obvious need and help the sick was telling and, to be frank," Greda's voice lifted, inspired at being able to speak freely to another she knew wouldn't be judgmental about something she had long repressed, "well, the situation became untenable.

I couldn't abide frothing around at home. After a while, one tends to move from a phase of sentimentality, if you like, to practicality, even pragmatism I suppose, terribly convoluted as all that sounds. One becomes older. Do you know what I mean, Richard?"

Superficially, he did, though just what she really meant intrigued him. A slim nod followed as he sought to re-align the conversation. "As you said, Edward's an enterprising man, an eye on everything. He's done well. I admire his get-up-and-go."

In reaching for the water jug his hand inadvertently touched hers, occasioning consideration of her wedding ring.

"It's been like this over the years. Nothing for a while, and then just turns up as if he's momentarily tripped off. I keep saying that. Perhaps it's a self-fulfilling exercise," she posited rhetorically not seeking his answer.

"He knows his way around, home turf and all that."

"Edward's familiarity with the lay of this vast peninsula continues to intrigue and fascinate me."

Richard might have drawn a jarring inference had he seen her expression as she rose and paced aside from him. Rather, from a distance, her lissom form earned the same close surveillance as her tone of voice, accomplished and as rich as the lead contralto from Handel's *Messiah*.

Greda surveyed him when next she spoke, this time betraying a tinge of nostalgia. "You know, we're appreciative of what's been achieved since you came here. The machinery is working wonderfully well, as it used to. Our boys think you're just terrific."

"I could never have done without them. They've understood it all pretty well, a friendly bunch—"

"Who would walk over the proverbial hot coals for you, perhaps because they saw a man all battered and bruised and yet, in a blink, you were down in the oil and grease as if having shaken off some minor fall."

"Well, I'm pretty much redundant now," he said, seeming to interpret that his time was running out. "Hard to contemplate how, but I'll really have to see about making it down to Singapore to pick up a ship. Of course, I wouldn't leave here until your husband returns."

Standing purposefully, she replenished the glass without a word in his direction. He averted his eyes and missed the trembling wrist. The sound of her heels reverberated across the floor disconcertingly.

"He'll be alright," Greda suddenly spoke. "There'll be extenuating circumstances. There always are." She was reflecting on earlier presentiments to quash talk of Richard's departure.

When she didn't further explain, he opined, "Once you hear from him, a decision about what's to be done here can be made. I mean, the way things are panning out so quickly with the war, your husband will have a first-hand picture and the facts on which to base any next step."

Now on his feet, he stepped away from her along the veranda as Greda continued to gaze wistfully across the spacious grounds. A passage of silence punctuated only by an owl's ominous hoot separated the shadow of her nearness.

"Sorry if I startled you," she resumed. "Richard, most of all I've noticed your generosity and patience with Jon. I listened in a few times when you were working on that engine and he was handing you tools and things. Then I saw him welding. Goodness, the questions! Must have driven you mad. I nearly warned him off."

He nodded appreciatively. "I'm glad you didn't. He's a good kid, quick on the uptake and keen. Wanted to try the welder and took to it like an old hand for someone so young. He's very likeable and respectful. The upbringing shows."

"That's what every mother wants to hear. Jon has grown fond of you, too. He told me so himself. As to your remaining here, well, that's for you to decide. I won't apply pressure." Greda bit at her lip. "You can—" She broke off, as a fatalism that nothing worthwhile ever remained the same overtook her. "Oh, sorry, I see it's late," and she bade him a peremptory, "Goodnight then."

Over the next weeks, her most predictable regime was silence from Faircrossman. A belief formed within her that lack of contact was not so much the product of his multifarious activities but a deliberate tactic calculated to put Greda in her place. She was in receipt of credible information from the hotel at Port Swettenham that Edward and his manager had stayed there on several occasions, the last time a fortnight ago. They had chartered a barge that involved a number of return voyages to Malacca.

After embarking on enquiries from some of Edward's acquaintances who suggested he might be on the road, Greda fell short of filing a missing person's report mindful of the consequences of having done so when he finally turned up.

Anxiety or annoyance at this prolonged uncertainty, Richard was not sure which it was, or both, developed into the theme infusing their regular dialogue, as did the ongoing speculation within the expatriate community that evacuation was not just a possibility but becoming inevitable.

Richard's disquiet persisted throughout the stalemate. He held that being in a married couple's home meant not taking anything or anyone for granted and treating their domicile as sacrosanct. This was the first time in his life that he had lodged in an abode not of his own kin for longer than a week. The uneasiness had been ameliorated to some extent by his setting out very early on to do more than make wages. Despite Greda's increasing reliance upon him as time passed, he determined to remain as detached as he could, at least during the day, by busying himself with estate duties, some well outside his remit. He developed a propensity to disappear whenever a visitor called and sensed she was alive to his rationale.

Internal arguments began to rage whereby he adjured himself not to act as one having assumed a status about this house that was neither warranted nor sought. Yet, each night after Jonathon retired, Greda spoke as if Richard was a permanent element of her existence. More frequently, the lead-up to these occasions had concerns regarding his father's whereabouts amplified by the boy. This was coupled with the grim, daily bulletins of the Japanese army's seemingly unstoppable acquisition of Malayan territory.

That she and he were being drawn together emotionally was undoubted. Richard's will to withstand that trend had been eroded to a point where further resistance was becoming impossible to cloak.

*****

Dusk on the ninth of January 1942 melded into darkness with scarcely more than a cursory interval of half-light. It allowed enough time to savour the mellow air at *Melmingreda Kediaman* and take in the insect and animal sounds synonymous with Malayan evenings. After an early dinner, Greda let the cook go and was tidying the kitchen. Richard's insistence on washing dishes was displaced by her encouragement of Jonathon's importuning him into a game of draughts.

When the English radio news was about to start, his position on the draughtboard was precarious. The boy remained in the games' room while Richard joined Greda beside the radio. The bulletin was ominous.

"For expatriates residing within a radius of forty miles to the south of Kuala Lumpur, there are risks to security. The northern capital is under threat."

It went on to report that some 'relocations' were taking place and, where possible, the army would advise individual estates. People were urged to exercise caution when moving about after dark as several armed and dangerous raiding parties had been committing acts of sabotage. In the more remote estates, immediate transfer to Singapore was recommended.

Greda was about to flick off the switch when she was halted by the words, "News Flash." The announcer spoke in a weighty tone.

"Following an ambush on a Telok Anson rubber estate, authorities are urgently seeking assistance to identify a badly wounded man whose condition is regarded as critical.

"He is described as European male, late thirties, of very stocky build, medium height and red-haired. No person fitting this description has been reported missing. Anyone who might be able to provide information is asked to contact the Kuala Lumpur General Hospital immediately."

She muffled a shriek using her hands.

"What is it, Greda?" She didn't answer for a time.

"The description almost matches Erik France, Edward's manager. I must phone the hospital straight away."

The gravity of the call was evident on her return. "He was brought in from near Telok Anson. Villagers found him some time ago alive by a thread. That's our northern plantation where they were sourcing latex, and it's almost inconceivable that he and Edward wouldn't have been together."

"Can you know for certain?"

"It all fits," she sighed. "Edward's just so foolhardy when it comes to things like that; first, be in denial that they dare come near his realm, and then take the view that he could fight them off." Her voice was quavering.

"Let's just take it steady. We need to find out for certain what's happened, and that means ripping up to that hospital to verify your suspicions."

Richard placed his hand on her upper arm, and she held it momentarily.

"We'll have to leave Jonathon. I can't have him exposed to all this."

After a further pause, she became agitated and began to prowl the room, each step more marked, her hands wringing intensely.

"Can I fetch you a drink or something?"

"No, I'll be alright in a moment."

Jonathon entered and gave his mother a perceptive hug, necessitating a restraint on her expressions.

"What's the matter, Mum?"

"Nothing, darling. We're going to take you to the Habbersfields where you can stay with Colin. We have to go to Kuala Lumpur."

"Is this about Dad?"

"No, Jon." It was Richard who spoke. "It's to do with someone who works for your Dad, that's all. We'll be back before you wake up in the morning, okay?"

Greda packed a bag for him and they headed over to the Habbersfield estate.

Eager to help, Joy and Ernest had also heard the broadcast and understood their predicament.

Richard swung the Plymouth onto the road leading to Kuala Lumpur and flattened the accelerator. It was unsurprising that Greda's mind was fixed on other matters. He wanted to reassure her that everything would be fine, but a form of words fitting the moment proved elusive. She nodded appreciatively when his fingers rested on her wrist. As they reached the outskirts of the city, she directed him to the facility in an emotionless voice.

Nursing staff had sought to refresh the room for her arrival, but it couldn't disguise the wilful odour of gangrene. Despite emaciated features, she recognised France in an instant and confirmed his identity. A stoutish, middle-aged sister took Greda aside.

"I'm sorry, but he's fading quickly. The doctor has given him morphine."

"Thank you, Sister," Greda said and knelt beside the bed.

"Erik, it's me, Greda." His eyes were closed, the lids flickering. She kept talking to him softly, patiently and composedly. Richard looked on from inside the drawn curtain.

She took his hand. "It's Greda, Erik. I'm so glad to see you. I—"

His whole body convulsed as a gurgling overtook him. She was surprised at the strength his hand imparted to hers, before a dreaded flaccidity settled. She used a cloth to cushion his chest. Minutes passed.

His lips moved and she whispered encouragement, "Yes, Erik, talk to Greda."

"Boss gave 'em, bad," he managed.

There was an appreciable interval as his breathing took on urgency but was becoming shallower. The margin separating life from death was indiscernible.

Greda tightened her grip, but this time there was no response. She bent down close to his ear. "Where's Edward, Erik? Can you tell me?"

Nonsensical sounds emitted as he strove to speak, then silence as France's breathing became more laboured. Like a stricken aircraft approaching the tarmac he glided between nothingness and a rattling quest for elusive aspiration. The clinician returned just as a nurse started up to summon him.

"Would you prefer to wait outside," he asked. "The sister will remain."

"Thank you, but I'll stay with him to the end. He's," she hesitated, "the last link left to my son's father."

"I completely understand, Mrs Faircrossman." A long, silent interval supervened.

That he continued to find breath was a miracle, and she hoped for another. As darkness began to disperse, Erik France died. She remained for a few minutes clasping an inert hand before drawing the sheet over his face.

"He didn't have any family as far as I know." She thanked the medical staff.

"We'd better get going, Greda," Richard urged, "for Jon's sake."

"Yes." With her taking the lead, the distance between them as they exited the ward increased. "Something has to be done to find out what's happened. Edward might still be out there, injured," she spoke with urgency.

Richard caught her hand and she turned to face him, thankful for the gesture as she paused to bow her head.

"This isn't like me, inflexibly contained and clinical. Now I'm unsure of what to do next. Jon has to be told about his father."

"Yes," Richard said soberly, "of course he does."

Her pale stare marked their walk through a deserted hospital corridor, and he motioned towards a nearby bench. Greda sat upright on its edge. Beside her and leaning back against the wall, he spoke in a clear, firm voice.

"Let's consider what must be done. Realistically, there's very little *you* can do, short of something very unwise. If he made it out of there, that'd be the last thing your husband would want." He paused. "I apologise for being blunt."

"No, you're being realistic."

"If he's well—if, assuming Edward's been—" He tried to correct himself. "Greda, I didn't mean—"

"Nor did I take it the way you thought I might, but it doesn't look good. Please go on." She tightened her hold on him and he rummaged for an assuring narrative.

"If he survived and was captured, prisoners have to be kept somewhere. It's a bit early to speculate about what arrangements the Japs have for detainees."

She nodded. "We might hear something more. If he's being held, he may be released, Edward's of no use to them. When they find out he oversees plantations, he'll probably be let go."

Richard fingered his chin. "Trouble is, nothing can happen from here. Singapore opens up possibilities of going through Army Command. Frankly, Greda, we've but little time to hang around."

"You're right of course, and probably also thinking what I am. Richard I've heard what they're capable of."

"It's dreadful for you, Greda, and unthinkable for Jonathon. On one view, so inconclusive, but his chances—"

"Of survival, even putting the most optimistic face on what's happened with Erik, they're remote. I recognise that."

Her frankness emboldened him to re-frame the actuality confronting them. "Each day moves inexorably towards the greater peril. It's imperative that you concentrate on doing what his father would insist upon. Your son's future, yours, too, demand it."

His words were calculated to impart assurance, yes, but they lighted upon her with such finesse that on meeting his eyes she trembled at reading them, much like she had just been addressed by a specialist before her first morning as an intern in casualty.

Though moistening, Greda's eyes didn't deviate. "We'll make a report to the police, and then not waste a moment in picking up Jonathon. Are you with me, my dear, sad Greda?"

Her absorption remained. "Of course I am. Thank you, Richard, I wouldn't do anything without you."

She leaned into him the more. They moved off towards the exit, her hand now fixed in his. She was quickening her pace and this time they were in tandem.

"Yes, police first, and then we collect Jonathon."

*****

The Habbersfield household had roused early as trunks were being packed. A late-night phone call from the army warned them to expect a visit confirming evacuation details. Indifferent to such momentous events, Jonathon Faircrossman and Colin Habbersfield were like any other boys of that age. Best friends and in the same room for the night meant being into every little adventure on offer. This morning they climbed the old Saga where, once inside the treehouse, each took turns bird-watching through binoculars. They were called to breakfast. Colin jumped down rather than using the trunk boards and dared Jon to do the same. He accepted the challenge, leaping out audaciously, but twisted his left foot when he landed.

Alerted by the ensuing commotion, Joy carried the lad inside. Swelling was immediate. The child braved off tears as ice packs were applied. By the time Richard drove up to the house, Jon was more settled. They were greeted on the porch of the single-storeyed colonial bungalow.

"I tried to telephone, but Fanny said you weren't home yet. While we were packing up, Jon had an accident," Joy related to an ashen-faced Greda. "It's not too serious, just a sprained ankle, I think. He's in bed. Is there news?"

Greda hurried in followed by Joy. Ernest pursued his wife's query with Richard, who took the planter to one side.

"I'm afraid it's worse than we expected, sir. Mr Faircrossman may have been caught in an ambush. The man we saw in hospital was his manager. He passed away earlier this morning while we were there. Edward Faircrossman hasn't been located."

"Is any sod out there looking for him?" Habbersfield growled.

"Before we left Kuala Lumpur, we advised the authorities. I can't be sure what they're doing but, judging by what we saw when we reported it, they've plenty enough to cope with packing up."

"Yes, as we have been and just about done, and as you'll soon have to. All a farcical shemozzle. Everything's beyond bloody repair in this hellhole of confusion, incompetence and error." Habbersfield shook his head. "We're waiting for the military to provide advice on the evacuation route.

They're going around to individual plantations, so they'll probably see you, too. Me, I wouldn't lay any bets on them doing anything. I've three young children to worry about."

Joy returned, telling Richard that Greda wanted to speak with him.

As he walked into the bedroom, she was re-arranging support around the boy's ankle. "We need to get him to the hospital. Apart from torn tendons, there may also be a fracture. They have an X-ray machine there."

"No cricket for a while, hey mate?" The child managed a wan smile.

Richard carried him out to the car, Greda leading to open the door. Joy was crying.

"Don't stress yourself. It wasn't your fault. These accidents happen. We'll head back home after this has been fixed."

"Dear, you have to get out. We're leaving as soon as we can. Again, I'm sorry about—"

Greda signalled with a finger to her lips and they left the estate. As they turned onto the road, an army truck entered the driveway.

Captain Binucane's mission involved face-to-face contact with the planters, confirming that they should evacuate from the Negri Sembilan area as the army could no longer guarantee their safety. He didn't look forward to the task. There was no easy way to concede a humiliating reversal, but the orders were clear, so he would make the best of it.

Binucane was not expecting any effusive thanks for his efforts. He also recalled the doubts he had privately entertained about how well the defensive preparations and countermeasures had been going. That would now be of little moment. He'd chosen the Habbersfields for his first call, opining that the somewhat cantankerous Edward Faircrossman was unlikely to be so forgiving when it came to propitiating explanations.

The sun had been up a full two hours when the truck rumbled up to the dwelling. He had fortified himself for every civilian reception and knew morning tea wasn't about to be served.

"Was that the Faircrossmans just leaving," Binucane asked the planter.

"It's her alright, off to the local hospital to get her son's foot treated. But, dammit have you people any idea? Don't you bloody talk to each other?"

Habbersfield related all that Richard had told him.

"Thank you for that update," Binucane responded apprehensively, and then, clearing his throat, "It's gratifying to see that you're getting ready to evacuate. The road south is protected. We've been on the hunt for raiding parties. They're unlikely to be anywhere between here and the main south road, but be careful. I would advise that you stay armed."

"Yes, I'll bring the kids' popguns. Bloody hell, why aren't I surprised? We'll be gone sometime today. I remember you telling us a few weeks ago in KL that all was going to plan. Some plan you have!" Habbersfield guffawed scornfully.

Binucane accepted the censure with a disconsolate nod of his head, a tacit acknowledgement that it was probably more broadly deserved. "My advice is to be gone by no later than three o'clock. Goodbye, and good luck, sir."

*****

The fifth metatarsal of Jon's left foot was cracked.

"Fortunately, it's undisplaced. We'll immobilise it in a plaster that he'll need to wear for a month or so," opined a plainly harried Dr Maganly, emerging from the X-ray room with the negatives.

"Oh, and not too long ago I spoke to a Captain Binucane who told us to evacuate tonight. What about you?"

Greda sighed. "Edward was in some trouble up north and is missing. Details are sketchy, but it's not looking good. Jonathon doesn't know. I intend to wait until nightfall. Perhaps the same officer might call at *Melmingreda Kediaman* with an update."

"What can I say, Greda?" Maganly shook her hand as they parted. "The army is providing some trucks and ambulances for the sick. Don't hang around too long, and God bless."

*****

General Yamashita was not given to harbouring magniloquent predilections about his capacity as a leader. His campaign had generated its own momentum. Like an unstoppable firestorm rapidly gaining real estate, even his supply lines were having trouble keeping up with the main advance. Resistance evaporated quickly and unexpectedly, and he wondered whether his troops might be heading into a trap. It baffled him, for this was nothing like what he had warned his officers to expect. Complacency, an inevitable corollary of such meteoric advances, could lead to eventual retreat.

A taste of resistance had occurred at the battle of Slim River, though a devastating defeat for the British and Indian forces followed. Among the guns, ammunition and other abandoned equipment, there were over five hundred serviceable vehicles. When he decided that a pause was appropriate, he told his chief of operations, Colonel Tsuji, that he wanted a comprehensive reconnaissance report about forward enemy movements. The general needed reassurance that these gains weren't a fluke. When Tsuji's report confirmed that the British were in complete disarray, the door opened to Malaya's northern capital.

PART II

All that is not eternal is eternally out of date.

~C.S. Lewis

Chapter 13

Sayonara Melmingreda

A s they entered the sure, macadam surface that had long guided all comers to the bungalow and estate of *Melmingreda Kediaman*, Greda was forced to confront the realisation that this would be the last time she'd ever do so. That sense of inevitability persisted when she couldn't get through to the Habbersfields. It continued as evening arrived and they still had no visit from the army. She had opted to delay their departure until the next day. If no further information about Edward's fate was forthcoming, Greda could satisfy herself that everything possible had been done.

Jonathon was informed of the decision to leave while she gathered belongings together. As they sat down beside his bed after dinner, he was told about what had happened in the north to his father's manager and that they could only hope and pray that some good news might arrive if they postponed leaving until the very last minute.

She held his hand and stroked him on the forehead as he pushed for details about the ambush. He brightened when she relayed how bravely his father must have fought, before beginning to whimper.

His mother pressed him tightly to her breast. "We have to leave, Jon, unless we hear something tomorrow. The army will do everything to find your father, but we cannot do anything ourselves."

"Mum, do you think Dad could be dead?"

Tensing, Greda turned her face aside. She wanted to assure her son that all was going to be well but couldn't say the words.

With tears, he addressed Richard, "Are you going to look after me and my mum now, sir?"

Jonathon shadowed his mother as she approached the window as if an answer to that query was lurking in the blackness. His saucer eyes were pleading.

"Little mate, I'll be here for you and your mum."

"Do you promise if you hear about him that you'll try to get Dad back?"

"Jonathon, my dearest son, we cannot make promises like that. We just don't know."

Richard faced the boy squarely. "I promise you this. Once we're told, I'll do everything I can to bring him home to you. Now, I want you to promise me you'll rest up, for we've a big trip ahead."

"Do we really *have* to go, Mum?"

"We can't stay, young fella, because it's dangerous and the Japanese are getting closer," was Richard's reply.

Greda arranged the bed, protecting his foot with comforters before lying beside him. Richard slipped away from the entangled mother and child to attend to the business of departure. He began preparing the only vehicle suitable for rough travel. The compact and durable truck was used exclusively for odd-job work on the plantation and came with a canopy that Richard fitted to the flat-top wooden tray. It was a mechanically sound, patchwork quilt of automobile that he had checked over thoroughly. Having no defined identity, it appeared to have been cobbled together from the shells of other makes. He filled the tank and two five-gallon containers; more than enough fuel to reach Singapore. In the midst of the preparations he was joined by a worn Greda, who apologised for not coming down sooner.

"Are you done?" her easier manner encouraging Richard. She positioned herself beside him as he leaned against the mudguard. "Sorry, I crashed with Jonathon for a bit."

"You needed it. As for this jalopy, she's pretty much ready," he said, trying to sound upbeat. "I gave her a thorough going-over. All of the essentials are there and we can leave the balance until tomorrow, if you like."

"You don't stop, do you?" she asked warmly. "Well, I've still a bit to do inside and should be done soon. It's going to be a longer trip taking the back roads."

The whole process at this time of night seemed to heighten the abiding sense of imminent loss, a life's work discarded, an uncertain future looming. She walked into every space that had housed her existence and marriage, amongst all of those things they'd worked to create. *Edward couldn't be dead*, was the enduring sentiment. She pictured him stomping about, arrogantly cursing the army, a less attractive quality when he was in the flesh, yet now almost endearing. Leaving hard-fought accomplishments when the principal shareholder could have no final say in the matter ignited a temporal fear against deciding anything herself.

It was also goodbye to her loyal staff and servants. That this had just dawned on her was an unpalatable reality. But Jonathon was the main priority, and that primacy trumped everything. She called her people together and candidly told them that if they were to remain there might be Japanese recriminations. All understood.

Greda excused herself to continue preparations. She accessed Edward's safe for the first time in her marriage and procured its contents. Sorting through them was a hollow and tedious undertaking, but she pressed on.

Underneath the last of the files and folded in half, she discovered a hand-written envelope. It appeared insignificant until she discerned a feminine influence in style. Fixed on what it might reveal, she removed the pink notepaper from which fell a seductive photograph of a young, exotic Chinese woman. With some trepidation, she began to read. Recounting an explicit sexual encounter, the author invited much more and signed off as, *Love and kisses, Carrie.*

Two recollections were triggered. The first was an occasion in the dining room when a photograph of a woman had fallen from Edward's wallet. He had retrieved the item abruptly, passing it off with, "I keep forgetting to give that to Erik. You know what footloose bachelors are like." The second was just weeks ago when she'd upbraided him following Richard's rescue.

Anger simmered within her, but Greda was not a woman given to expletives or peremptory reactions. She shuffled around her husband's office aimlessly, holding the note and photograph in one hand while placing the other to her brow, and then paused to read again the words that ripped her most of all, *Next time we can meet again at your place when your wife is working at the hospital.*

She scrunched the paper into a small ball, strode into the kitchen and threw it into the combustion stove, picturing the vulgarity of wanton trespass by a woman having intercourse with her husband. Her life here, her home, the savagery of his betrayal, all set against the accusation of inattention to domesticity was devastating. *I cannot play the victim, except of my own stupidity*, she reflected admonishingly.

Greda returned to the office. The safe held a large number of mixed banknotes. There was also gold, a useful commodity in these precarious times. She counted out equal shares of local currency for the workers, along with small portions of the precious metal. For each, the amount was more than they could have hoped to earn in two years.

She called out to Richard through the study aperture. "We'll leave it for now and do the top-up tomorrow," she said off-handedly, adding, "Jon would benefit by some extra hours of inactivity. I'd still like to speak to the army for *his* sake. But it's past time for a break."

"Okay with me. It'd be good to get any updates and give the young fella's foot as much of a reprieve as we can. You're familiar with the route, I suppose?"

She assented while surveying the remainder of Richard's exertions. In those few restorative minutes, the rancour abated, and she felt immeasurably boosted by his presence.

The next day, a dead phone greeted her. The two-way radio back-up also failed when she tried once more to contact the Habbersfields. There was still no sign of Binucane, a factor now assuming much less significance. They would travel that evening come what may.

Ah Fut was to use Greda's Plymouth to ferry the workers back to their villages, and she trusted that her instructions to render the car unserviceable would be carried out. The air was abundant with sadness. Despite telling her people she would return, each person knew that everything had changed. The master having disappeared was a matter they clearly lamented as an abominable thing for their mistress to confront. Unction had crept upon Greda as she assured them that she hadn't given up hope.

*****

Among the many strange appendages to the vehicle in which they were about to depart, the machine boasted two gargantuan doors allowing simultaneous access to the rear and front sections of the cabin. Suitably cushioned, the back seat permitted Jonathon to stretch across in relative comfort. They proceeded down the tree-lined driveway, pausing to discharge Greda at the main entrance. Momentarily, she gazed towards her home and then approached the sign. Nostalgia he could understand, but not the ardour of her attempts to dismember the object with bare hands, pushing, pulling, rocking and wrenching. The lopsided angle it assumed from these exertions became emblematic.

Moniker to stay for a little longer with the Japs to finish the job and heat a cooking pot, dwelling on the thought sardonically. "There's nothing left to say about *Melmingreda Kediaman.*" Her manner conveyed a contemptuous finality.

Richard commenced to drive while Greda stared sideways, biting at the knuckle of her index finger. Sensing that she preferred her own thoughts, Richard refrained from saying anything until the movement of her head in his direction and an absent-minded tap on his hand prompted him to speak.

"A bit of a tough one for you." He waited. "Options are few and far between."

A deliberative nod followed, and she seemed more relaxed. "Yes, on both counts."

"The Habbersfields obviously left yesterday, and it was inevitable. Anyway, we must look after the young bloke."

His ham-fisted attempt to propitiate her labile mood earned an appreciative pat on his forearm. Greda was a very tactile woman, a propensity that he rationalised as being incidental to her personality. The frequency of that physical contact had the effect of heightening his susceptibility to her and the need for its perpetuation ever unsettling.

"You're right, of course," she quipped brusquely, oblivious to his indisposition. Her mind had reverted to those she'd farewelled. "I came to love our people. They're not automatons. Beyond functional associations, one tends to develop real family feelings, not easily cast aside."

"You wouldn't be human if you didn't think like that," he offered upliftingly.

"But leaving them cold? It makes me wonder what sort of person I am. Do I really care for anyone other than those close to me, especially when I'm a doctor, for heaven's sake?" she asked with a degree of rhetorical flourish that startled him.

He glanced across, noting a perplexing combination of passion and detachment. "It's hard. They'll get on. Malaya's their homeland." He tried placating her further. "For what it's worth, I doubt the local population will hold any real fears for the Japanese. Best left alone, if they're smart."

She rested against the door, lost to his words. Despite travelling away from the advance, Richard recognised the hazards attendant on their journey. Positioned next to the driver's side door within easy reach, powerful, deadly and with a range of more than a mile, a fully loaded .303 rifle was a weapon with which he was especially familiar. Greda had also collected her husband's revolver.

In assuming responsibility for those riding with him, there was a personal redemption process involved. Since his recovery, Richard found himself unable to shake the conviction that the events in Kuala Lumpur fashioned the way his seagoing colleagues would ever remember him. Having let down those mates, he determined not to repeat the infraction when it came to Greda and the boy.

At her instruction, he turned onto a narrow cutting. Unsealed and at times rough, the timber track snaked circuitously behind the estate, a route which would emerge to connect with the Singapore road. It was slow going, the cumbersome truck having to avoid large potholes and washouts. In such conditions, the machine took some punishment and demanded his strength, but he appreciated that it was geared down and growled loudly, even when occasionally reaching twenty-five miles an hour.

His thoughts never strayed very far from the woman who sat close to him. From their first meeting, he was fascinated by a winning temperament. Her fortitude in the face of the dramatic changes illustrated another feature of singular character. Still, she retained a fragility demonstrated by actions and words showing reliance on him. Her voice created an air of familiarity and was energising. As he contemplated their present dilemma, he experienced a strong sense of anger towards Faircrossman. To feel so at a time when the man's life may have been forfeited caused Richard to wonder whether a seeming indifference to his fate was bound up in all he knew of him. What had Greda really lost, became the justification.

He was thankful when she removed him from these rationalisations. "Will you be alright for a while without a navigator? From now on, keep to this track. It'll take you about an hour to reach the main road. The map's on the dashboard. Jon's out for the count. Sorry, Richard, I'm wrecked for some reason."

"The reasons aren't hard to fathom. Go ahead, I'll be right."

Curled onto the seat with her feet towards the door, Greda inclined her head against his arm. When she adjusted herself to a more upright position, her cheek found his shoulder. Richard tasted the sweet, warm breath and he speculated on whether the movement was inadvertent. Persuading himself to think of Greda outside the prism of a relationship brought about by misadventure became easy. It ignited a reappraisal of everything that had happened, and the feel of her body did nothing to disabuse him of the conclusions he reached. Even if he had misinterpreted the signs, theirs was an enmeshment he couldn't avoid desiring. Still, he oscillated between a point of inner gratification at the heavenly place to which she had led him and one of abject disquiet.

The dichotomy was beginning to overwhelm him, and he had to break off. His jaw set, Richard pressed his left foot down hard on the sheeting behind the clutch pedal. If it had given way, such was his mood that he might have whispered he loved her. The sturdy steel resisted his impetuosity, yielding not a fraction of an inch, and was followed by a childish sigh from the sleeping form of her son. Richard let out a shallow breath with a rueful snigger. *Bloody fool!*

Indulging that misanthropic exercise, he'd become disorientated and pulled over to look at the map, careful not to disturb those near him. As the document was stowed beside the door, his hand touched the rifle, invoking a sensation that made him feel somewhat vulnerable against all the other factors that abounded. Night produced that two-way effect, shielding yet unnerving.

Richard had been a little unclear of the direction to take after passing a junction. He found the intersection on the map and was right to proceed straight through it. Their route was devoid of any vehicles.

The road, now little more than a two-wheeled byway, was badly rutted. Before he could slow down, they hit a deep washout, jolting his passengers awake.

"Sorry. Anything but this old tank would have snapped in two."

The truck started off again with a clunk. Straining to mount a rise, the clumsy vehicle bathed them in its lights. Just thirty yards in front were four ominous figures on bicycles, rifles slung over their backs. When their heads turned, Richard caught the faces of two wearing horn-rimmed spectacles. Revving the engine to an impossible pitch, he crashed it into second gear to gain momentum.

"Keep down, everyone!" he yelled.

He forced Greda's head beneath the steering wheel and gave it everything, at the same time arching his back as far as he could over her side as a shield. Splintered by the truck, the soldiers hurtled in different directions. Some dived into the pressing jungle. Richard struggled for a higher gear and slewed the vehicle to the right, smashing aside one of the men.

Greda clambered into the back seat to comfort her son. Gunshots and sounds like stones being pelted on tin, announced a hail of bullets ricocheting off the sturdy bodywork as the truck moved out of range. Now in fourth gear, he left them well behind.

"Richard, I can smell fuel."

"So can I, but I daren't stop until we get further away. Hopefully, it's just one of the containers."

"What are we going to do?" she asked, touching his collar.

"Let me think about that. If they're scouting on side-tracks like this, who knows what the highway will bring except no easy ride from here on."

"Look, there's a road." It was Jonathon's cheery voice that alerted them.

Richard steered in a direction that took a sharp turn to the right. A combination of dropping down through the gears, braking and a ton of luck saw the cumbrous machine veer off in time.

He advanced another hundred yards before halting and ruffled Jon's curly brown hair. "Well done, son."

Greda leaned over him with the torch so that together they could study their approximate position from the map.

"We missed this little junction, all except Jon, thank goodness," said his mother, directing a wry smile towards the object of her compliment. "I'd feel better here rather than the main south road. What do you think?"

Trusting that his own qualms didn't undermine any-thing he might say, Richard answered her.

"Ahead is a river. There's a turn-off to a bridge we'd need to cross, a distance of about three miles before we get there. It's too risky taking the chance of just blindly driving on not knowing what's ahead and we can't wheel around another way."

"Neither can we just sit here till daylight," Greda warned.

"We must cross that bridge soon to have any chance. I'll reconnoitre what's ahead."

"Richard, I couldn't let you do that alone. We really have to stick together," she insisted.

"I'd agree if we were sure what's ahead was clear and time was on our hands. It wouldn't work carrying Jonathon, especially if it all comes to nothing. By myself, I'm sure I could do it in less than half an hour round trip. We'll hide the truck good and proper."

She conceded his point regarding the boy but hesitated, anxiously searching for alternatives. "I don't like us being separated, that's all. Forgive my procrastination." A few more moments passed.

"Look Greda, I won't go if you—"

"Oh, just do it," she said suddenly.

A half moon guided him as Richard hacked at the bush with a machete, making a rudimentary cutting. The task became more difficult the further in he went, the jungle thickening up. He returned drenched in sweat.

"Here, put this on," she said, handing him a fresh shirt.

He drove as far as he could, cursing under his breath when a side mirror was ripped from its mounting by an overhanging branch. Turning the vehicle in the narrow clearing so it could be driven straight ahead when it was time to leave was laborious. When finally accomplished, he set about enclosing the truck with the newly slashed vegetation. "One of the containers was hit, Richard. You'll want to check with the torchlight of course; the candle's gone out."

"What's it about you with those store of one-liners like Bob Hope?"

She prolonged the humour by offering him a match, and then they were serious again.

"I'll take care of it," he said, grabbing hold of the drum that had been punctured just below its cap and moving it into the undergrowth. "It's best if you remain inside. I'll keep the small flashlight, the big one stays with you. Won't be long. If you really have to move, follow the track I'm taking left from here, but only as a last resort. The revolver's on the passenger side. I have the rifle."

She wrapped her fingers around his wrist. "Be vigilant, won't you, Richard? We need you. And hurry, please."

Her features were dim, but she was near enough for him to draw her close. Wanting to provide some comfort, he cupped one hand behind her neck, placing the other around her waist. Short breaths caressed his face and a faint moon revealed her eyes penetrating what so far he'd held in most stringent check, like a key releasing his soul. Its fleeting escape permitted their lips to touch for the merest second, before he straightened to clasp her forearms. In the manner that characterised his *raison d'etre*, Greda barely heard him say, "Thanks, I will," disinclined as she was to release him.

With one final squeeze of her hand, he was swallowed by the night.

The torch illuminated a path. Mindful of possible Japanese scouting movements, he took the precaution of enshrouding the light with his hand. When moonlight emerged to aid his progress, he flicked it off altogether.

The absence of nocturnal sounds was disconcerting, as if all had stilled while his activities were being monitored and set up for a fall. Then, not five minutes into his jog, he stopped abruptly, a large bent object he took to be a fallen branch impeding him. As he reached out, it began to move of its own volition. Richard dared not to blink. As thick as his wrist, its head reared menacingly. Flaring out like fronds of elephant ears was a king cobra. Instinctively, he whipped back, the rifle's barrel parrying its strike, and he remained rigid. Eventually the reptile lowered its head and slithered off, a retirement that permitted a resumption of breathing. Wiping away cold sweat, he pressed onward, experiencing an adrenalin surge that gave him the impetus to reach the crossroads all the quicker.

Gaining elevation, he saw the silhouette of a river courtesy of some lights on the southern shore. His mind began to debate whether they should motor towards that feature, but he scotched the thought, wanting to locate the bridge that must surely be within range. Another hundred yards on, its shape materialised in the distance. There was no traffic moving over it.

He paused on the top of a hillock and had just crouched down when a series of explosions rent the silence and illuminated the night sky. Reverberating in shockwaves, the ground shuddered, and he lay prone. Further detonations followed, and the bridge bowed like a coathanger amid cascades of sparks, thence to come crashing down.

Tactically, it made sense that the lights on the other bank must be friendly ones and the demolition the early harbinger of the central Japanese thrust. He despatched the tumbling feeling that being cut off from freedom engendered and focused on getting back to Greda and Jonathon, cocking the rifle in the process.

Five minutes into a determined run, he tripped on the uneven ground and fell, the safety catch preventing discharge of a round. As he started off again, a piercing shot rang out from the truck's direction and Richard extended himself to the limit of his endurance. But his ears were not the only ones to pick up the noise or appreciate its general location.

Chapter 14

Face to face

Jonathon had remained in the back seat while his mother leant on the pillar of the driver's side door. Greda wound the windows up, though not before the mosquitoes had gained a foothold, and her time was occupied fighting them off. Stifling conditions within the vehicle made everything feel infinitely worse. While she had taken the precaution of packing a jar of citronella oil, she fast realised that, as a deterrent, it required supplementation. A net, tied to suitable fixtures helped, but she soon discovered that any weakness in the improvised defences was quickly exploited.

Stretching herself along the front seat, Greda offered a prayer that Richard would soon return. Abstractingly, she imagined a fan whirring above her head as she drank lemon squash, an inane thing to contemplate at a time like this, yet even its transient effect enlivened her spirits.

A cheerless atmosphere generated electric tension. Being alone in the pitch blackness conspired to make Greda feel apprehensive. She took to flicking the torch on to check her watch, repeating the process several times over during the space of the next few minutes.

The first blast, almost shunting her out of the seat, was followed by more that sounded inordinately close. She sealed the boy's mouth with her hand when he sat up and cried out.

"Shush," her forefinger touching his lip, "You must stay quiet." *Now what to do,* she asked herself.

"I'm scared, Mum. When's he coming back?"

"We have to go after him, darling," she decided on an impulse.

Moving the branches hindering their exit, she wasted no time reaching in to lift Jon out, then replacing the camouflage. Taking him into her arms she gained the route taken by Richard before remembering the revolver.

"Damn!"

At the precise moment Greda turned, a deafening gunshot caused her to stumble.

"Stand still! Silence."

She recoiled from the voice and froze. The glare of a flashlight bore into her face, and Greda saw a bull-necked Japanese soldier in the vanguard and two others, one on either side of him, rifles pointed straight at them. Her mind worked feverishly to construct a plausible story.

Inchikowa pressed the barrel into her neck. "Sit," he commanded. Gripping Jon tightly, she complied. After grunting at the other two, a kerosene lantern was produced. One man held it while Inchikowa inspected them thoroughly. The lamp was then placed on an elevated stump, illuminating the figures around her.

A few moments passed before he spoke again. "You stand up, show respect to Japanese soldiers."

She held Jon all the while and quickly bowed. The Sergeant's features bore a portrait of malice. He wore a cap emblazoned with a yellow star. A splotchy face was impregnated with acne, and his chin sprouted a dozen strands of long, wispy hair. His breath, even from a distance, was noticeably fetid. As he moved his head closer, she shrank from it. Her arms instinctively tightened around Jonathon and Inchikowa wrenched the torch from her grasp.

He barked more commands; the sound akin to a person mustering phlegm prior to expectorating. The men sprang to attention. One retrieved a bicycle from nearby and disappeared along the path she had been taking. The face of the remaining man, when Inchikowa tacked on another dozen words, smacked of sneering triumphalism.

With the rifle still aimed at her, the Sergeant began in heavily accented English. "Where you come from and who this boy?"

Greda feigned understanding as a method of dealing with the inevitable interrogation. She resisted their attempts to pull Jonathon away.

"Look at his foot, see, son has a broken foot."

Inchikowa severed her grip and the other man took the boy. Jon began to cry.

"Please, sir, Japanese soldier love children. Look at plaster, broken foot, see," she gasped, then, composing herself, said, "It's alright, darling. We must do what they say, and please don't be upset." She pleaded with the soldiers, "The child's been sick."

"You, woman, what wrong with boy?" asked Inchikowa as he shone the light on the crepe binding protecting the plaster.

"It's broken. See the white cast, plaster, underneath. Look, Sergeant, please, I'm a doctor. You know, fix sick people. Foot broken."

Her brain was in overdrive, reasoning that Richard must be on his way. It was vital to maintain the conversation to avoid him stumbling upon them unawares.

"You want to know who I am. I'm a doctor of medicine and this is my son and we're lost. We—"

Inchikowa issued an order, then to her. "Put hands out."

"Do as he says, darling, just put them out in front of you. It's like a game and they're going to tie our hands up."

Cords were bound tightly around each of their wrists.

"We are lost and trying to find—"

"You no speak. Japanese soldier will speak first and then you speak. You down head for Japanese soldier. Him, too," the Sergeant said, pointing to the boy. He had forgotten his earlier question.

"Just lower your head, Jon, like this. Watch me. Can you see? Push your chin down on your chest." She bowed several times, placating Inchikowa.

Greda and Jon were led over to a tree. Roughly pushed against the trunk, another rope secured her waist. The hobbling Jonathon was put beside her with a corresponding restraint.

"Why you here?"

She repeated that they were lost. "Trying to find road so we can get to Singapore. We're so sorry to be trouble to you," spoke Greda at her most servile in a sing-song voice.

"Where car you drive?"

Greda inferred that they'd not seen the truck. "No car. We went across country and came on this road just before you found us."

Inchikowa cut her across the face with an open hand. "Silence! You lie. You dirty liar, English bitch woman!" he uttered ferociously, the blow causing her to gasp and she tasted blood in her mouth.

"You spy for British. Help Japanese, you live. You make fun Japanese, you die, and boy die first in front you eyes. Now tell me truth, where is car?"

An iron will stayed any reaction, despite the menace guiding the Sergeant's voice.

"It's true I live in Malaya with my husband. I work at the hospital near Serembam. He, my husband, was killed in an air raid and our house gone—" She was desperate to crib further time.

"You doctor?"

"Yes, respectfully, sir, I am. It is true. Spent many years in Malaya as a doctor fixing sick people."

"One man been shot, arm very sore. You fix now."

"Sir, may I talk?" She waited for permission, which seemed to mollify him.

"Speak now," he said, a little less contemptuously.

"I am a doctor and I work at the Serembam Hospital about twenty miles away."

The Sergeant mumbled again in Japanese. The man beside her removed a dirty fabric and shone her torch on a nasty infection on his arm.

"I—"

Inchikowa's rasping voice sheared across hers. "Be silent! Only speak when I say!" he roared, again raising his hand.

Greda thought a second strike was imminent and tensed.

"Hospital Seremban, you work?" His group had cased the facility earlier.

"Yes, sir."

He regarded her suspiciously as his hand returned to his side. "You fix arm?"

"Sir, with medical instruments I can try to find the problem."

The affected soldier bounded off again, returning with a small kit.

Holding out her wrists towards Inchikowa, she asked, "Speak please, sir." He nodded. "I cannot do anything with my hands tied."

The cords were removed. She located scissors, tweezers, scalpel, bandage and antiseptic, and then examined the suppurating wound.

"Remember, you and boy die, if say tricks."

"Of course, sir. I understand." Under intense scrutiny, Greda felt the skin around the infection, suspecting the presence of a bullet fragment. "May I, sir?"

"Speak!"

"Can you tell him something in his arm must be removed or he will get serious blood poisoning and die? It will hurt very much, but I must lance it to release pus. You need to hold him while I try to get it out."

He understood more than she realised. Inchikowa offered his subordinate the option of leaving it for another time, but he shook his head, pointed to his arm and nodded.

Her attention to detail impressed the Sergeant. Before she wielded the scalpel, the soldier was firmly restrained. Greda inspected the wound. Her overt intention was to show she cared to assuage Inchikowa. Her scalpel went to work, and the patient groaned with each incision. Alerting Richard actuated more extensive probing. She daubed the wound and resumed her exploration, removing a quarter-inch bullet fragment that had penetrated the bone. Cotton wool soaked up blood and pus, and she flushed the wound clean. Greda bound the area with a tight, neat bandage dispelling any doubts about her expertise.

With elaborate gesticulation and emphasis, she explained that the dressing must be removed and changed twice a day. The wound needed to be washed regularly. A fresh poultice of flour and water should be applied each time. She was not sure if the last piece of advice was taken in, but her prolixity was calculating

*****

Setting a blistering pace, Richard had not paused for breath and almost missed seeing the approaching cyclist. The lumpy outline wavered from side to side before seeming to right itself. Reaching for his knife, he slid on his stomach and crouched in undergrowth a dozen yards from the top of an incline where he was certain the rider would dismount.

Patchy moonlight gave him a bead on the uniformed man, rifle on his back, head down. Shooting the Japanese with the possibility of more in the vicinity told against any such action. He waited for the soldier to get closer, peering behind him for signs of others. As anticipated, the rider walked the bike up the last few steps. Richard sprang from behind. Armpit constricting his windpipe, he plunged the knife into his chest with repeated thrusts, breaking off well after the man's heart had ceased to beat. The faculties, from which such a combination of brute strength and lethal employment of the weapon were derived, escaped his comprehension.

Richard's frantic efforts to hide the body continued to render him insensate to what he'd just accomplished until realising that the warm, congealing substance on his hands represented the ebbing remnants of a human being's existence. Squeamish, he gouged at mud and leaves to erase the evidence from his person.

After pitching the bicycle to the opposite side of the track, he resumed a desperate pace, not daring to think what he might find ahead.

*****

Medical treatment had not left the patient any less churlish. Responding to his commander, the barrel of his gun was none-too-gently wielded in forcing her back to where the rope was reapplied, though no tie was fastened around her wrists. The Sergeant left the area, while the ingrate stood over the captives. In the few minutes that elapsed, all attempts at conversation proved futile. Greda desisted when the guard brandished the weapon within inches of her chest.

A loud series of shouts from Inchikowa saw him charge off in that direction.

"Jonathon, we have to get free." Greda was working frantically to loosen her bonds. She told him to stay calm, whispering that Richard wouldn't be far away.

The soldiers' reappearance saw their leader's demeanour incalculably more deadly. "You make fool of Imperial Japanese soldiers." He spat in her face.

"I don't know what you mean—"

He dismissed her declamations by serving up more expectorate and ordered that she be untied.

"I have something, see." He produced the broken mirror from the truck and pushed it at her. "You lie. You know what this. Confess first," he screamed, unsheathing a samurai sword and laying it beside the lantern.

"I, I've no idea what you're talking about," she uttered resolutely.

He growled at the other soldier.

Greda tried to remonstrate with them. "I'm not going to be separated from my son. Why can't he come with me?"

Jonathon began screaming.

"Silence!" Inchikowa bellowed. As he thrust the butt into her side, a shot rang out felling him, followed by a second replicating the first and the remaining soldier crumpled to the ground. Richard bounded into the clearing, a cursory look confirming an unerring accuracy. He helped her up from where she lay bent over with pain.

"Richard, thank God you're here! See if Jon's alright, could you?" She gasped unevenly, attempting to recover her breath.

He released the boy and carried him to his mother. Between them, they wrapped their arms around him and the child fell quiet.

"Are you sure you're alright, Greda?"

"Yes, I am. Oh, Richard!" Emotion overwhelmed her as she tried to speak. "It's not every day I have a gun rammed into my solar plexus."

A few minutes passed as they huddled together. "Jon, are you fine, and your foot?"

"Bit sore, Mum."

"Stay still for a moment," cautioned Richard, as he walked back towards the bodies for a second look. "They won't trouble anyone further."

"I don't know what would've happened if you had been a moment longer. They found the truck and I just—"

He brushed at some strands of her hair. "It was a mistake to leave you. When I heard that damned gunshot, I knew you must be in strife. The main thing is we're all alive."

Jonathon remained in his mother's arms. "No damage apart from a bruise or two. It was horrible. A vicious, spiteful lot, and once they stumbled on the vehicle, it was just a matter of time, and you—" Her voice faltered as she looked over to the crumpled forms. "Let's just get away from this ghastly place."

"Yes, come on." He blew out the lantern.

She tightened her arms around her son. "You ready, Jonathon?"

"There's no time to spare. The explosions were the bridge being blown to smithereens, and no prizes for guessing that we're on the wrong side of it. There are sure to be many more Japs here before too long." He lifted Jonathon and they scrambled back to the vehicle.

"Richard, stop for a moment. There was another soldier?"

He nodded. "Yes, I've dealt with him," he replied grimly. "These have got to be the ones we passed earlier. There were four and I slammed into one with the truck."

"A hue-and-cry will be on once they discover what's happened."

"Sure will, Greda. We'll take the truck up to where I walked and get rid of those bikes. Unless we find a boat, we have to work on another strategy. I'll have to check the map but what I saw has to be the Malacca River."

"I've no doubt it is, Richard."

"Okay. Well, if we can reach the port by following the river, there might be a show of getting to Singapore by sea."

Richard located an efficacious sinkhole for disposal of the bodies. He refrained from using torchlight in undertaking the gruesome task. Saplings were broken off and jungle debris piled around them. While doing so, his mind was fashioning their next move. Abandoning the truck was a risk, remaining with it a bigger one with its high visibility. There would be neither going back nor forward. In default of finding a boat, the best they could hope for was an uncertain trek west.

He was gulping in air by the time he returned and spent a few minutes detaching several engorged leeches from his legs. Greda was on the back seat with Jonathon's foot stretched out as Richard informed her that everything had been done.

"We'll see off this old girl after reaching the stream," he said, tapping on the roof of the truck. "So, Jon, soon you get to ride on my shoulders. How'll that do?" he asked spryly.

"I just want to go home," the boy moaned.

"We'll find a safe place for you. The river's our guide. We might get lucky and stumble on a canoe."

Greda winced whenever the vehicle was shaken and reached into her medical bag.

"Will you be up to walking for a bit?" he asked.

"Yes, the aspirin's working. I'm more sorry for myself than anything. I wouldn't volunteer to go through that again," adding tenaciously, "unless I had to. At least I've two sound feet. Between Richard and me, Jon, you needn't worry about even your one good leg touching the ground."

A mile further on, he stopped. They gathered their essentials into two knapsacks. He watched quizzically as Greda inserted the candlestick.

"There's no room for that silly thing," he offered teasingly.

"I'll thank you to pack your stuff and never mind about mine. Should I care to enquire the whereabouts of *your* Christmas present?"

The remark lightened him, and he couldn't help but wonder if any situation, no matter how dire, would ever repress her.

"It's in one of my pockets, I think," he quipped, and she pretended to box his ears.

He emptied water from the large container into a flask. They each had a spare set of clothes and ground sheets. She kept the revolver, and some ammunition was put into a side pocket of Richard's knapsack. He would carry the rifle and the machete was tied to his belt. His intention was to find somewhere safe to camp before dawn, then rest during the day and follow the river at night. Malacca was about thirty miles downstream. A friendly village along the way might provide other options. Getting to Singapore could be negotiated, as they had sufficient money to buy a sea passage.

Richard drove to the rise that dropped off to the river and they alighted. *The old girl doesn't deserve this fate*, he thought. He pushed it a few more yards until, of its own volition, the truck coasted over the embankment, gathering pace as the slope steepened sharply approaching the water's edge. A bubbling cauldron marked its demise under the leaden surface.

The remaining hours before daylight were critical. They needed to get at least half a mile past the shattered bridgehead, judging it a safe margin from any scouting parties. Richard kept to the bank, Jon on his shoulders. The boy's hands were interlocked under his stubbly chin and, though the knapsack was not heavy, movement was slow. He had to fight against slipping into the water, grateful for his rubber-soled boots. Greda was right behind him, her hand holding a cord secured to his belt, their pauses brief as dawn's approach accelerated. Finally, they were under what was left of the bridge. There was neither sound nor sight of any infiltrating soldiers as they negotiated the remnants of concrete foundations. Rough ground materialised into a track that descended to the river's edge. Mangroves clumped together in an unbroken line and had to be negotiated. Not knowing what lay ahead was disconcerting but, having left the main road well behind, Richard was a little more optimistic of finding somewhere to camp.

"Get down," was his reaction to the engine noise.

Jon was eased into Greda's arms and they huddled under a mangrove tree, narrowly avoiding the searchlight from a motorboat scanning the bank. A machine gun mounted on its bow, manned by two soldiers and three others at the stern with guns, provided a portentous reminder of the ever-present danger, the *Rising Sun* flapping above the stern.

Richard's mind leapt ahead. *There goes any idea of crossing over to the other side on a stray boat,* he resignedly accepted. With dawn almost upon them, finding cover was imperative. He was determined not to be scrambling for a hiding place at the last minute.

The path began to loop around, and they met the gnarled excrescence of an ancient tree that required each of them to crouch and pass Jon under. The path bore back and above the trail they had just taken and, conveniently, there was a flattened portion of ground where they could rest.

"Someone's coming," Greda whispered urgently. He undid the cord that joined them.

"Hang on and keep down!"

As Richard passed Jonathon to her, he lost his footing. Grabbing at the undergrowth proved futile, as he careered to the track below. Two sets of sturdy wrists fastened his legs, while his head had arrived so close to the water's edge that his mouth found oozing mud. All attempts to kick free proved ineffectual.

Chapter 15

With the sun in my eyes

"You never learn, Mr Kirnst! You should know by now that it helps to simply roll with the punches," Greda cheekily offered as she wiped mud from his face and admonished him for leaving her fingernails in disrepute.

They had fallen into good company. Richard's open-mouthed following of her verbal and visual exchanges with the fishermen was akin to that of a floundering man deftly scooped from an angry sea. He may not have understood a word, but the meaning was clear. The Malays took pity on the injured child. The shorter of the two gave him a sugar banana, while a bottle of coconut milk was pressed on him by the other.

The first had recognised her as the doctor who tended a serious infection from a fish spike at the hospital a year ago. His leg had been saved and she had given him some money to feed his family while he was recuperating. He was so grateful that he repaid the debt with interest after returning to his trade.

"So, this is the best we could have dreamed of, Richard. And there's more: a hideout in which to lay up not far from here. Jonathon, we're safe." She was overjoyed and hugged her son. "Getting to Malacca is next. Naranam will help. We go back quite a way."

"You look weary," Richard said, as first light traced stilted outlines of their whereabouts.

"It's what segues from elation and relief. Jon's desperate to curl up somewhere. And look at you, disgusting!" She continued to flick aside the clinging clay caked on his shirt.

He surveyed his clothes with a wry grin. "You're not wrong."

Naranam motioned them to follow him along a narrow path. Fifty yards on, they joined another trail, which snaked through a dense canopy of low-hanging trees and vines, gradually ascending from the waterline. They would never have taken such a path without their guides.

Ahead, set into the side of the embankment, well camouflaged from snooping eyes, was a fisherman's dugout retained by thick bamboo stakes fixed deep into the slope. Inside there was enough space for layers of nets, tackle and a small dinghy with a mast and sail folded along its length. Two bunks were set up on one side. On the other sat a crockery cupboard. In the middle rested a rough-hewn table with benches. A fireplace, large pots, several containers, a basin and towel were suggestive of cooking and bathing. It was rudimentary yet possessed a primitive functionality. *You could live here unobserved for months*, Richard thought.

The fishermen left, Naranam saying he would be back in a few hours. Jon occupied one of the wooden bunks with Greda beside him, and Richard, after changing his clothes, stretched out on a ground sheet next to the dinghy.

Unperturbed, Naranam returned with fish, vegetables and rice. He lit a fire, and before long sweet aromas filled the close atmosphere, rousing them. It was an unforgettable meal, steaming hot and as tasty as could be imagined. "Jap in Malacca, not one can trust," Naranam said in broken English and Malay. "Japanee spies everywhere and pay people who help get whites." He announced that it was not safe for them to remain there for longer than a couple of days—perhaps even less.

Greda translated. "He's worried that if anyone finds out he helped us, he'll be shot, along with his family. He says to be ready to move at any time."

This acted as a brake. Naranam again retired, requesting they remain inside. There was no need to move about, with food and water plentiful and little to do but rest up.

While Jonathon resumed a dominant slumber, Richard washed himself, taking warm water from a large, blackened cast-iron pot suspended over the fire. Then he drew supplies from a 44-gallon drum at the rear of the dugout and replenished the container.

Within no time, he had procured an unlikely-looking copper hipbath from the back wall and filled it with warm water. Greda reviewed these preparations with geniality. Testing the temperature, he told her it was ready.

"You surely don't expect me to climb into that thing?"

"I thought you might like to," he grinned. "Even eighteenth-century salvage relics have uses. I'll give you space and collect some more kindling."

With considerable amusement, she watched his fastidious assemblage of a little pile of inconsequential twigs.

"Richard, come on, we're grown-ups!" Greda said with a tinge of sauciness. "And what are you laughing about, you mercurial fellow?"

"Aw, nothing. I'll try to keep my eyes front."

"You'd better," she replied in a mischievous tone, "but don't wander too far away. Look what happened the last time you scarpered."

"Yep," he sighed.

"Not even just outside under the pretext of modesty. There's wood in the corner. But seriously, remember, no one must know we're here."

Removing her garments and laying them on a mat near where Jon was sleeping, she stepped behind the bath.

"What in the world are you going to do now, Mother Hubbard, surely not the laundry?"

She couldn't restrain her mirth as he adopted a backwards, crab-like movement, retrieved her clothes and began to rinse them in a basin of soapy water.

"Seamen call it 'doing the dhobi'. Remember, I've been batching a long time and it's second nature."

As the minutes passed, his endeavors to remain impassive were faltering. Feeling her eyes on him, he kneaded each item more vigorously, taking in deep breaths and expelling them audibly. He was acutely conscious of their proximity and the imagery evoked by the tinkling water.

Greda knelt in the tub and lathered her hair first with a tiny cake of soap. Hands cupped, she drizzled the revitalising liquid over her, rinsing off and repeating the process then pausing to study him.

Richard's concentration on the task had waned and his actions became less pronounced as his senses tuned into her movements. Quieter now, soothing, as he imagined her sitting down, incongruously yet gloriously taking care with her bath. Was there ever a time when Greda's aura of femininity deserted her?

He dwelt on the scene in which she seemed at home. As elementary as this wash-station was, it presented no impediment from which she might shrink or to which she might adapt. Greda encapsulated earthiness in perfect harmony with class—another characteristic of the woman he had come to idolise. He suppressed the temptation to steal a glance and moved to a bench near the front of the dugout. There he tied her skirt and blouse to a length of fishing net strung across for camouflage, before shuffling back to attend to the undergarments.

He didn't see the exquisite form of her breasts, when released, more bountiful than those shaping her clothing, rising as they did to meet nipples that were dark and prominent. Her hips, formed with a feminine bestowal of generosity, broadened from a narrow waistline. Hands and fingers, now scrubbed spotless, lay beside them to emerge at thoughtful intervals cupping and stroking the water in as considered a method as that of her mind when applied to this man.

Firelight formed mystical shapes on the bamboo retaining earthen walls, and the only sound, apart from the crackling of tinder, was that occasioned by the intermittent swishing of water over her body. His efforts subsided as if not wanting to clash with hers, and he forsook all attempts to ignore what she was doing.

Greda pondered whether he might entertain a notion to turn his head, relishing the thought, empowered by the conclusion she'd reached about Richard. Though intangibly contained in manner, he had revealed much more of himself than he might have cared to, judging by that unpretentious nature. His shyness she found compelling. He was also intelligent and insightful. She trembled at the handsome figure whose every attribute illustrated vitality and manhood. His strength smouldered, awakening feelings long since buried. Within this intimate mental dialogue, Greda was beset with a yearning she strived to contain. If only he would wrest her into his arms and make love here and now, all the present uncertainties, and even the wretched betrayal, would vanish, at least for a fragment in time.

While she struggled with these potent emotions, Richard was attempting to take hold of his own feelings. As the symphony of bathing lessened, so his desire returned. He felt a strange configuration emanating from her, too, but what? That became his dilemma, for he wasn't being asked to come to her. Greda wouldn't do that, but might she react adversely if he did? He visualised washing and kneading this woman with his hands and hers caressing his body, fingers and nails tracing a deliberative pattern on his chest, and then worked his jaw in a futile effort to expunge the image from his consciousness.

He kept his head down and resumed wringing each remaining item, purposefully prolonging the assignment, scrubbing back and forth, turning them over and inside out and rubbing ever harder, splashing noticeably and gritting his teeth, as if by doing so the forces within him might be extinguished. But nothing seemed to controvert his hunger for her.

"Richard," she whispered in a manner so unfamiliar that he imagined it was a ghostly embodiment of his visualisations. He continued with his tasks, oblivious to her movements and nearness. "My darling." Her hands formed a path through his hair and onto his shoulders. He trembled as he felt her breath on his neck and turned to look at her. Greda wore a thin towel, covering all yet revealing everything. Her legs were shiny and bare, narrow womanly feet nestling within sunbaked fisherman's sandals. Overwhelmed by their closeness, his head turned away. Encouraged by a corrective hand, his gaze lifted and, as their eyes met, they mirrored the bliss of reading each other's thoughts. Unable to repress the anguish overcoming him, Richard released the faintest tears of emotion. They bespoke the tormented feelings he held for Greda and the overpowering desire to take her.

Rather than a prelude to an enjoinment of their bodies, his sentiment was replicated in her and together flowed as the realisation that they loved each other, transcending any search for instant gratification. A prolonged stillness finally gave way to words.

"I'm in love with you, Greda." Dappled sunlight suffused the dugout, capturing the moment. "I love you deeply with the sun in my eyes."

"I know, Richard. I love you, too."

He kissed her softly on the lips. She responded with warmth and tenderness, the likes of which he had never felt before. More than flesh touching flesh, it was spirit within spirit. They embraced and kissed again, the towel providing a veneer of modesty between them for which he was thankful. Sustaining resistance if Greda were to feel him was an open question. That she had was the natural consequence of their embrace. She was content to savour his strength and the exquisite warmth it produced within her while fixed in his arms. A mutual recognition that their coalescence was a priceless gift formed on them and neither could unclasp the moment.

This man and woman knew and loved what they had found. With that, they were becalmed, hypnotised by each other, unspeaking, yet imprisoning a thousand words. They relaxed, smiled, and her serenity shone. Greda released him and he watched as she lay down, still wrapped in the towel, facing her son.

Richard's heart thumped. *So much for theory.* He sought the container of water and splashed his face liberally, not caring to avoid striking his cheeks in the process, an action that did nothing to repel his frustration. When he was done, the little crib on the other side of the boat was rearranged and there was some squaring up of a fishing bag as an improvised pillow. It took time for him to settle but, when he did, Richard slept the sleep of a man wholly gratified.

Greda was soothed by his threaded breathing, relishing a contentment within her soul which was without precedent. Their embrace had produced a phenomenon not replicated in the marriage and left her to ponder how and why it had been gifted. *Better now than never,* wasn't the flippant elucidation she might have chosen after thoughtful consideration, but its adoption parted her lips and elevated her chin. She was determined not to let this time for her be transitory, wondering whether life would ever be the same. Richard was her first spiritual love. From here on, she could never allow this realisation to sally from her. Edward's fornication and cruel betrayal had released her to think as she wished about Richard, to long for him to be inside her.

Greda's metaphorical transition crystallised. For its perpetuation, she concluded that she would never see Edward again. This was made easier when she revisited his debauchery. The 'voyage' with Richard, as she regarded it, had captured her mind from its inception that first morning in his sickbed. Greda was past the point where not permitting herself openly to love him would be a false denial.

Then, just as abruptly, a depressing notion swept over her. Did she really hold such a belief? Could she? Greda had done her best to try to assure Jon that his father was not lost, as had Richard. *Widow*, she sighed, *black widow, at that. Deplorable, wishful-thinking one*. These thoughts were flooding over her, cryptic, scrambled and wayward, and her inner self recoiled from them. *I must stop it*, she muttered almost audibly.

Greda read the inscription under the candlestick. This evocative gift inspired a reach into her memory. She began to re-enter life as a child at Christmas in Leatherhead in that exquisite Surrey countryside, visiting the cows with her father and watching them chewing their cuds contentedly as they huddled together against the cold in the milking shed. Outside, snow flurries peppered the bare fields like swarms of winged insects materialising as apparitions out of the greyness and then vanishing just as quickly on meeting her skin.

When Mother tucked her into bed on Christmas Eve, she was assured that Santa Claus was beginning his work and her requests wouldn't be overlooked—provided she had been good. Annually, she met this edict. A gangly and tall ugly duckling in those primary years, she never occasioned any trouble to her parents. In the early hours of that joyous morning, Greda woke to the crinkle of wrapping paper on the end of her bed. Then she would curl up into a ball and only venture her feet a short way down, pretending that no visit had yet been made by the old man in red with the bountiful white beard. This was a disciplined exercise that she undertook with practised relish. Greda would go back to sleep, then repeat the process over and over until first light, when the highs and the lows of the visit-or-no-visit fantasy were smoothed out by visual certainty that her stocking was brimful of presents.

Now, in newness of life, she was with the man she had come to love resting peacefully so near to her, yet so far from where she wanted him to be. Greda imagined he was lying with her, and dozed on and off in that translucent knowledge, only to realise he was still beside the dinghy. She repeated this a few times, the last occasion leaving her with a sadness no fantasy could expunge nor be assuaged by even fitful slumber.

Signs of darkling were emerging when she rose and drank some water, checking on her sleeping son. Gently, without waking him, she removed his clothing and washed it, hanging his shirt and pants beside the fire, which she had replenished modestly. Greda wanted to wear what Richard's hands had cleansed. She took her garments and dressed, glowing with pleasure, and then sat down next to Jon.

A thunderclap heralded an eerie downpour and the temperature plunged, prompting her to rise again. Appreciating their warmth, Greda sat for a while beside the embers that emitted a dull, red colour as she viewed the raindrops flecking off the green leaves outside like sprays from a fountain. She couldn't return to her bedding now and crept over to Richard, who was lying on his side. Slipping in next to him, one arm found solace beneath his head and the other held him tightly. Greda's body then entwined around his and, as soon as her eyes closed, she fell into the sleep of the little Leatherhead girl whose every Christmas had arrived at once.

Chapter 16

Getting to Malacca

Richard squinted in the dim light when starting up from his position, well slept and cognisant of voices emanating from the rear of their confined shelter. Greda, with Jonathon sitting on a box beside her, was buttonholed in conversation with Naranam in his native tongue. Such was the depth of Richard's slumber that he'd been unaware of the fisherman's return and embarrassed to see that nearly five hours had elapsed.

"Hello, the babe's awake," Greda remarked as he flexed stiff limbs.

Naranam nodded towards him, while Jon was preoccupied with a bowl of soup.

"Whoa, must've been out to it," Richard mumbled, feeling off-guard. "I doubt I've slept better since this whole thing started at the hosp— ah, wherever. I'm losing track."

For several hours Greda had lain in his arms. Although on a few occasions Richard had actually held her, it was evident he possessed no perception of that circumstance. This coloured her contentment as she surveyed him.

"I'm glad the two *men* had decent sleeps." She was regarding her son, who had risen only half an hour earlier, and then winked at Richard.

They sat down to eat; Richard effusive in his thanks for another fine culinary effort from Naranam. In addition to chicken soup, he had produced a rich prawn and vegetable curry. Bananas dipped in a sweet mango sauce followed. Greda's declaration that everything was delicious elicited Naranam's toothy smile.

Richard felt optimistic about their prospects. "I could get to like it here—and not just the tucker. Only I'd better grasp their fishing techniques to pay for lodging," he quipped.

"You haven't even baited a hook and see what you've caught," Greda's response prompting a rebuke from Jonathon about grown-ups talking in riddles.

Naranam's demeanour turned, suggesting that something was troubling him.

Greda translated. "The Japanese are in control of Malacca. The Allies have withdrawn, and the town is under their complete authority. They occupy every road, bridge and intersection."

Richard wondered aloud how they might get out without discovery and whether it was best to abandon the idea of a sea passage altogether.

Naranam seemed to understand and spoke to Greda, who translated. "He says it would be suicidal to cross the river and go overland."

"But how do you know all of this?" Richard asked, appreciating that where the British had fallen back of their own accord, the fighting would be concentrated on new positions.

This time Naranam replied in broken English. "Hear all things. I take you Malacca. You get to bigger boat tomorrow, dark spaces where you hide."

He added that his brother and the man tasked to take them to Singapore knew of a handy storage shed where they could stay for the night and hide up throughout the next day.

Richard was confused, so Greda elaborated. "A certain Arkoi owns the boat and wants one hundred US dollars. Naranam will give it to him in two lots, one at the start and the other on arrival. He told Arkoi we'll procure the balance at a local bank."

"That's pretty smart," said Richard, nodding in the fisherman's direction.

"Certainly is. Arkoi's committed to the Singapore markets, so he can't renege on his promise to take us," she added. "It does mean a fishing detour along the way, but that can't be helped. We aren't pining for a luxury cruise with cocktails on tap."

"None of that just yet, there's no going back now."

"Will we be leaving for the port tonight, then?" Greda posed.

"Darkness, weather good, little moon," Naranam acquiesced.

It was a sentiment she was content to share. "Thank God for him."

Greda told Naranam he would be reimbursed, not merely for what was doing, but for the risks being taken. He refused money from her, seeing this service as due recompense. Naraman left to finalise the arrangements.

Their meagre belongings were gathered as Jonathon dozed. Hours slipped by. Although not euphoric, they were upbeat about their avenue to Singapore Island.

"Too soon to be cocky, though, Richard," she said. "Something can always go wrong, and no guarantee we'll get there unscathed with so many variables."

Hearing Greda's voice anew had opened another chapter in his life. No need to harken back to what had been pledged between them the night before, not the slightest intimation of regret or hastiness, nor even a tinge of embarrassment.

Her head resting on his shoulder, she became meditative. "You know, over the years I lived in Malaya, people sometimes disappointed me, situations that looked fool-proof have unwound. But that's the walk of life, I suppose."

"Yes, always applies when you're relying on others, and even those you think you know and trust can let you down, often enough through your own foolishness," he pondered. "Learning that lesson comes by taking personal responsibility for the exercise of free will."

"Are you thinking of someone to whom you were once close, Richard?" Greda surprised him with her discernment. His embarrassment unmasked, she defused it. "You can say anything to me. Who was she?"

"Her Chinese name was Chin Ming, but she liked to be called 'Eva'. Why do you seem to be able to read my mind? Am I so limpid or is it just that you're, well, an incredible woman?" he asked rhetorically, studying her face.

"She hurt you, did she? You loved her?" It was a plaintive furtherance of the enquiry after his admission on the excursion to the Cameron Highlands.

To the woman to whom he'd so recently made the avowal of his heart, he was unable to concede having loved anyone else. "I trusted her and I—" He delved for a form of words to suffice. "I was, ah, weak."

"Richard, I thought I loved my husband. When we married, I trusted him. Things change. Disappointments arise, and everyone makes mistakes," she offered obliquely. "Edward will always be Jon's father. And he's gone. I have to face the truth."

Her eyes glistened, and his became directed towards the front of the dugout. In the wake of her recent profession of love to him, Richard experienced unease.

Greda clasped his face, aligning it with hers and whispering, "There's no shame in the lives we've both led before we met each other, but the future, that's ours, together, here, now and forever. You've got me, I'm afraid, and I cannot imagine my life without you in its centre."

"You mean that, Greda," he stated, rather than questioned. "It's hard to gauge that you're saying those words to me, but I do know I heard them."

"I lay next to you when you were sleeping, Richard, and I fell into a blissful repose, utterly serene, like I've not had for many years—maybe not since I was a little girl. I held you and you held me, even if you didn't know it."

"If only I'd been conscious of you," he kissed her warmly, "but then again, safer not to have been, as I don't think I could've remained altogether indifferent."

"Not that I didn't want to arouse you," she offered with tempting lips.

In the poignant silence, conflicting emotions worked within him. Richard discharged a salutary thought that a man surer than he might voice. Wasn't it a little presumptuous to conclude her husband wouldn't be coming back? His mind wanted only to relive her assurances. Still, he felt alienated by the notion that she remained a wife. Until her husband's death was confirmed, a future together remained enigmatic.

He returned to the kernel of her original question, "Eva, um, meant a bit to me and was intelligent, literate and well, accomplished. We, ah, wrote to each other many times after I met her on a trip to Port Swettenham a bit under a year ago. Call me immature but," he hesitated, "to be honest—yes, naively perhaps—I thought I wanted to marry her. She agreed, but over time doubts crept in."

He adapted the next portion of the narrative. Greda was earnest in expression as she took it in, outwardly as detached as an attentive journalist conducting an interview.

"Something happened that wasn't quite right. A stranger," he took in a deep breath, "ah, came to our hotel table, intoxicated, called her by a name that she didn't acknowledge and said he knew her. Later she passed it off, insisting there was nothing wrong. So I let it go. Well, long story short, she wasn't what I believed her to be. A lot was going on. You found me a pretty sorry mess and know the rest. Looking back, I sometimes think all I felt was, well, not pity, but a bit sorry for her. Thought I could help—the classic male ego; chivalry or something. And that's about it, really."

The moment he finished speaking Richard regretted unburdening himself. Was it artlessness that had led him to divulge such things to this sagacious woman? He toyed with muttering an apology until gaining redemption from her eyes.

Greda found herself drawn to his candour through the privilege he invested with her in reposing this confidence. There was no misspent anger, which she greatly respected, nor the slightest indication that he still retained feelings for the woman.

Their discussion terminated with the return of Naranam and his crewman. "Must go now, very quiet, please, boat leave."

They moved off down an alternative twisting path to the river. Richard declined Naranam's offer to carry the sleeping boy but accepted his warning to keep close behind him as the way might be difficult. The night was surprisingly balmy, but the track was treacherous after the late showers. A confused cloud cover shielded all but afforded intermittent moonlight, suiting their furtive slog.

As the party neared the water's edge, no lights were evident. They were rowed to a fishing boat and ushered to a space below deck. Richard wondered aloud what they would do if boarded.

Naranam, capriciously it seemed, comprehending much more English than what issued from his mouth, responded. "You here stay all times. See fish net, sails. Put over and boxes at front. Saw Japanee last night. So far not stop, but never you chance, must hide. Have me to deal trouble, pretty good talker," stifling a chuckle.

That Naranam could still resort to levity eased the tension. Richard retained the revolver; the .303 had been left behind. He spied another rifle leaning beside a bulkhead next to the wheelhouse. It was a rusty piece whose barrel had been shortened.

"Is this yours?" he asked, holding it up.

"Ah, yeah, bullet in, good shot for shark, maybe other thing, shark with hairy legs," Naranam snickered again.

The dinghy secured and anchor raised, the little inboard motor grumbled into life like a delusional gargoyle and commenced pushing the craft in a hesitant forward motion. The engine was underpowering the vessel and it would take all of the predicted time to make Malacca. Hiding places were arranged in separate locations under a layer of nets and sail sheets. Richard piled fish boxes and crabpots around Greda and Jon.

A chunky vessel, eighteen feet in length, just over six in the beam and with extravagant gunwales, it was built primarily for inshore and estuary fishing. Its superstructure had been added to over the years, and it was now used for a broader range of endeavours. Going to sea proper could only be undertaken in the most propitious of conditions.

It wasn't long before a combination of fumes from the exhaust, diesel leaks, and the inconsistent firing of the engine provoked a reaction from Richard, who called for some tools. With a torch in his mouth, he set to work on the moving parts, adjusting the fuel pump, which led to a stuttering motor before it became a more consistent hum. The engine revolutions grew steady and improved their speed by a knot. After tightening the joints and unions, the gasses incommoding those huddled below were negated.

The old boat leaked, too. Observing the disconnected bilge pump, Richard asked Naranam whether it had been used.

"Never. No good," the fisherman replied. Over the noise of the engine, Richard was given an elaborate explanation of the sale, the vessel's condition at acquisition, its predilection for shipping water and regular baling.

The bilge pump ran off the engine by a system of pulleys and belts. Richard stripped it down, greasing the moving parts and ascertaining that it was capable of doing the job. All that remained, he said, was simply engaging it with a lever, and this would keep the bilges dry as required. The crew would be relieved of having to bail with an added bonus of carrying more weight of fish. Richard wanted to give something back to Naranam and was halfway there.

To finish the job, the engine would have to be shut down. Naranam was wary about stopping. Assurances that it wouldn't take more than a few minutes saw him give way. Richard set to the task, but because it had been unused for so long, he was unable to extract enough elasticity from the primary belt for it to stretch and engage the pulley. Naranam hadn't anchored and an increasing current assuming its own mind skewed the vessel downstream and almost abaft their direction. Richard worked feverishly trying to loosen the bolts on the engine block to get the inch of movement needed. All except one had responded, and then the vessel stuck fast against a mud bank.

There was consternation on deck and demands for engine power. He gave the okay for the restart without completing the work, and further trouble ensued. There was but pithy energy from the battery when the start button was pushed and no purchase for the flywheel to be manually manipulated to effect refiring. Silence, interrupted only by lapping water and the ping of his hammer and chisel trying to loosen and clean the battery terminals, was abruptly overtaken by the tell-tale sound of another engine. Its elevated noise signified a much larger vessel powering towards them.

The deckhand cried to those below, "Japanee, Japanee!"

Naranam met Richard at the ladder. "Patrol boat. Give me tools, you hide. No speak, silent please."

Richard passed over the items, reviling himself under his breath. He piled additional fishing nets around Greda and Jon, moving them back to the stern and lay prone, covered by sheeting. Around him, Naranam arranged several squares of canvas. Scarcely daring to blink, he held the revolver as the sound of creaking timbers made it indisputable that they were going to be boarded.

There was much shouting in Japanese and then Malay, before Naranam and the commander resorted to broken English.

"We on bottom. Engine broke. Big trouble but I fix."

The heavy clunk of boots on the deck announced the Japanese presence on the little vessel. Naranam had taken the bold step of going straight to the commander, having smeared black grease on his face, hands and arms with a view to diverting them from snooping below. This strategy failed to deter the suspicious officer.

"Why you out now time? Fisherman go sea morning, not midnight this tide."

"Very lucky, find good fishing spot, better on late going-out tide and start incoming. I find fish and crabs, and private spot. And, please, sir, must be keeping secret," Naranam begged in a sycophantic tone.

"Give exact position, as Imperial Army wants many Japanese boats to fish. Fleet come here next week."

"Yes, can give, sir. Yes, sure. Engine there," said Naranam, pointing in a downward direction as a flashlight cascaded across the lower space.

"Know where engine, fool. I see for self. Why gun?" The commander pointed to the old rifle.

Richard lamented his failure to secrete it and prepared himself for a fight to the death if the officer came down to their confines.

Naranam fashioned an impromptu reason for its presence, adopting the guise of a simple fisherman plying his trade. Bowing low, he said, "For shark. Keep catch fish from big one and also get fin, sir, like famous shark fin soup? I get fin, very good eat. Get lot fin you anytime," he lied.

"You have shark fin here?" asked the officer, wide-eyed at the mention of this delicacy.

"No, sir, not here now, but go fish soon."

The commander turned to face Naranam, who had moved much closer, having sidetracked him from the search. Relishing the possibility of an unexpected bonus, he steadied in his descent backwards into the engine space.

Naranam warned him to be careful as the ladder was damaged. "Sir, get fin for you end of night, always when clean fish, some for you, sir? Much money if sell."

"I, Captain Sakeiwu. You remember if want keep fish. Shark fin give to me in morning or trouble," he snarled, making it plain that a poor night's fishing wouldn't suffice as an excuse.

"Sir, you see me at fishing wharf market sale. I give."

"If no fin, no mercy. I find you, cut off hand. We give boat Japanese fishermen."

Combining servile antics with adroit verbal manoeuvring, Naranam had reprieved his passengers. There'd be no full search, and Sakeiwu reboarded the patrol vessel. Engines enlivened, the patrol boat soon faded off upstream.

Richard was crestfallen as he emerged to comfort Greda and Jon, still huddled together. "That was a close one. You two alright?" he asked, reaching out to them.

Greda squeezed his fingers. Jonathon relaxed and offered to lend a hand.

"Thanks, Jon. I can take a hint, but I have to get this thing working fast, now," Richard said, returning to the job. "Better you both stay there until we get to Malacca."

With refreshed terminals, he hoped the battery might still possess sufficient kick. He had not abandoned trying to loosen the unyielding bolt and doused it with kerosene. Two light taps and the nut gave. Affixing the belt, engine power was restored. Adept seamanship followed, and a churning propeller released the vessel from the bank, with the help of pole pressure from Richard and the deckhand.

The marine engine sang like never before, and the bilges were pumped out. But Naranam's perturbation at the consequences flowing from Sakeiwu if the shark fin wasn't procured masked any indication of gratitude. Even Richard's apology was ignored.

"Will you be able to buy some shark fin if you don't catch anything?" he asked, pushing twenty dollars into Naranam's hand.

He waved away the apology and was thankful. Without the money his situation would have been untenable.

"All's settled up there at last," Richard shouted across to Greda, "though my interference almost scuttled us all. Our loyal friend, has, I fear, been compromised. He's going to have to meet that Japanese officer again."

Greda went on deck, conversed with Naranam and returned reassured.

"Don't concern yourself, Richard. He understands, his priority being to land us and get out fishing in quick time."

The sharp bump confirmed their arrival at a small jetty, bow first. The deckhand lifted Jonathon across to Richard, who had clambered off. Greda then joined them.

Nobody was around as Naranam led the way to the boatshed. He emphasised that they must wait there until contact was made. "Here key, not to lose, only one I give," he told them. "Where stay, you light far end—" He broke off to finish in Malay and Greda translated.

"He says inside there are four paddles leaning against the far wall and resting on some plywood covering an opening to the room where we'll stay."

Naranam resumed speaking. "Shut side door to lock self. Arkoi man come see tomorrow ready, food, water and sleep. So sorry, must get away."

Greda hugged the fisherman and thanked him effusively. Richard shook his hand.

"Hey, Mister Engine-Man. Fix pump, fix engine, I pay you, maybe," he laughed, rejecting the offer of more money. "Now get shark fins and fish Captain Sakeiwu. He like and think me silly bersetubah. What you say?"

"Bugger, Naranam means, Richard," Greda said, and he managed a self-deprecating smile.

"Yeah, yeah, old bugger. That way, get by. You careful. Japanee water much more now, not fools too big."

And then Naranam was gone. Tensely, they watched until the elderly craft had chugged from view.

Chapter 17

Occupiers

T he conquest of Malaya was not without fifth column
preparation of considerable ingenuity. Some enemy
sympathisers were established residents positioned
all over the peninsula and eased the way. Others were
strategically dispersed to foment trouble and promote the
cause of independence from Britain. Japan's long-term
objectives required a compliant populace.

Malcontents repeatedly emphasised that the Japanese
were true liberators, freeing the downtrodden Malays
from the yoke of colonialism and racism. The truth was
invariably different as the new subjugators took hold,
showing little respect for the rule of law and ruthless if
disobeyed or even questioned.

Assisting in this process were shopfront businesses
acting as staging points for the arrival of the Japanese
and the dissemination of propaganda and misinforma-
tion. Identifying ethnic Malay collaborators was another
important function. As well as exploiting simmering antipathy towards the Chinese and dispossessing them of
public prominence, it guaranteed the establishment of
stable provincial administrations friendly to Tokyo.

Located an overnight journey from Singapore, the Port
of Malacca enjoyed prestige in Malayan lore as a venerable
Portuguese outpost. It loomed as a strategic base from
which to both consolidate and secure that ultimate prize.

At the same time as Richard and Greda considered it
to be their optimum hopping-off point for an overnight
voyage south, another man and woman had ensconced
themselves in an inconspicuous two-storey dwelling a

comfortable distance from the town's centre. Since their relocation, Heenan had continued to draw from the Japanese Intelligence payroll. Apart from the ubiquitous assignations with Jamal Viranhi, Eva remained ignorant as to how his activities were now being carried out.

Having separated from the army amidst the confusion of Kuala Lumpur's abandonment and the constant pull-backs, he had completed the primary objectives set since the start of the campaign. When told by Jamal that he was listed as 'missing in action', he guffawed at the incompetence of his former employer. With new responsibilities bearing political import coming his way, Heenan was infused with self-importance while assuming the guise of a disaffected expatriate.

A consequence of his move into Malacca was that the relationship with Pinka had terminated. It was an inevitability with which he could live. Women who had succumbed to his charms found that his ideas and theirs rarely merged. Pinka wanted marriage. He'd vowed never to marry but relished the sex that came with Pinka. She might just have inveigled him to the altar, but his spendthrift disposition meant he had little discretionary money and, were he caught, no future other than the gallows. Heenan accepted inferior sex from the Chinese whore, as he habitually regarded Eva, trousering the extra cash that came with her.

His new identity afforded Heenan some clout in the Malaccan business community. An eye-catching Chinese woman with him from time-to-time didn't evoke interest as Asian mistresses were commonplace in Malayan life. Eva took on the appellation of 'assistant', one who accompanied him for business purposes and was easily passed off in that capacity.

During this interregnum, Eva's mind was never idle in its calculations of how she could finish Heenan. She'd revisited Nu telling her that the Australian had suffered grave injuries when he hit his head on the pavement during the fight outside the café, had been taken to hospital and passed away soon after. She refrained from questioning Heenan about it, but never accepted Richard's death as an accident. The forces that had incautiously motivated her one precipitate attempt at betrayal via Faircrossman were but a fragment of the hatred that seethed below the surface. Short of despatching him by thrusting a *parang* through his heart, she was determined to satiate the desire for revenge, believing that the most efficacious path involved his delivery to the British authorities without repercussions being visited upon her.

Eva was always mindful of the dire imprecations he had threatened for her family in Shanghai should she ever demonstrate recalcitrance. She continued to send financial support for them. Her brother remained in Kuala Lumpur, where he, too, was protected, provided she stayed loyal to the cause, and to Heenan's in particular.

Eva's options for the present were foreclosed. But that didn't stop her conjuring up ways to see reliance on Heenan removed in a manner that would preserve the integrity of the family and put an end to the infelicitous usage she suffered.

As a deserter, Heenan was an itinerant lodger and trap-setter, delighting in turning up without warning and, more usual than not, reeking of drink. This alone accounted for the horror with which she lived, never knowing at what ghostly hour those clammy hands would tighten on her neck, an artifice that he practised on occasion for perverted sexual indulgence.

Out of desperation, she envisaged running away, but the servants he'd employed were complicit in his intricate plans to shadow her. There seemed no chance of finding any pathway to freedom. Ironically, in doing his bidding, Eva had nurtured some contacts of her own and this gave her a chink of expectation. There was no longer any such thing as morality, just survival and endurance of whatever privation was necessary for her ultimate aims.

Since early December there had been no word from her family, and she'd become alarmed. Their method of contact was by mail and, when it became clear Heenan was being sent to Malacca, she had asked her brother to notify them and redirect any letters for her. For all Nu's failings, there was no reason to doubt that he would honour her request. Raising the question with Heenan, he had blamed the war and told her that once the new civil government was established throughout Malaya deliveries would be resumed. She didn't accept his explanation. Pressing him further, he growled contemptuously that she had better not aggravate him while her family was under his protection and, if she pushed too much, the responsibility for their demise would be hers.

There was little she could do to corroborate their wellbeing save for one clandestine avenue. She had a cousin living close to Shanghai who worked in the mail exchange. Eva penned a letter requesting any information she had about them, giving a return address care of the Malacca Post Office. Sometime after it was sent, she determined to check for any reply. Going out alone was not something undertaken with ease. She could never explain the reason for a trip to the post office.

That morning, Eva crept noiselessly from their bed, leaving him heavily sedated after a late night's carousing in the town. She fixed on an idea to deflect suspicion from her real purpose if it happened that he became aware she'd absented herself without permission. To date he had not protested about the state of her attire when in his company. It suited Eva to look as drab as possible to minimise his attentions. Her excuse would be to refresh her wardrobe with provocative clothes. She would tell him that they needed to reignite the spark and felt sure he would appreciate the sentiment.

Eva had just reached the door when, like a demented soothsayer, Heenan bellowed out an oath. She stood rigid as he lumbered down the stairs. He gauged her with distaste before his clairvoyance returned Eva a dividend.

"You look like an absolute fucking tramp. Instead of going to the fish market, you can damn well get a skirt worth taking off. Anything to lift that saggy arse and tits."

Another bawl brought a young girl running to his side with an attaché case.

"I'm feeling generous. Here's some money. Buy what I like rather than pissing me off with those frumpy rags you've been crawling around in lately. And do something with your straggly hair too." His instruction suited her purpose and she demurred with a bow. "And be warned: someone you least expect will let me know what you get up to if it enters your head to sneak off anywhere without telling me."

Heenan had always monitored her personal effects and acquisitions with manic zeal, demanding full accounting of every last tip she received and, in return, gave her the minimum allowance that he deemed sufficient for her needs. Such was this preoccupation that he'd caught her on two occasions with more money than he felt she should have in her possession and had confiscated it. Eva would never let on that those discoveries were deliberately set to avoid him conducting more extensive searches, for she had accumulated sizeable reserves in recent months. She took elaborate care to ensure the stash was well-hidden.

On this occasion, her tart reaction was that she wanted to look good for him, but in the past the servants had bought cheap clothes and pocketed the balance. This ploy produced an unexpected concession. She could go on the shopping expedition unaccompanied. He adjured her that she had two hours to achieve the task. Anything outside that scope would not go unpunished, reminding her that he would know if these terms were contravened.

After further grovelling submissions, Eva was able to extend the sortie by an extra half an hour. She was pandering to his vanity in the manner of her requests and saw his lip curling hungrily as he ran his eyes over her body. She gave him a coquettish grin, implying that he wouldn't be disappointed.

"I'll be here when you get back. We've much to discuss and may as well do it over a few whiskies," he guffawed, thinking it a very witty comment, when meaningful discussion was not an element of their existence.

Unable to listen to his voice a second more, Eva swept outside. She'd not taken many steps before detecting a servant, Dineh's, clumsy tailing. Setting out to lose her superficially appealed to Eva's sense of adventure. Mature consideration led her to discard the idea on the basis that it could easily be reported back as a case of deliberate evasion with consequences she daren't contemplate. She walked on at a steady pace, pausing at intervals to appraise her thoughts while feigning interest in garments offered for sale at the roadside and concluding, *Whatever I decide will never be failsafe*. Bribery would have to do, and she had enough to tempt.

In her brief tenure, Dineh had already witnessed Heenan's treatment of Eva. Knowing something of the girl's immaturity and circumstances, Eva thought that, in offering money, Dineh would gain more than anything she could ever achieve in the way of reward from the flint-like Heenan. Though he might try to wheedle her into disclosing an infraction on Eva's part, she was perceptive enough to appreciate that he would never forgive the lapse that had brought it about.

Eva drew away from her until she was out of sight. Among the street bustle, while Dineh's anxiety was raging and she stood searching the crowd, the object of her consternation came from behind placing hands over her eyes. The revelation elicited a shriek and had her sobbing in Eva's arms.

"What's the matter? Are you lost, Dineh?" Eva asked, trying to appear disconnected.

"I thought you were going—" she replied before stopping herself, realising she had said too much.

"You're following me?"

"No, I came here—I sorry, yes—but the master told me to and said if I can't stay with you my job gone and no chance to support my mother." She began to shiver.

"You'll not lose your job and I won't tell master what you've said, but you must do something in return."

Eva explained the need she had to undertake errands, ascribing destinations that didn't involve the General Post Office. The bargain was finalised when she pressed a dollar note into Dineh's hand with five more when she returned.

"So, Dineh, you remember what you must say if you're asked?"

"Yes, Madam, I not betray you. He very bad man. I meet you here two hours. Please you come back."

Eva had to be satisfied with this assurance. Dineh was not much more than a child, with a waif-like body and raw, dark eyes devoid of guile. For a second Eva could see her own reflection as she studied the young girl, prompting an empathetic hug and a kiss on her cheek.

"Make sure you keep busy while I'm away, Dineh. We're in this together and you'll be alright." Eva extricated herself from the brittle fingers and set a fast pace to recover lost time. Whether enough had been done to win Dineh's confidence was an imponderable until the moment might come for it to be tested. She decided that any misgivings were best expunged from consideration. The mission at the post office was her primary objective and thereafter she would make the necessary purchases. Beauty treatments might need curtailment. Adhering to a precise rendezvous with Dineh was her best protection against the possibility that she might panic and jeopardise the entire scheme.

If it came to an interrogation from Heenan, she would put up a façade and roll the dice. The drink might work for her at least one more time and unhinge his sixth sense. Luck was the vital ingredient she craved to divert his inbred suspicion. She looked back occasionally trying to be casual, and, seeing nothing, was certain Dineh hadn't repented of the bargain.

A residual energy dominated the streets; the crush becoming more pronounced as she approached the centre of town, slowing her to a weaving walk. As a relative newcomer to Malacca, Eva's capacity to make before-and-after judgments was limited. She didn't interpret any immediate change since the British authorities pulled out. The Japanese had infiltrated the port and surrounding areas without a shot being fired. Other than passing a squad of soldiers sitting in the back of a truck, there were few obvious signs of occupation. If the activity on the street at this hour of the day was any guide, traders were thus far unaffected.

As she neared the General Post Office, it was simple to blend with the large throng. Positioned outside was a bespectacled soldier standing to attention. Next to him rested a rifle with bayonet affixed and flashing as the sun's rays caught its shiny surface. He stared ahead impassively, paying no attention to the comings or goings, but even an innocuous presence influenced a decision to dispose of her task with alacrity.

Eva suspected there might be agents in plainclothes whose job it was to report anyone acting suspiciously.

From what could be seen on a speedy reconnoitre, she was satisfied there were no candidates fitting that description. Compressed in a line of people waiting to collect mail or buy stamps, she disciplined herself to appear as relaxed and natural as anyone else. Visiting the post office in Malacca was an ordinary routine.

She was right to be wary. Loitering adjacent to the queue was Jamal Viranhi, a man whose sole aim in life was to acquire pelf. He coveted it, sniffed it out in diverse places and, in its pursuit, never missed anything that went on around him. Not only did he recognise Eva, but Heenan's close confidante appreciated the nature of her connection with that estimable comrade. Theirs was an association of a different character to his predecessor's, being ostensibly a servile one. This pretence suited Jamal's purposes, preferring to be regarded as posing no threat to the supremacy his putative principal enjoyed. He was content to remain the serpent coiled inside the basket, always poised to strike when called upon.

When Jamal saw Eva, he assumed she was on an errand for their acquaintance-in-common and sidled across. She turned in a manner that was indicative of her having seen him yet avoiding any public acknowledgement. She may have had good reason to do so. The alternative scenario, as his natural disposition lent itself to habitual suspicion, involved her in an undertaking in which she sought not to be noticed. Stealth in her demeanour stimulated his curiosity. He slid out of sight and hovered in the vicinity, seeking a sign for resolution to the tiny riddle.

Occupied with the constraints of time and sluggishness of the queue, Eva hadn't seen the swarthy, omnipresent Jamal. Her anxiety became more apparent the closer she shuffled to the counter. When she was served, her request for mail for Chin Ming saw the harried clerk shake his head. Eva paused inconsiderately until the clerk became impatient to attend the next customer.

"Sorry, can you check for Eva Ming?" His frown prompted an explanation. "She's my cousin, you know, I may as well ask while I'm here."

Another search had him return with a letter withholding the item as she reached out. "Your cousin, you say? Where's she expecting a letter from?" he asked officiously.

"Oh, it's Shanghai, I imagine," she replied casually. "Her sisters live there and they always write."

Satisfied, he handed over the article. Jamal had seen enough. Eva darted out. A few blocks covering two hundred yards one way, then a left turn, scurrying past a series of intersections satisfied her that she remained inconspicuous. She chose a little tea shop, sparsely patronised and out of the central thoroughfare, to open the letter, there to read a detailed account of the family's arrest and subsequent disappearance. Their personal belongings had been collected separately, and the house where they'd been staying was now occupied by a senior Japanese official and his family. Lacing the final paragraph with profuse sorrow and personal experiences of arrests and removals, her cousin added that they would likely never be heard from again.

This was as clear for Eva as she could ever suffer to witness first-hand. Reading the last few lines again, she envisaged the cries of her mother and dear uncle, imagining the scene as they were dragged away. Seizing the chair until her knuckles discharged their colour, she saw her life dissolve. Eva reflected on the purpose of their going to Shanghai. Nanking, affording safety in the international zone, evoked a bitter memory. *If only they had stayed there.* Within her an overpowering rage was rising, like a volcano ready to spew, distended further through linkage to Richard's demise.

The protection of her family had been exacted at a price. Eva had continued to do whatever was asked, whether it was sleeping with Japanese collaborators in order to enhance Heenan's position or complying with his every unseemly demand. She had taken to drinking more than ever before to cope with the shame and blot out the mendacity of those around her. Her family's arrest couldn't come about without Heenan's knowledge. The fury of these disclosures instilled within her an unquenchable thirst for immediate retribution.

Her father was the only man she could now bring to mind in whom she reposed absolute respect. What would he do if his family had been butchered? *Never act on impulse,* she heard his voice. The advice reminded her to be circumspect. *A mindless hooligan lurches about like a mad dog.* Easy to say, but he might speak differently knowing what she'd been through. Eva was in a lip-syncing dialogue with Papa and hearing his steady erudition. If she was going to act, it had to be effective. That was his message. Her life had become as morally debilitated as Nu's and equally unsalvageable. There was now only one remaining purpose driving her, and she was determined to allow nothing to hinder that goal.

Chapter 18

Revelations

Welcoming their entry, a gassy cocktail of grease and paint dwelt comfortably with the fishy odour of the sea, no pungency offending less than any other. Chewed flutes of old propellers, carcasses of engines, dismembered parts and pump housings lined one wall, while tattered and smudged canvas was packed to the roof. Fishing nets, glass buoys, spars, ropes, hooks, lines and tackle were superadded to a storehouse of endless maritime paraphernalia.

"There's life after the war. What do you say, Richard, can you see us as partners in a chandler's shop?" Greda whispered.

"Provided your surgery's out the back supporting the float," he returned.

"I was going to say you've no vision, boy, but it might just work," her mouth on his ear, "as long as I'm not kept barefoot and you know what."

He cleared his throat and she squeezed his arm.

They found the open hatch. He went down first, the boy next, then her. The low ceiling was clad with overlapping sheets of rusty tinplate, the walls similarly adorned. It was about eight foot square.

Earnest assurances from Naranam that they would find bedclothes, food and water proved less than reliable. Three forlorn stretchers lay side-by-side, covered with mouldy calico. On the bowed shelf of an open cupboard riddled with borer reposed two rusty tins murkily labelled 'bamboo shoots', beside them a quart bottle of a brackish liquid and a stinking scrap of dried fish. There was a stubby candle and a half-spent box of matches.

"Ah, home sweet home," she offered spryly.

"You could say that. Fish you wouldn't give any self-respecting cat, water to soil one's hands, and who'll volunteer for bamboo mush," he rejoined.

The hatchway proved a problem requiring attention in case of unwanted snoopers. Richard covered the hole with a sheet of plyboard manipulated by a strong piece of netting twine and was satisfied as to its efficacy.

Access to the river was through an opening in the floor from where a barnacle-encrusted ladder descended to the waterline.

A stifling morning worsened as temperatures soared in the airless space. Jon hadn't been well from the moment he woke, complaining of severe stomach pain. He began vomiting until he was dry-retching. Colour poor, running a temperature and with his foot troubling him, he became tearful and withdrawn.

Potable water was essential, and Richard was impelled to contemplate disobeying Naranam's instructions. Greda, who at first resisted any venture into the open, began to waiver as their onerous confinement exacted its toll.

"Jonathon needs hydration. I wish you weren't going, but there's no other way," she told him as he finalised preparations.

"You'll have water soon, and I'll buy some food, too."

"And could you also try to get some medicinal aspirin? I've mislaid mine."

"Sorry you're not well, young chap. Just hang on for a bit and I'll find something to settle your stomach."

Despite the fact that he was heavily tanned and didn't evince the appearance of an Englishman, Richard's size remained a drawback. When he started out, his walk was measured, endeavouring to seem comfortable with the surroundings. He had been to Malacca before and took a general line towards the town's heart for half a mile before coming to a hill and seeing the masts of ocean-going ships to the west. Familiar with his position, he struck out for the sprawling street markets.

Purchases were accomplished without delay and he was on his way back when he spotted two Japanese soldiers sauntering among the marketers a mere twenty yards away. He effected to look preoccupied with a watermelon vendor. As they approached, he turned away and entered a shop, scrutinising several baskets piled high with salted fish, dried herbs and colourful spices. From the corner of his eyes he peered as the soldiers stopped to drink from green coconuts. An animated conversation with the trader who was trying to elicit favour from them dashed any optimism that they wouldn't tarry. When the expectant shopkeeper showed interest in him, Richard shook his head, turned on his heels and made his way back into the street. Taking the opposite direction to the shed, he increased his pace until the soldiers were out of sight.

The only European Eva had encountered that day was a tall, well-built man. Walking ahead of her, he carried two large bottles of water slung over one of his shoulders and a box of foodstuffs under his other arm. He walked with long strides and strands of brown hair protruded from under a broad straw hat.

Instinctively, she pressed hard so as to be a few yards behind him, and then eased back, careful to ensure her nearness hadn't alerted the stranger. His appearance may have been deceiving her, or was it a fairytale accompaniment to the mystical indulgences with her father during the distressing minutes preceding this sighting?

Her inclination was to just move off, putting her thoughts down to a vividly abstruse invention, but curiosity beckoned her, and she dashed up an alleyway with a view to getting ahead. Out of sight behind a canvas awning flapping against a pillar, she slid down onto the ground and removed a shoe feigning to shake out a pebble. Raising her eyes, she peered around the stone column. The resemblance from this vantage point was uncanny. Unable to let the man out of her sight, she willed it to be him. Eva had to know.

The street was far from crowded. As a means of determining whether anyone might have an interest in her activities, or even his, as he passed her, she doubled back, checked, and then paced herself to keep up with him.

He was maintaining momentum and she required swift movement to overtake him while remaining ever vigilant.

At the same time, Richard was reluctant to turn his head after the scare. Not knowing where the soldiers were heightened his disquiet. Already drenched in sweat from his exertions, this unease contributed to beads pouring down his face, but he had found the familiar long street whence he had come as he left the fishing wharves. He needed to cover one more block for it to be safe enough to peel off and go down to the river where the boatshed was located.

A relieving sigh was staunched by a woman barring the way. One hand was on his chest, the other pressed against his shoulder. For a fraction of a second he was minded to sweep them aside and slip away, but there was no prospect of doing that without a scene with the load he was carrying.

"Richard." Copious tears dampened her face. She clutched at his sleeve and he moved to one side, pretending to ignore her. She repeated his name, this time with an emphatic, "Richard, look at me!"

Dishevelled and shaking, she posed before him much as a desperate urchin in the back alleys of Singapore or an opium addict attempting to extract alms, only there was no whiff of narcotic or liquor emanating from her.

Willing to deceive himself, he tried to turn away again and said, "I'm sorry, you've made a—" until she challenged him thrice.

Denying her as a phantom proving futile, he shepherded Eva to a table in one of the shops, blocking his ears to the flood of explanations. With this wretched encounter came the vivid recollection of a contrarily disported woman late at night. Richard was dismissive, resistant to anything she was saying, and, but for the public nature of their meeting, would have made no attempt to cloak his disapproval at being waylaid by her. He ground his teeth and turned his face, then grabbed an arm roughly.

"Where's your boyfriend?" he asked curtly. "Ah, how uncharitable of me, I need to be more specific. The man in Georgetown? Was it Edward or Ted or something? Or how about—"

"Richard, please stop. I thought you were dead. Nu told me. The fall on the street, you hit your head. I'm trapped."

"Just like you were trapped by me," he spat out. "I want nothing to do with you."

"Richard, I beg, please, please listen to me, just for a minute," Eva beseeched him, her face blenched with emotion. He eased the pressure on her arm. "My family was back in China and he'd have had them killed if I didn't do as he told me. I'm sorry for what happened, but the man's wicked and I was scared. I'm afraid no more because I've just learnt my mother and my family are dead."

Richard shook his head disbelievingly. "Not the brother, Nu. He was very much alive last time I saw you."

"Yes, I know what you're thinking. Nu's no good. I was under his influence, too. Please, will you listen to me?"

There was not much else he could do.

"Oh, dear God, let me speak the truth. I just ask you to heed me and then go if you wish," she pleaded. Carefully and methodically she relayed a snapshot of her life including all she had omitted telling him previously, finishing with the contents of the letter from her cousin.

"How can I trust you? Yes, I see a letter, but it's in Chinese, and you could be telling me anything to help your story."

"I understand." She clutched his hand and dragged him into an area of the shop that accommodated a tearoom. Eva approached a white-aproned man who had just finished serving a customer. "Do you know me?"

The business owner was accomplished in English. "No, I've never seen you before. What's all this about?"

"Sir, can you please read this letter to the man here in his language," adding after catching his look of impatience, "It's very short and we'll buy things in your establishment."

The shopkeeper read the letter silently and then translated, Richard frowning as he did so. When he asked Eva if the letter referred to her family, she nodded. He shook his head sorrowfully, refusing money for his service, turning away when they sat down again.

If even half of it had some credibility, her current predicament began to make him rethink the rejection of everything she'd said. Immense man that he was, his size and deep voice evoking impressions of a hard, uncompromising character, yet tempered by her account, he relented, stroking the sweat from his forehead.

She recounted in greater detail what had occurred since their last fateful meeting, warning him that he was in considerable danger as there were spies everywhere.

"You're saying the man who bashed me in Kuala Lumpur is working for the Japanese, and was at that time?"

Unresponsive, she leant towards him, her voice hushed. "I've done things. Helped the Japanese."

"Answer me, damn you, was *he* working for them?"

She answered surely. "Yes, Richard."

"What? Heenan's a stinking spy, a traitor?" He regarded her in bewilderment.

"I'm sure he's caused many deaths, has no morality and nothing seems to stop him. It's only a matter of time before the Japanese take the whole of the country."

He was convinced she spoke the truth but was flabbergasted to hear it just the same. Eva emphasised that she didn't have much time, asked how he got to Malacca and where he was heading while eyeing the box of fresh food.

"Never mind about that," he replied abruptly, "what are *you* planning to do? You're still with this mongrel."

She stared into space, pursed her lips and trembled. "I'm going back to him, alright. I'll kill him for all he's done to my family, to you and to me."

"You'd never get near enough without risking your own life. He probably suspects you even now. You told me he had a servant woman hovering." Brows furrowed, his brain raced ahead. "If the military police were on hand, he'd face justice. No hope of that now."

Eva listened attentively, engrossed in him as much as to all he was saying. She felt succoured by a familiar modulation in his tone, where before there'd been scorn and derision. "Maybe you can trust this Dineh, but you've got to get away."

The effluxion of time was beginning to trouble him.

"Are you alright?"

"I have to go, Eva, there are things I must do." He gave out a few scraps of information to the effect that he was trying to find a boat to Singapore ahead of the invasion forces.

"I can help you," she replied, reading evasion as rejection. "I've some money and trusted associates. There are people who can get you a boat." She regarded him intently. "You want to bring Heenan to justice," she remarked intuitively. "I want to get him, too. I mean, once and for all. The British must know by now that one of their own has betrayed them and have a pretty good idea who it is." She deemed it prudent to omit particulars of her last engagement with Faircrossman. "What if we can work together? I'll get my revenge and so will you. He'll be hanged and I'll be free of him forever."

Again, he studied her closely, the determination to plot Heenan's downfall transparent. Vengeful, yes, but in his presence she had transformed from displaying a reckless foolishness to taking a stance that appealed to his sense of moral retribution.

"It's not my revenge, Eva. I would as soon have met him man-to-man. But knowing what he's capable of, I worry about what he can do to you," his concern now evident.

She fell into his arms, sobbing uncontrollably. "We'll get away, if you're able to forgive me for what I've done."

"You're already forgiven, Eva, and I'm beginning to understand what you've been going through." Gently but deliberately, he disengaged from her. "Ah, everything's different now and we can never be—"

She placed a row of fingers over his mouth, inwardly dismissing the import of what he'd just said, cognisant of his vulnerabilities.

"Is the place where you're staying discreet?"

He nodded. "Don't worry about me. But I really must leave."

"I must go, too. Can we meet here tomorrow? This should be done soon."

Richard wasn't about to tell her that in twenty-four hours he'd be in Singapore and there was really nothing he could do to help other than to wish her luck.

She smiled when he assented, still regarding him warmly. "Are you sure?"

"Okay, it's, ah, I'm a little concerned about being seen. I stick out a bit, as you confirmed. Off you go first."

He was relieved when she rose, squeezed his hand and departed.

A few minutes later, he entered the street. Attaining another elevated position, fifty yards away the cluster of fishing boats seemed more numerous than when he had left, with three and even four swaying astride and extending the length of the wharf.

Gaining the bank of the river upstream of the jetty and using the umbrella of mangroves, he waded laboriously in and out of their expansive roots until he was directly beneath a footway to the moorings.

There was no avoiding a swim, but to do so unobtrusively he followed a path under the criss-crossed pylons along an L-shaped route, keeping his supplies out of the water on some weathered planks he lashed together to form a raft.

Exhilaration when he entered the water after the oppressive humidity was short-lived. Jellyfish congregating in the shade under the jetty did not welcome attempts at dispersal. Cursing their painful stings, he followed the line of pylons to deeper water where the structure took a sharp left turn. He found the ladder and called for Greda. She reached down and retrieved the items from him. "Thank God," her voice hushed. "It's been nerve-wracking waiting."

"Couldn't avoid taking so long, more than a few inquisitive glances, and I thought it best not to risk being seen entering upstairs."

The water slaked their thirst and the medicine was administered to Jonathon.

Greda set about fashioning a meal of rice cakes, mandarins and dried fruit. She was flushed and speaking quickly. "The hours dragged by interminably. It's been murder here, but I felt Jonathon improved a little over the period you were away. I used seawater to keep him cool and his temperature eased."

"You look a lot better, young fella."

Richard stayed next to him and he seemed to brighten, nibbling on the fruit.

"I knew he'd be back, Mum. He never lets us down," He reached for a rice cake.

"Eat slowly, Jon," she said.

"Thank you, Richard, mister, ah, sir, for going out for us."

"What's all this 'sir' and 'mister' business? How about we just stick with 'Richard'? Yes, I know, your mum wishes to keep it formal. Some people call me 'Dick' as well."

"You mean I can call you Dick, too?" He sought his mother's approval.

"If Richard says so, go ahead, but I prefer the full version myself. It's a strong name."

"What, like Richard the Lionheart, Mum?"

"Boy knows his history, Greda. I'll have to find an old sword in that mess upstairs," he joked.

Subtly, the mood began to alter. Burdened by the unscheduled encounter with Eva, Richard picked idly at the food. A conviction that it could have no relevance to the plans in place for their departure did not erase his residual sense of unease.

Greda regarded his pensive look and, trying to appear nonchalant, asked if everything was alright.

"Ah, well, no problems," he replied jauntily. "I didn't meet a single Jap asking me for a smoke."

"Richard," she said, touching his arm to gain his attention, "there's something bothering you."

He sighed. "Can't hide it, eh? Actually, I, yes, did sort of run into someone, a person I never expected to meet again." He inhaled deeply before continuing. "It was Eva. I didn't know what to do." He slid a stretcher across the hole in the floor.

Greda's posture stiffened, presaging a search for the right words. Moving from a sitting position next to Jon to crouch over the bare-chested Richard, she saw red welts. "What happened? There, I mean." The tips of her fingers reached out to the inflamed areas. "How did you get these?"

"Aw, they're nothing. A few jellyfish in the way and, ah, they tend to sting a bit, but that's the least of my worries." Richard rubbed his hand over the marks and put on his damp shirt. "It was a hell of a shock running into her, here of all places. She accosted me in the middle of the street. I couldn't get clear." Without perceiving why, he was seeking exculpation.

"Well," said Greda, a pained smile creasing her face, "that's something. What did she say, Richard?" the query intoning a flavour of disquiet.

He poured out all that had transpired, avoiding mention of Heenan by name.

"She was emotional, almost distraught. I had no choice but to listen. After a while there were questions. I didn't mention you and Jon's presence or our leaving Malacca tonight. She offered to help me. We parted after an arrangement to meet again tomorrow and I felt pretty helpless really, and bit guilty for being deceptive."

"You did the right thing, Richard, ah—" Greda wanted to add a term of affection but, mindful of Jon's presence, checked herself. "She chose her own destiny and, yes, as you say, we have to feel for her, the way she was threatened and tried to save her family. But she's an intelligent and resourceful woman."

He had noticed her frown and was certain Greda harboured some reservations.

"Oh, yes, and this intelligent woman," her voice was tinged with irony, "must have wondered whether one day the game would be up, surely."

Richard lowered his head. "I couldn't say too much. I'm sure she'd never betray me. I should've told her I just can't see her again, but I'd like to get this, this—"

She found the word. "Traitor?"

"Yes, back to the British authorities."

"That's puerile talk, Richard. It's not up to you," she said abruptly, wondering where this notion was coming from.

"I'm sure you wouldn't say that if you knew more."

Not seeming to appreciate what he'd just said, she stood so her head pressed on the ceiling. "Somebody might have been watching. She could change her mind and out it comes. She's consorting with a very dangerous man who knows equally nasty people. As for you, trying to do something off your own bat, it's simply suicide to even contemplate. He'll eventually be caught. You're not the police!"

Her eyes flashed as she spoke, the colour in her cheeks disconcertingly florid. Richard hadn't witnessed such stridency before, and he felt a little sheepish. They had one task as daylight rapidly faded, and that was to prepare for their departure in a few hours.

"Okay, then." He was keen to change the subject. "How're you feeling, lad? Ready to go later?"

The boy won comfort from Richard's familiarity and responded appealingly. "Wish I didn't have this bad foot. I bumped the wall and it still hurts a lot."

"I understand, but try to forget about it now. It's going to be a long night and we need to conserve our energy. Hey, next stop the ship."

In their airless space, time was another enemy. Richard soaked a sheet of old sailcloth in seawater and rigged it to allow evaporation, giving some relief from the persistent humidity. The air cooled with a perceptible draught wafting up from the river. Jon had fallen asleep and Greda lit a candle. They had expected a visit from Arkoi by this time, but there was nothing, save the magnified gnawing of a rat, emanating from above.

"I didn't mean to snap at you." She was leaning over Richard, stroking his hair to one side as if combing, and then tousling it up again and curling strands in her fingers. "There's still something on your mind. Do you want to share it with me?"

He shrugged and showed his teeth. "You've me pinned again. I'm not sure I know where to start." He took her hand.

"It concerns Eva, I take it? Seeing her has caused a reappraisal?"

"Do you think I'm as shallow as that?"

"Sorry," she said and tightened her hand around his. "I'm not doing well. I declare that our first squabble has officially ceased." Her lips found his cheek. "Now you were going to tell me something."

"Well, Greda, I need to talk about what happened at the Cameron Highlands."

"Yes, where you spat the proverbial dummy." His grimace was met with a carefree sway of her head. "Oh, come on, Richard, lighten up! Do you want another apology, this time in French?"

"How many languages do you speak? Now it's your turn to laugh. Okay, well, you'd better brace yourself. I couldn't say anything back then, as I didn't think it was the time or even my business to do so."

"Richard will you please come to the point?" she asked exasperatingly.

"The officer, the one with your friend Pinka, was that Captain Heenan?"

"Yes, why do you ask?"

"He was the man who bashed me."

"You can't mean it, Richard! You're nodding. And that explains why—"

"Greda, you probably don't need this now, but that's not all. Heenan's the one involved with Eva. He's a dirty spy, a traitor, and now a deserter."

She sat up and drew her knees to her chest, clasping them and leaning forward as he straightened beside her. "What?" she asked incredulously. "Are you sure?"

"On every count," he announced with utter conviction. "Eva told me his name and the dots were easily joined when she revealed what he was doing."

"That's unthinkable! Oh, Richard. If it wasn't coming from you, I'd reject such an idea as absurd. Pinka has her failings with men, granted, but she's no fool. What on earth?" She shook her head, stared ahead impassively then wrapped her arms around him tightly for some minutes before speaking again. "I found him an unutterable bore from the start and was mystified as to how Pinka could've been taken in by such a blow-hard. Now I have it and—what's that delightful slang you Aussies use, fair something?"

"Fair dinkum?"

"I'm not sure if it fits precisely, but it'll do."

"Near enough. Seeing that fella sort of tested me at the time," he said modestly.

She held his fingers on her forearm, replicating a soft, pinching motion. "Richard, it's hard to conceive I've met someone like you."

He bypassed the compliment. "His was a face unlikely to be forgotten, and that obnoxious attitude! She's your friend, and I couldn't have spent as much as a second pretending. Even that smirk nearly sent me over the edge. Left with my tail between my legs, but you have to—"

"Absolute nonsense, you did. I remember what you said, male code for settling up outside. She returned to his hair, which felt like wire and whipcord, moistening it slightly with her kisses. "You'll need a haircut before too long. Did I tell you it's something I like doing?" she asked playfully before assuming a reflective pose, elbows on her knees.

"Well, one good thing: he's out of your friend's life forever."

"Yes. It's simply unbelievable how close she was to disaster. I saw the sneer, too, and wondered what it was all about. The more he spoke the more he damned himself, but she couldn't see it. Pinka probably thinks he's fighting like a hero somewhere on the front line. Ah, but whose front line? When this is all over, I'll tell her she tiptoed beside a precipice wearing a blindfold." Greda drew him down to her.

"We seem to camp with each other in ridiculous places, don't we?" he remarked.

"Well, if you accept me here in all my fetid glory, which I think you've done," she said, straightening her crumpled shirt and playing with the buttons of his, "I can't wait for you to see me in my chosen times, modes of apparel and place. With that, I'll say goodnight." They kissed before she slid apart from him. "We have to be careful with Jonathon."

"Of course we do, Greda."

Not long after finally succumbing to a fitful sleep, a hand cupping his mouth had him sitting up, alert. Greda, leaning over, whispered. "I heard a noise above, like gear being moved." Richard raised himself up sharply, stretched his arms and listened. "I can't hear anything." They waited in silence for a few minutes. "I'll take a peek."

He returned despondent. "Not a sign of anything. No one's been near us all day and half the night, then, when we're expecting a visitor, somebody just comes and goes. It's the obvious time to make contact. So, the question must be asked, where's Arkoi?" He drank from the bottle she passed him.

"This is the worst aspect; not even knowing what the vessel looks like or where it's moored." She was crouching beside him, her voice hushed.

"I'm going up to have another look around. We've a bit of a description of her, certainly as to size, and it's a fishing boat, though I imagine there are plenty of them about."

Greda was reluctant to release her hold on him. "Alright." She finally desisted.

Ten minutes later he announced with a degree of frustration that the mission had been ineffectual. "Nowhere to even start looking and I shouldn't have bothered. As far as I could make out, the wharf is deserted, save for two small boats."

"We just have to wait it out," she said, grimacing with a growing acceptance that their repatriation was no nearer.

"Come on, Greda, tomorrow's another day. We'll just have to recalibrate the gauges."

They embraced again with diminishing conviction. Lessening of the river's chimes against the pylons signified the ebbing tide, which became for them a ticking clock. Then the lapping ceased altogether and, along with hopes of imminent flight, their spirits were beached on the foul mud flat beneath them.

Chapter 19

Into the snake pit

Eva spared no time on returning. Bathing and makeup done, she descended to the living area clad in a tight red-and-gold silk dress slit on both sides, buttoned across her shoulders to a high collar, black belt and gold buckle accentuating her waist. Lace panties, the type he fancied, was her sole undergarment. Despite the forecast that he would be there, Eva was spared. For most of the time she'd been away, Heenan had sojourned at the old Malacca Club where transactions, mostly of a conniving kind, were entered into with local businessmen and sympathisers. His recently acquired status as a prominent planter provided him with eminent credibility when being viewed as an expatriate comfortable with the Japanese cause. They would bestow intelligence, as well as some under-the-table consideration, on his pretext that he was in a position to extract favours for them once a complete transition to local puppet rule obtained.

Halfway through a fourth gin and tonic, Heenan saw Jamal and whistled to him much in the way that an owner might summon a mongrel dog. "You can get another one of these for me and treat yourself," he called out, offering the price of both drinks in the one banknote.

Jamal took it without a word and returned with the obsequious air of one accustomed to disdainful usage. Still, he retained an appreciation of his utility, regarding himself as an essential cog in Heenan's machine. Jamal Viranhi was a misfit, physically and racially. Half-Malay, one-quarter Chinese and one-quarter Indian, this ethnic amalgam served him well as a master of all three languages of his derivation, plus a reasonable command of Japanese, more than adequate English and even boasting enough French to get by.

He was of indeterminate age, five foot eight inches tall, and sported a nondescript, if unusually urbane face dotted from chin to forehead with myriad tiny dark-brown pigmentations. He affected the persona of one perpetually anxious to please. Of lean and hungry build, with darting black eyes, an aquiline nose and a mouth that merged with sallow cheeks, he was an all-knowing, veritable Uriah Heep in coffee-coloured skin, with his affectation of humility, a man of shady business and an underlying distempered personality. He was shrewder than a crow feasting on roadkill.

"Come on, my little adder, what have you for me today? And it'd better not be more of the bullshit you've spewed up of late," the Englishman sneered towards Jamal as he clutched his glass, before lightening its contents.

Heenan gazed across the narrow beach to the passing parade of craft entering and leaving the harbour in the distance. His eyes lit on a salacious sight and, grunting lustfully, he whistled as a line of swaying young women carrying baskets on their heads sallied by, their sideways giggles titillating him.

Jamal prefaced most of his speech-making by rubbing his hands together and nodding incessantly. "Well, sir, we're very fortunate to have the mayor in camp now. He'll do anything to cooperate. I spoke to him this morning and his loyalty is unquestionable."

This richly pleased Heenan, knowing it would gratify the Japanese even more. Jamal noticed a smile curl around the scant lips of his superintendent as Heenan pressed him for detail about particular civic officials and the effect on them of the mayor's position.

"They'll go along with him, I'm sure." Jamal insisted greedily. "I've met with the important ones and confirmed this is the case."

"Anything else?" demanded Heenan, his manner appearing not overly ready to confer any compliments on his oleaginous underling.

Jamal recited a number of insignificant snippets about the police being in a state of limbo, needing some leadership as to what their role might be and whether they would continue to be paid.

"Alright, you've done reasonably well, but don't think it's finished. I want you to be able to report to me within the next twelve hours that everything's ready for the formal changeover by noon the day after tomorrow. If you tie that together, it'll be a big payday for us, so get off."

Like fanning away an offensive odour, Heenan dismissed the perennial hoverer with a backward motion of his hand. Still, he retained a grudging admiration for Jamal, finding him much easier to manipulate than the late Devis.

Within the space of a minute, he reappeared.

"What's it now?" Heenan growled.

"Sir, probably nothing, but your lady, sir, I saw her at the post office picking up mail."

Heenan sobered. Facing off squarely at Jamal, he insisted on a comprehensive recounting of what he'd witnessed, when he had seen it and whether anyone was with her. Consuming all of this material with a rigid concentration, Heenan resumed his seat, demanding to know the quantity of the letters, the names of the addressees and the origin of the stamps. When these interrogatories were met with, "Do not know," "Couldn't see," Jamal's unpredictable benefactor became incensed.

"Did you bloody-well ask the postal clerk about it? No! Go the fucking-hell down there, get back with answers, and be sharp about it if you know what's good for you."

Within an hour, Jamal returned. He commenced by referring to 'some good news and some bad news'. This had a pacifying effect on his superior, who listened without interruption. "Only one article; posted from Shanghai. The clerk couldn't remember the name but said there was something strange. She gave him a name and no letter was waiting and then offered another, the addressee. Oh, and just one more thing, sir, I should say that your woman seemed content to be unobserved."

"You've redeemed yourself, my friend. Here, go and get your queen a new dress," Heenan said mockingly, tossing him a gold coin. Jamal did not mistake the tone or the import. "But don't take too long in doing so, for I want you at the back entrance of my place, six o'clock. Stay there until you're called. Have you got it?"

This instruction was met with a cringing bout of nods and teeth-showing.

The fury that arose within him after being informed of Eva's activities at the post office eased as Heenan devoured his food. Then, he slapped his sides, experiencing a paroxysm of abstruse humour. He possessed information of which she couldn't have the slightest idea. Every question he posed would now be constructed like a cross-examining barrister at the Old Bailey, and he knew the answer to each one of them. But first he must accost Dineh to see what she understood about the day's events.

"Wait a while." He recalled Jamal. "I want you to go and fetch that Dineh. You know her, the domestic who works at my house. Bring the little bitch to me, bound if need be. Tell her anything except who she'll be seeing. Mind though, not a word to my skirt."

Jamal duly departed on a short drive to the rear laneway of the Heenan residence, stopping moments before Dineh exited the laundry shed. As a man who didn't trust anybody, not least his odious overseer, Jamal always did what he could to engage the confidence of those who might be of use to him, gleaning such tidbits as were forthcoming, advance warning of something that might be going on, anything that Heenan had chosen not to disclose and even his master's unstated movements and companions. All of this could be useful background should the occasion arise for its deployment. He never paid much, just enough to keep his informants interested. So there was neither hesitation nor surprise on Dineh's part at Jamal's appearance, and she readily approached the car when called.

"Little Dineh, sorry, I have some sad news. Your mother's here in Malacca. I saw her not long ago, asking for you. In a bad way after falling and must have an operation very soon or she could die. She needs your help. Leave everything aside. I'll drive you."

"Where is she? Will it take long to get there?"

Something in her demeanour suggested reticence or even suspicion. *Not misplaced*, he thought.

"Just a short drive, that's all. Don't worry about the master." He was trying to read her concerns. "He's out of town and won't be back until tomorrow."

"I should say to mistress where I'm going."

"Later, Dineh," he said, ushering her into the front seat. "I'll tell her after I drop you off, or maybe I'll bring you back straightaway with your mother if she's able to be moved. Your mistress will understand and know what's best to do."

Dineh was naturally trusting and, true to his word, Jamal had soon parked outside a cluster of huts where she had relatives, conveniently, in the vicinity of the Club.

"Just wait here while I arrange to have your mother brought out." He opened the rear door in anticipation, and she leaned out the window absentmindedly for some minutes before picking up a conversation in which Jamal was engaged outside one of the huts. Just as she reached for the door latch, a hand stopped her.

"Going somewhere?" An insinuating voice from behind brought a scream, cut short when a large arm fastened upon her neck. In a moment the vehicle sped off. "Not a word, not a sound, or by hell it'll be the last you ever make. We're taking a little trip down to the beach. Maybe we'll go fishing or even have a picnic. You might like a drink. I've even brought some pink gin," Heenan said, still holding her head. He reached over tapping the flask. "Here, drink some," pushing it to her mouth.

The girl was resistant. He repeated the action more forcefully so that she gulped a mouthful and then coughed most of it up.

"Be careful, Dineh, that's expensive liquor. Slowly."

Her hands shook violently as she juggled the flask.

"I'm sure Jamal has some beautiful treats you like—caviar, coconut sugar. Just the ticket for a little fawn from the countryside," he roared, chuffed at his sardonic wit.

They drove to Tanjung Kling, Jamal being directed to a deserted sandy inlet studded with coconut palms and the never-ending foliage of casuarina trees.

"Here will do. Jammy. Put a blanket down where Dineh and I can relax and have a sexy party after we cover the preliminaries and chit-chat."

The driver hastened to the passenger side, blocking any escape, before Heenan's grip was released and led the girl away.

"That's the boy, Jammy. Even brought some rope so Dineh can show us how high she can skip," laughter rending the deserted air.

Jamal witnessed not just a gin-sodden bully, but a pervasive, brooding malevolence, frightening even for an observer not bearing the brunt of his insinuations. Heenan's eyes were wide and bloodshot, his face bathed in a scarlet hue. Any sign of mercy emanating from Jamal would be interpreted as disloyalty. He must do as he was told without demur or sympathy. It was just another job. He tied her hands and walked Dineh under the largest tree.

"Now, my dear little rose-petal," menace pervading Heenan's monotone, "here's what we'll do. I'll ask some questions and you'll answer all of them truthfully. When we're finished, Jamal will take you to back to see your mother. Do you understand?" Dineh moved her head compliantly like a lamb craving reprieve from slaughter.

"Now, today I gave you a job to watch your mistress. Is that what you did?"

"Ye-ye-yes, sir," she stammered.

"Alright. That's wonderful. Now, don't be afraid. Just tell me what things your mistress did. There's a girl."

Beginning shakily, Dineh gradually grew in confidence as she detailed Eva's movements, assuring him she'd never ceased watching. There were the clothing stores where some items had been purchased; that Madam had spent a lot of time shopping, even drawing a comparison that she, Dineh, wouldn't have taken so long, that Madam had dawdled, at times looking at a myriad of wares, and entered several beauty parlours, emerging after a few minutes. There were refreshments at a tea café and visits to several hairdressers, but they were all busy. Finally, Madam had made her way back to their residence.

His lips curled and a half-smile attended Heenan's face when her recitation ended.

"Now, you're sure that's it? Anything else happen at all? You've left nothing out?"

The girl shook her head apprehensively, faintly suspecting that missing from the story was a portion of which
her tormentor might have acquired knowledge.

He continued nonchalantly, "You kept her under
observation at all times?"

"Ye-ye-yes, as I can remember, yes."

For the first time Heenan raised his voice and it
thundered over hers. "You'd remember, wouldn't you?"
She nodded. "You certainly would remember if she went
anywhere else. Didn't go to a bar? No?" She shook her head.
"Didn't go to a restaurant for a three-course lunch, not just
tea? No? Madam didn't meet with a man? No? How about
this: she definitely did *not* go to the post office?" He waited
for an answer. "Mmm?" was the taunt. Containing his rising
fury, the last utterance was barely louder than a whisper.

"No, sir, she didn't go to any of those places." Dineh was
crying and shaking convulsively. "I-I, would see her if she
did. Saw everything. I-I-I tell you truth."

"Thank you, girlie. I believe you. That's all I wanted.
You've done a wonderful job."

He shuffled around as if to return to the car, then swung
his clenched fist ferociously smashing her nose. Another
sickening blow with the other one ruptured her eardrum.

Rivulets of blood flowed as she moaned in agony while
Heenan railed at her, "I *know* you're telling the truth. I
know you are."

Jamal attempted to divert Heenan's attention from the
insensible form. "Shall I take her back to the village? She
won't bother us again."

"You'll take yourself off for a drive, my slimy one, and
come back in fifteen minutes to await my pleasure."

Jamal studied the ground as he walked towards
the vehicle, but a leering image, the epitome of evil
concupiscence, wouldn't leave him as he drove off.

Heenan's fingers traced a path across Dineh's brown
thighs, the hem of her skirt raised to reveal damp
underpants, and ended with his hand lodged between her
legs. She was barely seventeen and had known no man. This
one took the pleasure from which only a monster could

derive satisfaction, and then snuffed out any prospect of his being identified as the culprit.

*****

Waiting at the entrance to the track when Jamal pulled up, Heenan was scowling.

"Take me back to the bar. I have to wash this shit off me. And get me a clean shirt and trousers. These stink. I want you on hand when we visit Eva. You'll drive me there."

Jamal experienced reluctance in complying. Reflecting on a strict Muslim upbringing before he had abandoned religion, he was stabbed by a momentary pang of conscience.

Heenan laughed loudly and intuitively. "It's finished, my dear boy. That's what comes of those who take notions on themselves way above their station. You'd do well to understand." He relished the cowered look on Jamal's face. "Do you hear me?"

"Yes, sir."

"Come on, Jammy, I thought the subcontinental mind was made of rigid stuff. You have a weak stomach. Just go and get my clothes and stay out of the fucking way. Even doze if you like, but be in earshot in case I call for you. And don't ever disappoint me, Jammy."

When he returned to their abode, Heenan treated Eva's seductive presentation with pronounced indifference. Flopping into an armchair facing away from the liquor cabinet, he clicked his fingers over his shoulder and, when no answer came, called out, "Dineh! Where's that fool of a thing? Why isn't she here? That's what I pay her for. What do you know about this, Eva?"

Sensing a trap, she began to prevaricate. "Tell me what you mean, Patrick. Am I her keeper? What can I get you to drink?"

His lips tightened demonically. Ignoring her offer, he decanted a gin and tonic. With a show of bravado, Eva asked him for a whisky and soda while he was at it. Taking the chance afforded by his rare display of magnanimity in pouring her a drink, she drank a substantial portion and began to invent interest in Dineh's whereabouts. Moving to the back, she called out several times, went from room to room and walked to the laundry. Looking casually across the laneway, she saw the familiar outline of Jamal's car partly obscured behind a tree. *Must be nearby*, she thought, he not being one to skulk indolently in shadows unless under clear instruction to do so.

Heenan was becoming impatient and bellowed.

She entered through the kitchen, determined not to bray at the pending onslaught. "I can't see her. She didn't tell me she was going out and—"

Her fudging was short-shrifted. "We'll get along without her for the moment. Sit down and make no error in listening," Heenan said.

Eva complied, cognisant of the undisguised venom in his tone.

"Now, tell me with meticulous accuracy what you've done today. I'm sure you understand my meaning because—"

"Alright. I went somewhere not on your chosen list of destinations—the post office. And why? To get a letter from my mother that said they are safe and well in Shanghai." Eva read some flicker of a pain-free outcome in the surprise that registered in his face, inspiring her to decorate the chronicle further. "Now, is that so bad?" she expostulated more stridently, rising to illustrate her point.

She hadn't stinted herself in tilting the bottle before his appearance, whether in anticipation of any confrontation or not. Its influence Eva was fain to appreciate in this instance. Heenan eyed the ebbing liquid from the tall glass as she made a defiant show of savouring its contents. The immediate effect served the dual purpose of emboldening her further and dispelling fear of an immediate thrashing.

"You know how I feel about my family and you can't blame me for wanting to hear from them how they are. Now, I'm grateful for what you've done in protecting them. So whatever plan you have for me, do it now and get it over. I'm prepared to take the penalty for not telling you."

Eva had chosen insubordination, suggesting that nothing, short of extinguishing her life, would diminish a determination to assert herself. She found the effect liberating, not only by challenging him to do his worst, but by turning him from a picture of ugly retribution to one of smug satisfaction. He had caught her out but, evident from his attitude, a fact she relished more than anything else, was his obvious lack of awareness of her meeting with Richard. In the misty silence that followed, she charged her glass and sat down, crossing and uncrossing her bare legs provocatively.

He drank more himself before saying, "I like it when you're a bitch, when you stand up to me, and, mmm, those splits going right up to your arse. Why you bothered with knickers I'll never know. And to think you bought it all today to please me. One thing, though, my carnal little minx, if you don't mind—and heaven forbid me if you do—a minor detail. The letter, if you please."

"I don't have it. I burnt it after I came back."

"Well then," he drawled, detecting a blink at the request, "show me the 'charred remains', as the old Bill says. It's not that I don't believe you, but you know me. And no dawdling."

She swept into the kitchen, trepidation rising within her, returning to exhibit the ashes. Eva tilted the bin, showing him the fragments. "I would've kept the letter, but I know what you're like," she said, encouraged to expand her tale given the tactical victory.

"Not so fast." He seized her arm as she began to leave. "Tip them out. There's a good girl."

To her relief, very little could be identified, just enough for him to see Chinese characters on one tiny portion. She prayed that these would be non-incriminating.

"Jamal!" he thundered.

The saturnine figure materialised like an infusion of fetid air. Dread rose in case the authorship or contents were put at issue.

"Have a close look at this and tell me if you can pick out a word or two. That's all we have left of a letter Eva claims was written by her mother."

"It says here, 'All well Shanghai' and 'love you, Eva'. I can't see anything else, but wait," Jamal responded, taking further time. His eyes slid towards hers cunningly, "No, nothing more," and then narrowed as he waited for further instructions.

Heenan moved close to Eva's face. Squeezing her cheeks between his thumb and forefingers caused her to wince, but he was uncharacteristically equable. "You've saved yourself by being frank about what happened. Never do that again, mind, but I truly understand the motivation. You are no longer forbidden from going to town without my permission, for I'm satisfied with what you've told me. All independently verified, and never you mind by whom. Remember, I'll be told about anything you're inclined to get up to. Thank you, Jamal, you may leave now." He finished his drink before speaking again.

"Oh, and you needn't worry about Dineh. She's gone for good, just up and left. According to Jamal, the ungrateful girl told one of his confidants she preferred employment closer to the beach. Funny that, isn't it? Such unreliable help we get these days. You can look for a replacement tomorrow. Now break out the champagne and be damned quick in case I change my mind—about everything."

She didn't believe him for a minute. Heenan deflected further enquiry respecting Dineh's situation. The last of the bottle had been poured out along with much stroking of his ego. The defining inducement, where the tongue might be tempted to tell all with her mouth buried between his naked legs as he quaffed the dregs of his glass, produced only the tiniest elaboration, but damning nonetheless.

"I can say she mightn't remember all I did for her."

After Heenan had taken his fill, Eva was dismissed for the night and Jamal summoned to join him in the kitchen.

"I don't trust that harridan for a second," he relayed grimly, eyes still livid.

Opening another bottle of liquor, he indicated that Jamal might help himself to the tonic but to be abstemious with the gin.

"Jammy, my lad, you've plenty of work ahead. I sniff something. Log her every breath and here's some money for your lackeys. Carry out a very close and discreet surveillance of our little butterfly that seems to think its wings are broadening by the hour. One way or another, I'll clip them till the ends are bloodied." His raucous laughter was only stemmed when Jamal pointed a warning finger upstairs. "I want a detailed report on her. And don't fuck up like you did at the post office, if you value your life."

Jamal nodded several times, and then searched for his glass, taking a tiny portion of drink. He dared not abstract more but wished he could to assuage the horror he was experiencing in observing Heenan's face, a study in pathological brooding, akin to the crazed visage that had despatched the hapless Dineh.

Chapter 20

Chancers

Ever sanguine throughout an interminably humid night in what he had christened the 'cubby house', Richard was expecting the tap above their heads, signaling Arkoi's arrival. He succumbed to an hour's fitful sleep before the jarring cacopheny of another day of fishermen's environment stirred them all. One thing above all else had become clear: they couldn't continue to remain where they were.

Richard considered various options in turn, becoming more inventive as time skulked on. Stealing a boat in the dead of night, asking around to see if anyone knew Arkoi, canvassing other skippers and even trying to locate and re-engage with Naranam. Each proposal faltered embryonically. Indiscriminate enquiries meant risking betrayal.

From whatever direction these things were considered, he invariably returned to the only reasonable option and was fortified by the notion that Eva's help had been offered rather than sought. His preliminary assessment that he could trust her, firmed, accepting that nothing ever came with an iron-clad guarantee. The inchoate spectre of Heenan was always large in his reckoning in undertaking a second surreptitious assignation with her. But Eva was sharp, persuasive respecting her contacts and had left him confident that she could call on them. Her remorse for the past seemed genuine, if not entirely understandable.

That she still cared for him was a troubling element. The revelation of two other passengers for any voyage had to be made, and what might she discern from that? Then again, perhaps he was majoring on the minutiae. It was not something he needed to tell her immediately. He hedged between relying on Eva wholly, or just partially. Richard surmised that if she was able to track Arkoi down to revitalise the existing arrangement that might be the preferred pathway.

Greda's argument was that they might be left in a worse position than if he randomly appealed for assistance from piscators mending their nets on the wharf. At least he wouldn't be risking a confrontation with Heenan. Even the unlawful use of a boat had more merit, she thought, until he reminded her that the Straits of Malacca combined a hazardous patch of water to navigate in the best of conditions. Seaworthiness was a pre-eminent consideration and the chance of having sufficient fuel in a random selection was not good either, even apart from assuming a vessel could be unslipped without coming to the owner's notice or that of the Japanese.

Greda was that breed of woman who would, once a scheme was fully and comprehensively advocated, bow to reasoned and determined argument, especially if it emanated from someone whose opinions she respected.

"Perhaps I'm just dreading you parting from us again, but my head tells me you're right. As you say, we can't expect to get away with remaining here much longer."

His positive attitude reflected her concession. "I'll return by lunchtime at the latest with good news, guaranteed."

He kissed her cheek and tousled Jonathon's hair before opening the hatchway and exiting by the side door. The route he took into the market area was more circuitous than the one of the previous day, and he arrived at the teahouse several minutes late. He noticed Eva was wearing more makeup, but not enough to disguise shadows under her eyes. Radiating joy at seeing him, she poured tea from a large bone china pot.

"Everything normal. A few ructions overnight that had nothing to do with our parley, but I handled it." She turned her face one way and then the other, pointing with a painted forefinger. "No cuts or bruises."

"You shouldn't joke about that," he offered with feeling. "Yesterday you said you wanted to help me." He chose his words carefully, not wishing to appear overly eager. "I wasn't sure what to say to you—"

"You're too tentative, Richard. Do you think I'm silly? Let's get to why we're here. I know somebody, a captain of a small cargo vessel. He's solid." Eva felt no presumption in acquainting him with her scheme. "Now listen closely," she whispered forcefully. It was a side to her that he hadn't experienced. "The ship's leaving tonight. It's not openly listed as going to Singapore."

Trying to suppress his excitement, he asked, "You're certain about this fellow?"

Eva couldn't keep her hands off him. "Yes, I am. He's master of the *Fanno Maru* that's tied up at wharf twenty-three. Don't be alarmed," she said, seeing his frown.

"Oh, I didn't mean to appear so, just a bit jittery at the moment. Keep going."

"Richard, you're a lot older these days." She waited in vain for a response. "So, back to business. Last week it was the *Malayan Explorer*, and now a makeover to suit the exigencies, so unlikely to experience any difficulty leaving port."

He asked about the cost of passage.

"Money isn't in issue. You'll travel as crew. I told the captain of your qualifications and he said you can sail as chief engineer."

"Eva, that's all very well, but what about you? You can't go on living with that thug. You must get away, too, and—"

"Are you asking me to go with you? I'm not making it a condition of your leaving, but, Richard, we may still have a chance together." She urged her body against him.

This was the intimation he'd suspected but little wished to hear. It wasn't one he could blithely deny, even if instinct advised candour. Her volatility was to the forefront of his mind. If she thought there was the slightest hint of a romantic entanglement, the whole enterprise could be jeopardised.

She read his discomfort as rejection. "You don't want me to come, do you, Richard? I understand, really I do. I just want to hear it from your lips."

Was this a test question? he asked himself. There was a pragmatic side to her that he hoped wouldn't react irrationally, so he took a gamble. "Of course I want you to be safe. What sort would I be to think of anything else? Eva, um, we've had our time and it was good, but everything's changed since and—"

"I did love you then, Richard. I still do and always will. Now I've nothing to live for. Aided the enemy and reached the end of my usefulness. I hate them and loathe Heenan. He'll be punished one day. But I love you and need you!"

He dared not debate her motivations. Unable to curb her sobs, kissing his chest and neck, she came close to wailing, and he gently sealed his hand over her mouth.

There was but one thing to say. "Yes, you must come. You have to get away from him, and this is the Godsend." He connected with her eyes and repeated himself to make the point that such was his wish. "Eva, look at me. I want you to come."

The words, barely uttered, saw her lips claim his so insistently that he began to revile himself for succumbing to a reaction he should have anticipated.

She took his reticence as confusion and sat up straight, fixing him through her tears. "I know it's too soon. You're not ready for this. I'll wait, Richard, but I just want you so much."

A hapless embrace calmed her, and she relaxed in his arms.

She wiped her face and composed herself. Richard swallowed at the pitiable sight.

Eva interpreted his gaze as softening towards her. "I'm alright now, darling."

She produced a sheet of notebook paper and sketched a mud map of where he had to go, using the current location as a starting point.

"It's about twenty minutes' walk from here to the wharf. The ship will go on the stroke of midnight. Meet me at the bow half an hour before. I'll speak to the captain to make certain everything's arranged."

"I can't say how much I appreciate what you're doing, Eva."

She rubbed his forearms, stroked his cheek and regarded him with reddened eyes, willing another embrace before sneaking a look outside. On her saying all was clear, he departed.

Eva stared after him intently, hoping he would wave. He turned the corner with that wish unfulfilled. *Ah, but that's Richard now*, she thought, remaining ebullient.

Her plan mustn't fail. She remembered reading about men randomly hijacked aboard old sailing ships by other crew members to effect a complement. The irony was sweet. Captain Chia mightn't get the reluctant guest to work, but he would relish the significant reward for the traitor's delivery to the British authorities.

The next phase in the preparations for their midnight departure involved a bicycle ride over to the *Fanno Maru*. She pushed herself with the brisk and carefree air of a slave who'd been released from bondage. Her hair, loosened by the breeze, flapped its tresses across her face, unleashing little tingles and offsetting the oppressive air of the midday sun. A broad smile, the nature of which hadn't lit her features for a long time, was evident as she negotiated her way through the clatter and barter of the ubiquitous roadside vendors.

Joy tends to produce reactions, and hers was invariably reciprocated wherever she gazed, delighting in nodding to anyone who crossed her path on the busy thoroughfares and intersections as they led her towards the merchant shipping docks. She'd jettisoned caution and, like a punter's zeal after a succession of wins, Eva was inflated with an air of invincibility as she mounted the gangway.

The meeting with a brusque Chia induced a rapid deflation. Heenan, he insisted, had to be lured to an area proximate to where the ship was moored. He eschewed any suggestion involving his men any further afield and left her to work out how this could be achieved. "We sail to schedule, passengers or no passengers. You get him on the wharf and I can do the rest," he added.

"I understand," she sighed. "Oh, and I'll be coming with the engineer we talked about, Richard Kirnst."

Chia nodded. "Papers shall be prepared for Richard Baynes McCormack, my new chief engineer. And, of course, you'll bring the balance," he said, fingering the crisp, green fifty dollar deposit.

Eva's departure from the ship was in crestfallen contrast to her gangway ascension an hour earlier. The peddling was so unstable that at one point the bicycle almost overbalanced as she weighed her dilemma. Short of brute force it would be impossible for Heenan to be induced to come to the docks by midnight.

*****

With freshly developed photographs corroborating his dossier, Jamal Viranhi was possessed of the power of life or death. In this role, he bore the trappings of a man at the pinnacle of his craft, relishing the underestimation in which he was held by all who encountered him, chief of whom was the defrocked Captain Patrick Heenan. So internecine had Jamal's reach become in such a short time, that Heenan could be bypassed at his discretion and pleasure. That his controller lacked cognisance of this subtle alteration in juxtaposition tantalised him.

As his influence grew, so Heenan's was waning. Rapacious demands had alienated the people currently under Jamal's cultivation. His own position would be cemented if he didn't have to continually pick up the pieces of an abusive episode with local officials or arrange compensation for Heenan's damage to the property of businessmen or appease them after indecent dealings with their young daughters.

There were, Jamal reflected with conceit, degrees of wickedness and callous disregard for human life in all men. He wasn't exempt from calculated duplicity and ruthlessness that placed little value on the lives of fellow travellers, or anyone else, getting in his way, but he baulked at the wanton destruction of innocence. The nadir of Heenan's depravity was evidenced by the mutilated body of Dineh, her blood colouring bleached coral crusted in the sands. She was naked save that her top was threaded around her neck like a bowtie. Heenan had to be eliminated, but Jamal couldn't be seen as complicit in its facilitation. Before him was the substance of a plan ninety per cent hatched. The remaining ten per cent must, of necessity, involve him delivering the *coup de grace*.

There was another thing Jamal coveted with considerable relish. The safe in Heenan's possession contained a significant stash of gold and hard currency. To secure it, he needed to utilise every ounce of chicanery in his repertoire. One wrong move might not just foil his manipulations but also lead to a severing of his head, a fate dangled over him more than once.

Jamal was acquainted with Chia, as he knew almost everyone usefully connected with west coast Malayan trade and was aware of the captain's attitude to the Japanese invasion. Even potential protagonists or disagreeable spectators could become fair-weather friends if they shared a common purpose. With the contents of the safe and his nemesis out of the way, unassailable power and influence would devolve on Jamal in the vacuum created by Heenan's removal.

Eva's perfume had hardly dissipated before Jamal was seated in the captain's cabin, drawing upon a Cuban cigar bestowed on him by his host.

"I'm delighted to see you again, my new-found friend," the master beamed inscrutably. "You must want something, so make yourself comfortable. You needn't fret, our conversations will be private."

"So very suspicious. I was just in the area and—"

"You'll not mind my request that you come to the point. We're to sail tonight and there's much still to do, cargo to load—"

"Human cargo, perhaps," Jamal insinuated, and moved to placate Chia's frowning brow. "Come now, don't trouble yourself. I know all about it. Rodent guards on mooring lines serve one purpose, but your most important piece of uncollected ballast is that kind only I can deliver. He's large, belligerent, and worth a fortune to you, much more than the incidental services of a merchant marine deserter."

Chia was an eminently pragmatic man, blunt, straight-talking, a person who knew there was little to be gained by prevaricating. He also had a sound betting hand. "You deliver and I rid you of him?" he mouthed through compressed lips.

"Your point is taken. It's very simple, my dear Captain. You can carry the woman, or whoever you might want, on your little voyage without the slightest concern about being intercepted before you're two hundred yards into the channel, provided you lift the biggest prize of all. There's space, I take it?"

"You must already know that," Chia said.

"I know all, sir, everything. I also understand you wouldn't risk the ship or your life unless you knew he was in the bag, so to speak, but, without me to assist, peril abounds. That's why I'm here, so attend." He outlined the scheme to lure Heenan to the ship.

"You seem to know of the woman and the man she was with."

"You have the medley sweet, Captain Chia, and I'm hurt that you might wonder about the accuracy of my brief and what I've modestly mentioned already. But you'll be looked after, sir, I promise."

Jamal's darting, snake-like black eyes didn't inspire total confidence in the reliability of his representations as to the future, but Chia had seen them at work before in other contexts. When it came to plotting and skullduggery, he was without peer. The captain's sympathies ensured complete cooperation with him. Chia was backgrounded by Jamal on all aspects of the subterfuge. The quantum of the reward in the offing for a successful press-ganging sealed his acquiescence.

"You know my connections to the British, Captain," Jamal insinuated.

Chia nodded sagely. "I like the sound of it, but I'll want two hundred dollars once he's taken."

"Ah, Captain, you never disappoint. I'll see you tonight at eleven-thirty. And remember again the monetary considerations."

"Which are to be adhered to precisely the moment he's on board?"

"You'll have your down-payment and more when you deliver him to the British. He's to be handed over to a Major Newton, no one else. All will be arranged. Adieu, Captain."

Viranhi was satisfied and hastened off. One residual area troubled him. He must prevail over anything Eva might have in mind as far as enticing Heenan to the ship. Jamal was nothing if not a methodical man who weighed everything up before making a decision. He would meet with and selectively brief Heenan on Eva's manoevres before that individual returned to his domicile. The telling had to be handled with dexterity and assurance, whereby sufficient time might be purchased to allow Heenan's passion to cool.

Then there was the woman. Eva's involvement meant that, if things went awry, he could direct all the blame her way and save himself. She would be either an integral player or a sacrifice at the altar of Heenan's venom. In that event, plans at the wharf would have to change. He straightaway elected to inform Eva what he had in mind.

*****

Jamal's demeanour as he materialised in Eva's kitchen personified, once she overcame the fright occasioned by his unexpected appearance, an insidious and calculating quality that she hadn't previously experienced. Like a fractional opening of shutters, the slits of his eyes couldn't be narrower or more pervasive. His movements were pyretic, as if he was about to spring the greatest coup of his lifetime. Absent was the disconcerted air of the perpetually downtrodden servant.

"What I'm about to tell you is a matter of life and death. Yours in fact, and that of the man you met today at the teahouse."

Eva's face contorted in horror before she dashed towards an open window.

His fingernails tore at her flesh to prevent her from jumping. "Stop it, you stupid little fool!" he yelled, underestimating the reaction. He slapped her face. "Listen, I'm on your side. Do you think I couldn't read through those ashes? You want him handed over to the British, and so do I."

"You're lying! It's another trap."

She broke free from his grasp and raced to a drawer, grabbing a large kitchen knife. The gesture was futile for, while he effected the air of someone of insipid physical aptitude, his wiry frame, when tested, possessed significant reserves of strength. He latched onto her wrist and twisted it to breaking point. Wailing, she dropped the knife and fell to the floor. Her whole body shook in a kind of paroxysm. Jamal reached for a jug of water and threw the contents over her face. Eva sat up, her posture drooped in defeat as he spoke.

"You know what our good friend is like." Jamal told her precisely where he stood, as she watched on distrustfully. "And I've only to wink and you're finished."

For a moment he wondered whether that might be easier. Her demise would be inconsequential. The hardest thing was what he was suggesting.

"I'm listening," she said tersely.

He reminded Eva that they'd both suffered through Heenan's manipulations; that although his reasons for wanting him out of the way were neither altruistic nor congruent with hers, they could together develop a partnership of purpose to achieve his downfall.

"And don't forget, my sultry one, that the British might want to have a little chat with you at some stage for your part in the spying game. He won't hold back and will do anything to save his neck. I can just see it; you'll be the *femme fatale*." He permitted himself a sickly snigger that morphed into a despatch of phlegm through the window. "Do it my way and you become mistress of your own destiny. I'll put a word in. You just disappear in Singapore and get away from all this forever."

He observed her closely, baring his unkempt teeth in the fashion that she'd seen when he was with Heenan. There was no doubting his intuition that she was but a step away from acceptance as he reached into his pocket to produce the macabre photographs of Dineh's body. The memory of the attractive, immature young girl couldn't be reconciled with the despoiled and mangled depiction.

Trance-like, Eva rose and walked to the cabinet where the spirits were stored to down a tumbler of neat whisky. "Tell me what to do?"

*****

Elevated by familiarity with pleasurable sorties in most ports of South-East Asia, Richard loved nothing better than to go ashore and explore local markets. The object of these expeditions was to seek out exotic fruits and delicacies unheard of, let alone tasted, in his homeland. On his return to the ship, maladroitly lugging wooden half-bushel cases, often one under each arm, curious attention would follow him all the way to his cabin. Requests to sample the bounty had to be carefully overseen in case his supplies were exhausted before he opened his own mouth.

Such was the industry generated by these purchases that, on the *Erakai*, it raised the ire of the chief steward. In seeking Richard out and enunciating his displeasure that these developments were encroaching on his jurisdiction, all was defused when the second engineer diplomatically furnished him with his sources of supply, promising to be more discreet in future forays.

That 'collateral thought diversions', as he had cumbersomely dubbed them when confessing in bygone times to Willie O'Connell the existence of this phenomenon, made routine entries into his head baffled him. They arrived as if produced by some spirit, invariably when he was trying to solve a difficult problem. The capriciousness of these ephemeral bubbles was a puzzle he had lived with for most of his life.

O'Connell had told him then that the explanation was simple. "It's just you're a farkin' mad dreamin' bastard, nothing more."

"That's the classic Irish deduction, being such a race of nutters, Willie," he'd replied good-naturedly, "and maybe I am, but it still doesn't solve the marvel."

"And pigs fly to Londonderry in springtime. You've been at sea too long and need to go find a woman."

This was O'Connell's rationale for everything, and the recollection of their conversation reprised the very issue he'd raised. At the same time as the jibing amused him, the vivid image of his shipmate jarred as well. He posited where O'Connell was right now and, more especially, if he wondered what had led Richard to miss the sailing. Normally as subtle as a sledgehammer on white-hot steel, when the *Erakai* left Swettenham without him, he might have said a few *Hail Marys*.

Mercifully distracting, yet pointless as it was to contemplate the aetiology of these musings, there was the
beneficial effect on him. He was at last armed with something more than a specious hope of their getting out and
embraced the penultimate chapter of this nerve-wracking
uncertainty with renewed stamina. Richard was sustained
by the expectation that tonight he, Greda, and Jon would
be on board a ship taking them to freedom.

But such enthusiasm was not without dampeners,
and he fell prone to looking for the negatives. Within
the mix lay an element that couldn't be wished away. An
encounter between Greda and Eva remained a perturbing
possibility. Mentally, like the satisfaction to be gained
from fixing a problem with one piece of machinery, he
was constrained to confront the discordant clanging of
another about to break down. Greda would understand.
On the other side, Eva was much harder to plumb. She
would entertain suspicion of the unannounced passengers,
but Richard trusted that any concerns would be mitigated
by the pressures of the moment. Unless her antennae were
especially attuned, surely the revelation couldn't turn so
bad that she would jettison the arrangement. No matter
which way he balanced these potential pitfalls, in the end
it remained a possible hurdle with which to reckon.

The fear of misadventure in the critical hours ahead so
dogged his thoughts that Richard reconsidered, yet again,
the possibility of locating Naranam, who might know what
had happened to Arkoi. Like an endless rally in a tennis
match, eventually exhaustion won out and he pushed it
from his mind.

This time he would take a chance and enter the boatshed by the door. It must have been siesta for the fishermen, with a mere handful of idlers on the wharf. No one
appeared interested in him when he engaged the key and
went inside.

"Here man we look for long time," a stranger announced,
sounding as if Richard had kept him waiting.

Whether it was his preoccupations, the casualness of
the introduction or the fright of seeing a stranger not far
from where Greda and Jon were hiding, he didn't know,

but Richard's even temper fled. "What the hell are you doing here?"

He seized the man by his shirtfront and pushed him towards a staunchion.

"I, Arkoi, come here see you."

Two others emerged, one brandishing a pick-handle, the other a seaman's splicing spike. Richard wheeled his man around as a shield, keeping the pair in front of him. After the older man remonstrated with them, they lowered their implements.

Addressing Richard, Arkoi said, "Just come now, very sorry not yesterday night. Boat stopped and search by Japanese patrol. We back to port early morning. They ask me I see white man, woman and child. Not sure if they looking you. I sent someone here, leave note message. You got?"

"No, I haven't seen anything."

Arkoi retrieved a piece of paper from under a tin and handed it to Richard. The writing was confirmation enough.

"How was I to notice? There was a noise, but I didn't see anyone."

"Never mind. I be follow and they search when come here. Other boats also stopped, They know more, or maybe guessing, but take no chance and find it clear, be off other directions."

Arkoi sat down, chin cupped in his hands, eyes fixed on him.

Richard deduced that if he was being less than candid the shed would have been raided by now. "So where do we go from here? You're saying it's dangerous to take anyone to Singapore?" he asked, hoping Arkoi would offer an alternative.

"You need go soon. I think moment okay at shed. My men see who here, whether stranger people from afar. Cannot take risk anymore, my life, my future, for fishermen."

"Okay, I understand your position. You can appreciate mine. It's not possible to go instantly, but I'll leave here tonight."

"Better then. I very sorry cannot stay longer."

Richard scrutinised the dark-brown, leathered face of the old fisherman and read its inherent decency. He accepted the cash Richard pressed into his hand, producing a container of fresh water and a large papaya. "You take."

"Thank you. Here's your key, I shan't need it any longer. We'll be gone by ten o'clock and I won't be sorry to see the last of this place."

Arkoi bared his teeth and saluted.

Richard waited while the three fishermen gathered up some gear and left, closing the front door. He lowered the water, fruit and then himself below. An uplifting sight Greda made, such that he had to block the instinct to abandon all decorum and take her in his arms. He saw her relief as he clambered to the floor.

"I'm—we're so glad you're back with us. Someone called out and I was terrified, we just froze. I shouldn't worry, I know, but there it is. I was wondering if you were alright or been arrested or something else had happened, and then your voice—" She paused to catch her breath.

"Greda, this is a firm promise. The next outing will be together."

"It's so good to see you, ah," Jon looked questioningly towards his mother before going on, "Mum, I'm going to say Dick 'cause he doesn't mind. I'm a whole lot better now and she is, too."

As he scrutinised the innocent face, Richard thought of the loss he must be feeling over his father.

"I heard a little of that upstairs. We can't manage another night here," Greda declared.

"It's been tough, but our time in this cubby house is coming to an end," he said, going on to explain the late-night departure. "Another eight hours and we're on our way to Singapore."

Greda glanced from Jonathon to Richard. "And none too soon."

"You got it. As for Arkoi, can't blame him for being keen to free his shed from wanted fugitives!"

She knew Richard believed passionately in the escape plan but wasn't ready to provide unqualified endorsement. "If it's to work, then everything will be as you say, Richard, but to dampen things a little, we've been fortunate so far. Each step seems fractionally further out of reach of trouble, and I wonder, relying on this person—"

"We have to," he said, shrugging his shoulders. "Eva's our only chance now Arkoi has delivered his verdict."

"Why is she helping us?" asked Jon.

Richard attempted to satisfy the boy's enquiry before Greda spoke. "Because she doesn't like the Japanese. Now no more questions, alright?"

Full details were laid out as he pointed to the map Eva had scratched out.

"What I'll do is go to the front of the ship and wait. You and Jonathon need to stay in the shadows. I haven't told her about you."

"I wonder, though, if it would be better to bypass her altogether," offered Greda. "I can just go on board with Jon and plead to be taken to Singapore because I heard where the ship was going."

Richard reflected that it was unlikely the captain would bar entry to a woman and child given his apparent disposition. The idea had merit, but it forced his disclosure.

"Eva's coming, too, sort of desperate to escape this place, and I'm hardly in a position to dictate what she decides," he said awkwardly.

Greda was thoughtful in her response. "I'm worried about the woman, Richard. She's unpredictable and will no doubt want money too."

"Doesn't want money. She's been through a lot. But you're right to ask—"

"If you don't know her reaction, how can you trust her? Richard, this sounds precipitous and naïve, I have to say."

That she had spoken with conviction jangled his threadbare nerves. He took her questioning of the efficacy of a plan he was convinced covered all contingencies as a personal affront. This she had not intended to do, but her use of the word 'naïve' provoked an unusually blunt response.

"And what damn choice do I have, especially now we can no longer stay here?" he snapped. Then, appreciating that she'd posed some very telling points, he added, "Sorry for rounding on you like that, Greda. You must know I regard the safety and wellbeing of you and Jon as the paramount consideration."

"Of course I know that, and I shouldn't have allowed myself to parrot on. There's no need to be concerned at my reaction. I half-expected she would want to come."

He shook his head, contemplating her perspicacity.

"What's going on in that brain of yours?" she asked, airily.

"My head? You're telepathic, so why do you ask?"

They had developed an understanding that quickly stilled discord.

"Greda, the more I think about it, if we're to sail on that ship we all tramp on together. Anything else can follow later."

Arkoi's warning prompted a decision to leave the boatshed earlier than originally planned. Provided there was no obvious impediment to their boarding, it would allow Richard time to explain all to the captain. Greda had reservations about him disembarking again.

"I promised to meet her there at eleven-thirty and not turning up could place us in jeopardy," he insisted.

"You must do it, then. I'm a touch anxious."

"Understandable. I can't undo what's been agreed when she's taken it all this far."

"Alright, I'm a worrier, rather than a warrior. Enough of me and my predilection for pitching obstacles in our path."

She put her arm around Jonathon and held him tightly, drawing Richard in as she did so. The moment united them. She stroked her fingers wistfully around the back of his neck. A rumble followed by a thunderclap heralded the roar of torrential rain. Droplets seeped through the sheeting above their heads. Their huddle tightened as they tried to keep dry.

"Richard, I'm sure that by this time tomorrow night we'll be snug in Singapore, joking about how easy it all was and planning our next cruise."

Chapter 21

Pressganged

J amal had prepared a strategy in advance of the inevitable
fireworks. A singular capacity for insinuating himself
into the confidence of even the most implacable of
enemies stemmed from gaining an appreciation of his
foe's every thought process. Design rather than chance was
its hallmark and, in each case, adaptation to the individual
secured dividends.

The way to owning Heenan's mind when he'd been
crossed was to plot a piece of devilment so facinorous as to
outdo anything his extant employer could contrive on his
own account. Having discerned the panoply of Heenan's
pathological measure, it was this totemic tactic that Viranhi
employed in acquainting him with the embroidered
aspects of Eva's scheming.

An unexpurgated flurry of black oaths, tirades and the
pledging of a solemn troth where he alone would mete
out the requisite torture that included paring the flesh off
her body inch-by-inch with a rusty, serrated scaling knife,
followed the revelations.

"And one other vital little detail," Jamal's crafty
modulations serving to staunch the invective, "a way to
further satiate the vengeance you crave and justly deserve,
sir." He explained that Richard Kirnst's name could be
engraved on the trophy, but only by Jamal's securing Eva's
unwitting cooperation.

"What?" Heenan roared. "You mean she met with *him*?"
He was clenching his fists and grinding his teeth as the
proof was unveiled. "I've said it before, why didn't I finish
off that upstart colonial scum in Kuala Lumpur?"

"Well, my dear sir, now you'll have your chance, as she's going away with him on the *Fanno Maru* tonight. They're meeting at the front of the ship before it sails for Singapore."

"Jammy, I'll catch them in the act. You know what I want, and you'd better give me those heads on a silver platter."

"You shall have them, sir and, as well, my men to back you up. There'll be no escape. We'll get a tidy sum from the captain, too. He's been paid handsomely for his live cargo and that'll be forfeited, together with a substantial supplementation, otherwise it doesn't leave port, mmm?"

Jamal deemed it safe from the other's reaction to permit himself a chortle. This was stifled as the glowering returned, before, just as capriciously, Heenan's comportment assumed a chilling benignity. Its persistence pre-empted a stream of compliments; Jamal was a 'genius' and 'even more deceitful and corrupt than me', so elated was Heenan at the nefarious possibilities his compatriot had afforded him.

"Jammy, just keep very still for a moment, will you?" Heenan had produced a *parang* and stroked the flat edge across the horrified man's arm, like a barber honing a cut-throat razor on leather. "Maybe we're blood brothers," he enquired and paused to tilt the edge. His stare was so devoid of humanity or even its essence, of which he seemed to be positing a desire to commingle, that Jamal felt he was witnessing a manifestation of the Devil incarnate.

Pointing out that Eva might any moment surprise them, Jamal managed to extricate himself to avoid the infliction of a serious laceration in case the drink had affected the blade-teaser's dexterity. "I'll wait outside, sir," he said gingerly, evading the question.

Eva arrived with an air of indifference, inwardly feast-ing on the momentous events that were about to unfold. She swanned over to Heenan, who was spread-eagled in a large cane chair with a gin and tonic, leant over to kiss him on the cheek and related her activities for the day. She in-flated these with the tale of a visit to a beautician, inviting Heenan to smell her bare midriff, offered near enough to his face to receive a lurid lick in her navel, an abundance of French perfume inducing a smutty double entendre.

"Ah, skin so sweet and creamy as to be edible," he drawled insidiously.

She was ready for anything he might hurl at her—insult, compliment or questioning—but no sooner had she traced the back of her hand enticingly across his chest than he declared that there were private issues to which he must attend. She pouted a little, saying she appreciated his understanding, that it had been a long day and she was tired. The seductive tone of her parting whisper and the damp of her tongue in his ear sought to remind him of what lay in store upstairs whenever he cared to join her.

He was astonished at the convincing manner in which Eva carried it off. The longer she spent looking towards him in the same fashion, delaying her ascent, the greater he relished the conviction that she would never repeat such a performance.

Eva's exit saw Jamal's reappearance.

"What a delicate little flower, Jammy. By god, the bitch can play-act. Such a waste, really. I almost felt a good flogging would suffice to bring her back onto the path of righteousness, along with insistence that she witness what I intend for her miserable lover."

Jamal's response was limited to a knowing curl of his top lip, revealing nicotine-stained upper teeth so shaped and curved as to be easily mistaken for fangs. Heenan frowned, regarding the action as uncharacteristic, before his charge cottoned on and the familiar sycophancy returned.

"Sir, I'll take you down a few minutes early. I know you'll want to hear for yourself what those conspirators are planning."

"You've covered everything, Jammy. I won't forget what you've done for me. I so want to see them caress each other's bodies and hear about their plans for the future, and all their little sweet mouthings. This'll be rich. Almost splendiferous. Oh, young love, Jammy, how cruel to see it torn asunder and crushed."

Heenan guffawed again, this time so consumed by unassailable confidence that it prompted Jamal to make another count of the sailors Chia would have in attendance. *Surely three would be enough,* he calculated, adding in his own ruffians.

"What are you thinking about, my dear Jammy? I won't just be relying on your men, my earnest and honourably treacherous rogue." A lethal black pistol rested in the open palm of his hand. Like a gunslinger from a western movie, he flicked his wrist, caught the weapon and pointed it directly at Jamal's head. "I'm taking no chances with anything or anybody, Jammy. Did you know this little piece can bore a two-bob hole in a man's brain at twenty-five yards?"

*****

Richard crept outside the boatshed and onto the jetty. At his signal, Greda helped Jonathon through the door. Setting off at a steady pace with him perched on his shoulders, Richard's aim was to reach the *Fanno Maru* with time to spare. They kept to the shadows cast by scattered buildings lining a lengthy promenade that hugged the weaving shoreline. It was an ugly opening. Scudding showers came and went with short but sodden intensity. Despite provisioning themselves with canvas coverings crudely adapted as raincoats, they were soon wet through.

There was little activity for the initial half-mile with the fishing fleet having sailed. A few preoccupied souls, better weather-proofed than them, filtered by and were left behind. Pilfered remains of old fishing boats, most of whose innards had been reduced to rotten, misshapen hulks lay all around like corpses awaiting cremation. They, too, dwindled from sight leaving a bare, lifeless sump of ground; the sort where toxic waste had found a home.

As the mouth of the river distended, a sprinkle of lights rising in the distance necessitated that they veer off to the right. Progress from there on became slow and difficult. The ground was uneven, obstacles were hard to see, and pools of water required detours because of their unknown depth. Tripping, Richard staggered forward, almost losing the boy from his grasp and regaining his balance only through Greda's opportune and steady arm. Thereafter, he carried Jonathon.

They found the partially sealed road signposted by arrows on Eva's disintegrating map. More than vehicle-width, it meandered towards the berthing terminals. She had said that traffic later in the evening was unlikely, but also warned him to take no chances and avoid being seen. The advice was heeded. The road led them directly to the southern extremity of the merchant shipping docks. Rows of warehouses arrayed along the lengthy wharves provided some cover. Frequent pauses occasioned by increased activity made this another time-consuming and harrowing part of the journey. A number of ships were lined up along the half-mile wharf. Lorries were not their concern. Several were parked adjacent to vessels being unloaded. Rather, they were on the lookout for smaller vehicles undertaking security patrols. Only one such possible candidate was seen, but it turned out to be a utility truck piled high with bananas.

Finally, they located '23A' painted on a large warehouse and illuminated by a bright electric light. Pausing at the back corner of the building, Richard lowered Jonathon and whispered for them to wait while he broached the quayside. Alert to the slightest movement, he crept stealthily closer to the sleepy form of the *Fanno Maru*. Sparse light emanated from her and some degree of concealment was afforded as he hugged the front of a storehouse beneath the awning. The foot of the gangway was deserted, and rain began to teem down.

Seeing his chance, he tore back to Greda. "Come on, we've a show of getting on deck right now without being spotted."

"Let's get there."

They discarded their coverings and, with Jonathon in Richard's arms again, raced towards the ship. With the tide at halfway, save for the rain, gaining the deck was not attended with undue difficulty.

"Greetings. What have we here?" The voice of someone they couldn't see, bearing the clarity of a flute playing a subtle orchestral movement, startled them. They were under shelter, drawing in great draughts of air after the sprint.

"A boy, a broken foot and everyone's drenched. Welcome aboard." Chia came prepared with towels which were accepted with gratitude. "He can rest on the day-bed in the officer's saloon for the present." The lad, now clinging to his mother, shook his head. Under confined light, the neat uniform of the merchant marine signifying his rank was an agreeable sight.

"Captain, I'm your new chief engineer. The name's Richard Kirnst. I trust you don't mind us dropping in unannounced."

The master's hand was extended. "I thought it was McCormack, but no matter. Follow me to my cabin. Good evening, Madam. Your son?" Greda nodded. "You can all come then." His attitude seemed so unflappable that she wondered whether their exact manner of arrival had been foretold.

Jonathon insisted on hopping along the companionway while holding the rail. When they reached the foot of the sharp ascent to the stateroom, Richard hoisted him under his haunches.

It was an unpretentious space, befitting a vessel of that tonnage. A preponderance of almond-stained panelling decorated its interior walls, on which hung amateurish ships' paintings. Behind a desk covered with papers and charts was a well-worn leather chair and, to the right, a stairway leading to the bridge. A female steward appeared with steaming hot liquid and thick slices of buttered bread.

"I'd ordinarily produce my last discharge book, sir, but unfortunately I don't have it," said Richard. The statement earned an indifferent glance from the master, who seemed in no hurry to hasten their consumption of the refreshments.

"Ghastly night to be out. Are you feeling better now?" he asked in a friendly sub-continental twang after a period of silence.

"We are," said Greda, speaking for them all, "and glad to be here, too, if I may be a little presumptuous."

"Not at all, Madam, pleased to see you. Richard, just the name of your last ship will suffice. I've your articles here to sign. They're the shortest I've ever prepared, but formalities must be honoured even in these times. I'll at least get two watches out of you. My name's Bill Chia and these are?"

Richard introduced Greda and Jonathon. "I'm happy to sign on, sir, but I cannot sail unless Dr Faircrossman and the boy come with me," he said respectfully. "I've some money for their passage and—"

"That won't be necessary just yet. There's plenty of room, with a vacant cabin next to yours, Richard. We only carry two engineers and two mates because we're rarely more than a few days at sea and there are three engineers' cabins."

"So very appreciative, Captain," said Greda.

"No problem for me. I'm a friend of Britain. Did my Master's there so your delightful accent is Chopin to my ear, Madam. Love the old country, always will. Now get dry and settled. My personal attendant will show you the way. Richard, you'll want to speak to the second engineer and work out arrangements, but you can do that later. Let's talk first."

Chia signalled to the steward, who led Greda and Jon to their cabin clutching an assortment of dry clothes. A plump woman with a kindly disposition, she assisted the boy after a reassuring squeeze of Greda's hand. Screwed to the door was a faded sign bearing the title, 'Third Engineer'. Inside, a single bunk ran fore and aft adjoining the outside skin underneath a standard porthole. A mattress had been brought in and the bed made up. Jonathon was changed into fresh clothes several sizes too large for him and slid under crisp coverings.

When Richard arrived, he wished for a camera to capture her radiant features. Greda was studying his as he spoke.

"Chia said it's best you remain here for at least an hour after the ship sails, not that you'd want to do anything else."

"Only that I'd kill for a bath; but I doubt there's one handy. I won't go anywhere, so you're safe."

He laughed and then mimicked a mock bow. "For you, almost anything, but yet another fancy bath, ah, no. Still there's a bathroom and shower on this deck."

"Thank you, Jeeves, that's perfect," she smiled, savouring her new surrounds.

"But seriously, I'll leave you to it." He found that hard to say. "It's a little better than what we've been used to, though not quite the Ritz. I must speak with the captain again, and there's that matter to do before we sail."

She followed him for a few steps beyond the doorway. They hugged and she rested on his shoulder.

"Shouldn't be long," he said breezily.

When Richard returned to the master's suite, Chia was with a squat, muscular man wearing a cloth cap and grey overalls. He waited at the doorway while they conversed in a language that was unfamiliar, save mention of his name. The crewman departed, acknowledging Richard with a brusque nod as he passed.

"That was my bosun, Kwoli, tidying up a few things before we sail. Sit down." Richard entered, declining the offer of brandy, and commenced to tell the captain of the assignment at the bow.

"I'm aware of course," Chia replied. "Kwoli will be around. You'd have gathered I'm very anti-Japanese, although outwardly, when it suits, we pose in a different way." It was apparent the captain liked to talk. Richard waited for more. "Amazing, isn't it? A can of white paint, an able seaman who doubles as a welder and signwriter, and allegiances are transformed overnight. A ready supply of flags of convenience, too!"

Richard recalled for Chia's edification the encounter with the Japanese lieutenant on the river several nights ago and the warnings from Arkoi. "That character was surly, suspicious and pretty unscrupulous with it."

Chia batted away any concerns with practised nonchalance. "Yes, I know Sakeiwu from Penang. He may come on board after we enter the shipping channel, but won't stay long, and no search will be done. I've developed a fast friendship with him. He's fond of saying, 'Many little fish taste better than one big one,' when lamenting his meagre salary from the Emperor."

Richard appreciated Chia's discerning character. Misgivings entertained before boarding the small coaster under the command of someone about whom he knew nothing had evaporated.

"You will take her out with the other engineer for the first half-hour."

"Thank you, sir."

Richard was about to leave when Chia asked, "Ah, the lady and the lad, all settled?"

"Yes, and very appreciative of what you and your steward have done."

"Part of the service, Chief, and call me Bill. I doubt if I've carried a more handsome passenger even impressing those damp clothes. How did you three link up, and where's her husband, may I enquire?"

"Long story, but, in short, they helped out when I missed my ship after an incident in Kuala Lumpur. Dr Faircrossman cared for me. Mr Faircrossman, we were told, was in an ambush and is missing. We had to get out and have been on the run since then. All sorts of incidents along the way," he offered vaguely. Chia seemed to be keen for more detail when Richard noticed the chronometer and was reminded of his appointment with Eva. "I see the time. I'd better be going."

"Good luck," said Chia, which struck Richard as an odd thing to say.

On the wharf, Richard nodded to the bosun, who was conversing with several crew members. It was pitch black except for the dim, reflective light from the ship. He skirted to the rear of the warehouse to wait before proceeding to the bow. A sprinkle dampened his brow. The heavy, salt-scented atmosphere milled around him as if about to disgorge some unevolved urchin. A beating in his chest felt like a bass drum being pounded, instilling apprehension of something lurking in the shadows capable of perceiving his presence. Richard had no reason to expect any trouble but conjectured whether being armed might have provided some extra margin of comfort.

Holding his watch closer, he saw that it was almost eleven-thirty and moved towards the front corner. The wharf number lamp had been extinguished, but he channelled himself in the bow's direction utilising the side of the building. The faint light on the forecastle pole, guided him across to the rendezvous point. There, his feet shifted uneasily. Convinced his watch had stopped functioning, he abstractedly tapped the face several times. Growing anxious as the minutes passed interminably, he began pacing back and forward from the bow line.

Then, he heard his name called from the shutter doors of the warehouse.

"Richard, darling."

Eva swooped on him gracelessly and he shuffled backwards. Taking her forearms, he laid them down, though she still pressed her body on him.

"There's something I need to—"

She was silenced. A voice supervened, one he'd never forgotten.

"Well, well, well."

Eva's eyes widened. She squealed and turned into the glare of a flashlight.

"What have we here?" Heenan sneered as he emerged from behind the discarded casing of a ship's boiler. "A late-night sewing circle? A game of bridge on the bridge of the *Fanno Maru*?" He laughed boisterously, a predisposition befitting him whenever his presence was least likely to be expected.

Both confronted their intimidating antagonist. Eva, deathly mute, a hand felt for the dagger tucked into the rear of her trousers. Richard suspected deception until the ensuing tirade disabused him.

"How could you have been taken in by this fucking whore of a thing?" Heenan spat out. "You didn't learn your lesson the first time and ran away like a stuck pig in the Camerons. What now then? I can assure you the cruise is off, so it's a toss-up as to who'll be fed to the sharks first."

As Richard's feet began to shuffle forward, Eva fastened onto his belt staying him. Heenan ventured closer, near enough now for Richard to see the gun in his right hand, the torch in his left.

"You can say what you want with that thing aimed at me."

"Aha, the little lambkin speaks, like a mouse this time. No, that's too kind. More like a drowning rat. Keep it coming, I want to hear all about you and the little arse-princess here. That's where she likes it most of all, ha. So, what's it you two are up for, hmm? By gad, Aussie, you get around. Where's that upper-class bitch, by the way?"

Richard ground his teeth but said nothing.

"Aw, didn't work out? Shame. Well, this one's always on tap, and plenty of others have greased that dry gully before us, cobber." Heenan taunted, seeking a reaction that might resolve his quandary about whom he would despatch first. "I've got it now: we're going to take a romantic interlude, a threesome maybe. She's used to them, matey. 'Oh, Richard darling,'" he mimicked. "I'm really disappointed. I thought you Australians were supposed to have balls. You're a pussycat. Well, you like the pussy, but that one's poison, as you'll find to your cost before I'm through."

"I'm sure we can sort this out," offered Richard. "If it's money, then—"

"Ah, a bribe. Hear that, Jammy?" He'd raised his voice. "This pathetic clod thinks he has the wherewithal to buy his life. He'll get no fucking change there. You see, Eva, do you really think shit like you could persuade my loyal lieutenant to abandon his post? He told me what you tried to cook up. Jammy, you're on. Come out and show yourself to Eva for the last time." There was a noise behind Heenan, but the summons went unanswered. "Jammy, step forward with your men and greet these folks, will you," agitation creeping into his voice.

"Yes, Heenan, here I am."

The use of his surname and its mutinous overtone produced pustules of sweat on Heenan's top lip as he waited for penitence. "Jammy, don't fucking play games with me!"

Jamal's derisory laughter caught Heenan's attention, and Richard's boot sent the gun flying across the planks and into the water.

Eva screamed, "This is for you!" and burst between the men with her knife, thrusting it forward. But Heenan was nothing if not the quintessential street thug. He stepped aside. Eva misplaced her balance and as she lurched over, Heenan crashed the stout steel torch into the side of her head. A sickening crack preceded her fall.

"You miserable swine," Richard yelled, as he drove his shoulder directly into Heenan's chest with a power that knocked the man backwards, leaving him gasping and writhing on the decking.

Richard challenged him. "I won't sink the leather. On your bloody feet and let's see how you go."

Their positions had reversed, but Heenan was not yet finished. Counterfeiting injury to aid recovery time, he laboured to a shaky upright stance. Keeping his head down, he exploded into life with a flailing roundhouse swing that Richard's left hand easily deflected. His counterpunch struck Heenan cleanly on the jaw, knocking him down.

At that instant, several crew members set upon Heenan, dragging him away from the edge of the wharf to which the protagonists had moved so perilously close.

"Chief, Bosun Kwoli here, you alright?"

Richard kneeled to clasp the stricken Eva's head, blood issuing from her mouth and nose.

"Yes, I'm okay," he finally replied to Kwoli. "That thing will pay for what he's done. Can you get him aboard? I'll explain it to the captain."

"I can do that for you, sir," Jamal answered and then called up to Captain Chia, who was looking on from the bridge. "You provide lodgings and basic meals, I trust?" he laughed.

"On M.V. *Fanno Maru*, yes, we do."

"Very well, he's yours. Mister Richard, the captain will hand him over to the police in Singapore." The voice was the same one that had responded to Heenan earlier. "A beautiful right cross, if I may say so, my dear friend."

Richard had ceased to listen.

Heenan was gagged and trussed up. A sailor on either side gave him much-needed stout support as his knees began to fold under him. Before boarding, the men stopped on a command from Jamal and the gag was removed. A spotlight was flicked on. When his eyes adjusted, murderous rage greeted Jamal's victorious stare.

"Jammy!"

Heenan's bull neck straightened before he slumped back into the arms of his captors.

"Enjoy your voyage, sir. And say hello to General Percival for me."

The ship's horn heralded imminent departure.

Jamal slipped an envelope to Kwoli and then sidled over to Richard. "Hello again, sir. Jamal Viranhi at your service, and very humbled to be so. I've heard much about you and your companions' exploits, but the praises sung were wholly inadequate."

Richard passed Eva to the bosun, who carried her up the gangway, before turning to the man, puzzled by his sudden interest in him.

"I hope she'll be alright. Oh, poor thing," Jamal muttered, not giving Eva as much as a second look. "You're Australian and working on the ship?"

"Yes," said Richard circumspectly. In no mood for talk but drawn in by Jamal's insinuating knowledge of passenger manifests and purposes, he was constrained to listen as Chia, still observing from above, seemed to be affording some leeway past sailing time.

Viranhi at last desisted, apologising for stalling the departure. "You'll have good sailing, Captain. Sakeiwu is taken care of, and if you have time, please inform your prisoner that his business interests will be assiduously administered from here on. Goodbye, Mr Kirnst."

Chapter 22

Cruises and cargoes

To the relief of her owner and navigator intent on an uncomplicated departure, the *Fanno Maru* cleared the approaches to Malacca, turned hard to port and set a course for Singapore. The vessel's alter ego, *Sibya*, replete with red ensign flying stiffly astern, made a steady eight knots into a moderate south-westerly wind and choppy, confused sea half an hour out from her moorings.

Richard took the first half of the watch. Having become acquainted with the dispositive mechanical arrangements in his allocated realm in a fashion even more mechanical, he ascended to make a tour of the auxiliary machinery and safety equipment.

Trance-like, he negotiated the boat deck through to the bow on one side, completing the circuit by taking in the starboard gear. The lifeboat was unpretentious but seaworthy, as was the emergency raft lashed to the safety rail at the stern. Next, he started the fire pump. The last task involved him descending the vertical ladder to the tiller flat. Once back in the engine room, he satisfied himself that the motorman knew his job. In any other circumstance, Richard might have been absorbed by his new but familiar environment. This morning he offered perfunctory interaction with the job, noting only that it was functioning as expected.

His countenance remaining furrowed. He sought to ascertain if there had been any change in Eva's condition since she passed into Greda's care. Before doing so, beleaguered by the prospect of revisiting her parlous state, Richard prayed for an early release from her suffering.

The officers' saloon had been refitted to serve as an infirmary stocked with an elementary supply of medical items, including an oxygen apparatus presently in use. The patient lay on a bunk mattress, pale, desperately ill, her breathing on a vain search for depth and clarity. The blow to her skull suggested serious damage and internal bleeding. Her heart rate was fragile, a condition meeting the criterion of 'critical'. Eva was otherwise placid, mirroring deep repose.

Greda observed her relatively young, still face and an inkling of recognition arose. Unable to pinpoint the source, the notion passed as the responsibility of dealing with a woman hovering on the brink of life and death actuated each step in the curative process.

Gauging the gravity of Eva's condition was not as confounding as doing something about it. Surgical intervention was imperative to relieve the pressure on her brain. Even if successful, she might be left with irreversible damage. It was a procedure Greda had never previously attempted. On several occasions she had assisted neurosurgeons, and, in theory, it was not difficult. What was absent in equipment and experience, she didn't lack in self-belief and adaptation. The presence of Vernon, the second mate, with elementary training in treating injuries, encouraged her.

As Greda weighed up the risks, Richard, swallowing water to moisten a dry throat, watched unobtrusively from the doorway. He observed as she monitored Eva's fight for life, attending primarily to the regularity and strength of her heartbeat.

When he offered Greda a drink, she betrayed anxiety. "I'm not sure she can be saved. An operation is her only chance. I'm fairly certain she has a cerebral haemorrhage and, unless the pressure's relieved, she'll likely slip away."

"You must try it, Greda. Is there anything I can assist with?"

She wanted to hear this. "I'll need to improvise, as there's only basic equipment here. Principally, I require something to drill a hole, capable of penetrating bone and no larger than the diameter of this tube. Both must be sterilised."

Richard soon returned with the items. He had given a prolonged burst of steam to long-pointed pliers, a drill, the bit and the tubing, before dropping them into methylated spirits. A boiler suit and a crepe mask comprised Greda's surgical attire.

Trembling as he exhaled, Richard glanced from her to the still form. "If anyone can do this, it's you. I checked Jonathon and the steward is looking after him. What else do you need?"

"A modicum of luck and the ship's medical officer here as my right-hand man. May take a while." Her attention returned to Eva.

He next joined Chia on the bridge. Prolific navigation lights dotted their port and starboard sides. "I expect the Straits hold no fears for you," Richard said casually, trying to relieve a fixation on the events unfolding beneath them.

"I knew some skippers who took that approach and lost their ships. Never one for me."

As they chatted, Chia informed him that a few sporadic attacks on merchant shipping had occurred in recent times. "Nothing lost that I know of, but it seems they have a penchant for torment, if they've nothing else to do."

"That's all the more reason to keep a lookout."

"How's the woman? I didn't want to get in the doctor's way. Is there any hope?"

"Just holding on. Depends on the operation. Good of you to have the second mate help and doing his watch for him. What about Heenan?"

"Under guard and locked in the bond store."

"That was something, for you to take him at my request."

Chia cleared his throat. "My motives for doing so weren't entirely altruistic. I was forewarned by Jamal Viranhi that a wanted man might be a passenger tonight."

"And the reward, I suppose—"

"I had no idea you or that woman would be caught up like that." The chart suddenly captured Chia's attention. "Ah, Viranhi was to get him there. I'd do the rest. Perhaps I could've been clearer. I assumed you knew, but it spiralled out of control."

Richard accepted Chia's statement as the nearest he would get to a concession that some matters had been withheld. "So, what happens to him now? Were the chance offerred, I might work on a few ideas of my own in the interim."

"I've alerted the British authorities. There'll be a reception committee when we dock. This fellow's been keenly sought by them since his desertion. By the way, an ambulance has been booked to take her to hospital."

Chia seemed to have covered everything. A question arose about Heenan's connection to Eva coming to light and the prospect that she might be treated as complicit in his treachery. In Richard's eyes, the vicious assault had to amount to exculpation of sorts, and he would speak for her if the occasion were to come about.

On his way back to the engine room's floor plates, Richard checked on Jonathon again to find him sound asleep. The next level down contained the bond store. A man was standing guard outside. The temptation to seek entry and deal out further retribution to the occupant almost got the better of him as he looked through the grille at the top of the steel door. There was a faint-coloured globe burning inside. He remained long enough to discern the huddled form on a wooden bench.

In the saloon, Greda's expertise had been put to the ultimate test and not found wanting. Her diagnosis was correct. She'd inserted the drain. The vital signs suggested that Eva's condition had stabilised.

Several hours passed before Richard returned for an update to find the second mate standing over her. An intelligent figure, Vernon reassured him, extolling Greda's work. "Woman will live now. Doctor gone to cabin," he said.

Richard reached her door and tapped lightly, whispering her name.

"Come in, Richard." A desk light was on. She was freshly showered, wearing a man's shirt that draped above her knees and was drying her hair with a towel.

"I want to say what you've done is remarkable," his face mirroring the admiration of his words when he saw the tell-tale signs of fatigue mingled with reticence. "Are you okay?" He placed a hand on her shoulder.

"Yes, but *she* has a long way to go before being out of trouble. Vernon told me we'll arrive early afternoon."

"Yes, and Chia said an ambulance will meet us. The hospital has been made aware of Eva's situation."

"If she can get through the next day or two there's a real chance. Better try sneaking some rest while I can, in case something else comes up."

Richard resumed his watch. With a view to a swifter passage, the captain ordered an increase in speed and the vessel was making a neat ten knots. Against the hope generated by the successful surgery, the synergy of his surroundings lent itself to philosophical deliberations. He remembered once reading prose about a 'cruise romance' that went something like, *The sun rose upon their approach to disembarkation the same time as it began to set on all that had gone before.*

Once in Singapore, what would happen? Eva would go to the hospital. The Heenan business was the prerogative of army intelligence that might require testimony at a court martial. The military imperative was still upon them. Either the British were geared to resist the attack or had made contingency plans that would see the repatriation of women, children and other civilians. They would have to find somewhere to stay and ascertain the full picture in a place where there was a civil administration. Eva's surprise re-entry into the picture was an uncomfortable conundrum, and this probably showed. Greda was perceptive. He trusted her to know that his love was immutable.

At those same moments, Greda, after lifting Jon into the bunk, lay on the mattress nearby, also reflecting on the future. They had already traversed the possibility of evacuating together from Singapore. It was hard to look too far ahead, but being separated from Richard was inconceivable. As these matters played on her mind, exhaustion won out, releasing her from them.

Captain Chia had retired, too, as the conditions outside moderated. Turning over the navigation and watchkeeping duties to his chief officer, he catnapped only, a practice at which he was adept in these waters. Two hours into the watch, with dawn upon them, the first mate heard an aircraft making an approach from the north-east, flying very low towards the starboard quarter. The bashful light did nothing to obscure a red ball under each wing. Through binoculars, he saw the Zero bank to the right, circle and do another pass, this time directly over them from the stern. Then it climbed and disappeared towards the Malayan coastline.

He placed an immediate call through to the captain, who sighed wearily. "Yes, I heard. Strange to be checking on us. I'm coming."

Any trust that this reconnaissance amounted to idle curiosity was abruptly dispelled. Three Japanese fighter planes in formation flew towards them from the same direction. Two peeled away to fall in behind the leader. Loud blasts and water spouts shooting up like fountains on the starboard side announced cannon fire. One crashed into the hull, raking the superstructure and smashing the glass surrounding the bridge.

"Down!" Chia screamed.

All dropped to the floor for cover on the port wing. After the explosions, a piercing howl from the helmsman was the last sound he uttered. When the smoke cleared amid the splintered deck, Chia rushed to inspect the man. One leg was severed above the knee by a piece of shrapnel torn from the coaming and had been deposited on the chart table. His other was hanging by a few sinews. The man died in his captain's arms.

"Hard to starboard, Mister!" screamed Chia.

Attempts by the chief officer to comply with the order and steer the ship on a weaving course met with little response, suggesting damage to the rudder.

Below, the chief engineer saw the bridge communication light flashing and took the captain's briefing. Lights started to flicker as Richard hurtled up the ladders like a man out-sprinting an enveloping cloud of poisonous gas. He appeared at Greda's cabin, cognisant of acrid smoke. She and Jon were huddled on the floor with a mattress covering them, the boy shaking uncontrollably as she covered him.

"Greda, Jonathon, it's alright, I'm here," he roared above the din.

"In heaven's name, Richard," was all she could say as she tightened her arms, face and neck, shivering in terror.

"They'll be back. They're out to sink us. Get into warm clothes, bring what you can carry and be prepared."

They saw to Jonathon first and had just completed dressing themselves when screeching engines punctured the air. Several explosions jolted them against the bulkhead. Smoke was enveloping the cabin and the lights went out, leaving a wavering battery glow. Richard retrieved two lifejackets and fitted them to Greda and the boy.

"Do you have one, Richard?" Her voice was drowned out by more thudding of shells. The ship began taking on a list.

"Forget it!" he yelled, "We have to move."

He grabbed the bedclothing and opened a fire hydrant. There was enough of a trickle to dampen it. With Jonathon wrapped in one of the sheets and the other around Greda, they moved off, almost colliding with the captain, who had staggered into the companionway. He was bleeding heavily from a head wound.

"We're sinking. I've given the order to abandon ship. Some at stern. Chaos, bridge destroyed, fire everywhere, steering kaput, officers gone. Kwoli at lifeboat. Must get out."

Greda steadied Chia when he stumbled forward and tried to staunch the laceration.

"Save the boy. Going, taking water fast. It's leave now or we're finished."

The smoke suffocating the accommodation space underpinned Chia's assessments. With Greda and the captain behind him, Richard passed their few belongings to her and descended with Jon to the lower deck where the bosun had released the lifeboat from its derricks. They entered as Kwoli readied the winch.

Richard turned to him. "Bosun, where's Eva?"

It was Chia who spoke. "Who knows if anyone could've survived that last hit."

The vessel was listing forlornly to port when the lifeboat collided with the water. Kwoli shimmied down the fastening lines and they pushed off, Richard rowing ferociously to clear being sucked into the vortex of *Sibya's* sinking. The planes made one last pass. A violent explosion followed a direct hit on the fuel tanks. When the spray and smoke dissipated, all that remained was a bubbling cauldron surrounded by a fiery slick. The ship had vanished beneath the waves.

Kwoli relieved Richard, who began scouring the water around them.

"All gone, Chief."

Richard shook his head in disbelief. "Seems that way. It's incredible. No, wait. Something's over there, debris I think, at two o'clock, about a hundred yards."

Kwoli's forearms, an anchor tattooed on his left and a square rigger on his right, strained as he closed the distance. Before they reached it, Richard cried out.

"There's someone in the water!"

"For God's sake!" Chia swore. "It's the Britisher. Leave for the sharks."

"Sir, do you mind?" Richard's insubordination was not challenged as he called out to Kwoli, who had begun to pull away. "Can you just hold for a second, Mister? We've one more."

"So good Malaccan current allow drift over," puffed Kwoli through clenched teeth.

"The last thing we'd want to do is disappoint the executioner," rejoined Richard.

The bosun fashioned a lasso, and Richard was not fussy about the methods he adopted to secure it to the obdurate rescuee. It pleased him to see arrogance having finally deserted the pathetic, bare-chested figure trailing spindly legs like the remains of a harpooned mammal. Richard made good use of the painter line for additional restraint and lashed the balance of the rope to an anchor stay.

The bosun continued to jerk on the oars, taking turns with Richard. Chia inspired their hopes of being picked up when he told them an SOS had been sent.

Half an hour later, relief came into view. All except the prisoner were soon taken aboard a British merchantman that had witnessed the attack. She motored over to search for survivors after the Japanese planes had become specks to the north.

The accent of the leading seaman directing the operation to get them aboard was the most melodious Cockney Greda had ever heard, its derivation a poignant reminder of England. And right now she pined for it, longing to take Richard to her homeland.

Two of the crew were detailed to make the final pick-up. Greda, Jon and Chia were taken below decks. Richard and Kwoli tarried until Heenan was hauled aboard with a rope and harness before being lodged in the grease and bilge storeroom.

PART III

Love beareth all things, believeth all things, hopeth all things, endureth all things.

~1 Corinthians 13, 7

Chapter 23

British Intelligence

Singapore Intelligence officer was the first person to board the ship carrying the bedraggled rescuees from the waters of the Straits of Malacca after the vessel docked at Keppel Wharf.

Major Reginald Newton, as crisp, proper and immaculately arranged as a dinner setting in Maxims, introduced himself. At forty-one, and standing an erect five foot eleven inches, he bore the landscape of a man born to occupy first place in the portrait section of an art gallery.

Laser eyes of emerald hue appeared equipped to dismember any façade while he, as a perpetual receptor and propagator of information, true and false, remained as inscrutable as a ream of blank paper. Fine, dark hair flirted with minute strands of grey and a pencil-thin moustache as black as boot polish decorated a sharp face whose complexion was flawless. Newton was not just the quintessential English officer abroad in uniform. He was a manifestation of everything for which the British Empire stood.

Chia, resting in the rescue ship's dining room, his head still swathed in Greda's bandage, was occupied by his crew's fate. The loss of his ship and its cargo, both of which, he confided, hadn't been insured, would seal his ruin.

"You made it, Captain. I shall not obtrude upon your feelings by saying, 'Singapore welcomes you,'" offered Newton after presenting his credentials.

"Kind, Major," Chia said, pushing his shoulders back and grimacing. "If I was a soldier, I could say that those bastards will feel my wrath in good time but, for me, revenge will plot its own avenues."

"Indeed." Newton was impressed. "I've had a chat to the prisoner below. Laid on the charm in a manner least expected, such a curious fellow. Said it had all been a shocking mistake. Actually claimed to be a rubber planter and tin merchant from Selangor, naming himself Edward Faircrossman—"

"The hell he did!" Richard interjected, aghast.

"Just a moment, please." Newton bridled at interruptions. "I'm addressing Captain Chia. Convincing, too, and very persuasive. Am I correct in assuming this is the first time he's declared such a thing?"

"Yes." Chia growled at the effrontery of the assertion. "I've absolute verification of his identity." The major waited until he calmed down.

"Did *he* admit to it?" enquired the major.

"No, but an associate called Jamal Viranhi vouched for Heenan and instructed me to hand him over to you," Chia responded.

"May I speak with the associate?"

Chia was startled at the question, recalling what he had been told by Viranhi, and answered in the negative. He related the events leading up to Heenan's capture by the wharf, including the attack on the Chinese woman, who had played a part in his demise, and her fate.

"The involvement with Heenan is known. We might have tried her as well, but she would have been facing a lesser indictment to the one I expect to be presented against him. Are you sure she's lost?"

"I cannot be certain. He was the only survivor we saw in the water. Other boats were in the area."

"Did Heenan offer any evidentiary proof, documents or the like to support his claim?" asked Richard insistently.

"And you are?" the second interruption being as unappreciated as the first.

"Richard Kirnst," he answered.

"It's alright, Major, this is my chief engineer," said Chia.

"Ah, Mr Kirnst, yes, I had overlooked that." Richard wasn't so sure but waited for him to continue. "Actually, he didn't. Has no identification on him at all, but he seemed to know about Faircrossman. I wonder how that could be," Newton fished.

"Damn it, I know him and so does Dr Greda Faircross-man. Since she is the wife of the man Heenan claims to be, I'll bring her here if you like."

"That won't be necessary, Mr Kirnst, one of my men will attend," said the major, as he motioned to a subordinate.

Greda returned with him. The major bowed, introducing himself. "What a terrible ordeal for you and your son."

"We survived, Major." She was sensing an announcement. "You wanted to see me?"

"I don't wish to add to your distress. You have experienced quite a lot in the last twenty-four hours. I have to follow protocols, however, and there's something I am bound to raise. Regulations require—"

Irked by pedantry, she asked, "What *are* you trying to say?"

"Could I have a moment; Captain, Mr Kirnst?" After they departed, Newton informed her of the claim.

Greda was confounded by this development. That Heenan was in possession of anything concerning her husband fired within her all manner of questions, principally whether he had met up with Edward or was aware of his fate, or both.

"Before Mr Kirnst, my son and I left the plantation, I was informed that Edward had been intercepted and possibly shot by Japanese insurgents and was missing. I accepted the information to be true. No one has seen or heard from him since. I believe my husband was killed or," she hesitated, "at least so badly wounded when he was ambushed with the other man, who has since died, that the prospects of ever finding out what happened are remote. Do *you* know something more?"

"I'm afraid not, Mrs Faircrossman. Furthermore, the claim by the prisoner is false. We are aware of who he is. Our records are supplemented by the account from Captain Chia. Might you have a photograph of your husband, something recent?"

Greda had retained several family portraits in a leather satchel and selected one. "This was taken in the last twelve months." She specifically recalled the occasion, Faircrossman lounging against his car before heading off to Penang.

"Do you mind if I copy that? It will be returned. A few days are all we'll need."

She consented to his request. "Major, I'm sure you appreciate this new information means a great deal to me. I need to know as much as I can—whether my husband is alive or not. Heenan might know something. You must try to find out what that is as carefully as you can and not let him—"

"Dr Faircrossman, I'm informed you are a medical doctor. I would never presume to tell you how to conduct consultations or dispense medicines." Newton had a habit of pausing to emphasise a point. "You won't mind my saying I've been an intelligence officer for fifteen years and surgical questioning is my specialty, no pun intended."

Superciliousness repelled Greda, and her disdain for Newton was redolent. "I didn't effect to tell you how to do your job and have no qualms at all about your capacity, Major. Rather, I'm anxious to find out what's happened to Edward. Heenan's an appalling character. He was involved in a relationship with a close friend of mine."

"Female friend?"

She could see that he was very well briefed and nodded.

"I may have to take that up with you at some time."

"What?"

"No need to be alarmed, Mrs Faircrossman, it's just routine. With every respect, I have acute understanding of the position you're in," Newton stated in a vain attempt at less formality. "You have my absolute guarantee that any relevant information I glean concerning your husband will be obtained as a priority and, subject to security considerations, relayed as soon as humanly possible."

"Then I'm indebted," she said somewhat acidly, as he stood up to usher her outside.

Newton ordered his accompanying soldiers to remove Heenan from the ship and took his leave. "We'll be in communication again, Dr Faircrossman. Here's an address where you can find me," he said, handing her a card. "If you'd be so kind as to attend there at about this time tomorrow, I might have more for you."

Greda and Richard watched from the upper deck as Heenan, casting a perfidious glance in their direction, was led handcuffed to a waiting car that soon after was swallowed by Singapore's bustle.

Richard intended to take advice from the shipping agent respecting accommodation as the survivors disembarked on Keppel Wharf. The man fitting that description carrying an attaché case was about to board. Mr Ang, an educated Singaporean whom Richard had met before, was well-versed on prevailing conditions. As to finding a place to put up so far unaffected by the bombing, he was encyclopaedic as to neighborhood, style and even price. Richard also mentioned the plight of Captain Chia and his bosun, who had been standing nearby. Their spirits lifted when the agent indicated that positions might be available on the *Pantaan,* expected to dock in the next day or so, as third mate and able seaman respectively. Despite Greda's urgings that he visit the hospital for a thorough medical examination, the prospect of losing a potential berth was foremost in Chia's mind, and he told her warmly that she had given him all the treatment he required.

She afforded him heart-felt compassion. "Thank you, Captain Chia, and your bosun, you've been marvellous. I'm certain you'll both find your feet again. It's a dreadful loss for you."

"Same goes for me, too, Captain," said Richard, moving to take Chia's hand in his.

"Much less loss than yours, Doctor, with your husband gone and his businesses overrun. There'll be other ships and cargoes. Good to sail with you, Richard." Chia added with a twinkle, "One day you'll tell me the story of how you missed that ship, yes? And may I say, madam, you have the most expressive hands I've ever seen." He fixed on them resting in his, before rejoining Kwoli.

The onset of evening dictated a prompt decision. Near Orchard Road, a locality consistent with Mr Ang's recommendations, they found a serviced semi-detached two-bedroom dwelling. A new concrete bomb shelter underneath convinced them. The wallpaper was flaky. A tap dripped onto an ingrained rust stain in the sink, and a ring around the bath seemed to be a permanent marker of the acceptable water level. Both beds sank appreciably in the middle. But the place was otherwise clean and fresh linen plentiful.

"It keeps getting better, Richard," warned Greda with a wink.

The landlady brought a plate of Chinese vegetables for Jonathon. Once fed and bathed, he was receptive to the soft mattress. She recommended a walk in the cool and said her niece would be happy to remain with the boy now that he had settled into bed.

Arm-in-arm, they sauntered along Orchard Road, taking in the lights, the street cafés and the stalls; an altogether surreal atmosphere. She spoke first.

"Does anyone really appreciate that the Japanese are on their way down here or that a fight to the finish might at some stage take place? Is there a soul who seems to care?"

Richard reacted similarly. "It's business as usual with no finger writing on the wall at Belshazzar's feast. Speaking of which, how about we get something to eat?"

The Singaporean repast was exceptional, coming after their abstemious fare of late. Drink was plentiful, with adjacent diners unstinting, and the mood was animated. Europeans, as well as a few army officers, were sprinkled among the patrons. It was Richard and Greda's inaugural social outing together. Only on returning to the apartment and discharging the carer with a coin, was the occasion solemnised.

"Do you realise the significance of what we've just done?" Greda asked, her face sparkling like tinsel. She answered for him, shamming being put out by the mystified look on his face. "You old drudge! That's the first time we've ever been in public as a couple, not that I was expecting a corsage and chocolates."

"Do you want me to pop back out for them?" he asked breezily. They relaxed for a time, drinking tea in the tiny kitchen. "Tomorrow we'll have to work out our next move." He was speaking generally, unable to broach the sole matter occupying his mind.

"Our next move indeed, and I know you don't mean this place is already getting on your nerves. But life seems to be going on, if tonight was any guide," Greda contemplated as she approached the window facing the street, hoping Richard would refrain from saying anything just yet.

"We can't keep skirting it," he remarked, prompting her return to sit in front of him.

"Richard, of course I have to know about what's going on. I had a discussion with this Major Newton. It seems possible that Heenan could have information about Edward. Whether directly or third- or fourth-hand is uncertain. I owe it to Jon, to myself and, well, to you, too. Having said that, Newton doesn't think Heenan can be relied on for very much. And Eva cannot tell—" She noticed Richard's breathing. "What is it, my darling?"

"Just over a day ago, Eva was arranging a ship and looking—" The word on his lips was 'exhilarated', but he smarted at that image. "Now, she's forfeited everything." The ironies weren't lost on either of them. "Life and death, there it is, when you think about the conundrum. Without her blood being shed, we might never have heard anything more of your husband." He was reprising the tripartite connection.

Greda apologised. "Oh, I didn't mean to be so insensitive about her."

"You weren't, given my foolish adherence to candour."

"Don't change." Her fingers caressed his face. "Anyway, tomorrow I have an appointment with Major Newton. I gather they'll not waste time with Heenan after the interrogation."

"That's probably true." Richard studied the wall, his mind in overdrive, before continuing. "So, he'll be tried for what he's done. Did the major say anything about Eva?" he asked, surprising her.

"Nothing really. Newton's a shrewd operator and I inferred he knew a lot more about them than he let on."

He drank more tea as if each intake abetted his cognisance of reality. If there was some scrap of evidence suggesting Greda's husband was still alive, there could be no plans made. An admixture of duty and honour had overwrought him. Distractedly, he began to think of what work he could do in Singapore to assist in any capacity, for there was no question now of their leaving immediately. Greda's almost casual aside about volunteering at the hospital was subtle evidence of that. And honour? He'd never set out to alienate the affections of someone else's wife. These weren't issues to be treated glibly, as he made plain to her in careful and measured terms while she listened in silence.

With any hint that Edward might not have perished, Greda began to experience the whispers of conscience. Unquestionably, she had come to love Richard. Could fate so decree that something as natural as this was wrong?

After they separated to their bedrooms, introspection followed. Greda changed her clothes, becoming very conscious of Jonathon's presence. Lying next to him, her back was turned upon the adjoining room. The paradox for her was that Richard had been content with separate sleeping arrangements. She wouldn't have refused if he had asked her to remain with him, yet neither was his pronouncement unexpected.

Now that a question about Edward had emerged, disquiet beset her. Until its resolution, she steadied herself endeavouring to weigh obligations to Jonathon respecting his father, until she heard the seductive voice of Carrie speaking from the wretched letter. It was enough for Greda to want to regard Edward as removed from *her* forever.

*****

Singapore's Tanglin Barracks, though starved of space, contained a number of dank, almost airless areas commonly requisitioned for retaining broken items, spares and stores. Emptied of its contents, one such venue was chosen for the interview. Even after modification for its interrogative function, the room, selected by Newton, was a spartan affair. Freshly painted battleship grey over red-brick walls gave it tang, visual and sensory, and one tiny window above the door permitted some light. But as a place of gravity for a traitor's expurgation, decorum and trappings were otherwise absent. It was not more than nine feet square, with a high ceiling from which a solitary cord and strong light bulb hung.

Towards the rear of the room rested a scratched and serrated wooden desk, drawer on each side, where the

inquisitor sat, his face squarely a half-yard opposite
Heenan's. The prisoner was parked on an upright stick of
a chair that squeaked when he shuffled his rump. Newton
reclined into the padding on the only piece of furniture
that might muster interest at a second-hand market. Still,
its English oak cried out for a coat of shellac.

Witnessing the formalities was a lance-corporal incongruously holding an Owen sub-machine gun. Behind the
interrogatee, a warrant officer, possessing an inchoate familiarity for Pitman shorthand, sat on a cast-iron stool, notepad
perched on his knee, pencil stuttering in anticipation.

Heenan's audacity of the previous day had evaporated on account of his softening-up by a no-nonsense subordinate acting in concert with Newton, one Lieutenant
McKenzie. He had told Heenan it was no good denying his
identity as they knew everything about him, even showing
him a series of photographs of his subversive attendances.
One, in particular, saw him and Eva seated in the lounge
bar of the Eastern and Oriental Hotel deep in conversation
with an Asiatic fifth columnist who had since been caught
and executed. McKenzie had gone on to say that any fili-
bustering would make matters worse. Some redemption
might be found in providing the identities of persons with
whom he had dealt and were sympathetic to the enemy's
cause.

Casting all legal niceties aside, such as the admissi-
bility of confessions after promises or inducements, the
lieutenant added that the best Heenan could hope for, if
minded to cooperate, was life imprisonment. The more
names he supplied, the greater the likelihood of a reduced
tariff. After this blunt assessment of his prospects, Heenan's
bravado crumbled. He provided a written list of the operatives with whom he had associated. As these tumbled out,
gratuitously he even volunteered the names of other collaborators in Singapore itself.

Major Newton, briefed on all these admissions, was yet
to be convinced that they comprised the full account. But
he was encouraged by the progress McKenzie had made
with the prisoner and expected more would follow with
an alternate mode of questioning. Of especial significance
from an intelligence perspective was the knowledge that

all of those nominated in Singapore were already under suspicion.

Newton adopted a nonchalant and foppish demeanour. He affected the air of an ignorant, disinterested spectator at a football game, framing questions in an ungainly manner, sometimes almost as an afterthought. During the course of the examination, every so often he would slip in a seemingly innocuous fact or two and gauge Heenan's reaction before moving to obtain further elaboration of the activities the spies were undertaking. The satisfaction Heenan thought was registered in Newton's face led him to expand. The interrogation then focused on the planter Faircrossman, whose identity he had forlornly attempted to assume.

"Yes, the man was captured somewhere up near Selangor, and I know for a fact he was imprisoned because I saw him in the camp. He'd been shot in the leg and was tied up, but didn't see me, of course. He was being grilled by the Kempeitai and an intelligence officer."

"What, a major or something?"

"Yes, as a matter of fact that's true, and I couldn't believe my luck because I recognised the Englishman as one of Eva's lovers. She'd managed to wheedle some pretty useful information from him about the planters' plans for dealing with their estates in the event of the occupation. I knew all about him because she told me he was from the Selangor estate."

"And you were saying about not believing your luck?"

"Well, there was a sort of resemblance between him and me. He's that bloody tanned and we even have a prominent mole on the right side of our respective necks. I made a mental note of it at the time."

"Oh, is that so? Why did you do that?" Newton was yawning indifferently.

"No reason, really, except one needs to be resourceful."

"Yes, that's right. I'd never have imagined—" The major trailed off as if interest was deserting him along with the tenor of the narrative. He shuffled papers, fumbled with the contents of his pockets, talked about rugby and boxing, yawned, and apologised, moaning that all this was 'frankly tiresome'.

Heenan had become convinced that the major was a complete dullard and he was benefitting from their exchanges to the other's detriment. His chin twisted, a sign he thought might be unappreciated, but he couldn't recognise any perceptible change in the officer's attitude. One thing of which he was certain; the British wouldn't dare convict, let alone execute, him without a formal hearing. And he also knew that, with the rapidity of the invasion, time was running out for that mechanism to be put in place. Fudging with the military establishment was proving easier than he ever dreamed of and the prospect of being able to elongate the process until the island fell seemed within reach.

Newton continued; "Did you say you'd become that what's-his-name planter and with some false papers it might have worked? But I'm told you didn't have any."

"Well, I did, but they weren't on me at the time that scum Jamal betrayed me. Remember him, won't you, he's a traitor, a double-crosser and a murderer. If he tries to make out he'll help you, watch out. He murdered my servant girl after raping her. He's a revolting slug of shit. You need to mark him carefully and—"

Newton turned in an unhurried way to the note-taker and adjured him to, "Take that down word-for-word, for future reference."

"So, after that you went to Malacca. Oh, and what became of the Englishman, Faircrossman, was it? You didn't see him?"

"He's dead!" Heenan declared with considerable emphasis. "Do you think I'd get papers in his name and be prepared to pass myself off as him if he was alive? He was shot after the interrogation. I was told by Major Kano himself he'd ordered the execution and ensured it was carried out."

"Mmm. What date was it, do you know?"

"Just a second, let me think. Ah, yes, that would've been the thirtieth or thirty-first of December, no later for certain."

"You're sure of that? Good. You spoke to some Japanese major and received confirmation?"

"Kano, yes. He was, ah, a most reliable source."

"Well, thank you very much, Mister—ah, forgetting myself, I should say, Captain, for you have not been stripped of rank—are entitled to respect and a trial conducted according to law. You have been most kind and helpful."

Newton stood up and glanced behind Heenan, motioning with his head to the transcriber that the interview was at an end, and then ambled around the room scratching his head for several minutes.

This unnerved the prisoner who was searching for some sign of approval. Droplets of sweat began to form on Heenan's forehead and run down his face. He was unsure whether to stand or remain seated. "What happens now? You must be pleased with what I've told you." The scribe picked up his pencil again. "Look, I was threatened with a slow death if I should disclose any of these things. I lived under constant fear for my life. I had to do it; you make one mistake and they trade on it. They threatened Eva—Chin Ming—and her family, and I've been protecting them back in China, you know? She's done much worse than me, though. She prostituted herself to them."

"Did she survive the sinking," Newton chimed in.

"There were two people in a raft, but it disappeared in the explosion."

"Thanks for your help. Anything else?"

"Just that I've worked hard for Britain and have been treated badly by everyone. Ridiculed, I was, my colour—called me 'nigger bum', filthy racial slurs and—"

They ceased to hear him as rambling incoherence took hold. Spittle seeped down one side of his mouth and the veins in his forehead were quivering. A realisation took shape that he may have been duped into telling all for no gain, for he could get no sign of encouragement from Newton and was ignored when he tried to catch the lance-corporal's eye.

"I can give you lots, tons in fact. I need, ah, let me have a week or two to think about it. It's hard to remember but in, well, a few days—" Looking from man to man, Heenan's face contorted grotesquely.

"The Military Court convenes at ten o'clock tomorrow morning to determine a *prima facie* case. A lawyer will be appointed to represent you." Newton had reverted to the archetypal intelligence officer. "You have paper and ink. Write down anything you think of in the meantime. Lance-Corporal Reilly, take him away."

Newton was not worried about any violent reaction as he viewed with scorn the removal of the pathetic, manacled traitor.

Chapter 24

Jobs and shipmates

Richard had anticipated that his first morning in Singapore might entail some casual fact-finding respecting the island's capacity to withstand the invasion. This would be followed by a pragmatic evaluation of what their next steps should be. But, as the flaccid wire base squeaked, he awoke with a piquant reminder of the sole matter dwelling on his mind.

Several hours ago she had bade him goodnight, and he doubted whether Greda's commitment could have been more fulsome. Still, her eyes could not conceal the miasma of conflicting considerations swirling between them. The question of Edward's fate couldn't go away by its own accord.

Richard was driven to speculate on whether knowledge of her husband's infidelity would make a difference to how she viewed the future. Her Church of England upbringing permitted divorce where one party to a marriage had committed adultery. But why flirt with such ignominy? He would not under any circumstances tell Greda what he knew and was ashamed for even allowing it to enter his head.

Thankful for tentative light, he vowed to clear his head of this dissonant imbroglio. Suppressing the sound of his movements, Richard washed, shaved and dressed. Prior to venturing outside, he penned a note to say he'd gone to fetch breakfast.

Sounds of the new day greeted him. He was glad of the exercise, and its betterment to his soul soon took effect. The jam of humanity was evident. Motor vehicles and bicycles were out, along with a number of rickshaws.

Exotic spice-filled vapours from a collection of roadside cooking stalls, its vendors attracting customers on their way to work, were taken in. Becoming at one with everyday normality, he nodded at passers-by.

The previous evening, Greda had elaborated upon local acquaintances in the medical fraternity and of her intention to pursue those contacts, certain there was a much-needed void for her to occupy. She was going to call at the General Hospital and also enquire whether Jon could be schooled, if only for a short period. Her appointment with Major Newton was set for mid-afternoon. At Greda's request, Richard would accompany her while the boy remained at the apartment. Any attempt to work out a means of leaving Singapore was premature until the outcome of her meeting. Richard imagined that, in a city as British as this one, decisions about mass evacuations were for the governor in consultation with the military command.

Richard was also determined not to be idle. He would start by finding the Civil Works Depot, trusting they might be glad of some assistance in the engineering department. Watching the activities about him as he strolled, he couldn't help absorbing the feeling of confidence that customariness produced. The prevailing sentiment seemed to be, 'We're alright; no need to panic.'

It was not yet seven o'clock. Traders applied finishing touches to their stalls, while doors and shutters on shops opened, and he paused to examine the array and nature of produce on sale. Old habits seemed to hang about him like a favourite shirt as he purchased a mangosteen. Flames and the comforting clang of wood on wok followed a breakfast order and the avuncular trader was rewarded by his beneficence. Increasing his stride back up the hill to where they were staying, he was arrested by a voice from behind.

"Hey! Is that you, possum?"

Instantly, he swung around. The dark, wavy hair was perfectly arranged; the body had added a few pounds, an obvious indicator of his well-known fondness for expensive wine. Here was his most enduring seagoing pal, one whom he hadn't seen for several years.

"Bryan 'Kiwi' Williamson, the last person I thought I'd ever run into!"

"And likewise to you. Looks like you're on a mission; chow?"

"Yeah, you're welcome to join me. I'm just up the road."

"Forget that. What the bloody hell's going on?"

Richard gave a rundown on how he came to be in Singapore.

"You were wrecked by the Japs and lived to tell the tale. As to me, I was sent here to join a ship in late September. The old tub was diverted to another port for repairs and last time I heard it was still there. I waited, saw the agents and then another tramp I was supposed to hook up with disappears without trace. Dry-docked, I had to do something and got a job. I'm a maintenance engineer with the Works Department. Pay's piss-poor, but they gave me a flat as part of the deal; about to leave for work when I saw you."

"Well, mate, you might see *me* there soon. Can I visit you later this morning?"

"I'm not always at the depot, but here's the address." Williamson jotted it down. "It's Cavenagh Road, not too far from here. I'll let the boss know you might pay a visit. They're in dire need of some decent help and, with so few being qualified, the power station's a real show for you."

"Thanks, I—"

"Remember your first ship and me the third?" Richard knew there was no applying brakes to his reminiscences. "Well, that was the summit of my achievements, just a junior engineer. You studied and got ahead."

"Well, yes and no," Richard responded self-effacingly. "You were, and no doubt remain, a top engineer. Still much you could teach me, I'll vouch."

"Maybe about sheilas, mate, that's one thing that's eased the pain of my dilemma, stranded without a berth in the Far East. She's a gorgeous little Singaporean girl called—" He faltered as he tried to think of her Asian name. "Ah, what the hell, Suzy is what I call her. Only eighteen. Came to wash my clothes, clean and cook, and now she does all that and a bit more, too, and I'm as happy as Lothario on heat."

Laughter followed, as Richard recalled Williamson's dreams of being waited on hand and foot by an Asian angel. It went back to their early days on the Australia to New Zealand run. He was about seven years older, tall, well-built, a ruddy complexion and boyish good looks. He had a ton of cheek, but was ever the loyal shipmate who, in those early days at sea, would stand up for the new engineer being tested by a truculent crew.

Auckland-born Williamson was a diligent worker, unafraid to get his hands dirty. But the transformation when exiting the engine room was stunning; immaculate deportment and a snappy dresser, his hands devoid of the slightest trace of grime with effeminately manicured nails when a shore excursion beckoned. For all his high-brow mannerisms, liberality became him in his eagerness to teach 'young Dickie' and then 'possum', as he so dubbed the novice, the layout on his first ship.

He was a little older now, to be sure. The distinctive navy-blue uniform of the merchant marine engineer officer had been, temporarily at least, consigned to mothballs, but Bryan was no less debonair in a white silk shirt, keenly pressed fawn pants and shiny dark boots. Apart from that little more flesh, the only real change was a slight thinning of his sooty mane of curls, now interwoven with a suspicion of salt. When reminded of that distinguished blend within diminishing locks, he protested it was hard to obtain colouring agents that would not 'damage hair follicles' and 'no self-respecting axle' would be content with the local grease, incapable of creating 'the illusion of body'. This occasioned more hilarity on Richard's part, Williamson's phony frown soon giving way to his old comrade's mirth.

To have actually run into him in circumstances in which Williamson was now making a go of an alternative existence away from the sea was more than a mere piece of luck. It was, Richard thought, almost predestined.

"You'll come down and have dinner with us tonight, won't you, poss'?" he requested, as he kick-started the motor bike. "We've got plenty of good tucker."

"I'm sure you have, mate, and I'd really love to, but I have company."

"Ah, a woman. Dickie. What's happening to the staid and timid stick in the mud I once knew?"

Richard reddened a little and this was not lost on his compatriot. "I do declare the boy's won a heart," he pressed mischievously.

"Maybe lost one, Bryan. It's a complicated thing," Richard countered with a shrug of his shoulders. "I'd need a while to fill you in and you're heading off. She has her son with her and—"

"Doesn't matter, Dickie, you're all welcome. I get home about five, you come down at six. I can't wait to meet her."

"Thanks." Richard vacillated. "Ah, we'll have to see, a fair few things to do today. But I'll meet up with you at the depot before then, probably when you finish work. So, yeah, catch you later."

"Look forward to it, poss'. See you then."

Even on a motorbike of some antiquity, Williamson was able to embrace the style that educed for Richard the many happy memories of their voyages and shoreside follies. As his old friend retreated into the hum, he shook his head several times, chuffing amusedly at his nicknames, terms he hadn't heard since those early, heady days, mulling it all over and grinning to himself with the contentment that seeing Bryan again had brought.

Back at the apartment, over breakfast the day's plans were set. The young woman who had attended Jonathon previously arrived with the landlady. Richard was exuberant as he related the encounter with Williamson. Greda shared his happiness.

"I don't know what you'll make of him, but I'll be watching this cove very closely at dinner. Expect to be ladled with charm. He's well accustomed to being the cynosure of female attention," he added with a smile.

"I'm sure to warm to anyone of whom you speak so highly. He sounds a likeable charmer, if not a rogue. I'll enjoy testing his reaction, if I should choose to deal out some flattery of my own."

They reached the street with rickshaw operators vying for custom. Straight after their remarkably tall contractor began his commission, they heard explosions in the distance. No one seemed to be paying much attention to the intermittent air-raid warning, which sounded like a steam train's whistle. Soon they began to engage with other traffic, now demonstrating some urgency in negotiating bustling streets. The Singapore General Hospital lay several miles to the south-west. There were no obvious signs of property or road damage along the route.

"Do you want me to wait for you outside, or shall I meet you later at the barracks? I'm happy to hang around," he asked when they arrived.

"Thanks, but no. You head off to that works place. It's fair to say things here will be pretty busy, and perhaps I'll be able to help out for a while."

"I'll vouch that you're pressed into service. See you there at three o'clock."

Once through the main entrance, Greda was confronted with an emergency case in the corridor. She bent over a stricken man and, using her hair ribbon as a tourniquet, managed to stem the bleeding from a nearly severed radial artery.

"Dr Faircrossman, I'm confounded. There really is a God. And here you are doing my work." The voice belonged to Dr Alexander Congreve, an emergency surgical registrar whom Greda had known since university. "Here, throw on a gown. And, Nurse, get her a stethoscope, will you please?"

"Dear Alex, what can I say? You'll have me for a few hours at least."

"More, if I have my way."

*****

Now on foot, Richard jogged from New Bridge Road and continued until Government House. As he mounted higher ground, he could see smoke curling up from the general location where they had been berthed the previous day. Finally, he reached the depot situated on the other side of Bukit Timah Road and spied a small building with a large sign that read, 'Works Manager'. There, a prim, middle-aged woman, seemingly oblivious to his presence, was sorting papers and filing documents. She was, he surmised, hoping he would go away by feigning ignorance of his existence. Several clearings of his throat constituted a vain gesture to attract her attention. Spectacles perched on the bridge of her nose, she began clicking away severely on an ancient typewriter. Behind her was a large pane of frosted glass through which he could make out the distended silhouette of a man at a desk. He leant on the counter with both hands and coughed, this time loudly. Without looking up, the woman pointed to another sign reading, 'Push button and be seated'. He duly complied. Minutes passed and he was advancing on the buzzer again when a jovial fifty-ish Londoner appeared, asking him his business in a manner that was disarmingly friendly.

"I'm sorry to bother you at a time like this. I'm Richard—"

"That accent? Got it." The man was quizzical until, like a switch being flicked on, his face displayed a keen interest. "I remember, Williamson told me. You're the Aussie engineer. You're not bothering me at all. Everything else, and these damn Japs and Miss Henschell here, bothers me, but a real engineer! You've a double Chief's ticket, haven't you?"

The superintendent stared past him, forestalling response. Richard nodded. "Now, come in and sit down. No bother, no bother at all," he kept repeating effusively. "What can I do for you?" Cutting Richard off, he continued, "I know what a man with your experience can do for us. We've a power station to run, so far unscathed. Some sheds were blown up the other week and we lost spare parts and two of our best men. When can you start? Tomorrow would be good. Shifts are twelve hours, sometimes longer, the pay frightfully below what you'd earn at sea. No digs at the moment, bother—other areas to look after—water supply, pumps and sewage, the whole gamut."

Richard waited upon the unexpurgated summary of the enterprise with some amusement. The man knew nothing but public works. A crumpled shirt strove to contain his torso, a faded blue tie exhibited a fragment of bacon, his sleeves were ingrained with dirt and grease and his trousers, once grey, bore oil splotches and were hitched up by tatty braces. Even the shoes were strangers, one brown, the other black. He looked more like a vagrant than any man Richard had ever encountered.

"Oh, and don't mind me. I'd normally apologise about the state I'm in, but beyond that now. I've a little crib out the back. Wife's been gone a year, couldn't stand the place. Can't say I blamed her. Miss Henschell sorts the pay out, don't you, Miss Henschell?" he said, raising his voice. "You will tell, ah, what's your name again?"

"Kirnst. Ah, Mr Suggiss, is it?" Richard asked, reading a nameplate.

"Sorry, forgot to introduce myself." Perpetual hand-shaking tested the elasticity of Richard's elbow. "Call me Cyril, almost everyone does. Now here, about the pay and all that—"

The redoubtable paymistress appeared and returned his request for assistance by issuing orders of her own. "Get him to fill in the book. Our new chief engineer, I gather, Mr Suggiss?"

The manager nodded meekly, underlining the pecking order.

"Is that all you want to know about me?" Richard asked incredulously.

Suggiss grunted. "Dick—you don't mind if I call you that? When Bryan recommends someone, I needn't ask too much more. Familiarise yourself with the plant. Steam and diesel there, so your qualifications are just the ticket. Mostly we get around on motorbikes. David Yip will run you up. It's the main power source on the island, along with two diesel stations." He made a call over the intercom. "Attention! David, David Yip, to the office. He'll answer any questions. I've a meeting with the governor and the Military Advisory Board at one o'clock."

"Just one query, do you have work clothes and boots?"

"Oh, yes, you arrived here only yesterday with very little, Bryan said. Go to the stores with David. Here's a requisition and get what you require. I'll be on deck, as you sailors say, probably all night, if you need anything else."

Richard knew it was time to go when the protuberant belly, like an extension of the man's blancmange face, swept passed him to confer with the unflappable secretary. In a less than flattering address, Miss Henschell declared that she would not be at her desk for him to stand over unless he attended to his body odour forthwith. He begged of her one last favour as he dictated a letter from the eight-foot distance she acerbically decreed he maintain as a precondition for taking it down. The contrast between the two couldn't be more pronounced, she the officious spinster in spotless starched frock and he ordained in sweat and grime. Yet underneath her prickliness and outward show of disfavour, Richard sensed respect and admiration.

Near the office, a bright little face announced itself. "Hello, I'm David," offering a blackened hand with fingernails bitten to the quick.

He was originally from Hong Kong. With a seagoing background from the age of fourteen and completely self-taught, David Yip had risen from the rank of greaser to junior engineer within twelve months. He had gained considerable experience on large ocean-going ships over the next ten years, before his vessel's extended stay in Singapore during an overhaul changed his life. Love-struck at the sight of a waitress in a Yum Cha restaurant, theirs was a painfully cautious courtship until his ship was due to sail. A sanguine proposal of marriage was accepted, and he resigned his position.

Yip had quickly adapted to shore-based engineering, where he excelled in every department. He could strip down any engine and rebuild it with alacrity. When time dictated that necessity beget the mother of invention, adaptability and initiative were the child of pressure. Suggiss recognised his brilliance, but Yip was hindered from attaining formal qualifications by a self-effacing reluctance to become more proficient in English.

The transformation from shy, infatuated twenty-three-year-old to proud father of five was accomplished in six years. David fascinated Richard. He was a boyish thirty, no more than five foot three inches in height, yet deceptively strong. Then there was the beam that occupied the entirety of his face, imaging a man radiating contentment and who only saw the best in his fellow human beings. Frequently genius accompanies a disposition not to suffer fools lightly, but Yip just kept on smiling.

The motorbike on which Richard was bidden to take a seat looked like a misshapen hybrid of a late-1920s Triumph and an early-1930s BSA. In Yip's hands it was soon careering around the various job sites, Richard competing for room with an assortment of tools in the sidecar. He couldn't have asked for a more thorough itinerary. As they stopped near a burst water main, among the mayhem Yip bounded off to a nearby manhole with a bar and spanner and staunched the flow to a trickle.

"See crew for this one after we get to power station," he said when they reached that destination. "You look while I fix," and he was gone.

Yip returned just as Richard's familiarisation was completed. Without the slightest hint of perturbation, they tore off to the earlier pipeline casualty, where a crew was engaged in feverish activity. There Richard was able to catch up briefly with Williamson, knee-deep in muddy water and operating a welder.

"I'll see you tonight, Dickie. You're all coming, I trust?"

Richard signified hesitant assent. Before he could add anything, Williamson had tipped the helmet back over his face, the blue arc forcing him to avert his eyes. There was urgency in everything he had seen on this most revealing foray. An entertaining debriefing session with Suggiss followed acceptance of the position.

"Consider yourself hired as of now. Go and do what you have to do and then be ready for the challenge first thing tomorrow," Suggiss said good-naturedly and rattled his hand again, motioning for him to go about his necessary business and then waving him back. "Oh, before I forget. The last chap's car was going to be yours, out the back, wrecked him as well. Poor sod had no luck. David will lend you his bike. But I'm onto it and there'll be something better, just wait a bit."

Richard seemed to recall some mention of his predecessor's heart attack had earned the sobriquet, but ellipsis was a facility with which Suggiss seemed bountifully blessed.

He wondered whether his work history had come up. "You should know that my previous position ended in some difficulty—"

"Stuff and nonsense. I know it all, having spoken to that damned awful sod Oram regarding your last vessel. Vilified you to hell and that was enough for me to conclude you must be just my man."

Chapter 25

Decisions

Arriving at Fort Canning early, Richard announced himself to a spruce orderly who advised that Newton had been unavoidably detained. After he idled about outside, an ambulance swung into the driveway and Greda alighted somewhat later than the appointed hour with an apology.

He took her hand and kissed a pre-occupied cheek. "There's no call for urgency. Major Newton won't be available for an hour."

"Oh, then time to compare notes. Seems like you've been busy," she observed, examining his hands, exhibiting a preference not to meet his eyes.

"And you busier," he replied, pointing to a telltale blood spray at the hem of her dress.

"Suborned on the spot, am I right, Richard?"

"Not just for a few hours either. Looks like a full-time job. They're stretched. The superintendent's battling to maintain power utilities and mend burst pipes. Somehow he took to me."

"I'm not surprised at the conclusion he reached, but, seriously, while I'm used to hospital emergencies, that was chaos. Some shocking cases were brought in. Children with shrapnel wounds, frantic mothers screaming for babies for whom there was no help, and a serious shortage of qualified medical personnel. Staff are being run ragged."

"You'll go back then, I imagine?"

"Yes, and you know, even in that frenzy things became clearer. Richard, I might have waited until the Newton business was done."

He studied her guardedly, "What's on your mind, Greda?"

They ambled along a circuitous path lined on either side by unruly rows of mock-orange bushes. Oblivious to their presence and puffing coarsely on a cigarette, an ancient man wielding clumsy clippers was shaping them into hedges. The walk terminated at a rotunda shaded by an overarching Royal Poinciana tree in stunning golden bloom.

As they sat down, Greda took his hand, and this time her eyes were set. "Let me be very candid with you, dearest. I've been thinking about this since last night and perhaps I skipped around it even after the stuff about being frank and straight-talking. Until I have definite confirmation of Edward's fate, I can't leave here unless we're forced to." Her hand loosened before disengaging altogether. "As for Jonathon, after what I've seen, I won't place my son in harm's way by having him stay here. Children are being evacuated as a priority. Some nurses I met today have already sent their kids to Australia and elsewhere."

She rose and measured her paces reflectively, then spun back to face him as if to emphasise her point. "Everything has to be for his sake."

To suggest Jonathon might leave without her was a momentous pronouncement. That the decision was inextricably linked to the future of their relationship registered in a manner he could no longer shirk.

"You understand, don't you, Richard?"

"Yes, I sure do," he said, intent on the gardener.

He heard her voice, but she wasn't there, as his mind raced onward. Presentiments were released like airlocks in a submerged object. Could all they'd said to each other become redundant? Substance in a marriage was always open to inferences, benign and malign. However, an only child remained a potent visual reminder of a family unit. Here was a boy of character, the product not just of Greda but of his father, too, the image pivotal in reaching a conclusion consistent with his instincts. The word 'honour' resurfaced, one she hadn't mentioned and needn't have. It tooled her vows and he heard its discordant reverberation presaging attention on the future. Her voice wrested him from these disconcerting realities.

"Richard, you're the most decent man I've ever met, and nothing has changed between us, inside us, has it?"

Her quest for reassurance seemed to redound on them and the unspoken 'nothing ever will' hovered in his mind.

"No. It's the right thing. I'm totally convinced," he said, secreting an upward twitch of his eyebrows.

He had regained himself when she secured her gentle face on his. "Perhaps we can discuss with the major about getting Jonathon away from this mess."

He was thinking of how fate had dealt them cards from mismatched decks, "Of course, Greda."

"I'll contact my sister in Sydney straightaway. She visited us in Malaya a couple of years ago, and Jon adores her."

"He's fortunate to have a loving aunty," he offered absent-mindedly.

She nodded. "It's a huge trip, of course. One of the nurses I met today, whose two children are younger than Jon, waved them goodbye in mid-December and they're in Brisbane with her brother's family. Her experience convinced me he'd be alright, but you would know better. What about rough seas?"

Reflexively he told her that no passage across that expanse of water could be insulated from bad weather, especially at this time of year.

"The ships have destroyer escorts," she said, seeking his averment.

"Singapore's under threat, Greda. Perhaps the greater risk is remaining here."

"After today, I'm with you on that. But we'll ask Newton."

An unconvincing calm hovered. The methodical clipping became a noisy imposition joining with a crow's discordant screech while each nodded expectantly, willing the moment to pass and wishing the other would speak.

Finally, it was her voice reaching out to him. "I can't express how much your understanding and support has fortified me."

Richard ground his teeth and cleared his throat. "We'd better go in. The major should be ready by now." Her embrace searched him.

Returning, they were ushered through a maze of corridors before arriving in the presence of Newton and Lieutenant McKenzie. The major's countenance was funereal, and he deflected Greda's initial 'any news' enquiry with a wan invitation to be seated.

"Dr Faircrossman," he added stiffly, "I'm sure you're not here to listen to either platitudes or speculation, and I'm sorry I can't be more certain, but I'll come straight to the point. We've reason to believe your husband might still be alive. I'm unable to put it higher than a chance, mind you."

The room was silent for an appreciable time, the clock above Newton's head signifying the stilted moment. Richard, unable to bring himself to look at Greda, seemed hypnotised by the brass pendulum's inexorable motion.

"Was Heenan able to tell you that?" she eventually enquired.

"I'm sorry, I can't go into any detail about the specifics of the discussions I've had with the prisoner. Suffice to say our intelligence sources might be found wanting if that was our most reliable font of data. However, all material we receive is collated, assessed and weighed against the known facts and those that lie in the category, I suppose, of uncorroborated information. What we know about your husband lies, at best, between these two. I cannot offer more, for I don't want in any way to elevate your hopes on the one hand or dash them on the other."

Greda accepted that the major had a job to do, and perhaps his *modus operandi* was calculated to make everyone to whom he spoke feel as if they were under intense scrutiny, but this bureaucratic verbiage was intolerable. Mustering all the composure she could find, she replied, "Major, I'm making a decision of such magnitude regarding my son that I can't tell you, with all due respect, how infuriating I find the tone, content and tenor of what you've just said. Please, can you tell me whether or not I should put my son on a ship sailing to Australia?"

"I'm struggling to see how this relates to what I've—"

"Mr Faircrossman loves his son, who adores him. Unless you tell me otherwise, I have decided that my boy must leave, and I should wait. Is it likely Edward could reach Singapore and—"

"That I cannot possibly say. Lieutenant, I'll speak with Dr Faircrossman alone. Mr Kirnst, do you mind going with my aide? He'll arrange for some refreshments."

Greda and Richard exchanged glances before she asked, "Is that necessary?"

"It's alright, Greda." he tilted his head towards Newton and then back to her. "I'll be down at the cafeteria or whatever."

Newton resumed after the door was closed. "I didn't mean to embarrass you. There are topics you may not wish covered in front of a passing stranger."

"Richard's not a stranger. I've already told you my son and I owe our lives to that man," Greda fumed, finding Newton's insinuations less than agreeable. "Now, as there's something you seemed desperate to expatiate upon, just come right out with it. I *am* a grown woman."

Her emerging frustration had an assuaging effect on him. "I never intended to patronise you, Dr Faircrossman," he shot back, fixing her with eyes so unnerving that she gave way and regarded the wooden floor. "Now we shall go on. The woman known as Eva, you were treating her for a serious injury inflicted by Heenan, had you ever seen her before?"

"What sort of nonsense is that? How would I have?"

Newton left her to ponder the query while he removed a photograph from a brown envelope.

Greda scrutinised the clear image of a relaxed face and began to equivocate. "I, I'm not sure, perhaps I have. It's possible she came to the hospital where I used to work. There were hundreds of patients with family members in tow."

"Has your husband ever mentioned an Asian woman with that name?" Newton probed.

"My husband? Definitely not. What are you telling me?" she demanded.

He continued unflappably. "What about the Australian, has he ever spoken concerning her?"

She flushed, a sign he took to be an affirmative. "Why don't you ask him yourself?"

"Oh, I intend to, Mrs Faircrossman, I most surely do."

"I've no idea where you might be going with this or what you're conjecturing, but it's leaving me entirely cold. If you're inferring my husband or Richard is spying for the Japanese, I reject that with the utter contempt it deserves. I saw Richard kill two soldiers with my own eyes and—"

"Come now, Dr Faircrossman, you're more intelligent than that. I'm suggesting no such thing. But I want to show you something that has managed its utmost to baffle me. Before I do, is it correct that your husband visited Penang in the last six months or so?"

Reverting to her professional title was, she thought, a puerile technique.

"He visited Penang regularly. I told you that when I handed over the picture."

"Ah, I'd forgotten," he drawled.

"You did no such thing."

"Dr Faircrossman, our endeavour is to try to find out what has happened to your husband. We think, somehow or other, he eventually fell into enemy hands. You formed the view that he must have been ambushed given that he and his manager were travelling up north. Heenan has told us something of this as well."

She began to speak, but he waved her away. "No, don't ask about that again. But I'll tell you this. From all the sources we do have, we can't say for certain Mr Faircrossman has been killed."

"But that gives me nothing more than you've already offered. Please, can you tell me if he's alive and where he is, if you know? Please," she begged him.

"Off the record, Doctor, I'm more inclined to think he's out there, whereabouts unknown, but I won't be held to it. Whether he's in captivity is another issue."

For a moment Greda detected amelioration in his manner, as if the mask of inscrutability had now mutated into a living and breathing edifice. But no sooner had she asked, "Why do you think that?" than his expressionless appearance resumed.

"I'm unable to answer your question, and I don't want you to conclude I've held out to you any official hope as to whether he's alive or even well. Of course, it goes without my saying so, but none of us is entirely safe here on the island, in the jungles of Malaya or anywhere else."

She sighed wearily. "Thank you for telling me what you know and think. There's something I've remembered about that woman. In relatively recent times there was a photograph, a likeness I think, though I can't, ah, be sure."

He urged her to go on.

"It's just that, well, Edward came back after one of his trips and a photo dropped out of his wallet. I was curious. When I first saw her brought onboard the ship, you know occasionally one gets an instant thought that a person looks familiar, and now I think that's where I might have seen her before. Edward said he'd forgotten to pass it on to his manager. I wondered, but then just left it. I imagine anyone would wonder, Major Newton."

Without removing his gaze from her, a drawer opened as if he had pushed a button. The epitome of mystique, from fingers that seemed more accustomed to tinkling ivory keys slid several black-and-white photographs across the desktop. "Do any look like the woman?"

The first picture wasn't quite front-on. Greda studied the plate before putting it down. "It's not a particularly good photograph, but there's a likeness."

As all the images were presented, one couldn't lie. Tantalisingly, he revolved the last photograph. It was the shot to which she returned again and again, not least because it depicted two people arm-in-arm, the woman from the safe accompanying her husband.

There was an awkward delay before he resumed. "This woman was who you were treating before the ship was sunk?"

Her acquiescence went almost unrevealed. "I'm trying to understand why you've drawn this out. Was it to sheet home that my husband had another life besides the one he shared with me? Is there an award for a wife who's borne infidelity? But I do know Edward loved his family. And it doesn't change my determination to find out if he's still alive." Greda succeeded in outstaring Newton.

"I'm sure it doesn't, Mrs Faircrossman. There's something else of which you may wish to be appraised. We were always very interested in the activities of this woman. When your husband was in Penang the last time, the Australian, your Mr Kirnst, was with her. Did you know he was another of her many, ah, acquaintances?"

An expansive breath before responding did not conquer her feelings. "He mentioned a few things, but, as a seaman, would have no knowledge of her movements," she replied measuredly.

"Did he tell *you* he was ignorant of her activities, Dr Faircrossman?"

A distasteful question and, despite the varied emotions she was experiencing, Greda deflected it forcefully. "I won't discuss the confidences we've shared. They have nothing to do with this situation or my husband."

"But I just said, and perhaps you misheard me, that your husband happened to be in Penang when the Australian and the woman were also there. In fact, they ran into each other and had a discussion before going their separate ways."

"You're saying Edward met Richard in Penang?"

"Of that there cannot be even a flicker of doubt. We have them shaking hands."

Greda took the photograph from him and stood as if riveted. Newton read people carefully. That was the nature of his business. Her features metamorphosed from bewilderment to calm acceptance. That her husband had been involved in an affair was not news. Greda remained unmoved, save for the tears moistening her eyes and the barely perceptible nod of her head. Intuition and discretion told him to refrain from further enquiry.

At that moment an orderly knocked, entered and handed Newton a sealed envelope. She saw it was marked 'TOP SECRET' and he swivelled sideways in his chair to study its contents. Turning back to face Greda, he slid the paper inside a file and replaced the photographs in the drawer. He lifted the telephone receiver and within a few minutes Richard re-appeared.

"I needn't ask you anything, Mr Kirnst, at this stage," Newton placing emphasis on the last three words. "It has been a trying day. Now, on the issue of evacuation: do I understand you're staying on for the moment?"

"Yes, I am." Richard tried vainly to meet Greda's eyes. "It's a long story and the relevance to us being here now is pretty marginal. Let me just say I've been nationalised for the cause. I'm going to be looking after the power station."

"You mean to tell me you're returning to the mechanical trade?"

"Yes, in a manner of speaking. Mr Suggiss has appointed me chief engineer."

The major straightened in his chair. He recognised worth in the Australian from their moment of introduction, despite an innate disposition lending aversion to favourable first impressions. "So that makes two of you holding the fort, if you will, with Dr Faircrossman being sorely needed at the hospital. It shows some mettle to stay on, the more so, Doctor, because, as you told me earlier, you're desirous of seeing your son evacuated on the next ship to Australia." Greda appeared to be in a dream and he repeated, "Doctor?"

"I'm sorry." There was a slight movement of her head. "You alluded to my son?"

He nodded. "I'm of opinion that the sooner he's out of here the better."

Newton confirmed the ongoing evacuation of families and children. When asked how soon a passage could be arranged, to her surprise he took it as an instant plea for assistance. The promise to do what he could marked a transformation in attitude.

"Major, I didn't mean to importune you into helping us."

"Nobody importunes me, Mrs Faircrossman," he replied with deliberative consideration of a desk calendar. "I'm in regular contact with a Captain Ross, to whom I'll speak the moment you leave."

Greda was startled by Newton's munificence. "Thank you."

"Madam, you mentioned that your sister lives in Sydney. Do you have a telephone number on which she can be contacted?"

"Yes, but I can't recall it off-hand." She gave him her name.

"Never mind, let me try this." Newton had the Sydney telephone exchange on the line within a few minutes. "Mrs Fay Carter? Yes, this is Major Newton calling from Singapore. I have Mrs Greda Faircrossman, here. She wants to speak with you."

It was evident from their conversation that she was greatly relieved. They had not been in contact since late December and her attempts at communication with the plantation had been futile. She would be only too happy to look after her nephew. A telegram detailing the arrangements would be sent forthwith. Greda was adjured to be careful and to leave if the situation deteriorated, but her sister understood her reasons for remaining.

"Well, that seems to have been settled," said Newton, as Greda put the phone down. "Now, what I intend to do is speak to someone who handles such matters. There are always unaccompanied minors on these trips. Your son will be thoroughly cared for and supervised. I am confident I'll be able to get him on the next ship leaving Singapore."

"So this means imminently?" Greda asked, experiencing trepidation.

"Yes. You must see that the boy is prepared and ready by seven o'clock tonight. I believe there's a vessel sailing at eight PM for Sydney, which is convenient, if I can link this—" Newton stopped, thinking it imperative that Greda not leave his office until the arrangements for the boy's passage had been finalised. "Just a minute, would you?"

He picked up the phone again and asked for Captain Ross. "This is a long shot. He's very hard to reach sometimes, so we may have to wait. 'Ross. Hello, it's Reginald, old fellow. I've a passenger for you, top priority. No, he's ten and unaccompanied. His aunt is in Sydney. Mother's a doctor and required to stay. Father, well, that doesn't require explanation for the moment. You'll be able to manage it? Superb. And I can count on your discretion?"

It was all settled while those opposite him sat open-mouthed.

"My car and driver will pick you up at 1900 hours. I may see you both later. Could you give me your son's full name?"

Newton took three sheets of paper with his letterhead at the top, inserted blue carbon paper between them and wrote several lines. Near the bottom of the page, he printed a few words and then signed each sheet, placing his stamp over the signature. "Here's a letter from me authorising Jonathon Harold Edward Faircrossman to travel as an unaccompanied minor on the Motor Vessel *Sydney Breezes* set to depart at 2000 hours today. Mrs Faircrossman, underneath is an endorsement that you must sign. An original, a copy, and one I retain—you know what the British are like—whereby you, as his only parent capable of doing so, consent to Jonathon sailing as aforesaid and being delivered into the custody of his aunt, Mrs Carter of Lane Cove, on arrival."

Such was the efficiency with which Jon's passage had been finalised that Greda began to wonder aloud whether she had enough time to explain it all to him.

"You will, Madam, and you must. Let me tell you, it's imperative that he leaves while it's within our remit to send him, rather than in a last-minute crush or perhaps not at all." His tone was potent.

Greda shook hands with Newton, who bowed, remaining in awe of her and trying not to show it. "In my eyes, you've outdone yourself, Major. I'll not forget, and you, as the perspicacious one, won't mind my observation that, until a short time ago, I viewed you as an absolute prig."

The major permitted himself a wry smile, snookered between compliment and disparagement.

Chapter 26

Farewells and hails

Bryan Williamson tendered a glass of champagne as his other hand held open the front door. When told that Jonathon was being evacuated in a few hours his ebullience contracted momentarily, but he flat-out refused to hear of a withdrawal from the arrangements.

"That'll be tough on his mother, and we understand the need for time to say goodbye. Dinner can wait. Come straight down whenever you're ready. It'll be good for both of you," he pressed.

Richard's hand gestured towards him awkwardly. "No promises, mate. She's yet to tell the kid."

"We'll be waiting, Dickie, for both of you, mind."

Jonathon's head was resting against his mother's chest when Richard returned.

"He knew something was up. My impenetrability is about as shambolic as a puppy's at dinner-time, and he insisted on the full account."

"Dick, did you agree?" Jon asked ingenuously.

"I did, mate. This was a very hard call to make and you have every right to wonder why it's necessary. Just a short while ago, someone from the army told us a ship's due to sail tonight. He said it's too dangerous for you to be here. Your mum and I have seen how bad it is. All the children are leaving, mostly to go to Australia."

"Not safe for me? Then it's not for you and Mum either. I want to stay and—" He began to cry.

Richard took a rescuing glass of water to Greda as she strove to hide her emotions.

He sat Jonathon in his lap. "Young fella, has your mother mentioned to you that your father is the reason?"

"What do you mean about Dad? Mum?"

"Sorry, Greda," he baulked. She nodded towards Richard, accepting the intervention. "Today the army told us your dad might—well, could be found. No one can say for sure, Jonathon, but this changes everything."

"Dad's found!" the boy's squeals were unrestrained.

"Your mum had a long talk with Major Newton. He's what they call an intelligence expert, very smart, alright. They know things no one else does."

"Jon, you would want me to wait for Dad, so," the words almost eluded her, "we—he could come back. Wouldn't you be gl—"

"I want you and Dick and Dad to all come home together."

Greda derived solace when she perceived no apparent reaction from Richard. She continued. "But we only say 'could', remember, as neither the major nor anyone else knows for certain whether your dad's okay and where he is and that's why I—we," she corrected, taking Richard's hand, "have to stay, but you can't be here with all these bombs falling."

"I'd be in the shelter," the boy tried again.

"Jon, lad," said Richard as he moved closer, "you trust me, don't you?"

"Sir, I love you."

Greda reciprocated with the water. "I'm on your mum's side," he said with effort. "We're making the very same decision your dad would if he were here," he struggled to suggest, and then forcefully, "you're heading off to Sydney tonight, Jon. So come on, I'll help you pack. The car will arrive soon and it's the major's. That's how important you are to Army Intelligence."

"Wow! Am I really that important? Mum, Dick can pack my things with me. I really love Aunty Fay too. I can't wait to see her and my cousins as well. But I'll miss you." The swiftness with which his resistance crumbled surprised his mother. When he tried out the new crutches Greda had brought from the hospital, only the voyage seemed to be on his mind. "Look at me, Mum! I'll be able to get around the ship with these easily."

The day-sitter returned with last-minute clothing purchases for the trip. Greda folded them into his port. She drew strength from the interaction between Richard and her son, numb at the pending farewell, but beaming with pride as they went through sketches Jon had made during the day. One, depicting an engine he'd helped Richard assemble at the plantation, earned considerable praise.

"Some day you'll be an architect or designer."

"I want to be like you, Dick. When the ship starts, I'll ask the engineer to let me see the propeller shaft turning."

"Best you do that a couple of days out, when things are quieter."

While Greda sat beside Richard on the edge of the bed resting a hand on his shoulder, Jon regarded them knowingly. As he dressed and put the last of his belongings inside his case, she became serene. Richard faced her quivering eyes as she whispered, "Thanks. I'll never forget what you've just done."

The major's black Vauxhall arrived not a moment later than expected. At the wharf's checkpoint, there were no delays upon presentation of Newton's document.

"What bright young sailor do we have here?" asked a bubbly sixty–ish purser in a starched blue and white uniform positioned at the top of the gangway. She was handed the paper with his name on it. "So, this is Master Jonathon. Welcome aboard the *Sydney Breezes*. And here's your mum and dad?"

"No, just Mum and our good friend, Dick. Dad's coming on a later ship."

This was not an occasion for explanations.

Newton's arrangements smacked of efficiency, giving them the opportunity to get the boy familiar with his allotted cabin and the ship's general layout. While Greda spoke to the woman charged with supervising the children in his group, Richard took Jonathon to the halfway point of the engine room, opening the fire doors to peer inside.

Pointing to the six huge, round heads that marked the cylinders of the main engine, Jon was open-mouthed at the sight. "Gosh, it's hot and noisy!" he yelled.

"It'll be much louder when the propeller comes to life. I'd take you down to the plates, but those ladders are steep. We don't want another bung foot!"

She was a chunky, riveted old vessel whose best days were behind her. The builder's plate read '1918', but no rust-bucket, being a cargo and passenger steamer of the type that plied the world's major ports.

"Watch out for yourself, Jon, won't you? If it gets rough, stay in your cabin. Have some of the chewing gum I gave you. That'll stop you from getting seasick. And don't eat too much."

"Sir, can you look after Mum, and please get Mum and Dad away from this place before the Japs get here? And you, too," the boy added. "I want you to come to Sydney as well. Will you promise me?"

"Mate, as I told you another time, I'll do all I can to find your dad so that everyone can be on the next ship to Sydney after you."

Three other boys his age were vying for bunks when they returned. Greda looked anxiously at her son and, for a second, Richard wondered if she might change her mind.

"This is Mavis Metyard," she said finally, as the introductions were made. "She'll be looking after Jonathon."

The pleasant-faced spinster offered a schoolmarmish greeting and Jonathon looked sheepish.

"Evening, Miss Metyard. He's a good boy and will give you no trouble. Here's a friendly tip from an old seaman. At this time of year, the north-west monsoon is active and, if you strike bad weather, it'd be wise to keep the boys inside."

"Much appreciated, Mr Kirnst. We've already been briefed on that front. It's something of a first, looking after boys on a ship, although I've had a good deal of experience teaching them on dry land. But we've an abundant supply of games, and they'll have regular lessons too."

That observation produced a disgruntled murmur from all the prospective pupils.

"Here's a report detailing Jon's injury. The cast is not due to come off until after you dock. Mrs Carter, my sister in Sydney, will meet him."

"Don't worry, madam. My eye will be on Jonathon."

A bell rang, followed by a Scottish-accented voice bellowing, "Alls ashore that's stayin' ashore."

"Now, Jonathon," said his mother intently, "please be careful, my dear son. Do what Miss Metyard says at all times and don't go on deck unless she's with you, and no roaming. Remember your crutches and try to keep off that foot."

"Yes, Mum," said Jon, consuming the plethora of instructions.

There were hugs and kisses all round, the significance of the parting not quite bearing on the boy. Richard and Greda retreated to the quayside, where they could see him waving from the top deck, attended by the flaxen-haired Metyard. Greda prayed for his wellbeing, clinging to the reassurance given by Newton that a destroyer would escort the *Sydney Breezes*.

She wept, blew kisses and called her son by name. Having slipped its moorings, the ship eased away from the wharf, guided into the channel by two tugs before its engine rumbled into life. They waved until it became little more than a diminishing collection of lights being drawn like a magnet into the blackness.

He was behind her and Greda leaned into his encircling arms. Amid the pain of parting and the sense of grief this separation entailed, a glut of emotion continued to buffet her. When the last light vanished and they turned to leave, she could not have loved Richard more.

*****

"I'll tell them you're not up to it and be back shortly."

She was contemplating the empty bed, only to appreciate his presence when Richard tentatively announced again that he would put in a brief appearance at the Williams' abode. She urged him to take whatever time he liked.

"I'll be alright," she said, squeezing his hand.

He opened the door and stepped outside.

"No, wait, damnit, I'm coming, as soon as I touch up this streaky face."

The couple were greeted effusively and made to feel they had been there since the first cork was popped. A stunning banquet was laid on.

The host savoured his drink like the dilettante he was, effecting to take the golden nectar as if it was passing his lips for the first time, ever the connoisseur rather than a philistinic imbiber.

Carefree banter lifted their spirits. His enchanting girlfriend was anything but the dutiful appendage Richard had imagined. Suzy was a true spark of domestic efficiency, a skillful culinary artist, charming, educated and mature beyond her stated years. He concluded she was probably closer to twenty-five than eighteen but would not disabuse the mercurial Williamson of his splendiferous illusion.

"I used to lug French champagne from ship to ship, you'll remember, Dickie."

It was the first time Greda had heard that affectionate term and she rather liked its usage in context, seeing further shades to him from these historical nostalgias. She was determined not to let her inner sadness infect the occasion. Richard was relaxing, too, recognising in Greda's expressions generous enjoyment at this reunion.

"I remember, alright, always reserved for your doting admirers, never the coarse gullets of shipmates, except perhaps a wee taste once or twice!"

The hint that females may have benefitted from Williamson's largesse as part of a finely practised method of seduction was not lost on the perceptive Suzy.

"I protest at this innuendo. No, my delicate little orchid, he didn't mean I only drank Dom Perignon with persons of the opposite gender. There were important meetings and, ah, now where were we?"

Nobody dared jump in to speak.

"Yes, I remember," his third portion having been decanted from the second bottle.

"I knew you would," cut in Greda unable to refrain from nudging him.

"Thank you, my dear. I'll have to watch myself with this girl, Dickie," Williamson's affectation noticeably more pronounced. Upon Greda registering approval to his accent and appellation, he couldn't desist from enhancing the timbre.

"As I was saying, the store was added to over the years and from time-to-time the odd one was uncorked. What's your take on the 1928, Greda?"

"A subtle bouquet, exceptional quality, perfectly complemented by Suzy's cooking," she replied, her glass untouched, "and what better company to enjoy it with?" Her voice quavered.

"The last few hours have been difficult for Greda, mate." Richard was studying her as he spoke. "Perhaps we should be getting home, being past midnight."

"It's alright, Richard. I like to hear of the old times, and what Bryan and Suzy have gone to the trouble of putting on has been just right."

"Well, the one thing I'm not going to do is leave any of this," holding the bottle aloft, "behind for those unsophisticated oriental palates to quaff and—"

"Do you think it's really near that point from all you see here?"

Greda's was an interruption to which he lavishly acceded. "Please go on, my dear."

"Are they about to close in? Do you have any inside information?"

"I give us probably a month at the most, unless those planes we've been promised arrive, but all we receive here's empty rhetoric and weather predictions. The forecast is always wrong. Here's my own prognosis. We'll all be scrambling to hop on the last ship unless other plans can be formulated. So, Greda, in the meantime, are you going to work at the hospital?"

"Yes. They need doctors. Richard has a job lined up and you're here toiling away. Surely you could have left by now, Bryan?"

"I could, but I'm certainly not going without my girl," he said, winking at Suzy.

Her eyes glazed at him. His request for the 1930 bottle was firmly declined, demonstrating an exertion of will that impressed their companions. "No, we'll have Chinese tea. Think of guests, who need to work in few hours, like yourself."

"Isn't she a treasure? Suzy, darling, show Greda where I keep it cellared. We can part with a few. Dickie, old mate, how about a cigar?"

Greda answered his query. "Very kind, Bryan, but perhaps another time. This has been wonderful, and it's been lovely to meet both of you, a pleasure and a rare insight all round. Richard, I know you still have a fair amount to catch up on, so stay. I'm on early and, if yesterday was any guide, today can only promise more of the same."

"Take a bottle or two, won't you, Greda? I'm down to my last two dozen, so what the hell. Better still, I'll give them to Dickie. Really just adorable to make your acquaintance, Dr Greda—it's Faircrossman. Yes, unusual name, so very English and charming." Williamson took her hand ostentatiously, bowing slightly and raising it to his lips. "You see her home, Dickie, and don't be too bloody long! Your son will be looked after, Greda. It'll be a breeze on the *Sydney Breezes*."

She conceded a smile while planting a kiss on his cheek. "Thanks, Bryan."

Richard followed her outside. "I can go back with you. I'm happy to call it quits."

"It's fine. Just watch me from here. Goodnight, Richard. Make sure you get a good rundown on the way things truly are. Bryan's very keenly in local touch and he admires you."

"I didn't think it was that obvious, even though he mentored me, but he does love banging on about the old times, especially those in which he features."

Meditatively, she traced a forefinger along his hairline and down to his cheek. "I love you."

"I won't be too long. Sure you're okay?"

Greda answered with a nod and took time to nestle into him, then disengaged to walk up the hill and ascend the stairs to their apartment without looking back. Richard returned to find Suzy serving tea.

"Now, mate, will you take a port? No? Tea? Right, so tell me what plans you've got. As I said, we'll all have to get out of here soon, and that beautiful creature loves you. I noticed she was wearing a wedding ring."

"Yes, she's married, as I thought I'd told you."

"Did you? Oh, anyway, go on."

"No real plans. Obviously, this is a bastard of a time for her. Until our arrival in Singapore, it seemed to all that her husband had most likely been killed. I, to be perfectly frank, well, loved Greda from the moment I set eyes on her. It was one of those miracle things, almost too miraculous and—" He scrambled for words. "Ah, hell it's about fallen apart after Greda's meeting with an intelligence officer earlier. Now that her husband may still be alive, the next step is speculative. Her son says he wants me to find his father and for us to all live happily ever after."

Williamson sounded a deft tone of compassion. "Bloody gut-kicker, hey, mate?"

Richard shrugged his shoulders. He proceeded to provide more detail of what had happened since the Heenan flogging and the overland trek culminating in their escape through Malacca.

"But you can't just sit here waiting for him to turn up. You're never going to know while the Japs are coming down here at a hundred miles an hour. Are you certain the Army's going to help out? Sorry, but they've more important things on their plate."

"Greda seems to think so," he responded, rising to circle the room much like a prisoner walking the waiting cell with advance knowledge of the jury's verdict. Williamson motioned for him to sit down, but he continued to pace distractedly.

"Dickie, I've got to tell you my estimate of a month was probably exaggerated. It's near the end of January. The establishment here's pathetic. They tell you so very little. One minute the British Navy is showing off two of its finest ships. We go down to see them off amid much fanfare. They're sent away and the next thing, disaster. Why? Because there's no plan. And that's the never-ending story. No air cover there, precious little here. Thousands of lives and many more lost since the bombing started in earnest. It's a cruel hoax. And some of the new recruits they're sending up to the front lines, as green as; their chins covered in bum fluff."

Richard paused to consider his words. Williamson's uncensored summation swept aside the earlier characterisation.

"I can't blame Greda for wanting to find out about her husband now she's been advised that there's a chance. She told the boy, and he looks at me with his big brown eyes, expecting a family reunion in Sydney."

"Sit down, Dickie. Your fretting's making me nervous and I need to think. You'd be tempted to make something up, tell her the whole thing's a lost cause and just head off. But I know you couldn't do that and, deep down in my soul, neither could I."

Richard resumed his chair, slapping Williamson on the back. "Fretting, eh? Don't mind me, mate. Anyway, have you got any ideas for getting out?"

"I thought you'd never ask," Williamson answered enthusiastically. "You've already met David Yip and seen how he operates."

Richard nodded. "A very impressive little bloke he is."

"Well, his wife and Suzy are distant cousins. I've heard the Chinese are being raped and massacred wherever the Japs go. They're not safe here. And he has five young kids. Now, we've made a modest investment in a small ship. The main engine was stuffed but, between us, David and I put in some big hours fixing it, begged, borrowed and, well, I won't say stole—liberated some spares and it's pretty much ready to go. Looks a rusty old scow, but she's seaworthy. The engineering plant's in good shape and—"

"What about fuel, charts, navigation and supplies? How far are you going?"

"We've some juice, but it needs tons more for a long trip. That was part of the deal when we purchased the thing. In fact, it was to be scuttled and we bought it for the value of the bunkers left in the tanks. We don't have a skipper or charts, but we're working on that. Food's not a problem. There'd be plenty of space for you and Greda. We're aiming for Darwin by way of the Dutch East Indies. Because it's not a large vessel, about eight-hundred tons and pretty nondescript, it won't invite the attention a bigger ship might."

Richard was attracted to the notion of evacuating in such a vessel. With its shallow draught, small size and unkempt appearance, it would be unobtrusive, yet not so small as to be unable to ride out bad weather. Finding a skipper and a mate capable of navigating and completing such a voyage would finalise the ship's complement. He immediately thought of Chia and Kwoli and recounted Chia's part in bringing them to Singapore, the loss of his coaster and the reward in the offing for his efforts in handing over Heenan.

"He and his bosun might do the job. Chia knows his way around. There'd be a price of course, but that'd be for you and him to work out."

An inveterate optimist, Williamson was ecstatic to hear this, cuffing him on the ear with, "Dickie, this is brilliant! David can do almost anything, but, look, to have a qualified master. Might this skipper and his offsider be found at the Seamen's Mission?"

"That's where they were, unless they've already picked up a ship."

"I'll go down and find out tomorrow. It's Chia, you say? Do you mind?" He didn't wait for an answer. "I'll grab David, if I can find the bugger. Maybe you can tell Chia first to give him the drum, as he might think me a nutter if I go cold. David and I can then see him. I'd imagine his preference would be finding a command rather than anything else. He'll probably need some enticing once he sees our old girl. David will handle that."

*****

1–5 February 1942

With his Army at the gates of Singapore, General Yamashita was unusually sombre. The British and Commonwealth forces contained in the tiny island were all that lay between him and the crossroads of the Far East.

After approving the battle plan for Singapore, he addressed his commanders:

> *Life is desired by all men; death disliked by all.*
> *But this day, standing on this earth,*
> *if we meet death,*
> *which we all must welcome once, one day or another*
> *will we not be happy that it comes*
> *while we are participating in this battle?*

His newly appointed headquarters was in the Imperial Palace of the Sultan of Johore. Strategically of immense significance, it stood on the northern side of a narrow, fast-flowing expanse of water separating the Malayan Peninsula from Singapore Island. The naval base at Sembawang and the Tengah airfield loomed within easy reach.

At the eastern end of the red brick and green-tiled building, a five-storey tower was accessed by climbing a spiral ladder. From there, Yamashita could observe the entire front for the amphibious advance. Having regard to Singaporean topography, it also commanded a view of the impending battle for the heights of Bukit Timah. With powerful field-glasses, he studied the movements of men and equipment. For the Japanese, this was the Sultan's strategic treasure house, a gift that kept replenishing their intelligence for the forthcoming assault.

In the British Colony, there was a large group of listless, dispirited and poorly trained men with morale deserting them and discipline breaking down. Many lounged about, got drunk and some harassed civilians. Robbery and violence abounded.

Coming and going from his headquarters outside Singapore was the Commander-in-Chief in the Far East, General Wavell. Within ten days of Tsuji's and Yamashita's plans being drawn up in the palace, Wavell, then on his last visit to the island, would cable Churchill to tell him that the greatest catastrophe ever to befall the British Empire was about to unfold.

Chapter 27

A last waltz

Asolitary, defiant frangipani tree garlanded in pink
seemed to scorn the desiccated remnants of its
cousins occupying a moribund line along Beach
Road. Coconut palms were equally forlorn, like mon-
archs whose jewels had been debrided from their crowns,
with some beheaded altogether. Of the many European
bungalows at Tanglin, few had escaped unscathed. Widespread targeting of Chinatown had wrought much destruction, and even the grounds of Government House
were pitted with craters like traps on a golf course awaiting the introduction of sand fill. One obliterated face of
the clock on the Memorial Theatre testified to the effects
of the pounding.

Elsewhere, normality strived to prevail. Every night
at Raffles there was a dinner dance with the orchestra
playing eight in the evening to midnight, so announced
the daily advertisement in the *Straits Times*, promoting the
general edict from the Governor of 'business as usual', as
evacuations grew apace.

Richard and Greda, overborne by their respective
duties, had not seen each other for some days after their
apartment was hit when both had been on duty. Because
of the exacting hours of their respective workplaces, an
instant decision was necessary. She had moved to available
nurses' quarters at the hospital. He had shifted into spartan
accommodation adjacent to the power plant, remaining
on twenty-four hour tenterhooks. The space doubled as
his office and communication centre.

Meanwhile, as greater numbers of wounded people taxed the hospital's capacity, reserves of morphine were becoming compromised, and even basic items such as bandages and plaster of Paris were seriously depleted. The situation was exacerbated when a Red Cross convoy had been strafed and vital supplies were destroyed.

Against their chaotic environs, contact was problematic. Telephone lines, even specially devised ones, were not immune from disruption.

Never far from Richard's mind were speculations about whether Major Newton had updated Greda regarding her husband's whereabouts and that, by design, he was being kept in the dark. The insecurity besetting him had reached such a zenith that only the vehement work regime imposed by the exigencies of his position provided a cloak in which to withdraw. Even that wasn't enough, and he started to question his capacity to carry out his responsibilities. After an incident where he barked the skin off a finger when his hammer's trueness miscued, he slammed his tools down. Composure was only regained by recalling that she was dealing in lives rather than machinery and thereby couldn't afford the luxury of a hissy fit. That image spurred him into action.

Richard had resolved to see her and, just as he was conjuring a means of doing so, Williamson's motorbike made an impromptu appearance. Explaining the impasse to the affable engineer, whose zest for romantic intrigue was unrepressed, Richard's reservations about absenting himself were swept aside with an obliging offer. Already generously trimmed with liquor, he had hoped, as the clinking of bottles in his knapsack revealed, that the visit might take on some convivial dimensions.

"I'll look after the job for you, Dickie. I told Suzy I'd be here the night, after the little treasure gave me a leave-pass, as she was going to see David's missus. But you know me, mate, a slave when duty calls."

"You're sure, Bryan? I don't want to make my issues your headaches."

"Hey, we're all in this, poss', and my purpose in coming was by no means limited to having a few grogs. I've mentioned previously that David and I moved our floating Jezebel in rags by tug to Keppel the other night. We've a good thirteen-footer ferrying us to and fro, and it's studiously hidden. Which reminds me, Chia and his bosun may opt in. They're pretty rapt in the ship and they can make up their minds while living on board courtesy of our grub and bedding. We're not mugs mate. If that's not an inducement, buggered if I know what is. Righto, my friend, I'm blathering on and you've more serious business to transact with that beautiful dame."

"Mate, I can postpone this. What you're saying has to be worked through if we're—"

"Save it for when you get back, Dickie. That dazzling doctor needs you, poss'. Like Suzy, she's a woman to die for, so piss off now, in case I thwack your head with this wrench."

Richard goaded Williamson to 'give it a try' before knuckling him on the forearm. "Just a couple of hours will do it, Bryan, and hey, not too heavy on the bubbly."

"I'll be here, sober as an unshelled peanut."

"Yeah, and as comatose, too," Richard joked, starting his vehicle.

Being close to ten o'clock, he couldn't avoid noticing numbers of enlisted men aimlessly wandering around in groups. Almost without exception, the idlers were vocal, purposeless drunks spoiling with disaffection and regarded him with a singular degree of belligerence as he drove the Jeep emblazoned with its Works Department British insignia. Some were in the uniform of Australian regular soldiers and he wondered whether the antipathy arose from an assumption that he was an Englishman.

Nearing the hospital, he stopped to avoid a group of three wearing slouch hats, sidling across the road and contemptuous of his presence. They were unsteady on their feet and each held a bottle. One thumped his fist on the bonnet. "Fuckin' pommie bastard," he roared.

Richard turned his head to avoid their glares and waited, noticing the trio stagger in the direction of the spacious hospital grounds where, he imagined, they would be sleeping it off. On pulling away, he heard them continuing to yell and swear after him.

As they were near the facility and looked like trouble-makers, he mentioned their existence to a desk clerk on his arrival. That functionary responded acerbically, "We've no time here to worry about such things. Go and talk to the police, since you obviously have little else to occupy yourself."

Greda spied him in reception. Exhilarated, her impulse to surprise was curbed by the looking glass. He waited a full fifteen minutes before she reappeared. When he rose, her face lit up. In a fraction of time their electricity fused.

Her lustrous black hair tied with a bow, she was wearing a white-and-pink floral dress featuring a fitted bodice, sweetheart neckline and full skirt. Greda followed his eyes, which studied her in a manner she found tempting, and her body reacted. She knew the absence of her wedding band had not escaped his survey.

"Not mine, I'm afraid, but adequate. I borrowed this ensemble from one of the girls. Hope you like it. Oh, why do I ask? You would eat me out of it now, if I let you!"

It was a tantalising riposte. Her classic feminine elegance eclipsed evident fatigue.

He fumbled to remark, "I might."

"Since you are reasonably spic and span, am I correct in assuming you've permitted yourself some free time?" she enquired with rakish formality.

"Yes, to assuming I found some," his rejoinder colouring her features.

"There's no way I'd permit you to see me in hospital regalia, so I detoured, though not before I stole a pretty fulsome peek at you." Her dark, full eyebrows arched as she spoke and he smiled at her boyishly, shaking his head. "By the way, I have my own little flat now, with a bathroom, too. Part of a few private domiciles for doctors. I graduated from the nurses' digs, though, with such company they weren't so bad."

"I can't say how pleased I am to be with you, Greda."

Hand-in-hand, they sashayed outside before he lifted her effortlessly into his arms. As soon as their lips touched, hers parted to receive him.

"I've thought of little else but seeing and feeling you!" she cried.

They held each other as if some hidden force bound them. Her body regained the ground, but there was no indication that she wished to separate from his. The warmth of her mouth, its inviting taste and the exigent need she conveyed took him by surprise. Transfixed, the moment encapsulated something beyond their emotional relief at seeing each other. He kissed her tenderly again, almost in remorse for visualising an alteration in her affections.

"Richard, I love you so dearly. I've missed you in ways you couldn't imagine. There was simply no opportunity for me to send you a message. Before I saw you, I was pretty much done. Now I'm alive and intend to retain my *joie de vivre*. The next emergency will have to wait." She searched his eyes earnestly. "Is there anything the matter?"

"I was worried for you, with the bombardment and everything, but I didn't—ah, I wasn't sure that, well, whether you may know—" Richard stammered.

She held his face in her hands. "I haven't heard anything from Newton. Not a word. Nothing at all about—" He sketched her face and when she spoke, detected a hint of disdain, "about him."

"Your husband, yes," he managed. "This must be really gnawing at you."

"It's getting at us both. There comes a point when one has to say 'no more can be done'. Jonathon must have one parent and I'm very much alive, for now."

"You shouldn't be so flippant as that."

"You're right, but it would be senseless if he lost both through sheer folly. And you, too—I refuse to call you Dickie—Richard. You wouldn't still be here if it wasn't for me. It's time to get out."

"I couldn't be anywhere without you, Greda. Over the last couple of days, I imagined him back or that you knew something but were unable to bring yourself to let me know."

"If he comes now, and I cannot conceive of that happening with the Japanese just a few miles away, but if he does come—" She sighed. "I've thought of nothing else for days. I'll tell him I'm in love with another man. I can't be his wife any longer. It's something that must be—"

"Please, Greda," his hand squeezed hers, "I know you love me, and that's what counts." She nodded, taking it wistfully and stroking his wrist with her fingertips. Somewhat airily, he added. "Fancy us choosing to partner up now, like two birds twittering between artillery barrages."

"Yes, fancy." Greda's eyes flickered at the imagery.

Concluding that his attempt at levity had faltered, Richard continued circumspectly. "I guess this is neither the time nor the place for gushing. Our love will endure."

"You're so right there. It will, darling."

"Come on, enough of this."

His arm settled around her waist. She tilted her head towards him, and they glided to the Jeep.

"What do you think of it? My boss managed to trade it from some Yank."

"Just the roadster for a night out in this air," she replied with consummate ease.

"Now, if this was my hometown, I'd whisk you up to Picnic Point. Remember, I mentioned it being at the top of the Toowoomba Range, with views of the world. You can sit or walk around. There's a path perched on the edge of the escarpment leading to a little pavilion, a place where lovers—"

"Make love, I hope," she chimed in gaily. "And you *will* take me there one day, Richard."

"As God is my witness, yes, and on a full moon, too. When this is all over, there are so many things to show you," he replied, bursting to expand.

They drove off, momentarily lost in their own thoughts. He entertained a vague notion of heading in the direction of Little India before another idea occurred. "I've never been to Raffles. Shall we risk it? You know the place, and perhaps we'll have one of their famous Singapore Slings. It's always open, I gather?"

"Yes, around the clock, darling. But the Slings are on me—and no arrows, except the ones in my quiver."

Greda was never so carefree. An arm through his, a hand brushing strands of hair from her face, abandoned to these precious moments with her man. A reckless breeze caressed them as they rocked and bumped down to Beach Road.

She led him to the Long Bar, sparsely occupied at this time of evening, where they sipped their drinks before moving into the Grand Ballroom. The orchestra was playing, and couples were dancing. Every person seemed jovial and friendly. It was crowded, but they found a table cloaked in a white cloth, immaculately pressed, on which sat a crystal vase. Theirs was the only setting with a red rose, its perfume rich and endless.

Glasses clinked together as they toasted with the simple phrase, "To us."

Greda led him towards the dancers.

"You seem to be initiating all the moves tonight."

"I haven't even begun to initiate, Richard."

Their gazes fixed on each other until he averted his eyes, blushing self-consciously.

Recalling his late teens, when he had attended rough-and-tumble bush dances and stood around watching, never game to ask any girl to take a turn with him, Richard hesitated, "Haven't done this before in my life."

Increasing her pull, she brought him to the centre of the floor. The orchestra was playing a slow waltz. It was dark and smoky, windows shrouded with black, chandeliers extinguished and subdued light coming from oil lamps positioned on pillars around the room. The walls and ceiling were alive with the shadows of couples moving in harmony with the music.

"Just follow my lead." Taking his left hand, she steered his right arm around her waist. "The magic sustains as long as you listen and let me guide you."

It was an inauspicious debut as his feet faltered and criss-crossed. Greda drew him closer, enough for Richard to be conscious of her bosum. With each misstep, she encouraged attention on her eyes and forgetting about whether he might stand on her toes. Before long, their bodies synchronised, and they were gliding serenely across the floor as one. Gradually a brash sureness emerged, emboldening less restrained movements.

"Oh, come on, Richard, you *have* done this before," she teased. "Making out it's your virgin dance, while all those country girls were falling at your feet, rather than you treading on theirs!"

He pleaded innocence, looking straight at her, and she reacted with a comical, questioning frown. He started to laugh, mildly at first. This had an infectious effect, as they descended into prolonged and uncontrolled laughter so raucous that it drew glares, especially when their steps upset the rhythm of others nearby. Nothing now impeded them and, with a more up-tempo piece and enthused by his newly acquired legerdemain, Richard mimicked a nearby couple. As he reached for Greda's right hand, she anticipated the movement, spun gracefully full circle and took another step, before turning again, laughing carelessly and dancing on. After the next tune, they returned to their table breathless and she fanned her face.

"Whew, I haven't broken out like that before, and all those disapproving stares. Did my dress really flounce over my head and was that woman expecting me to perch a leg on your shoulder?"

"Maybe both legs while I held you upside down!"

"Then damn it, I should have! Our debut at such a venue, this could become a habit, and as for those little pirouettes—'twirls', you said." Greda was child-like, yet exuded a sensuality that challenged his restraint. "It really was a first for me, Richard. I've never danced that way."

A waiter hovered and they exchanged glances, weighing the idea playfully, before his persistence prevailed when she nodded. "I'm game if you are," and Richard needed no importuning in requesting champagne.

"We'll have to think about leaving soon, but, you know, Greda, I just don't want this to end. It may be the last time we're here, and I want the memory to be preserved forever."

She nibbled at his neck, managing to whisper that he had already achieved his goal, before wailing sirens muffled her voice. Within minutes, bursts of anti-aircraft fire and detonations, rumbled in the distance.

For some in the confines of that august venue, these events inspired a rush into shelters within the establishment. For the majority who remained, the lamplights now suffused almost to extinction, the raid became a spontaneous signal for the orchestra to strike up the national anthem, played and sung with gusto, lustily followed by

There will always be an England. The familiar lyric was led by a bountifully proportioned Welshman with a baritone voice to match. Everyone joined in, Richard last of all after hearing Greda's mellifluous contralto tones, recalling the words *Red, white and blue, what does it mean to you*, although little else beyond *a million marching feet*, from his days at school.

When it was finished, the Welshman boomed, "I want you all to charge your glasses and drink a toast to the King."

People reached for bubbles, beer, spirits or anything else they could find, poured their drinks, tinkled their tumblers, clinked their bottles and long-stemmed glasses and, with a resounding chorus of voices, replied, "The King!" Richard ordered more champagne and they drank in unison, savouring their intimate celebration. For the avid patriots, a recharge and a defiant, "Long live the King!" was followed by three hearty cheers for Singapore and, when one in their number called out, "The sun never sets on the British Empire," they all downed their drinks for a second time.

Neither Richard nor Greda was of a particularly nationalistic bent, finding displays of country pride and chest-thumping even *passé*. He, the self-declared cricket aficionado, might ordinarily have regarded this spectacle as an uncomfortable reminder of the bitter bodyline series a decade earlier. Yet such was the essence of the occasion that they two became symbols of an alliance that historically had always arisen when confronted by adversity. In this milieu, each was as much to the forefront as anyone else. Here was an outpouring of a very different flavour, and Richard's momentary reflection on the things that divided his country and hers were promptly cast aside, united and facing the same sinister foe. Nobody in that company could exempt themselves from the common cry. And so, they, too, were gathered up in the moment that had evolved into much more than mere bluster.

It was a demonstration of all hearts standing firm, such that if a dozen armed Japanese had walked into that ballroom there and then, they would have been set upon by every man and woman in the place, dealt with in short order by the crush of hands or whatever improvised weapons were within reach, and hang the casualties in the process.

Still they were not done, as the crowd, rebelliously downing their replenished glasses, danced on in a fervor obliterating all other considerations. The players, too, had brought their instruments to life, having instructions from the management consistent with the British tradition that, barring a direct hit, the show must go on.

Richard and Greda were on the verge of leaving when the all-clear siren whined again and forced an immediate reappraisal. He posed the question as to whether she should go back to the hospital and he to the power plant, but she would have none of it. That could happen 'all in good time', were her words. Untying the bow, Greda shook her hair free with as much defiance as anyone in that space. Her eyes betrayed the removal of the ribbon as a metaphysical release of what had once tied her. She surged outward, casting it asunder without a backward glance, waving and wishing the music would never stop.

With radiant tresses sailing around her astonishing features, Greda's purpose needed no adumbration. When squarely facing him, the colour coursing through her cheeks was replenished by the sensuality of his lips, their kisses freeing an unrestrained passion. His recently uttered words of it being the last time lingered in her mind. Within this lambent moment, she would fervently disagree. A whole future lay ahead and it was one where unbounded happiness was their preserve.

"There'll be another Raffles, Richard. Now, indubitably now, it's time for *us*, so beyond time. You must know the desire of my heart." Her eyes, her mouth, her body were transporting their spirits to but one destination.

Chapter 28

Jamal's contract

Major Newton had managed four hours repose in fifty-six. He kept to his desk during the air raid, a relatively short one with its target the hill at Bukit Timah. A large bomb had landed in the hundred-acre grounds surrounding the sumptuous domicile of the Governor Sir Shenton and Lady Thomas but, as with the Raffles patrons, they were like fixtures.

Thereafter, any thoughts of a reprieve from his duties evaporated after a signal from Jamal Viranhi, one of his last remaining operatives behind enemy lines. In recent times Viranhi was proving to be capricious, the pattern being a series of unanswered messages, then a sudden resumption of contact and elaborate dissertations to explain himself. Newton didn't have to like such a breed of man, but he suffered Viranhi for his ingenuity and originality, if little else.

Jamal's survival dictated that he remain acutely aware of everything that was going on around him, not just events relevant to his dealings with the British. Where intrigue was concerned, he was like a ferret. Information was sniffed out and devoured, mental notes always made, memory ineradicable.

After being told an important Englishman was sheltering in Johore Bahru, Viranhi had located Edward Faircrossman. The correlation between this name, the one Heenan had sometimes adopted in Malacca and that of the doctor's, engaged Viranhi's acuity. He immediately sent Newton a coded message telling of the find and relating a medical condition, chief of which being an infected leg wound. Sick and immobilised, unless he received proper treatment his life was in peril. Viranhi was swift to be self-serving, adding he had procured some quinine on the assumption that the man's other symptoms were consistent with malaria.

Newton asked whether he could be put on a boat and brought across to Singapore without being discovered. Viranhi, anticipating the query, replied that no such craft was presently able to be procured in sooner than two days. He observed that the resolve of those looking after him, mindful of the fate that would befall them if they were discovered, was beginning to falter unless some 'outlays' were furnished.

Armed with this material, a direct link with Viranhi by radio was established. "And what suggestions do you have?" The major was chary of asking such a question, knowing the answer would always require distribution of scarce resources and payment of money. Viranhi put it in the crudest of terms, 'cash for delivery'.

But this was no ordinary citizen. Rather, he was someone who had assumed a prominent role in cooperating with the Army Command in the early days of the invasion. These facts were unknown to the Japanese as far as he knew, and Newton was most certainly not going to acquaint Viranhi with them.

The major had played an unsavoury game in his discussions with Greda, characterised by a somewhat transparent insinuation respecting her husband's patriotism in the context of his liaison with Eva. When he surmised there was nothing to suggest improper behaviour, he was unprepared to concede the fact, such was his strict adherence to intelligence protocol. At the tail end of their interview, Newton received a note confirming that Faircrossman had approached the British authorities about Heenan's treachery. Besides the liaison with his mistress, which appeared to lack sinister intent, there was nothing to indicate the planter was other than a loyal subject doing what he could to further British interests. From that point on, Newton had recast the tenor of his dealings with Faircrossman's wife.

Viranhi told Newton the Englishman could be brought to a rendezvous somewhere near the Causeway. He had imposed a 'not negotiable' proviso that required the delivery to him in person of a large sum of money for 'expenses'. But Newton was not prepared for the next demand.

"And I'm sure, dear sir, you won't mind me mentioning one other request—no, may I say 'condition'. The Australian man, Kirnst, must bring the money to me, as he's the only one I know by sight. I don't intend making any unscheduled visit to Singapore, understanding dear Mr Heenan does not pine for my company."

"But that's impossible. I can't requisition this man to undertake such an assignment. He's a private citizen," replied Newton.

"There's no other way, I'm afraid, and, if it isn't soon, we might be too late. I'm sure you want to help the lady doctor, my kind sir. Mr Faircrossman has asked about her and his son, and I told him they were well. I also informed him about the Australian and how he'd managed to get them away, with some help from me."

The implacability of Viranhi's position and the finality of his demands were unmistakable. Newton appreciated his inequality of bargaining power but posited another angle.

"I'll do what I can, but it doesn't have to be him. There are others I can vouch for, and you must know we've no intention of forcing you back here. We all benefit from continuing cooperation."

"You'll forgive me, sir, if I sidestep your overtures and assurances. In my business, it pays to impose one's own strictures and to create, as you English say, binding rules, or are they mutual obligations? Maybe both," Viranhi replied insinuatingly. "I've found this an absolute guide to my continuing prosperity and good health. You understand, don't you, Major, sir? It's him or no one."

For a moment Newton entertained the thought of ceasing to deal with this man. Viranhi's usefulness was suffering from natural attrition with the invasion's approaching denouement. He could probably use the occasion to conjure some trap and, in the process, save the Crown the gold that the enterprise was going to cost, but the cards were not falling to suit his preferences and the risks of losing Faircrossman were too great. To complicate things further, Viranhi had made it clear that any rescue mission couldn't be delayed beyond one further night.

Over the next two hours, Newton deliberated about what to do. He had been unable to contact the Australian at the power station, having spoken to Bryan Williamson, who was evasive about his whereabouts. A final desperate pleading as an issue of life or death forced him to relent and reveal that Kirnst had gone to the hospital. This was the lead Newton required.

The cordiality that obtained between the doctor and the engineer had not escaped Newton's keen purview. Such was obvious from their affinity in his presence, highlighted by transparent endeavours to appear indifferent to each other. It was hardly surprising when any two people were thrust together by events beyond their control. Nor did he think their relations posed any obstacle to how Kirnst might greet this extraordinary request. What appeared plain was their conjoint desire to explore every avenue to locate her husband, hence the waiting behind, sending her son to Australia and Kirnst's support of that decision.

Newton would make clear that it was for him to accept or decline and that Viranhi had insisted on his involvement as a condition of Faircrossman being handed over. Suspicion as to why that might be crossed the major's mind, but he didn't regard it likely that any danger existed from Viranhi. Newton reckoned that the lure of a continuing financial association after British evacuation was infinitely more attractive to Viranhi than its sudden cessation in the event of failure to follow through on his promise. The greater risk involved ferrying a person from occupied territory across a tricky mote of water in a small boat.

Satisfied he had balanced all relevant considerations, Newton set to work on the logistics. He needed a reliable craft. The idea of using a fast launch decked out as a fishing boat was superficially attractive, but engine noise might draw fire on the rescuers. It needed to be big enough for Kirnst and one other person in addition to the incapacitated Faircrossman.

Newton had no hesitation about who that would be. He summoned a tough Gurkha Rifles veteran from the barracks, the type of man who would unhesitatingly grasp the opportunity to participate in this action as another step in his development as a soldier of distinguished pedigree.

Modest in stature, immensely strong, ruthless, resourceful and brave, Ranghati would be the armed back-up for the Australian and remain as invisible as a big cat stalking game. The presence of the Nepalese soldier amounted to a lethal deterrent.

Moon and tides were another factor. Impossible to row against an hour or so past running out, the waters would be equally perilous on the incoming surge. The distance depended on the area to be chosen for embarkation. Newton pegged Kranji and the nearby Woodlands in the north as the staging-points. From a chart, he noted a designated high tide was scheduled for the next day just past one AM. An hour either side of that mark would give a rescue boat without an engine a two-hour window in which to make the journey and effect the pick-up. This was adequate for the operation.

Newton would travel to Kranji to coordinate the mission. If Kirnst declined, there would be a stalemate, for a 'no-show' was not an option with a person like Viranhi. Newton trusted his instincts that Kirnst would accept.

*****

Whether it was the Singapore Slings with champagne chasers, the dancing, the rousing displays of singing, or a combination, the tremors about their future were expunged, replaced by blissful anticipation. Richard and Greda drove back to the hospital without rush or urgency, drawing on the night air's palliative infusion.

On the streets, the only change Richard discerned to that of when he had set out some hours earlier was the absence of itinerant soldiers. Such was to be expected, given the hour. Faircrossman's revolver was always with him these days, for no other reason than he had become used to being armed.

He slid it under the seat before they went into Raffles then re-positioned the gun next to his feet when they returned, prompting her remark, "You're continuing to take precautions, I see."

"It goes with me everywhere. Experience teaches in these uncertain times. You don't know who or what's about."

Just as their faces freshened, subtly, the atmospherics seemed to cool and then become pained after he began acquainting her with Williamson and Yip's preparations.

"Bryan has been in negotiations with Chia and Kwoli, and they've agreed to be part of the venture. The ship's well-provisioned, a great prospect of reaching Australia unscathed, and, with the Japs just shy of invading Singapore, we need to consider that now, Greda."

Hesitation obstructed her reply. "Just so, Richard, but aren't there other ships leaving almost around-the-clock?"

"You're still holding out." He sighed in frustration. "It's not going to happen, Greda."

Richard broke off. He checked his speed in approaching the open hospital gates. A soldier, rifle at the ready, appeared in front of them, signalling him to stop. Richard complied, though he sensed something was amiss. No guards had been posted there earlier.

Two other uniformed men materialised from behind the stone pillars on either side, each levelling his weapon. They were the same group he had seen earlier impeding his path, except then they weren't carrying guns.

"We ashya to stop 'n' remain where ya are in da guvna's name," slurred a single-striper with a familiar accent, the same man who fisted his bonnet. "I wanchya to state yer bizness and explain what yer doin' in posseshun of a miltry vehicle."

Richard searched for a calm response. "I'm just going to the hospital. This lady's my wife. She could be having a miscarriage and we need urgent medical attention."

"Ya 'ear that, lads? I'm all ears, so what's 'er bloody problem?" His demeanour, unreceptive to an answer, he continued to ramble. "If it's attenshuns the buggers want, then it's bloody attenshuns they'll get alright, ya can bank on that. Attenshun be damned. I'll give 'er me attenshuns in a minute. I'll guarantee ya that, missus. Me intenshuns are pure as the driven snow, I ashure ya, lady." He laughed for a few moments, then looked darkly at his compatriots' apparent reticence to join in. "All's I think, and these boys 'ere know, is yer both spies."

They hoped for the arrival of an ambulance or a nightwatchman.

"Don't speak, but be ready," Richard whispered, shuffling his foot to bring the revolver within reach.

"Now, ya just stay where y'are or I'll let ya have it," the spokesman continued, brandishing the point of the gun uncomfortably close to Richard's head. "You, hey, missus, get outa ya seat and come 'round 'ere into da light and let's 'ave a look atcha."

Richard touched her hand to signify she should comply, muttering, "Do as he says."

"Now, boys, I wanchya to guard this big 'orrible lookin' bastard 'ere, while I give 'er some of *my* attenshuns. I got me first aid. I'll 'ave examinashuns of 'er, eh, Josh, while ya watch this prick. Then yer turn next, ya ugly grub."

He leered at Greda as she alighted and walked in front of the headlights. "She don't seem too preggo to me, boys, no gut on 'er, but how would I fuckin' know, eh? Spose s'up t'me ta find out." Laughing, he took a long swig and pitched the bottle down the hill, nearly overbalancing, but corrected himself before Richard could react.

"Harry, mate, we'd better be careful near the 'ospital, we're pretty much in the open, ya know," mumbled the distinctly more sober Josh.

"Good thinkin' cock. I got me torch 'ere, so ya stand by and I'll be over there in the bushes. I gotta look at ya, missus, so get over 'ere'n take that gear 'n' knickers off. I'm not Superman, don't 'ave x-ray vision. Keep 'er covered, will ya, Mick? I gotta get me duds off too. Wouldn't be fair, would it, lady, if just one of us was starkers?"

"I am not taking anything off, you inebriated, dreadful, wretched creature."

"Did ya 'ear that, boys, with that plummy pommie accent, too? 'I am not takin' anythin' off, you 'ebrated, dreadful, wretched creature,'" he mimed. "I ain't wretched, am I, Mick? Or too dweadful either and 'ebrated? Is that a posh word for bein' a bit full? Bloody oath and fuckin' desperately retchin' for a root maybe."

He tore the front of Greda's dress. She reacted instantly, raking her nails across his face, and he released a bellowing oath.

Richard seized the split-second he needed to spring from the jeep, revolver in hand, kneeing the soldier who was covering him in the solar plexus and whipped his temple. "Get going, Greda! Run!" he yelled, and watched as she headed for the hospital. To the other man he roared, "Now, drop that gun, you dog. On your stomach."

Richard placed his boot carelessly on Josh's head, but he was far from subdued. In trying to gain his feet, Josh twisted his body and Richard fell, but not before kicking the soldier, knocking him down and out.

Knife in hand and teeth bared in a deathly, snarling grin, Greda's assailant rushed the prostrate Richard, whose pistol cracked into service. The bullet shattered the soldier's kneecap, leaving him rolling in agony on the grass.

Richard sprang up, pointing the weapon at the last man. "Now, do you want some of this, too, Mick? Get down!" he screamed out, firing another round. Crouching over, Mick became compliant, interlocking his hands behind his neck.

With the group's leader writhing and holding his bloodied knee, before any coherent reaction from the third recalcitrant, a smattering of people, including several security personnel, arrived on the scene.

"The screecher might need some medical attention, although the priority for a cur like that is very low, and this one, Mick, well, he looks like he's going quietly," Richard reported. "Has anybody seen Dr Greda Faircrossman?" he called out.

"I'm here, Richard." A nurse's red cape was draped around her shoulders.

"As if we don't have enough to contend with," he said through clenched teeth. "Are you okay?"

"Yes, but it's you I'm worried about."

As they moved towards the hospital reception, the impolite clerk, now contrite, intercepted them. "Excuse me, sir, I've an urgent message. You're Mr Kirnst from the Works Department?"

"Yes, but this situation was not of my making—"

"You're required back at the power station by the manager."

Richard looked at Greda impotently.

"It's as will be," she said. "You have to go."

"Damn it. Damn bloody everything." His exasperation was short-lived as she pressed her palm onto his cheek, her words stilted by the presence of those around them.

"There'll be another time, a chance for us Richard, soon, believe me."

*****

"No hits, job well going," was the Asian greaser's response as Richard pulled up. He pointed phlegmatically towards Bryan Williamson, comatose in a lounge chair outside the office, the neck of an almost empty bottle of champagne still retaining some unity with his left hand. Nothing could wake him, nor did Richard want to, as he rummaged around on his desk for any signs of the urgency that had been impressed on him. By the phone lay a note he recognised as having been written by his colleague stating that Major Newton had called and wanted to speak to him. He dialed the number and a voice shorn of its customary polity was heard down a crackly line.

"Ah yes, Kirnst. I need to see you. This is a matter of the utmost priority."

"What's it about?" Richard was perplexed by the request at this time of night.

"Can you come to the barracks now?"

"Why, yes," he replied hesitantly. "I should confirm my absence with the manager though. How long will this take?"

The question went unanswered. "I'll arrange for that approval without you troubling yourself. My car will arrive in four minutes."

Many different scenarios coursed through Richard's mind as he was taken to Fort Canning. One was more troubling than any of the others. The major ushered him into his office without any formality. He seemed in no mood to bandy words.

"Sit down."

"No worries, Major," Kirnst acquiesced, trying to appear unruffled. The least importunate prospect he'd entertained for this peremptory summons was that it had a connection to Heenan. But as Newton's keen eyes bored into him, it provoked a guilty intuition of awareness on the major's part that he'd been cavorting at Raffles with Faircrossman's wife.

"I'll come straight to the point. I've established the whereabouts of the doctor's husband."

Richard's shoulders flexed hard against the chair as if his chest had been poked by a hot taper. He attempted to assume a dispassionate aspect.

"Well, that's a turn-up. Here in Singapore? When did he arrive?" reading in Newton's demeanour more than sublime curiosity at the rapidity of his responses.

"If it were so, you wouldn't be here now. He's across the causeway on Johore Bahru."

"Is his wife aware of this?"

Newton sensed his disquiet. "No, nor will she be told just yet. He's quite unwell, probably suffering from malaria, and has a very bad leg, which means he cannot make any distance on foot without assistance."

"Are you sure he's alive?"

"I've no reason to doubt it. You met Jamal Viranhi in Malacca and might recall speaking to him just before you left. He was quite complimentary about you in our discussions."

"I vaguely remember something but, Major, so what?"

Richard was surprised that the challenge didn't earn a frown.

"Viranhi can bring him to a handover point tentatively proposed at just west of the Causeway."

"Yes, well, that's all very interesting, but what has it to do with me?" He took several deep breaths before adding, "I'm pleased for his family and, if I can help in some way, I will. However—"

"I won't beat about the bush, Mr Kirnst." Richard gave a curt nod. Newton began to enunciate the job of repatriating Faircrossman, and about the delivery, to be paid in gold and on an inflexible condition.

"He wants me! Why?" Richard asked in amazement.

"I've wondered, too, but then he said he knows your face and trusts only you. He thinks Faircrossman would be more at ease going with someone familiar to him. But, otherwise, you might be able to enlighten me, although it hardly matters. I thought that, because Viranhi had developed a rapport with you—"

"'Rapport' wouldn't be my term. I did speak with the man. I guess he noted the way things were handled when we nabbed Heenan. Come to think of it, he did ask a few questions. I felt a bit uneasy, although I can't now think why. He was overly friendly, at times even fawning, but it was a pretty shocking event. I'd just seen a mortally stricken woman carried away. She worked in with him to trap Heenan, and he knew about Mrs Faircrossman, the boy and the fact that her husband was missing."

Richard began to remember more of the discussion with Viranhi, whom he had assumed to be an ally, but then reflected that he may have been incautious in being so forthcoming. "You obviously seem to know this cove. Can you trust him?"

"On balance, yes. He provided an accurate description of Dr Faircrossman's husband, even down to a mole on his neck. Nonetheless, to be perfectly candid, I'm not sure I have much choice, and that's where the dangers assume some significance. I've discussed with my commanding officer the nature of the proposed mission and also sourced a formidable member of the Gurkha regiment. If you volunteer," Newton's voice dripped with emphasis, "he'll be your guide to the rendezvous. As to the drop-off and exchange, Viranhi was insistent that you be alone. I'll have him think that demand was being observed of course, for I would never put anyone in that position, no soldier, no civilian and no officer."

He contemplated Richard with magnanimity. "And while I'm on that topic, you'd better ready yourself further. It's an additional instruction, an army requirement if you like, one with which compliance is mandatory or the operation won't be taking place. You must be commissioned. Your identity would be changed for obvious reasons."

"Whoa, Major, that's going mighty fast, I'm not qualified to be an officer, not even an ordinary private," Richard said, shaking his head and forcing a smile.

"You're refusing, then?"

Richard fidgeted and then stretched both arms out in front, dovetailing his fingers in a gesture defining both indecision and perplexity. "No, I'm not saying anything. How's it possible for me to be commissioned?"

Newton looked at him, his deep-set eyes, ringed with black shadows, unblinking. "You're superbly fitted. The extraordinary journey overland, the liquidation of those guerillas of which the doctor lauded you, the confrontation with Heenan, and I've a report from Suggiss saying you're a born leader of men. Do you want me to go on? And need I mention what transpired a short time ago?"

Richard shook his head in bewilderment, "Yes, I have eyes everywhere, Mr Kirnst. Those men you dealt with single-handedly, the 'stragglers' as is being put about, deserters and cowards the lot of them, worse than wild animals," Newton's language especially strident. "And you hold a chief engineer's double certificate. Ordinarily that qualification would mean automatic entitlement to the rank of captain, which is the designation that will be conferred, if you accept and do this thing. Of course, it's your choice."

How simplistic everything sounded, summarised by the astute intelligence officer, not shy of bestowing some flattery. Richard shifted uneasily as the major considered his reaction. "I'd at least like to think about it, or do you need an answer on the spot?"

"I can give you some minutes," he replied bluntly, then almost as an afterthought, "and the other important thing to consider is that the army has taken over the running of public utilities. You would continue in your current engineering role but henceforth as a commissioned officer having overall responsibility for maintaining the power plant. Anyway, it's your call and while you consider the proposal it will permit me an opportunity to obtain a tenth cup of coffee. I imagine you won't dismiss strong and black? No milk to hand, I'm afraid, or sugar either."

Richard was sapped and weary, not so much from the absence of any rest for close to twenty-four hours, but now burdened with condign responsibility. This was a service morality would forbid him from declining. True, he was somewhat chuffed about being offered a commission in the British Army, which, judging by the military exigencies imperilling the colony, was going to be one of the shortest careers he'd ever enjoyed, even with the opportunity to keep the lights on a little longer.

In acquiescing to the mission, he would be instrumental in an action destined, through success anyway, to link the woman he loved with her husband. The very notion defied every dream entertained when dancing with Greda so short a time ago. He had reconciled the dilemmas, weighed the conflicting considerations and resolved there was nothing standing in their way. And an opportunity to take her back to Australia beckoned. Richard did not wish Edward Faircrossman any ill fortune, yet, even now, he found himself reviling the arrogance of a man who had taken his wife for granted. This was a doleful excuse for an individual, consorting with Eva, almost young enough to be his granddaughter. Faircrossman, who knew better and had so much, thought so little of his family then.

Delicately, other notions supervened. Richard was being asked to attempt something no one else could: save that husband and father. He re-lived the boy's recent proposition of them all being together. Jonathon would quickly forget that when his parents reunited in Sydney. For a time, Greda might long to have his arms around her, but even unhappy marriages had a habit of transitioning through their peaks and troughs. Being constrained to linger in Singapore through romantic illusions about undying love had blinded him to the residue of feelings personified by their son and a long period together. Believing Greda might have held a strong suspicion that her husband had been unfaithful but overlooked the indiscretion assisted Richard in his counterveiling assessments, as did her hesistancy at the hospital gates.

There was no choice to make, yet its wretched ethics overwrought him.

So, like the boy who had been taught in Sunday school at the little country Methodist church, Richard sought guidance, entreating his Maker that the task ahead could be achieved and Edward Faircrossman saved. Mostly, he beseeched for the courage to say farewell to Greda forever.

The major remained silent for some minutes, seeing a man not reliant on fate alone, but seeking the guidance of a higher power. Newton's service knew all too well it was the resort of almost every soldier confronting his mortality.

Richard rose, and abandoned himself to a reckless exhilaration. He swallowed the coffee and blenched. "Now, about those captain's stripes?"

"Epaulettes, Mr Kirnst."

Chapter 29

Rowing to Johore

Sergeant Deepak Ranghati was an organic man-of-war, so much being evident from a cursory glance at his physique. Standing only five foot six inches tall, head and shoulders beneath Richard, each other physical attribute beamed immense strength: a cannonball head atop a parapet neck, bulging biceps, sinews tying forearms to wrists rippled when flexed and squat legs with calves as broad as a foremast. When he saluted Richard, now kitted out in khaki, Ranghati's jaw, unusually square-set for a person of Nepalese ethnicity, jutted out like a blacksmith's anvil.

The greeting that followed their introduction evinced modesty as well. Richard doubted he had ever met a more intimidating individual, having been forewarned by Newton that this 'efficient killing machine' was the only man for the task ahead. He felt like the skipper of a cricket team handing the bright red cherry to the world's fastest bowler who knew precisely what was required on a green top.

Newton, Ranghati and Richard drove to Kranji and thence to Woodlands, arriving as a sly evening was setting in. A *kelong*, from where their boat would be launched, guarded a discreet waterway through the mangroves that opened to the Johore Strait. Here they would lodge until given the signal to move. Richard peered across at a sprinkle of lights, lost in a count and wondering how many represented enemy encampments.

Irregular showers from an expectant sky came and went. This afforded the best protection they could wish for, if the conditions held. There was little breeze. Forecasts had been encouraging, although all knew that clouds could just as suddenly dissipate and even a waning moon remained capable of giving up their movements.

They inspected the boat. It was sixteen feet in length, robust and replicating the lines of a nineteenth-century whaler. In the middle was a seat for the oarsman, as well as one to the stern. Forward of its centre line was an area where a gurney had been rigged to accommodate Faircrossman. The gunnels were high enough to provide some shelter for any figure in that position, yet its draught was not so projected as to cause undue difficulty navigating the shallows on either bank or the creek chosen for the rendezvous. Ranghati, covered by a tarpaulin on the trip over, would be lurking at the stern.

Once the tide was halfway in, the boat, tied to one of the stilts, would be floating. For the first twenty or so yards, Newton would guide it beyond the mangroves and into the waters of the strait itself, with the distance to the opposite shoreline almost a mile.

The bulk of the Japanese forces were thought to be encamped further west of the Causeway than the exchange point. Viranhi had argued that soldiers preparing for invasion were the least interested in monitoring departures, and it was the place nearest to where Faircrossman was hidden, but gaining this section of the mainland required greater rowing for the rescuers. Newton wanted to mount a crossing close to the Causeway given the lesser expanse of water and comparatively easier launching and landing areas. Ultimately a compromise was reached that had the exchange just over one hundred yards west. Based on intuition rather than on-the-ground intelligence, Viranhi's protestations and assurances aside, it was where patrols were least likely to be encountered.

The greatest peril lay in the changeover itself. The significance for Newton of the selected position was the presence of a well-concealed narrow creek with reasonable egress for those bearing a man whose condition was uncertain. Viranhi assured Newton that the planter could hobble and that bearers would assist in the transfer.

After some further wrangling, the exchange was set for fifteen minutes past midnight.

Ranghati had a variety of weapons stowed in the dinghy, chief of which were two fully-magazined sub-machine guns, a revolver and six hand-grenades. Richard became hypnotised by his feathered honing of the *kukri's* blade on a stone, only returning it to its scabbard with forbidding satisfaction after testing its utility. Newton questioned Richard's weapon of choice, the non-issue revolver, but his subordinate wouldn't countenance parting with it since the piece had served him so well.

The final briefing from Newton was explicit. "Should discovery occur before you get there, the mission is to be aborted. You must avoid being captured at all costs, even if you have to swim back to this side and abandon the planter. If there's any suggestion of a change to the deal or fresh demands, or, dare I say, indicia of treachery, Viranhi is to be liquidated. Sergeant Ranghati will deal with such contingencies. "Faircrossman's repatriation is the priority, subject to your own welfare. There's an element of discretion. I cannot anticipate every eventuality. Know what I have in mind and you'll understand everything that needs to be done." Detecting Richard's perturbation, he added, "highlighting risks and exigencies is necessary and appreciating them will see you through." He also made it clear that there was little to be said about Viranhi by way of redeeming features, save that their relations to date had been without mishap. Richard called to mind the man's Machiavellian traits.

"Sir, this isn't a case of me going lukewarm. I neither expect cast-iron guarantees nor am I regarding this as an evening's crabbing," the observation yielding elasticity in Newton's static features.

"Well, that's as it should be, Captain. Caution must rule, but Viranhi will want a full return for the service. That would be difficult if he were to tip off the Japs. Nor is he the type to share, having an adept knowledge of simple mathematics, where one into his fee equals his return for service but another party might put the whole in jeopardy."

"We will get Faircrossman out."

"You can do it. Avoid any shooting unless it's absolutely necessary, for that would spell real trouble. I needn't observe that capture would not be healthy, and you aren't expected to lay down your lives if things go awry. Now, rest up. Expect to be called in two hours."

Richard tossed and wriggled and then lay awake. Curled up on a groundsheet as if he was bivouacking on a chaise longue before a game of chess, Ranghati's blissful slumbering from the opposite corner of the hut gave him heart. Both were dressed in fisherman's clothes.

He thought of the boy. Jon had told how he wanted to be like his father, go to university and reach similar heights. He spoke of being with him everywhere when on vacation, his father's influence seeming to push the lad in a business direction in advance of his years. Jon had related their visits to Port Swettenham, where he learnt how the enterprise worked and explained the regimen for tending to the trees, harvesting their latex and planting new sections. He drove the old plantation vehicle under his dad's supervision and once, to his mother's considerable consternation, without it. As they talked, Richard couldn't help but take in Greda's expressions. Sometimes embarrassment shaped her face after Jon heaped copious plaudits on his father and she steered the conversation to the sea. The boy liked that talk, too.

Outside, the cacophonous night symphony rose and fell eerily, and inflowing eddies lapped the stilts. Ranghati sprang up wide awake and ready when Newton ascended the stairs. Below, their boat knocked, tolling their hour to leave. Richard found it uncanny that those disparate sounds managed to prevail over a choir of countless frogs croaking in opposition to all other nocturnal murmurings.

Ranghati told Richard he would be over the side when they were within a chain of the creek's mouth. It was an area with which he was familiar, and his compass would direct the other's rowing so the entry could be reached with pinpoint accuracy. Richard laid a rifle with full magazine in the bow and his weapon was tucked behind his back.

The weight of gold surprised him when Newton lifted it over. "Remember, don't part with it until you have Faircrossman strapped in. But, again, if it comes to your safety or that of the target, its disposition has to be secondary. Your primary task is to rescue the planter. Good luck. Pull hard. It's an hour's turnaround. I'll have a squad of armed men here and ready to act if you need to fight your way back."

Newton guided the craft between two lines of black twine tied on either side of the little channel. Less than a mile away a smattering of lights flickered. The sky was quilted by heavy cloud as the craft was pushed out. Richard, in the central oarsman's station, commenced to pull against an appreciable incoming current, taking care not to create a wake. He hadn't rowed since a spell as oarsman in the eights during an inter-school regatta, but this was an entirely different sortie. The modest tidal movement proved useful in muffling the sound of oars meeting water, but progress was not earned easily.

Their course had been chosen very deliberately to avoid detection. It took them several yards away from the camouflage of overhanging trees lining the bank of the island and roughly parallel to it, until they reached a position almost opposite the entrance to the creek entry on the other side, as the compass dictated. The water depth along this route was not consistent and in one section they bottomed. Ranghati, anticipating the problem before they stuck fast, slipped noiselessly over the side to pilot the boat into deeper water. That he regained the craft without appreciable disturbance was, Richard surmised, an exceptional feat.

Now the critical tacking position had been reached, the left oar was deployed to bring the boat in a direct line to their landing place. Finding the point of entry was not something that could be achieved solely through reckoning alone, as Newton had warned, having arranged for Viranhi to signal with three flashes to guide their approach. If in five minutes there was no visual, he would repeat the action.

Time was on their side as Richard worked the oars. Ranghati was whispering instructions to keep it on course. Near-silence had to be maintained, yet a noise inflicting most anguish was the drumbeat distending Richard's chest. His sense of disquiet was heightened when Ranghati, now in the water, began trailing the stern.

Reversing his body, he peered straight over the bow, straining to discern the hoped-for signal after noticing the hands of his watch had parted company from the vertical position. Close to the edge, as the seconds passed endlessly, he wondered whether he would need to turn the boat side-on to the shore.

When the flashes came, he was uncertain how far the boat was from their objective but then discerned the creek's mouth. One further pull and the bow nudged inside. Richard resorted to a smaller implement, for oars were useless in this confined area. By now, assistance from the stern courtesy of Ranghati, had ceased and, as he closed in on the rendezvous, his paddle became the sole means of propulsion. Incoming tidal movement served to take him along the tiny waterway. Just after passing through a gap so narrow that he used both hands to grab overhanging branches as a guide, the creek opened into a lagoon wide enough to permit the craft to be turned around completely. This was the spot, but there was still no follow-up signal from ashore. He cushioned the craft against a tongue of bank, stepping off to secure the tieline to an upturned log.

"I see you've made it, Mr Kirnst." The insinuating voice issuing from the blackness startled him. Richard shielded his eyes as he identified the form stepping forward. "Remember me, Jamal Viranhi at your service, sir. And you have my present?"

"That goes for us both," Richard's assertive response unsettling him.

"Of course, my dear friend, in good time," Viranhi replied suspiciously. "You surely don't think I'd come here alone," a rhetorical riposte rather than a question. Viranhi turned away to converse with an unseen person. "Here he is. Say hello, Mr Edward Faircrossman."

Richard could see the silhouette, his arm around a man supporting him, as they edged to the waterline. Torchlight on his face and body confirmed that Faircrossman had lost considerable weight. He wore tattered grey shorts, a filthy, holed shirt and was barefoot. His left leg from the knee to the upper thigh was swathed in stained bandages, the odour emanating from the wound pronounced.

"Thank God you're here, old man, but how?" The less robust voice underlined his fragile physicality.

"Explanations can wait. I must get you bedded down and away. Try not to make a sound." He took Faircrossman's right arm.

More instructions were issued by Viranhi. Richard pulled the line securing the boat as far as it would go and stepped into the water. With the assistance of the other man, he lifted the Englishman onto the stretcher.

There was no sign of Ranghati, but that fact didn't trouble him. He could stalk around like a Sumatran tiger as he chose.

"I'm very thankful you came by yourself. It seems one can trust the British after all. Now, something for me, regretfully, I must ask again."

The box was placed on the ground in front of Viranhi. He went through an elaborate pantomime of feeling its weight, opening it, kneeling down, shining the light on its contents and tipping them out to examine each individual sovereign.

Richard squatted beside him. "It's all there. Every last one."

Viranhi waved the torch irritatingly in Richard's face. "We mustn't be impulsive. I'm a patient man. You be, too, and wait until I'm satisfied the bargain has been fulfilled. Just sit down." He patted Richard's lower back. "Oh, and what's this?" In a split second he had removed the revolver, flinging it into the darkness. "I sense duplicity."

"Protection only."

Viranhi thrusting the barrel of his pistol into Richard's ribs was his only response. Viranhi issued a torrent of orders to his associate. Richard cursed himself for not having been more alert. Was this just a staying action from a nervous conniver while the coins were counted? Trying to sound calm, he asked Viranhi whether he was satisfied with the quantity and quality of the pay-off, but his question was ignored. He tried to draw solace from a belief in Ranghati's proximity and his having understood every word uttered.

There was nothing immediate he could do but play along, again attempting to engage his adversary. "You'll find the sum complete, solid gold sovereigns of the realm."

The moon chanced to appear, revealing Viranhi's repulsive face which complemented a severe case of halitosis as he spoke. "Well, it's all there. I'm very grateful. And you have your man. He'll soon be in clean linen."

"Good. Then the deal's done. We seem to be concluded here. Time's going, the tide's beginning to turn," Richard said briskly, conscious of the prodding steel.

"It's already turned for you, Mr Kirnst. You'll be elated to know there's a price on your head. Something about the murder of soldiers on bikes up-country near the Malacca River. I daresay you recall the occasion?"

"That's ridiculous, I've no interest—"

"You protest too strongly, my dear sir. Shall I enliven your memory? His Eminence Hirohito has desired your company for some time. I know all things, so don't act surprised. It didn't mean anything until I heard, most pertinently, that the wanted man had been travelling with a woman and a boy. Remember now? When you undertake executions like those, you ensure no one is around. Malayan jungle has many eyes and mouths. You must know they sing for tiny pence. And everything was clear, but most of all the large reward I found irresistible. You see, Mr Kirnst, I've few scruples, if the price is right, and in this case it was you and the Englishman, I would go close to doubling my emoluments. And that awful surprise at sea, how sad for Eva."

Richard's attempt to regain his feet was stymied by the butt of Viranhi's pistol. His body wavered more in shock than anything else, knees squelching the soft ground before he sat, cognisant of blood trickling down his face. Viranhi spoke to his accomplice, who withdrew.

Just twenty paces into the blackness, an iron forearm flexed, snapping the man's neck as if it was a twig and as noiselessly.

"Now, Mr Kirnst, slowly up, sir!" Viranhi said abruptly. "Up now, do what I say, for you're my prisoner."

Viranhi called out insistently in Malay.

"I'm sorry to inconvenience you, Mr Faircrossman, but you won't be taking that trip after all with your Australian friend. I've changed my mind. You're going to fall into the water. How about we tie you to the anchor rope? You'll have a chance to swim over to the other side. It's only a short distance for we'll take you halfway across—"

Beyond the sound of a deathly gurgle, the rest of the sentence never issued from his throat, which had been cut from ear to ear by the Gurkha's flashing *kukri*, crumpling him like a carcass in a back-alley abattoir.

Richard had scarcely appreciated Viranhi's execution when Ranghati told him they must leave immediately. "Are you alright to row, sir? I see only scratch, and so keep lookout."

"All dead? Is that what you're saying?" Richard asked incredulously.

"Sorry, Captain, couldn't bring Viranhi back. He would squeal, I certain of it, and Japanese swarming around us no time. And after these plots here, the major not want him. I just tow his body out into deep water and do to him as he was going to do to Mr Faircrossman, but he's beyond feeling anything, and sir, here, give box back to our major. I push you off."

*****

Newton ran his fingers through the sovereigns and deigned a faint smile at the success of the mission. Viranhi might be floating in the South China Sea for all he knew or cared. He could have been useful locked away and under interrogation, but to speculate was redundant. In hindsight, insistence that Kirnst be involved in the rescue was, Newton had to concede, an intelligence lapse, given that he overlooked Richard's status as an individual wanted by the Japanese.

From Kranji, Newton accompanied the Englishman in the ambulance, taking him to the Alexandra Military Hospital. Apart from his leg wound, he appeared to be in better shape than Newton had imagined.

Responding to questions regarding his wife and son, Newton was circumspect, merely saying they had made it through to Singapore and she would come to see him presently. "Dr Faircrossman's working at the General Hospital and is unaware of your rescue. I should just emphasise that she had the opportunity to leave Singapore, but wouldn't do so until definite word about you was received and—"

"You needn't tell her I'm here, her constancy no doubt on display in Mr Kirnst's company," Faircrossman cut in abruptly, "and what about my son, damn it? You seem to be avoiding that issue."

"He was evacuated some time ago." Newton returned imperturbably.

"Alone? That bloody stupid woman; how could it be so?" he expostulated. "Why wouldn't she have gone with him and why didn't you make her? What the hell are you hopeless army people doing?"

Newton's patience was being tested, and he shot back with pronounced vigour.

"There's no need to raise your voice, Mr Faircrossman. Your son is being well looked after, along with the many other children evacuated with him. I personally arranged for his passage. The ship is steaming to Sydney under destroyer escort. Once he's disembarked, your sister-in-law will assume his care. Try to understand, your wife faced an agonising dilemma and she chose to wait and find out about you."

"I'm not interested in your palaver. The wellbeing of my son's all I want to know about."

Newton was used to dealing with buffoons. This one was arrogant, too, and it was time to discharge a volley in his direction. "Then you won't be interested in hearing about Carrie, although she was someone with whom you were involved?"

There was protracted silence as Newton regarded the other man intently. The light in the rear of the vehicle was not so dim as to disguise Faircrossman's discomfiture. Like a chess player, he froze, unable to formulate the next move without sureness of its efficacy.

Sensing the absence of bluff, he started to smile, resuming in a modulated tone, "You're a man of the world, Major," he drawled, "Army Intelligence, you said earlier. Experienced, I imagine. Know what it's like to be away from home for long—"

"You'll permit *me*, I decline your palaver also."

"What about her, then?" Faircrossman had dropped the mask. "Yes, I know Carrie, and I suppose you have her back there singing like a canary. What's she saying about me?"

"As a spy for the Japanese," was Newton's canny retort, eager for an indignant reaction. "You must have been aware of her activities, hmm?"

"That's ridiculous! What sort of fool do you take me for? Are you implying she was using me to get information for the enemy? I was their prisoner, shot at! You see this stinking bloody leg, don't you? I escaped." He raised his voice again. "I'll have you know that I'm acquainted with officers at the highest level of the British Army. You'll answer to your superiors were I to inform them of your outrageous imputations."

"I needn't impute, Mr Faircrossman. It's not illegal to have an Asian mistress. But the threats you make demean you. I shall, for the present, put them down to your having been through protracted privation. It was I who sanctioned your rescue, which put several lives at risk, including the Australian's."

"Ah, well, he owes me one," snorted Faircrossman dismissively.

Newton sighed. "You can also thank the initiative of one of my best men, and congratulate your wife that you're here most of all, for without her representations on your behalf, well—" He paused for effect, deliberately overplaying her input. "I'll just say, seeing you here now and listening to you, I have my doubts whether I would have troubled myself, if not for my orders. I have many other more pressing matters with which to deal."

Faircrossman knew there was little point in furthering the conversation along the dangerous route it was taking. "Of course," he said, on the defensive again, "between gentlemen like us, my wife would know nothing of the woman, ah, Carrie, I imagine?"

"Perhaps you should ask her, Mr Faircrossman."

The ambulance was entering the built-up areas of Singapore town, a full five minutes elapsing before Faircrossman spoke again. "I'm sure, if she did anything wrong, it wasn't really her fault, you know. She had family in China and things were very hard for them. I'd be willing to vouch for her on that score." Newton didn't reply. "You understand, Major?" Still silence, before Faircrossman cribbed further. "I'd like to speak with her. Are you able to arrange for Carrie to visit the hospital discreetly? We don't want her and Greda running into each other." He truncated his laugh when no reaction emanated from the front of the vehicle. "Ah, might be a trifle awkward, Major. Are you with me?"

Newton's response was terse. "Indeed, though you mightn't need to fear that happening."

"I'm grateful to you, then, Major," he hesitated.

The vehicle stopped at the entrance to the hospital. Newton was at the rear when the doors were opened. He signalled an orderly to bring a wheelchair.

"You haven't answered me, Major. So, can you have her see me privately?"

"I apologise to you, sir, if I've been disingenuous. No, I can't let you see Carrie presently, in an hour's time or even a day's. You needn't worry about any awkward meetings; for she didn't make it. Good day. I'll just pass on your appreciation to the men who risked their lives to rescue you."

*****

During the morning of the ninth of February, 1942, a radio broadcast informed the island's residents that the Japanese had landed on the north-west shores the previous night. The report was accompanied by overtures that the incursion had been confined. Operations were continuing, it said, to mop up the remnants of the force, suggesting it had been a bungled attempt to gain a foothold.

Behind closed doors at Fort Canning, the military and strategic reality was far from even approaching normalcy. The north-western sector was being defended by the twenty-second Australian Brigade, supported by the eighth Australian Division, under the command of General Bennett. Relations between he and General Percival were at an irretrievable juncture. The latter had cabled General Wavell that the enemy had penetrated five miles inland. The situation was serious, and Percival was marshalling his forces for what would be a final stand.

Tengah airfield had capitulated that afternoon, and Colonel Tsuji, wandering through the officer's mess, beamed with pleasure. Noting clothes and suitcases strewn around and warm bowls of soup on the tables, he told Yamashita the enemy was in disarray. The Japanese general climbed a low cliff to gain his first foothold on the island. He was watched by a bedraggled group of demoralised prisoners, who, a few hours earlier, had been holding that very ground.

Meanwhile, Percival spent the evening in his office next to the British operations room in Sime Road. Sleep for him that night, when he finally set about it, would prove elusive, with the incessant clatter of typewriters and raised voices bellowing down feeble telephone connections. He cut a lonely figure. Discipline among his troops was breaking down and strategic territory was being ceded with barely a shot discharged. The loss of the airfield followed the relocation of the few Hurricanes left, ending the last semblance of air cover. Percival had become convinced that capitulation was just days away.

Denialism, redolent in the wider community, walked with complacency. While people expected to see widespread damage from bombs, key buildings that remained intact were regarded as some indication that the defenders were containing the advance and eventually the enemy would be pushed back into the straits. The central business district was relatively unscathed, and Raffles glided on. Fire stations were functioning, albeit with increased workloads. Port infrastructure had been hit, while buildings along the waterfront were largely unmarked. The most potent change was that shipping numbers in the harbour were nothing to what had been seen in the bustling pre-war days. One of those remaining ships was a dishevelled, eight-hundred-ton hulk languishing at anchor in Keppel Harbour. The *Pelangi*, its name indistinguishable on the bow as rust streaks had debrided the letters, demanded to be broken up as an act of mercy. In a calculated ploy to give all who saw her another reason to think she was in imminent danger of foundering, a pronounced list had become evident.

Chapter 30

Reappraisal

An unsightly swelling on Richard's forehead responded to the application of an ice pack during the first hours of his return from Kranji. He couldn't afford rest and attended at the power station in civilian clothes to check on the machinery, before returning to the barracks where Newton had arranged permanent quarters. Eventually, he managed some thankless sleep. A dream found him on a ship about to sail when Greda, vivacious and carefree in a white skirt and pink blouse that left no room for conjecture, boarded hand-in-hand with Faircrossman. As becomes honeymooners, they gamboled in a grand spectacle, she being carried across the cabin's threshold. Her husband's kicking the door shut against Richard's face shook him free. In unfamiliar surroundings, his headache grew immeasurably worse when he rose and dressed for the scheduled appointment with Newton.

"On time, though far from being lachrymose after your sortie, Captain Kirnst," the other muttered laconically, yawning and retrieving a bulky file from his cabinet. "Jamal Viranhi. Well, that's to be archived or, more likely, destroyed. You'll be interested to know our man's under army medical care. I'm told he's comfortable, and his leg is being assessed."

Richard seemed on the point of saying something, but Newton wasn't finished. "You must be done in, power station under your aegis again, though there's no disguising the weighty matters caressing your mind."

"I was there incognito. Thanks for setting me up in these digs."

"Well, come on, let's hear it."

"Have you told her that he's back?"

"No. Do you offer a suggestion?"

"I'd prefer that you waited a bit."

Newton blind-sided the observation. "Didn't particularly warm to that Faircrossman character. We save his life and he wants to make mine harder by hinting to go upstairs. I feel a little sorry for his wife. Very disagreeable; the sort of upper-class haughtiness one expects in the circles in which I'm sometimes required to mix. I suppose he's been knocked about a bit, but ingratitude never earns exculpation. Now, let me speak of the antonym, for that's what he owes you: his eternal appreciation. How *is* the head, by the way? I see the swelling's gone down."

Perversely, Richard chose to defend Faircrossman. "He wasn't like that before all this. Just chockfull of self-importance. The head, sir, yes, it's working. I'm lucky to be blessed with a hard nut."

"That's good. Now pay attention, Captain. Military intelligence personnel will commence being evacuated tomorrow. You're included, too, given you've a mission under your belt and that they're after you. Our orders have come from Percival himself. End of operations in the Far East is imminent. The Rising Sun has landed and isn't setting anytime soon. We were fortunate to get away from Kranji when we did."

"I see," became the measure of Richard's mood. "Sir, I'm unsure what I'll be doing, but I won't be leaving here until the Faircrossmans are tucked up and away. I've promised that to the boy and, ah, to myself."

Newton would ordinarily have regarded such a statement as tantamount to insubordination but saw, from the look in his eyes, that what Richard had said didn't stem from any challenge to his authority. "Captain, I don't wish to sound officious, but let me repeat, that was an order from the top, through my colonel to me. Of course, there may be ways around it."

"Sir, I need to tell you a few things. I might be a 'commissioned officer'," Richard emphasised sardonically, "but you can appreciate, and I know, it was a one-off. I'm not going to desert or anything. Far from it. I want to keep to what I was doing here as long as humanly possible."

Newton reacted with avuncular disposition. His new recruit was deflated, as they all were, but in his voice lay resignation of a philosophical kind that he hadn't previously recognised in the man's make-up. "It's the woman," he queried.

Richard's eyes circled the room before he continued. "There's a plan in place to evacuate a number of people on a small freighter. I've been invited to join the enterprise and happen to think it's a good idea. The ship's pretty much ready to go; to Darwin at least, if not Sydney."

"Might it be the old listing thing anchored off? The *Pelangi?*" the major asked with a wry smile.

"Is there anything you don't know, sir?"

A barely perceptible nod preceded, "Go on."

"You remember Captain Chia? It seems he's a sure bet to be its master, with Kwoli as mate. You've heard of Bryan Williamson with whom I once sailed, and there's a local Chinese engineer who makes up the hard core. He's taking his wife and five young children. There'll be room for more. Greda's aware of the venture and, now that her husband's back, well—"

"You appreciate that I can probably arrange a clearance. Seems like a good plan and, if you must fit into it, do so. I'm sure my colonel will approve, if I were to give the okay to cover the commission situation."

"I did fit into it, but things have changed. I can't go. The problem is, everyone must think I am, most especially, *her*."

"But why must she think that? What does it matter?" eyes again in penetrative mode.

"You pegged me, sir. I love the woman. I believe if she had any inkling I may not be sailing, she'd refuse to go. So, as I see it, there are two possibilities. This is where I need your help, sir."

An orderly entered with coffee that was placed on Newton's desk. "Go on, let's hear them," the major said, as he passed a mug to Richard. It was too hot to drink but the aroma revived his spirits.

"Thanks. One is that I simply play along and say we'll all be sailing, including her husband. The other being I effectively disappear from this point on. Major Newton, you might say to her, for example, that in my capacity as a commissioned British officer I've been sent on a top-secret operation and am already out of Singapore. She respects you. That would end once and for all any hope she retains of leaving with me. Or perhaps paint a negative light that I've simply gone, leaving it up to her to chase down Williamson and work out her own arrangements, and you only became aware of them by accident. You might also hold out the prospect of me being returned to Australia on the mission's completion, to give her some hope we might meet up again. I don't know, I'm just—"

"Steady on a moment, you're flailing my friend. That clout unhinged your brain." Newton regarded him thoroughly, before stepping to the embrasure of the window overlooking a moribund drilling quadrangle. "If I were minded to love a human being, she's the one woman I could not go past."

Richard wondered if he had misheard and watched as the Englishman searched skyward. The major was a difficult man to read. Smokescreens, the concave, the convex and intrigue were his vocation, displaying the enigmatic corporate façade, facilitating subtle cross-examination calculated to discover the facts. Here was an inward reflection, but by the time he faced Richard again, unfathomability had regained its familiar opulence.

"You were saying?"

"Sir, I just want to do what's best, and it must be the right thing."

"I agree that everything has to be carefully handled. I'm sensing it would be unwise for you to elaborate with her. On the other hand, she'll know soon enough you played a significant part in her husband's repatriation. The good doctor will demand answers."

"I don't wish to see Greda. With his survival, anything I do or say in her presence is done or said in his, whether he's right here or two hundred yards away."

"Understand," Newton said, almost looking through him. "One might wish the other chap possessed half your timbre," he trailed off. Sensing Kirnst's introspections were prompting a release of inhibitions pertaining to a subject of which he had never canvassed, Newton hastened to add, "Never mind, keep going."

Perplexed, Richard avoided his eyes. "They're a family unit, no matter how much one can snipe from the sidelines. My present inclination is to bow out of sight, if you don't mind, sir, and perhaps let you offer the reasons for it."

Newton didn't pause to reflect. "For the moment just stay put and don't speak to her until I get back to you. There's one other thing: Williamson has been trying to contact you through me. I've had my staff fob him off. If you like, I can arrange to have him brought to see you. Like most in the colony with any nous, he's aware the Japanese aren't far away and, from what you've told me, wants to push off soon."

"Thank you, sir. That's appreciated. Please just give me a couple of hours before you send him up. That will allow me to sort out a few other things in my own mind. Perhaps it's better to hear from you before I see him."

"Look, what I'll do is review everything before I speak to Dr Faircrossman. There isn't much time. She has the right to know her husband is here and, if not for his recent presentation, would have been made aware by now. You've told me what's on your mind, and yet another problem is thrown up. Now there's so little left to do in my department other than sift and destroy files that I may as well become a full-time agony aunt."

Noticing Richard's frown, he muttered a grudging concession. "Yes, clumsily put, I know, Captain. I'll play the rest of it by instinct, if not by ear, and give you an update later. You will meet with Williamson. One way or the other, the Faircrossmans look like they'll be going on the freighter, and it's clear you've ruled it out."

Richard nodded.

"As far as what you can tell Williamson, and anyone else, not very much is all I can say. You can't go into the rescue of the Englishman. The cover I've created for you will operate such that, with the concomitant breakdown in the civil administration, it was essential for you to be commissioned. To be effective in that role, you have to possess the power and the discretion to oversee the continuing function of utilities and essential services for the army, including protecting capital infrastructure from possible acts of sabotage. As a civilian with limited powers, you couldn't hope to handle those things. Can you follow all of that? It's akin to martial law. Your engineering expertise warranted the commission."

"Respectfully, sir, I'm happy to adopt any reasoning, conflated or otherwise, as a justification. Bryan will be surprised. I'll hear from you in due course?" he asked.

Newton nodded. "That's certain."

Saluting his superior was substituted by a meeting of their minds and the shaking of hands as they separated. There was no hint of a rebuke. A sliver of private light peeping from the opacity of a one-way street, a mutual fondness and two-way respect had transcended the nuances of rank.

*****

The rapping was unmistakably militaristic presaging the door being opened, the forerunner of hob-nailed thudding through his quarters. As the electric bulb lit the room, Richard, aroused from slumber, eased a hand gingerly over his forehead. A pot of hot tea and a plate of sandwiches was placed on the side table.

"Courtesy of Major Newton, sir," said the boots, crisply saluting. "The major also advised that you might join him in his office at 2030 hours. And there's Messrs Williamson and Yip outside waiting to see you. Shall I say you'll not be long, sir, and ask them to wait?"

"Yes, thank you, ah, soldier. Ten minutes, then show them in, please." Richard was still adjusting to issuing orders and the crisp deference emanating from the ranks.

The sandwiches found their repose easily, as did the hot brew. A quick shave and wash followed. Reinvigorated, he spied the newly ironed uniform in the wardrobe and dressed. He applied a final buff to the black shoes, presenting a mirror sheen. The fastidious Williamson was certain to scrutinise every article before bestowing an opinion, applying his most astringent inspection to the calibre of Richard's footwear.

"Gidday." Richard greeted them at the door, which opened into an anteroom furnished with a round wooden table and three chairs. Hands were shaken all round and backs patted in camaraderie. "Come in and join the party."

Williamson looked him up and down, a sardonic smile creasing his face. His stare rested on the insignia decorating his shoulders, before he made an elaborate display of stooping to flick imaginary fluff from his shoes. "So that's the drum, Dickie. We've been combing the whole island while you've joined up to this hapless pommie outfit. How could you?"

Yip became his sidekick. Exhibiting an open-mouthed expression akin to a row of piano keys, he made a great show, bowing effusively with the denouement fixing himself in a rigid stance, topped off by an extravagant salute. "They not feeding you well and beat you, too!" he said, finger pointed at Richard's forehead.

He joked that a drunken soldier had taken a swing with a piece of timber, and then called out for more refreshments. Both visitors began to speak at once, before he assertively cut across them using the explanation consistent with Newton's direction. "I'm sure you blokes have a few questions. There's not a great deal I can tell you. I've been inducted because the army felt it was necessary to have an officer coordinating everything. I was called in suddenly and offered the appointment, so here I am, courtesy of martial law edicts deeming Suggiss redundant. Apparently, he was pre-warned by Government House and the military the day I joined. Many briefings and so on, I can tell you. With service personnel running the show, at least both your workloads, such as they've been, will ease off."

Williamson, detecting evasion, was not disposed to enter into idle banter. Here was a very different situation to the one contemplated when they had discussed the plan to leave Singapore, and he was nothing if not blunt. "Let's stop the verbiage, Dickie. Does this mean you're not leaving with us now you have to answer to a chain of command?"

Richard strove to construct a reply. "My boss knows in broad terms of the plan. He hasn't vetoed my participation in it by any means. Timing, though, is pretty critical. You'd know about the landings in the north-west?"

"Yeah, bloody heard alright," Williamson snorted face-tiously, "along with the inflated accounts of 'containment' and 'in a matter of days things will return to normal' shite.

Dickie, we're not moved by all this baloney and you can see what I'm thinking. We're pretty much ready. Thanks to David, the ship looks even more decrepit, not even worth an idle bit of strafing, and that's the way we want to keep her until the last hour, when we'll crank her up, right her, and boom."

"Ever the sceptic, eh, mate? Well it's sure justified this time. As to your old thing out there, have you a sailing date?"

"I think we should push off by Friday at the latest. It's been put back once already when we didn't hear from you. David and I have been full-on with preparing the scow for sea. Everything's dissolving and we can't delay much longer. By the way, to make Australia, we need more fuel. There's ample for the Dutch East Indies. I thought we might have enough for Darwin, but Chia's charted a zig-zag course to avoid the trade routes where shipping might be harried by Jap aircraft, and it means additional sea time. We'll require another thousand gallons at a minimum. It's not been easy to come by, let alone shifting it out there, although David has a barge lined up. I'm starting to say my prayers about getting the diesel by legal means at any rate, and—"

"Hint taken. I'll have a word and see if I can help out. There are still a few storage tanks intact, and we have our supplies. I'm told there's more than enough. We're not planning to leave any behind."

Williamson returned to the original question. "Come on, 'fess up. What are you proposing to do, Dickie, and how about Greda?"

Richard rose and fixed his gaze on the fan whirring in the corner. "I've a problem, Bryan. Her husband's in the military hospital," his voice choking.

"Bloody hell!" Williamson appeared behind him and gripped his upper arm, a gesture Richard appreciated. "That's, well, incredible," before returning to the table, shaking his head and parting his hair abstractedly.

"She doesn't know anything about it. I guess there'd be room for him, too?"

"We can make space for another ten, even twenty in a pinch." Williamson studied every action of the other man before Richard resumed his seat and their eyes met. "But what *are* you saying, Dickie?" The strain he was carrying couldn't be hidden. Williamson summed up the situation with apparent ease. "We're on concurrent courses, poss'."

Richard sighed. "Yeah, like when we used sign language in a roaring engine space, always knowing the other's mind." He was moved by his mate's intuitive nature when there was no follow-up question. A moment passed before he spoke again. "That's the way I'd prefer it, Bryan. I've sort of closed the book and I don't intend to tempt its reopening."

Williamson chose hyperbole in his response. "Now listen, my grand-poohbah-Aussie-captain-turned-pommie-bastard officer." Yip's toothy display soon wiped the severe look from Richard's face. "You must promise me one thing: you have to get out of this shithole, mate."

"The Army's told me I'll be looked after."

There was a knock on the door, the orderly entering to inform Richard that the major would see him forthwith.

"Thank you. I'm on my way. Can you blokes hang on, probably, not much more than half an hour?"

Williamson assented, accepting the assurance that the tea would be augmented by more sandwiches. David passed, indicating that he had to get back to his wife and family as they were fretting every moment he was away from them.

Richard took the long way to the major's office as it afforded him time to gather his thoughts.

"Sit down, Captain," said Newton, motioning him to a revolving wooden chair that creaked as he filled it. "I've considered at length all you've told me. Anything else you want to mention? By the way, I've still not spoken to Dr Faircrossman. As far as the husband is concerned, he should be fit to travel."

"Bryan is in my quarters at the moment. Their venture's about ready to crank up. They need some fuel though, and pretty quickly."

"How much?"

"About a thousand gallons or so, sir. It's to cover an alternate—"

"Forget the explanations. I'm sure you'll be able to find that amount for them. You know where the fuel dump is, so it's in your capable hands."

"Thanks, sir."

"Now, I assume you've ascertained whether they have room for Faircrossman?" Richard nodded. The major continued. "Good, and you're not going to disappear or do anything else. You should speak to her—"

Richard remonstrated with Newton at this juncture and took in a deep breath. "I really don't think I can, sir. I'm simply unable to face—"

"You'll have to speak with her, so toughen yourself up for that. You're an officer now, remember. I am scheduled to leave Singapore, too, this coming Friday, so undoubtedly I'll be seeing her before then. It's inevitable that you'll need to before it comes time to get whoever on the freighter."

"As you wish, sir. Bryan has said he'll help out with all the necessary arrangements as required. I'll be prepared."

"Good. I assume you've not changed your mind about sailing with her and, yes, him and the others."

"Well, no," Richard replied disconnectedly.

"Now, about your own repatriation," Newton continued, "there are no excusals or exemptions. All non-combatants are listed to sail on the *Empire Star*. That ship will be taking a large number of evacuees."

"I understand, sir. I recall you saying we're in a different category to regular soldiers, although, with respect, you far more so than I. There's a sense of cutting and running with which I'm not entirely comfortable."

"Yes. Well, yours is not to reason why."

The Newton protocol was never far from the surface. Richard thought the concept of rules and regulations was a state of mind as much as a state of fact, but this was the military, and he had sworn allegiance to the King. His admiration for Newton was not dented on that account. "My new identity, sir, that's official now, is it?"

"Yes. You're Captain Frank Joseph Alderson. Remember that, in case you need to. Once we clear out of here and, depending on what you want to do thereafter, you'll be restamped and resume your true name. Why do you ask?"

"Oh, ah, no real reason," Richard said phlegmatically. "I'm just a little, ah, fazed."

"Get used to it. You'll be heading back into the old line of work at least for the next few days. That's not my department, so I wish you well. I'm going to slip over and see how Faircrossman's going. Do you want to join me?"

"That's probably a good idea. I might just dash back and tell Williamson what's happening. I can brief him on the man's condition afterwards. Ultimately, he has a right to know about the health of his passengers."

"I'll meet you there." The major reached for his cap and they left together.

After seeing off Williamson, Richard entered the Military Hospital, coming upon Newton in conversation with a doctor whose face was imprinted with perpetual fatalism. "There's been a dramatic deterioration in the patient's condition since I spoke with his treating physician earlier. The infection hasn't yet responded to penicillin, so discretion suggests that saving his leg is problematic."

Richard groaned and Newton shook his head. "Has a time been set for the operation?"

The surgeon checked a timepiece. "It's going to be done within the hour. He's been delirious since his fever worsened."

"Captain Fitzmaurice," said Newton, motioning for Richard to join them. "I have to go. This is Captain Alderson. I shall see you both later."

"Things are pretty grim, I gather, Doctor?"

"Yes, very, Captain. The infection has spread. We need to amputate above the knee. Delaying the procedure could be catastrophic for him."

"Do you think he'll be fit for evacuation in a day or so?" asked Richard.

"Captain Alderson, Mr Faircrossman has been through quite an ordeal and, despite that, was surprisingly well when he first came in. It's a concern that a severe fever developed. If he comes through, he'll require close medical supervision."

"I see. That could be—" Richard began.

"His wife's an experienced doctor. Now, I'm extremely busy and will let—"

"Captain Fitzmaurice!" A frantic nurse's summons saw the surgeon sprint down a corridor after her.

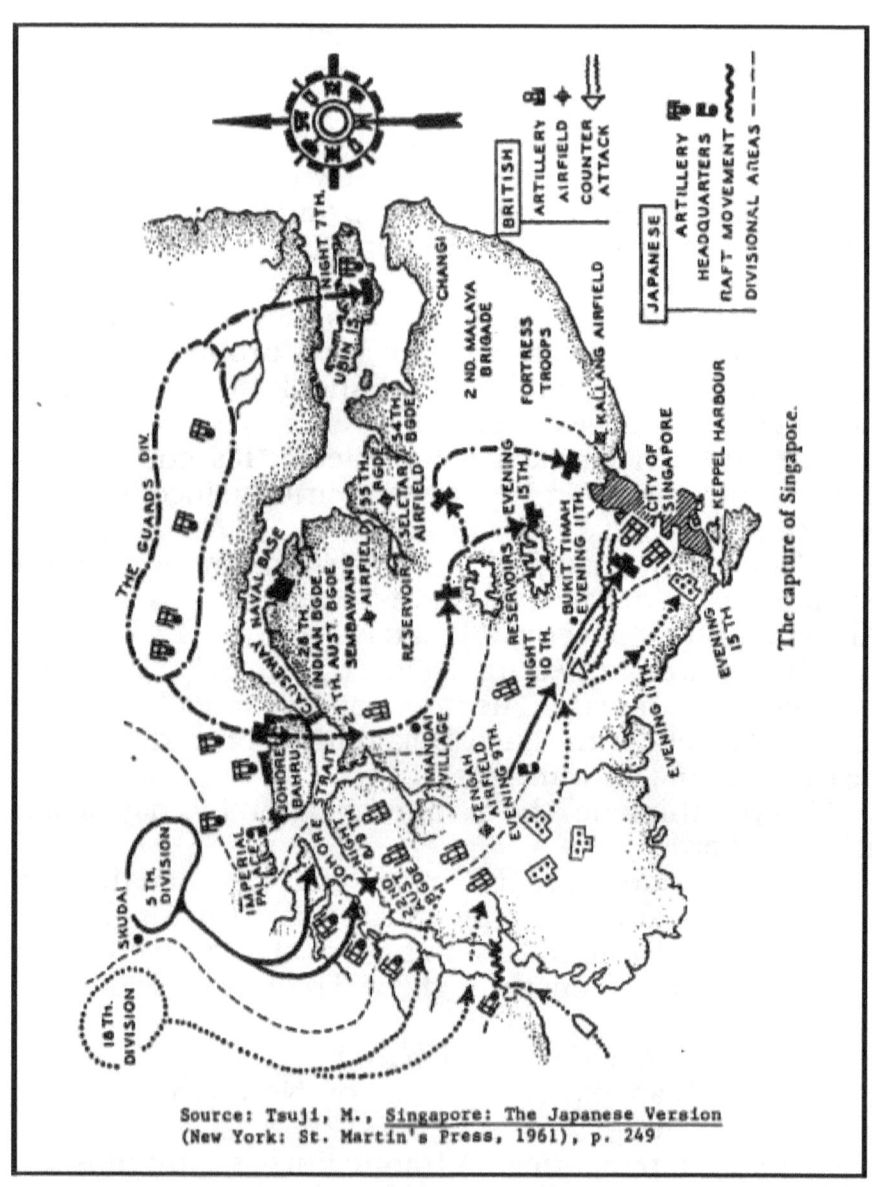

The capture of Singapore.

Source: Tsuji, M., Singapore: The Japanese Version
(New York: St. Martin's Press, 1961), p. 249

Chapter 31

Costings

With Richard gone, the crew of the *Pelangi* still needed extra bunkers, but now they had a role on the ship to fill as well. David Yip had done all he could to procure the former commodity, but shortages had resulted in an exorbitant asking price. He had more success conjuring up an apprentice sailor. The young man was a distant relative and protégé of his from the Works Department who was capable of acting as a trainee engineer and deckhand. Chia had found an experienced motorman when told it was doubtful they could count on Richard Kirnst. For the procurement of a substantial quantity of distillate, Williamson knew his colleague would not fail him.

Meeting again at Fort Canning, he assured Richard that Faircrossman could be properly accommodated, having regard to his condition. He ventured to reopen the idea of Richard's participation in the voyage, presciently omitting to mention Chia's hiring.

"I won't revisit that, Bryan," he returned bluntly.

"David's got a keen young all-rounder lined up, so we can live with it, I guess, but there's a sick passenger," Williamson pressed.

"I'm no nursemaid. Greda will be there, and Major Newton's sure to find other help. You've room for another medico and a nurse."

"Alright, whatever you say, Dickie, but keep your hair on, you pig-headed bugger. Always were. You're getting out, too, aren't you?"

"Yes, there are contingency plans. The *Empire Star* sails late on the twelfth. Have you heard of it?"

Williamson nodded. "At one stage thought I might've had a job on the old thing. So you'll be on board when it sails?"

Richard nodded. "I'll be there, according to the Major."

It was a curious way to frame his answer, Williamson not entirely convinced. "You'd better be. Now I need a big favour. Are you able to wangle some diesel, like about a tanker load or a touch more?"

Richard grinned at the Kiwi. "I wondered when that was coming."

They collected David and headed to the supply depot in Bukit Timah Road. Richard's remit extended to ordering shipments of fuel about the island for public usage and, in this case, it would be on the pretext of augmenting supplies for the power station. An officious-looking lieutenant, along with two armed sentinels, faced them at the entrance. Richard appreciated immediately that the officer would not cede his authority meekly. Their identity papers were demanded before any discussion was countenanced. Superciliously satisfied, he declared no lorry driver would be available until 0700 hours. Richard's protests, as well as his requisition form, went unheeded.

"Oh, I see you're new around here. We have procedures, as you should know," his condescension rankling.

This fool would not be suffered without some incident or other, thought Richard. "It's 'Captain' to you."

"Captain, I'm sure you understand how stretched we are."

"I'm responsible for—"

"Just a minute!" the lieutenant snapped, looking at a ledger. "You obviously have sufficient supplies to get you through to tomorrow afternoon. I authorised a fuel drop there only two days ago."

Williamson stalked away indignantly to avoid becoming embroiled in the row. He examined a tanker whose gauge registered the requisite quantity. The keys were in the ignition.

Richard's patience was evaporating. "What's your name? Stand still when you're spoken to. I'm not asking you to supply a driver, for I've no need of one!" he countermanded.

"Well, you cannot have the lorry. My orders are clear, and the fuel will be delivered in the authorised manner tomorr—"

Williamson started the engine and gave it everything.

"Stop that man!" the lieutenant yelled to the guards.

Richard shouted back at him, "Just lift the barricade, I'll take responsibility—"

"That tanker must not leave here without authorisation. I'm warning you. Open fire!"

Each guard discharged a round as the truck crashed through the boom gate and continued down the road.

"You'll be hearing from my superior, Captain."

"And you from mine, you little twerp!" Richard palmed him aside and ran to the Jeep. Yip drove off in the wake of the lorry.

"He'll go straight down to the wharf. Let's get ahead and you can line up the barge," said Richard.

Williamson waved as they overtook.

When they pulled into the loading dock, a sentry saluted stiffly as Richard alighted from the Jeep. He almost forgot protocol, with a belated acknowledgement, but also appreciated the need to be forthright. Yip's racing off occasioned some consternation.

"Don't worry about him, Private, he's acting on my instructions. Furthermore, there's a fuel tanker not far behind. This is urgent. Let it pass without hindrance."

"Yes, sir." The man jumped to attention and saluted again.

Soon after Williamson parked, David appeared, cutting the engine and leaping from the bow onto a ladder. The two men connected the pipes. There was a fall of about ten feet, and the gravity-fed transfer of the fuel to a motorised barge directly underneath the wharf was soon accomplished.

"What are you drinking up there, you lazy sod?" Richard called, expecting a robust reply. It was the bullet hole in the door that alerted him. Williamson was slumped over the steering wheel. "David! He's been hit!"

They lifted him out and saw his shirt was soaked in blood, but he remained conscious.

"We'll have to get you to the hospital, mate. Forget the barge." Richard held Williamson in his arms.

"Forget jack shit, possum," Williamson ground out through a bout of coughing. "We're getting that out to the *Pelangi* now."

"Bryan, you need a doctor."

A trickle of blood issued from his mouth. "Lose this diesel and the trip's wrecked. I need nothing, Dickie, although you do, you hopeless, lovesick fool. I'm going on board. We've got a doctor coming. I can wait, but I'm not forfeiting this junket for no bastard."

Helped by Yip, Williamson wobbled onto the barge, where he lay down, head in Richard's lap and eyes wavering. "Let's go, David," he said, looking anxiously at his wounded comrade.

At a modest two knots, the glorified punt ambled out to the nondescript *Pelangi*. Once the barge was alongside, the fuel had to be pumped up by hand. Kwoli joined with Richard and Yip to hoist Williamson on board. Chia was speechless after examining him.

"Get those bloody bunkers done, will you? I'll be right here," Bryan groaned meekly.

The others took fifteen-minute turns to operate the pump, while Richard remained beside his cherished mate.

"This is crazy, Bryan, I want to—"

"Now just listen, poss'. My sea bag's aboard and there's some money, pretty much all I have. That's for Suzy. She's having a little one, old son. David and Chia get the *Pelangi*, but ten per cent of the profits go to her and my young 'un. I get Davy Jones' locker. They're my wishes and tell Chia. I know you're not sailing. David's got someone and so has the old man. Yippy can run the job single-handed anyway."

Tears filled Richard's eyes when Williamson struggled to speak again. The faintest of smiles lit his greying face. "Always were jealous of my locks, Dickie. Some of us, yeah, poss'. Always the Sunday school kid, hey poss', never the rogue? Go for it, Dickie, get on."

The others gathered around and Yip kneeled close to him, mouth open, weeping great tears. Richard had almost given him up, but Williamson opened his eyes and, spotting the inimitable rows of teeth, managed a slight smile.

"David, see to Suzy and my kid. I don't want her hooking up with some white lecher bastard like me." A fading sound in a vain search for articulation was his last before he died.

Three hours remained until daylight. Richard had washed his uniform and rejoined Chia on deck. The captain bear-hugged his erstwhile engineer before breaking the silence. "We're sailing tomorrow night and privileged to have you again as chief, this time for a real voyage. But what uniform's this? Not the merchant marine."

"No, it isn't. I know you've got back-up, Bill."

"Kwoli won't be cooking, I promise, and we'll always salute."

Richard appreciated the sentiment but couldn't return it. "Whatever happens, David Yip and his offsider will be here, too."

"From the merchant service to the civil one, and now significant rank in the British Army, what will be next?"

"There'll be a recent amputee as passenger, along with Dr Faircrossman, his wife and perhaps a nurse or two."

"I knew she was coming; almost but not quite *déjà vu*, Richard. I'll make sure there's a larger cabin for them. What are you thinking? You're surely not staying here?"

Richard cleared his throat. "I have a bit to do yet. Is the ship up for this voyage?"

"Doesn't seem much, but I've been all over her like a man contemplating marriage, and she has a lovely body. If there's a fault, it's the tomboy look from the lack of makeup, if you get my drift. Pun intended."

The analogy was apt and, at this time, the mood suited him. It was hard to say goodbye. Did that twinkle in his eye betray insight? Probably, but he was the epitome of discretion.

Chia remembered seeing Richard and the English doctor together on that ill-fated voyage from Malacca. In the first moments after his ship's demise, he witnessed the trussing up of the baleful prisoner, the reward for whose capture and return now forming part of his equity in the *Pelangi*. It was an action he wouldn't forget for, without the Australian, he would never have been able to present the cheque. He had watched as Richard had shepherded the woman and boy into the lifeboat, ministering to her as if she was the only person who had ever touched his heart. No fool was this ship's captain.

"You'll give him a decent burial at sea?" The words almost choked him.

"Richard, the New Zealand flag will be strapped to his shroud. I'm so sorry."

*****

In the mirror an image formed as his dishevelled own. When he blinked at the horror of Williamson's sudden death, willing a purge of the last few hours, Richard saw his shipmate as the coiffured contradiction, greasy mechanical ingenuity with class and style. He determined this was the way he would forever recall his mentor and swallowed hard, hearing the voice, *Get on, poss'*.

Army life, he was destined to appreciate, suffered no post-mortems, *Easy come and go,* was the motto, and it entailed an endless stream of paper, requests, requisitions and functionaries. He was only just starting to penetrate the surface in the capacity of new 'chum', as he overheard one staff sergeant remarking of him to an underling. Not to be thinking there might be an end to it, poked under his door with several other missives was a note from Newton enjoining him to come to his office at 0900 hours, with a postscript that he had still not spoken to Greda. It allowed him enough time to bathe and change. He subjugated all that had just occurred with the army dictum.

At half past eight, he was dressed and savouring steaming cocoa. A sheet of paper in front of him, he jotted down some observations in preparation for his meeting with Newton. The *Pelangi* was to sail at 2300 hours, and a good deal of preparation needed to be done between now and then. Nothing, he concluded, could be accomplished by vague and dreamy ideas. He then penned a letter, placing the smaller envelope into a larger one containing a note addressed to Newton.

With the appointment pressing, Richard dashed over to the Military Hospital for the latest on Faircrossman's condition. The surgery had been successful, opined Fitzmaurice, the jargon of 'resting comfortably' applied. To the increasingly common question at this moment in Singapore's history about whether he could be safely moved that evening, came a perfunctory response iterating that it would be better if he was kept at the hospital for another week. There were no guarantees that the sutures and, in turn, the integrity of the wound, would not be compromised in any transfer. "The fundamental requirement is providing proper care over the next ten days. He has a reasonable chance with good management."

"Thank you for taking the time to speak to me," Richard said as he departed.

"Oh, and I understand his wife's been informed."

A chill overtook Richard. He resolved to shake free of it, striding briskly to Newton's office. The major was completing the last of his administrative duties in Singapore as Richard was ushered in. Scattered on the desk was an unruly assortment of documents. Newton scanned each one, concentrating intently, allocating them to various dispositions within his view, while fielding telephone calls of a nature that signalled the closing phases of security operations under his auspices. One large pile of papers was summarily despatched to a metal bin whose proximity to a container of kerosene suggested their imminent fate. An aide removed the items outside, and the contents were rapidly incinerated.

Richard viewed the flames reflectively. A small pile was neatly arranged inside a folder by the same functionary and, as each document was so directed, the process was repeated in rapid order. When the aide departed again, with Newton consumed by his task, Richard managed to secrete his envelope within the surviving papers. The major raised his eyebrows as the last of the calls was dealt with and took the classified material, placing the folder in his attaché case.

"Richard, I have secured passage on the *Empire Star*," he said, handing him officially stamped passes. "You need to be by the Keppel wharf no later than 2230 hours. I'll be sailing." Newton scrutinised his face before continuing.

"You're not entertaining any second thoughts about going that way, are you?"

"No, sir," he hesitated, expecting to be upbraided on account of the incident at the fuel depot.

"Dr Faircrossman has tried to phone me a few times, but I've removed myself from discussions with her, allowing Sergeant Tubbs to take messages. I can't prevaricate much longer, and I'm far from comfortable with this," Newton said with a hint of reproval.

"Thank you, sir, but it seems she may be aware anyway. I just spoke to Fitzmaurice. I'm happy to go and see her forthwith and simply say I was commissioned into the army as a noncombatant engineer to look after—"

"No," Newton commanded firmly. "I—

A commotion outside the office interrupted their discourse. A woman could be heard quarrelling. It was a voice that sent another tremor through Richard.

"Listen to me, I know the major's in there, and I demand to see him immediately!"

Newton rose imperturbably and opened the door. "It's alright, Tubbs, admit Dr Faircrossman."

He resumed his seat. Greda strode determinedly through the doorway and stood close to him. "How dare you try to avoid me? I am told my husband's at the military hospital and his leg has been amputated. You know something of this, I take it?"

The question was sufficiently answered by Newton's nod, but he hastily added, "Yes, it's true that Mr Faircrossman is at Alexandra." Newton subsumed the irritation engendered by a complete lack of security.

She glared at him fiercely.

Richard, whose presence she hadn't perceived, spoke. "Hello, Greda."

She spun around, looking at him imploringly and surveyed his uniform. "Richard, what in heaven's name? Thank goodness you're alright! I was terribly worried when I hadn't heard from you." She reached for his arms. "I don't understand what any of this means, but you're here, and that's all that really matters to me."

Newton chose to ignore the unfolding scene and removed himself. Whatever he said to the Sergeant was suppressed by the creaking door hinge and definitive closing.

"So, you already knew?"

He felt like a prison inmate behind plate glass during a stranger's visit and collected himself before responding, "Yes, Greda. Your husband," he said, with some emphasis on the spousal denotation, "is here."

"And what precisely do you know?" He bowed his head, feeling a sense of shame. She answered her own question, "Quite a deal, it seems," exasperation evident.

He chose to ignore the inflection and moved towards the desk with his back to her. "Greda, this is what you've been waiting for. His fate was the reason for not leaving with Jonathon. Your son wanted his father. There is, well, finality. We must now talk about the second part of Jon's request, getting you away, because the freighter sails tonight."

She sank at his alteration in manner. "Getting *me* away from here? And who else, Richard? I take it you—"

"Well, you and *him*, of course," he said, with a trace of bitterness in his voice that did not escape her notice. "Arrangements are being put in place to get you out to that ship. I'm seeing to it."

"Richard." She moved over to him, engaging his eyes. "I'm not leaving without you. I cannot. I won't."

He pulled away and leaned both palms on the desk, decreeing, "You will go and must go. Don't you understand what I'm—"

"But our promises," Greda said, regaining her composure, "that night when you held me, and I told you I was yours. What do we do about that, Richard? I can't live with a man for whom I feel nothing, not even pity." Tears emerged on her cheeks, yet she remained serenely calm.

He surveyed the woman he loved, exerting a Herculean effort to maintain his own self-possession, noting her face was unusually pale and dark folds of skin were ringing her eyes. Seeing no corresponding moderation in his features, she leant face first against the closed door and tried to stifle the sounds now coming from within her breast. As he came behind her, she felt his proximity and turned to hold him with every sinew she could muster.

That he could not reciprocate with the strength she desperately sought led Greda to release him and take the proffered handkerchief to wipe her face. Greda sat down. A glazing shadow overlaid her face. She stared at the empty wall, finding no respite, but then turned back and searched again for some indication that he might be weakening. Finding none, she shook her head resignedly.

"Have you stopped loving me, Richard?"

He regarded her as would an insensate automaton.

She continued in a voice laden with irony, "So this is what it's come to. I invited you into my heart and, sure enough, true to life's slavish, excoriating principles, fate has delivered its scant return."

Still no words came, as something inside stayed his voice. Contractive pain, the like of which he'd never experienced, rose from his stomach and compressed his chest. He gasped for breath and tried to disguise the indisposition by clearing his throat and turning his face from hers. A lengthy quiet ensued, neither knowing what to say. The air was pregnant with anticipation. Their emotions, cloaking the room, strained for expression.

Finally, Richard brought his clenched fists to his side, standing very erect, and broke the silence. "Um, he'll need medical assistance for the voyage," he faltered, taking stuttering breaths. "They'll be sending a nurse or two to help."

She chose not to hear him and said, "I know what you're trying to do. Listen to me. You are sailing, aren't you, Richard? I don't mean with me. It was always part of the plan, come what may."

It opened a means to defuse the tense atmosphere. "Well, someone has to keep the engines running. I wouldn't leave it to those other scallywags." The words almost gave him away.

He had relaxed and she became the Greda he knew, nestling into him.

"Not sure what you'll think of me for confessing this, but my wish is not to see Edward now. I'd prefer to wait until we're all on board and underway. Do you understand that, Richard?"

He nodded gravely. She was reading his thoughts. The seeds of the admission that he wouldn't be going with them had been duly planted. As they continued to regard each other, he began to waiver. One voice told him that he had to go and protect her. The contrary echo said it wasn't his business to be entertaining such proclivities. She had her husband to look after. And still another voice told him that taking passage on the *Pelangi* would be tantamount to noncompliance with orders, given that his departure had been booked on the *Empire Star*. However, knowing Newton, Richard was certain no report of his going AWOL would ever be promulgated.

On cue and without ceremony, that figure of discernment resumed tenure of his office. Newton nodded towards them, Richard taking the opportunity to say that they had things to do. Greda appreciated the imminence of their leave-taking. Newton was, if nothing else, unbendingly predictable in attitude and he shepherded her to the door.

She took the major's hand, surprising him with a grip belying her willowy frame. "I'm grateful for everything you've done. All I seem to do these days is extend my gratitude, like an old record. Rather, I think I should be administering rebukes, perhaps even a not-so-gentle cut across your face. I'm pretty good in that department, you've no doubt heard."

Newton disclosed the makings of a perceptive smile.

Motioning towards Richard, Greda bit her lip, the only device available to disguise the inestimable turmoil within her. "By the way, Major, getting this fellow into uniform, a captain at that, too, didn't happen by accident. And I see he's been fighting again. Who was it this time, the cook? Is he going to be reprimanded?"

In a different setting, her comment might have disarmed the tension pervading the room. A strained inelegance hovered as Greda and Richard left Newton's office and soon they were hurtling back in the Jeep to the General Hospital.

He casually mentioned that she would need to be ready to leave by ten o'clock. "Ah, I'll come back and we'll head down to the wharf."

When they arrived, Greda stared into space, pensively quiet. As his head turned, she met his gaze, entreatingly. "You're coming with us, aren't you?"

The question surprised him. He shifted his haunches and wondered whether she might discern equivocation. "Of course I am. The ship can't sail without me."

She seemed relieved, accepting of his answer, and leant over nuzzling her mouth into his neck. "We'll get back to Sydney and I'll tell Edward our marriage is over. He's lost his businesses in Malaya, but he's hardly without resources. I want nothing from him. And you don't have to worry."

She thought of her husband's affair with the woman known to both men, and continued staccato-like, almost dreamily, "He'll get on. It's been over for a long time, a blessed release. A nurse can look after him, and Edward's sure to marry again. I'll explain it to Jon. He likes you. This is destined to be, I know it is, and I'm going to make you happy, Richard. We've plenty of time to work it all through. You needn't worry about anything. There's one person I think of day and night and that's you, my darling. I know that now's not the time to ask, but what on earth are you really doing in that dreadful—figure of speech—outfit?"

Caught up in her sanguine soliloquies, she was oblivious to the tumult in his eyes as they kissed goodbye.

"You're right about the garb. It's a long story, and I'll tell you everything later, but must get back. My job, you see," was all that he managed as they parted, and he fled, drawing on a conviction of reckless abandon back to the barracks, at sea as much as on land.

Greda sat down to collect herself and to look back. In the short time they had spent in Singapore, neither had ventured into discussion pertaining to details of the bedlam encompassing their respective work environments. She had met the obdurate imposts that her Hippocratic Oath demanded. If not for the joy experienced at saving a life, the setbacks in being rendered, at times, largely ineffective would have crushed her.

The functioning of the General Hospital itself as a gazetted institution for the treatment of the sick and the injured, in contradistinction to a backyard ambulance station, was becoming increasingly compromised. Never more so was this evident than in the previous thirty-six hours when two direct hits had wreaked unspeakable carnage and the hospital's integrated whole was besieged. Quite another issue was the personal danger. Greda had been less than a minute clear of one of these blasts. On the northern wing, following completion of her rounds, a cluster of patients lodged in cramped spaces and suffering from diffuse traumatic injuries were obliterated. The Matron's sturdy workstation had saved her but extinguished the lives of nurses to whom she had moments before offered words of comfort and encouragement.

Her personal anguish was not because of the sight of smashed and broken human beings incongruously strewn amid the rubble of what had been a pristine place, nor was it occasioned by the desperate efforts to clear the debris in the search for survivors. Rather, when uncovering the lifeless forms of the nurses with whom she had shared quarters and become very close, Greda was overawed by an indescribable grief. One of the dead was the very same sister who saw a son and daughter sail off to Brisbane and had been influential in her decision to evacuate Jonathon.

The pressure of work and such tragic events told on Greda's aptitude for coherent reasoning. Watching Richard's furious withdrawal, she felt ashamed for the loss, not simply of poise, but of control of her feelings. She couldn't take back what had fallen from her, but wished it had been spoken in a way that was less demanding and, she reflected penetratingly, not so downright selfish.

Added to this was the inability to fully process the reality, rather than merely the fact, of her husband's survival. As she started packing her few possessions, Greda began to experience the actuality in which she resided. Guilt chastened her for not going straight to see Edward when she had learnt of his return. It was originally her intention, but she detoured to Newton, given over, it now seemed to her, to protest too much for not being informed of what she did not wish to hear.

Her emotional relief at seeing Richard had completely taken away any desire to proceed with the visit afterwards, apart from receiving confirmation of Edward's successful surgery. Incapable of self-reproof, she was perplexed by this arbitrary detachment. Now, however, there came on her a realisation that could no longer be repressed. As much as she might have wished it away, Greda conceded surprise, considering his state of fitness, if not admiration at her husband's resilience when contemplating what must have been the trek taken to secure his repatriation.

Given that seeing Edward was becoming inevitable, she conjured in graphic terms the recollection of his betrayal as dominating her resistance to doing so. This permitted analytical coolness in the processing of the next steps. Beyond handling what needed to be done to facilitate his transfer to a ship and ensuring he would be looked after along the way, she was numb to all other considerations. His losing a leg she tried to subsume.

Until she'd been given the news, Greda had willed that he was gone and never to be found. Contemplating the situation now extant after the veracity of his survival, she could only conclude it had become impossible to disentangle her emotional investment in acceptance of his death from the love she had found.

With freedom stripped from her, how could the broken wreck of their marriage be reconstituted? One thing Greda did know: she would never find it in her heart to love her husband. She reiterated that the dissolution of their union had been coming long before that fateful occasion when Richard had appeared, bruised and bleeding, by the roadside. What had ensued was an unfolding gift that each had found in the other. Had they become one, she was sure this morbid internal debate wouldn't be taking place.

But, in one of those cruel turns of destiny preying on a woman who, up to then, had been dutifully adherent to her vows, the conflict outside the hospital gates had forestalled all she had been anticipating. Whatever she could now reflect upon as to the abiding ecstasy, contentment and perpetual unity that moment might have produced no longer mattered, removed so far as she was from it. Greda could forever dwell on having been taken to Everest's summit without attaining base camp.

She dreamed on at this point. Their eventual sexual congress wouldn't be a letdown. Rather, throughout their lives together, Raffles would remain a poignant reminder of a fragment in time when the love that lived within them was forged like steel. Her willingness to give herself to Richard now faced the test of doing so in the knowledge that Edward was alive. Rebellion against the instincts seeking to restrain her rose up and then simmered for a time before she capitulated. The sweetness of a life of complete love and happiness anticipated for her eternity had metamorphosed into an empty delusion.

For Richard, things had changed, apparent from his reaction to their seeing each other again. A patent sadness or even remorse was evident in his smouldering, almond eyes, full of a love that could never fade. She intuited hesitation in his touch akin to a sense of resignation that this couldn't be. Greda was driven to certainty that, even if it lay within her to try, there would be no dissuading him from the conclusion he had reached. That much was clear no matter how earnestly she thought about it in amplifying her affection for him.

Her mind continued to vacillate on how the disbanding of her marriage could be effected without rancour or ill will, but each time she arrived at the same conclusion. Happiness and personal desires may be searched for too keenly, may be loved unwisely and, in their singular pursuit may cost too much, destroying in the process the very fabric of love woven in its manufacture.

Through this wrenching analysis, Greda became convinced that Richard could not—no, would not—sail on the same ship as she and Edward.

Chapter 32

Finality

anging, regarded as the most fitting reward for those
in uniform convicted of treason, was not an option
at this, the penultimate chapter in the colony's
history. Newton was charged with the responsibility of
ensuring Patrick Heenan's death sentence was carried out.
As the time drew closer for the departure of the *Empire
Star*, so did the performance of this duty in respect of the
condemned man.

He had not spoken to Heenan after the initial interrogation. Beyond giving oral testimony, Newton had absented
himself from the court martial. The sentence neither surprised the major nor, outwardly at least, perturbed Heenan.
The smugness and conceit characterising the man's demeanour after his interrogation had long fled him.

As Newton proceeded to the cells, accompanied by
Lieutenant McKenzie and a corporal, he felt strangely
apprehensive about this final encounter. He thought of
what was to follow. The door being unlocked, the shackled
prisoner then taken to his place of execution. Practically
speaking, there could be no burial. Newton and the
men with him were constrained by deadlines. The place
decided upon as the point where the traitor's life would be
forfeited was a secluded section of the harbour confines.
This was a crudity with which the major was far from
comfortable given his Sandhurst breeding, but he had his
orders. The man was to be shot, the body weighted down
and dumped into the depths.

The two men exchanged glances as the shackled Heenan
was taken from the cell to an army Jeep. He seemed to

crave some acknowledgement of both his existence and his impending fate, but Newton, as imperious as always, declined to oblige.

On being secured in the vehicle, he spoke in the manner of a man desirous of verbal engagement as if he might gain sympathy. "Well, I suppose this is it, Major?"

Newton effected not to hear him and refrained from uttering a word. He had to say something official when the time came and contented himself with the notion that Heenan would surely know there was little else he could expect to hear as his last breaths were taken.

They arrived at a location over a mile east of the *Empire Star's* berth. It was a disused wharf with precarious planking. Walking in single file, the lieutenant designated to fire the fatal shot was directly behind the prisoner, whose hands were held in front of him, while Newton led the way. The corporal was wheeling a trolley bearing an old engine block with a chain secured to the crankcase.

"Stop here," said the major, as they neared the edge.

The moonlit reflection off the water below confirmed where the remains would be submerged. It had once been a deep mooring and, with the weight of the engine carcass, there existed no prospect of the body surfacing. Calm transfused the atmosphere as the chain was locked onto Heenan's ankle, a task the major delegated to the non-commissioned man.

Newton began to speak in a censorious manner. "The British Military Tribunal, having found Patrick—"

"Major," Heenan broke in, fully appreciative of his fate, yet still lacking contrition. "I have but one request. Am I allowed to make it?"

"You may speak, prisoner," Newton responded coldly.

"I ask that no notification of my execution be formally given. I only have my mother and simply want to be listed as missing."

"I cannot guarantee anything like that. However, these are unusual circumstances. There will be no formal announcement, since that is ordinary operational procedure in this type of case. I'll do what I can to ensure your request is passed on. I'm a man of my word."

"Thank you, Major. I believe you are. Now, just get it done. I'm ready. Can my face be covered?"

A hessian sack was placed over the prisoner's head and secured around his neck.

Newton spoke the fateful words, adding, "You have been tried by a duly constituted Tribunal and convicted of treason. The sentence is death and I am authorised by the orders made within its jurisdiction to carry out the punishment."

An explosion punctured the night air, as just one shot to the back of the head discharged Newton's obligations. Heenan's body plunged into the water, a second splash proceeding from its cast iron companion. For Newton, this rebarbative dispatch would not rank among his most illustrious assignments while serving in the British Army.

*****

The invaders were encamped on the outskirts of Singapore and a lull descended over the town. Surrender was thought to be imminent. The deteriorating morale of the defenders couldn't be hidden, with evidence of mass desertion. As darkness advanced and quiet fell on the front lines, on the twelfth of February in every precinct it was realised that the sea provided the only escape. The ensuing panic became ubiquitous as civilians streamed down to the harbour.

At the quayside containing the *Empire Star*, dozens of unattached soldiers had also gathered and were demanding entry on board. There was no real prospect of the ship's crew restraining these men. Military police tried valiantly to control the line, but the numbers overwhelmed them. Mooring lines provided avenues for many others.

The master, Selwyn Capon OBE, surveyed the scene during final preparations for departure. The previous day he had received instructions from the British Navy headquarters in Singapore to evacuate women, children and military personnel officially authorised for passage. His was a cargo vessel designed to take twelve passengers in reasonable comfort. Before his eyes, an hour shy of sailing time, having already been inundated by hundreds of legitimate passengers, the ship was now encompassed by unruly mobs.

Anticipating a logistical nightmare, Capon had sent his chief steward and third mate ashore to collect provisions. Both were exceptional barterers, and they achieved considerable success in the markets where traders were doing brisk business, relishing the inflated prices the rampant demand had brought for their goods. As departure drew closer, Capon had cause to wonder whether the additional supplies would adequately provide for the teeming numbers pushing hard against the riveted seams. Seeking out the chief steward, he was assured that, with a careful degree of rationing and an ordinary passage to Calcutta, they could cater for 1500 people. Drinking water was the vital commodity. Seawater would substitute for bathing during the voyage.

By now, Newton was on board. He found the wheelhouse, where the master was poring over charts, looking flustered. After ascertaining Richard had not yet arrived, Newton advised Capon that he was expecting two more of his team.

"Not wanting to harry you, Captain, but up here I've a good view of the boarding, if you'll permit me," he said. "I must keep an eye out for my men."

Capon was not going to argue against the request of this imposing officer, hoping the major's presence might define some semblance of order, but as the surging throng enveloped the ship, it was beyond anyone's capacity to fully arrest the tide.

"I must warn you, Major," his voice rising above the din, "I've strict instructions to sail precisely on time. There are many hundreds of lives for whom I'm responsible and more streaming aboard every minute. I appreciate the importance attached to the evacuation of your personnel, but my orders originate from a much more senior level. We're to sail as scheduled and without exceptions."

Newton understood. He had been surprised at Kirnst's and Ranghati's absence. As he peered into the crowd, it was impossible to detect either individual among the many enlisted men and civilians crammed together. The situation was deteriorating even as they watched. Among the crush of legitimate boarders and some anticipatory indigents, both saw marauding soldiers with the one object of gaining the decks of the ship at any cost. Such was their intent that, in whatever manner they could, including threats and intimidation, they were determined to dash the hopes of others more deserving of repatriation. Even women with children were not immune from their depredations. But trying to stop the soldiers would put civilians at risk.

In addition to the melee at the quayside, smaller craft of all types and persuasions had been stolen or commandeered. Such was the incoherence of some of these seizures that capsizes were frequent.

*****

Never once during the fifteen-minute drive from the hospital did Richard, at the wheel, or Greda, beside him, dare to glance at each other. On the wharf of the inner harbour, two nurses, who had volunteered to join the voyage on the *Pelangi* alighted from the car and he assisted with their luggage. A desultory figure lingering, as their voices trailed off, Greda could suffer the tension no more.

He responded to her summons with, "Yes, Greda, what is it?"

She recoiled from his business-like tone until, apologetically, he took her arm and they moved to the privacy of the far side of the vehicle.

"Richard, I understand why you can't go." He was momentarily lost in a hazy recollection as her breath sweetened the air. She placed her hands in his. "It's right. We, well, had our crowded hour of glorious life and I shan't forget those times as long as I live." Her eyes glistened as she spoke, but the voice remained perfectly modulated. "What are you going to do?"

He was salvaged by the question. "I'm shipping out with Major Newton to India on the *Empire Star*. It's leaving tonight, too, and there's, um—we have plenty of work to do. I'm beginning to enjoy the adventure of army existence; bit like the merchant service really, just different clobber." He continued to speak, hoping to forestall any prospect of intimacies being exchanged between them, still unable to fix her eyes. "Never anywhere too long and variety—"

"Richard, I'll always love you. In another time—"

"Excuse me, sir, madam." It was Ranghati. "Problem. Ship's boat was collecting—" and then he lowered his voice to a whisper as they moved away from Greda. "These peoples everywhere. David Yip tell. Has sunk. Some deserters swam out as we coming in. There was fight and boat tipped over. David, he told me go another boat, maybe."

"Geez, we're going to have to see if we can get everyone aboard the *Empire Star*." The Gurkha frowned. "What, you don't like our prospects?"

"We have passes, sir, but not these. We try."

As Ranghati finished speaking, the ambulance bearing Edward Faircrossman arrived. Richard was mindful that Chia couldn't delay the sailing. "If anyone can get hold of another boat, it's that little bloke Yip."

"Hope so. Have small time to get to ship before sail if we row. Beg pardon, sir, as I know you row good," was Ranghati's grunting concession to humour.

Within a few moments Yip staggered into view, breathless and in a very agitated state, fresh from the harbour waters. Ranghati rushed to his aid.

"David, you little beauty," Richard exclaimed, as he helped support him. "When I heard about what happened, I was certain you would make it."

"That's nothing. Got away quickly, but was long swim to my friend. He has other boat, very small," Yip managed to say before being shaken by a paroxysm of coughing and vomiting. "No room for sick man, just another three besides me. Must go soon, Richard. Wife, children wait for me. Sorry for trouble."

"Can it possibly take one more? You need protection, and Sergeant Ranghati here will provide it. There's no man like him. He'll shoot any person who interferes."

Yip returned to flashing his teeth when acquiescing. Ranghati hesitated, but Richard's nod towards the Gurkha brought him straight to attention. He saluted with a resounding, "Yes, sir!"

"Good luck, Sergeant, goodbye. And, David, thanks," Richard said, shaking both their hands. "I'll take Mrs Faircrossman in the ambulance with her husband."

"Sir, what medical services?" asked Ranghati.

"They'll have plenty on board the *Empire Star*."

A small dinghy with an inboard motor chugged up beside the wharf, the sole occupant throwing up a line, whereupon David placed a wad of damp notes in his hand. The man nodded intently and disappeared into the night.

Richard assured the nurses they would be safe with Ranghati leading the group. "You'll taste Australian steak long before we do."

His words brooked no dissent. All were now caught up in a frantic quest for survival. The boat motored away.

Greda remained apart from the nearby ambulance.

"Looks like we'll be voyaging together again after all," he said. "It's as well."

She lightened a little, before entering the rear beside her husband. It was the first time in two months that Greda had set eyes on Edward. In the darkness, she could only distinguish the outline of his face and felt emotionless. He'd been given a strong sedative to settle him for the duration of the anticipated transfer.

As they moved off, pensively, Greda looked at the man she loved in the front of the vehicle, then back again at the supine form before her. The odd streak of light delivered a surreal sense of inevitability and she lowered her head in resignation. Greda saw the heavily bandaged stump and touched her husband's forehead.

Richard, fixed on the process in boarding, took the passes in hand, deleted his and the Gurkha's names, substituting in their stead Greda and Edward Faircrossman, possessing a fatalistic intuition that his future was sealed in a manner predetermined. Certainly he knew his orders. Given his rank and the circumstances, there was unlikely to be any barrier to his embarking, pass or not.

But in a dissociative state, it mattered little to him whether he left or stayed. He had interred the notion of a life with Greda, reaffirming that his mere presence, even in the relatively short voyage to India, would be more of a long-term hindrance to her than any transient advantage. At that moment he cast a surreptitious glance in her direction. The timing was exquisite, Greda stroking Faircrossman's forehead, the gold on the third finger of her left hand serving to forge his analysis.

The ambulance crawled its way through to the gate and was waved along by two guards, divested of weaponry and overcome by the numbers converging on the place. They forced a pathway to a position adjacent to the gangway.

Richard checked his watch and noted that the ship would cast off in fifteen minutes. People were striving to clamber on board as he alighted. The riotous scene unfolded before their eyes, as some who had tried to get aboard were forced back, resulting in a complete logjam halfway up the ramp. How those superintending the boarding were able to discriminate between people eligible to sail and others was, from his perspective, impossible to fathom.

A little girl who had been separated from her mother was distraught and screaming for help. Richard hoisted the child high above his head to avoid her being trampled by a uniformed man who ignored his order to stop. A rope was lowered, the girl harnessed to it and she was lifted to a tearful reunion.

He returned to the ambulance to see Faircrossman, semi-conscious through the jolting rush to the harbour, being eased out on a stretcher and positioned on the roof of the vehicle.

"He'll have to be closely monitored, sir," said one of the medical orderlies to Richard.

"I can see that for myself," he replied tersely. Standing on the bonnet cupped hands over his mouth, he yelled above the row, attracting the attention of the first mate. "Hey, Chief, we need a cradle to get the patient to you. His leg's just been amputated, so he must be handled gently. You heard me, didn't you?" The mate placed one hand behind his ear. Richard bellowed out, "The fellow's leg been recently amputated, and we can't risk reopening the wound."

The chief officer yelled back, "Has he a pass?"

Richard could hardly contain himself, responding exasperatingly, "Bloody passes, when all these others are gatecrashing the ship."

"What was that, sir?" said the mate.

"Yes, he's got a pass!" Richard thundered back.

"Right you are, Captain."

A cradle was steadied, and slings were attached. The stretcher was raised with a commendable degree of precision and Richard watched with relief as it was lowered to the deck. Blowhorn at the ready, the master was about to order departure. Time importuned Richard's every action. After the bags and medical kit followed, it was their turn as he, leading, and Greda clinging to him, began the scrummage and then a thrust onto the gangway.

"We're coming up, Chief." he yelled, but his words were lost in the cries and jostling of those around them. "Here are the passes, Greda."

He reached back and gave them to her as the press increased. The chief officer, set to unfasten the lines, had abandoned hope of trying to stop any more from boarding.

From the rear, Richard heard loud swearing. "Get the fuckin' hell out of the way. We're a special detail assigned to come aboard. Obstruct us and ya'll be shot. We're here to protect the ship."

Recognising the soldiers from the hospital gates, Richard seized Greda under the arms and propelled her in front of him. Valiant attempts to keep together were thwarted as the masses wrenched her hands away from his arms. He turned to block the deserters.

"Stop! I order you to stand fast and throw down your weapons," Richard shouted.

"Well, lookie who we 'ave 'ere," was their retort.

Reaching towards his holster while trying to hold back the wild-eyed pair eager for revenge, he was overcome by their surging forwards. Clubbed in the chest by a rifle butt, Richard was tipped over the rail to land heavily on the wharf. In the melee that followed, Greda screamed, unsure what had happened.

Now on the boat deck, Newton had seen it unfold and rushed to prevent Greda from attempting to return down the gangway. Its holding ropes were being disconnected by the mate and an able seaman, intent on removing the persons still trying to fight their way onto the ship. The keen-eyed bosun operating the winch allowed the structure to tilt, discharging its remaining adherents.

Thrice the ship's whistle was blown, and the captain's voice boomed from the bridge. "Let go for'ard," followed soon after by, "Let go aft".

"It's no good, Dr Faircrossman," Newton said, his arms restraining her. "There's nothing we can do. The safety of the ship is paramount now. Hundreds of lives are at stake and the captain must carry out his instructions."

"You surely aren't serious? We cannot leave Richard! I won't!" Greda tried to push past him. "What sort of a monster are you? I thought there beat a heart, but it's ice that flows through your veins."

"Someone will look after him. He's resourceful. He'll survive, I assure you."

The vessel slipped its moorings. There was no placating her. She managed only to utter, "Richard, I love you," before accepting Newton's embrace.

Chapter 33

Inside outside

15 February 1942

A party of British officers tackled the hill to the Ford Motor Works at Bukit Timah. Theirs was in the manner of a ceremonial procession to the formal surrender of Singapore. Presenting themselves in unblinking style, they strode as if anticipating a stirring exhortation from Churchill. Eyes fixed straight ahead and steadfast in step, it could only be wondered what was really coursing through their minds.

Major Wild bore the Union Jack. Next to, rather than in step with him, two Japanese officers in high boots and swords sheathed, dwarfed the Englishman in conquest, if not stature. All the while and drawing the astonishment if not the sympathy of a sprinkling of onlookers, the gaunt, worn and stooped figure of General Percival picked his way distractedly at the company's right.

It was nearing four o'clock in the afternoon when the officers assembled inside the car factory, now functioning as General Yamashita's headquarters. A long table had been set up in the canteen. The victors and the vanquished faced each other in a surreal montage.

Yamashita sat on one side, looking resolute, but manifesting more than a trace of humility rather than appearing the exultant conqueror. An undisguised insight into what the other soldier was enduring seemed to elude his faded counterpart.

The British general seemed unable to look Yamashita directly in the eye. Questioned through an interpreter as to if he had seen the terms of surrender, Percival sidetracked that issue by asking whether he could keep a thousand men under arms to ensure no further looting would take place. He was firmly told that the Japanese army was in control of the situation and he need no longer concern himself with these matters. Percival lowered his eyes and shifted in his chair. It was time for clear speaking, as the British general began to equivocate.

Yamashita at this point demonstrated the characteristics that had carried him to such a decisive victory when he declared that the attack would go forward. "If we cannot come to an agreement, make no mistake about it, that is what will happen."

Percival again wriggled uneasily, searching for an avenue where some face might at least be maintained. "I would like you to postpone it," he asked timidly.

Yamashita remained unmoved though not devoid of understanding. "The attack will go forward if we cannot come to an agreement," he repeated.

The broken Percival, sensing that he had to deploy another element to justify some remnants of control over the impasse, responded with a forlorn plea. "Because of the rioting in Singapore, I would like to keep one thousand men with arms. If there is a night attack, you put me in a difficult situation."

His counterpart decided that it was time for an ultimatum. "Do the British intend to surrender or not?" Yamashita demanded. "I need to have your answer."

Percival hesitated, testing the patience of his interlocutor before equivocating further. "I wish to have a ceasefire."

"The time for the night attack is drawing near. Will the British Army surrender or not?" Yamashita replied, speaking, as if for added emphasis, the next words in English, "Yes or no?"

The vanquished general had little left with which to argue but managed to persist. "Yes. But I would like the retention of one thousand armed men sanctioned."

The makings of a concession appeared on Yamashita's face when he replied, "Very well."

Percival had won a pyrrhic victory. General Yamashita would go on to discuss the timing of the surrender, pointing out that, if an earlier hour could not be agreed, he would have to hold Percival and Shenton Thomas as hostages.

By this stage of the proceedings, Percival had morphed into a filament as he signed the document presented to him. Singapore thereupon ceased to be the jewel in the British crown.

*****

Holding an abstruse gratitude towards the men who had pitched him from the gangway, he rationalised that Greda may have felt unburdened at the eventuality, sustained in that view by an image he was unable to erase, the reappearance of her wedding band.

When the command came to lay down arms, Richard realised it was only a matter of time before his duties at the power station would terminate. He didn't have long to wait, as a squad of Japanese soldiers brandishing fixed bayonets stormed the facility. They bound his hands and led him to the cricket ground where thousands of other men were assembled prior to the long march to Changi Prison. Most were bewildered and wondering how in the name of heaven the sudden capitulation had come about.

Several months into Richard's incarceration, news was promulgated by their captors of an 'exciting new opportunity' for men who wished to volunteer for work on the Siam/Burma railway. He had no intention of volunteering for anything, but it was soon evident, after the limited degree of interest, that conscription would be the next order of the day. Able-bodied men possessing the merest aptitude for engineering or capable of swinging a pick and shovel would be sent there. His vocation was known.

Not long after arriving at the cutting, Richard received a visual understanding of what was in store. The camp itself was primitive and cramped, illness and jungle diseases already rife.

The depredations of confinement and onerous work practices began to take a fatal toll on the prisoners. They were under the control of vicious and palpably sadistic overseers determined to complete their project on time and indifferent to how that goal might be attained, especially as to the expendability of human fodder. One by one, friends and colleagues surrendered to dysentery, malaria, beri-beri and other tropical diseases, compounded by malnutrition.

Richard clung on by unflagging resort to the memory of the unalloyed love he had experienced through Greda. Over time and continuing personal privation, she metamorphosed into an illusory being, patiently awaiting his liberation. This sleight of mind enabled him to subsume his outrage towards his captors. The thought of her and their time together became the only mechanism by which he could be uplifted as the extremes of captivity forged their indelible scars.

1942 rolled into 1943. The ever-dwindling slave-force hung on through willpower and any other means. Increasingly, Richard found it almost impossible to conjure up any thought beyond the next morsel of food. One man to whom he had grown close was William 'Billy' O'Leary, an Australian civil engineer. They were dubbed the 'Siamese twins', not only on account of their physical similarities, but also as they were rarely out of each other's company. Whether it was working side-by-side, cracking banal jokes while hacking away at the solid rock at Hellfire Pass or talking far into the night to maintain mental integrity, they kept their sanity.

Richard continued the ruse of British nationality consistent with his rank and standing, deft accent facilitating the process. He created an elaborate cover that he had spent time in Australia but was originally from Leatherhead. It pleased him to draw on Greda's childhood tales, all the while dreading that the charade might implode. Interest in his background and nationality faded, as the primary focus of all prisoners became their own survival.

O'Leary he confided in, including his false name of Frank Alderson and the risks if his true identity emerged. Still, the deception left him vulnerable. After one of the men rumoured to be involved in the execution of a Japanese colonel during the battle of Slim River was hauled away and never seen again, he decided escape was his best option. One night he took O'Leary aside after his mate commented on his hoarding of scraps of food.

"I'm getting out, cobber, and damn the consequences."
He outlined his plan.

No amount of pleading on O'Leary's part would dissuade him from doing what he intended. "Frankie, you're dead meat out there," he warned.

"I'm dead already, mate. In fact, you're that mad it's not me ya talking to, but a ghost. Listen, fella, you can have those few bits of grub. I'll be getting more than you can dream of. Look at us, carbon-copy shrinking sticks about to snap."

"Forget it, Frankie. I'm a bit stronger than you anyway."

"Be buggered you are. Whether I make it or not doesn't matter. You've a lot to lose, with your wife and kids. I'll get out and she'll learn you're having three meals a day, hot baths and Sundays off. Have you got it?"

"I get *you* alright." O'Leary grinned. "But wait another couple of days. You're fragile and shitting yourself again through the eye of a needle."

"It comes and goes, mate. The date can't be postponed. I'm meeting this native girl outside the wire tomorrow night, two hours after lights out, and that's in stone."

Richard's disappearance prompted predictable shrieking among the Japanese guards. This was followed by abuse and rough handling and, at the interminable parade of miserable humanity, denunciations from the commandant. The prisoners were harangued that those minded to think of escaping were committing a capital offence. They would catch the absconder and decapitation would be the most pleasant release to the punishments that could be expected.

At the end of a further week, the camp's population was assembled once again before the toad-jowelled commandant, looking exultant as he disdainfully regarded two crumpled forms in the mud.

"As I warned, here we see what happens to those who escape Japanese hospitality and anyone who decides to help. Let this be a lesson to you prisoners."

He barked an order and meagre shrouds were removed. The wasted, decomposing remains of a naked man and woman lying side-by-side, faces unrecognisable, their

heads grotesquely tied together with barbed wire symbol-
ising the joint enterprise.

"This is Captain Alderson and his lover. They finished
their lives as scum," the commandant declared, pointing
with a long cane to indicia of torture, "the reward for all
who cause trouble to the Emperor."

Within a fortnight, the surviving Allied prisoners were
transported back to Changi for the remainder of the war.
Most wished they had tried what Alderson had failed to
achieve, rather than enduring the living purgatory of two
more years in that abode.

Chapter 34

The letters

The sixth of February was an anniversary Greda would never miss. Four years had passed since they danced together in the Grand Ballroom at Raffles. She was given over to recall how, after an awkward debut finding his feet, Richard had proficiently mastered the steps. They drank Singapore Slings and champagne and, she conceded with a trace of private amusement, became a little tipsy, toasting King and Empire. Four years since the moment when no announcement needed to be made of the love that they knew encompassed their hearts, captured and encrypted by circumstance, tattooed in time and place.

Now all still as fresh in her memory as when it was happening, she leaned on the barrier at Picnic Point. Greda looked out over the escarpment to the fertile, cultivated plains of the Lockyer Valley. The distant paddocks were laid out in perfect rectangles, like a giant chequerboard of market gardens, emerald green with lucerne and oats, and black where newly ploughed, stretching as far as human eyes could see. The symmetry between Richard's take on "the world" and this living quilt was so remarkable that his voice still traced every contour.

Rain over the past week had refreshed the immediate surroundings after a long, dry summer. Wherever she looked, stands of rich, crisp shoots had sprung upright like feather spears. A kangaroo with pouched joey was nudging away contentedly at a thick clump mere yards away. The honeyed essence of freshly cut grass filled the atmosphere and, for a moment, she wondered whether this was the time of day chosen by those tasked with collecting samples of mountain air for the tourist marketing ploy. It was not quite the busy lovers' retreat just yet, as from prior visitations she knew it promised to be. The last rays of the sun were sliding away, transforming the lands below her into widening and lengthening shadows, latent twilight providing serenity.

Greda was not the sole receptor of this panoply of peace. Occasionally young people drifted past hand-in-hand, lodged at a vantage point and exchanged smiles. *Perhaps they had their own special memories*, she reflected.

One couple in their twenties paused nearby, the woman offering a friendly greeting and observation of how tranquil the place was. "Aren't we privileged and free with all that fighting over?" It was evident she wanted to proclaim her new-found happiness. "We've been husband and wife just six months. Married here three weeks after James came back from the war and expecting our first child in August. We're like doves."

"That's wonderful," Greda whispered, swallowing uneasily.

"Are you alright?" the woman asked, touching Greda on the wrist. "Hello, I've met you before. You're Dr Faircrossman from the hospital. You saved my mother's life when her appendix burst, and she was terribly sick. I didn't get to thank you, but I'm doing it now." She gave Greda a spontaneous hug, patting her arms.

"You've no need to do that. It's my job, and sometimes there are good outcomes. I'm so glad your mother has recovered. Back to full health, I trust?"

"Yes, she is." An awkward silence lingered before she spoke again. "I hope you don't mind me saying it, but I was so sorry to read in the paper about your husband's passing, and around the same time you saved Mum. He suffered so much."

Greda nodded. The tears couldn't now be stemmed as she muttered a hasty, "Well, goodbye then," to avoid embarrassment, and traced the rolling parkland, the lush turf cushioning her feet beneath the majestic Australian eucalypts. They all vied for command—iron bark, spotted gum, bloodwood and the incongruous blue gum trees with red wood inside the bark, those Richard had described perpetually guarding the area like giant sentinels.

Edward Faircrossman had survived three and a half years after their evacuation. Malaria, in combination with the psychological impost from the loss of his leg, exacted a significant toll on his physical and mental integrity.

Although saddened that Richard was left behind, Jon had been overjoyed at his parents' return. Greda had envisaged that the special relationship with his son would be a great source of strength for Edward, giving him a reason to adapt to his handicap and live and watch the boy mature into a young man destined for success. Jonathon made exceptional progress at secondary school, and a scholarship beckoned for the degree in mechanical engineering at the University of Sydney.

Greda downplayed the sacrifice others thought she had made by unstinting attention to her husband's health needs while encumbered by professional duties. Edward's days were spent in idleness, continuing mental decline, ill health and a rapid descent into alcoholism. It soon became obvious that his bond with Jonathon would never be the same as it was before their separation.

Spousal relations reached a turning point early on in those trying and bitter years, when he found a letter she had written to Richard. The name on the envelope, *Captain Frank Alderson*, initially mystified her husband, but, in the body of the letter, all was made clear. Its discovery set the stencil in his emotional disinhibition for the balance of his days. Over the remaining period of Edward's life, Greda believed the scars seared into his brain by these revelations were more profound than his bodily infirmities. His treatment of her in those last years, meted out mercilessly and almost daily, she accepted as just punishment for her love affair. He memorised the words she had written. Whenever the mood took him, like an actor in a radio play, he indulged a passion for mocking recitation of each 'tender, precious utterance'.

Jon became a boarder at the Grammar School after the family settled on acreage near Toowoomba and they were forced to spend more time alone. Faircrossman luxuriated in piercing the more intimate lines her way, phrase by phrase: *I adore you and will love you for the rest of my life. You are the man who awoke in me my womanhood. You are my all and you will always be inside me in spirit.*

And so the mantra went on, like a *parang* plunged into her soul, with its blade twisted and turned spitefully. Except when Jon was home on vacation, the only respite from his abuse came during her working hours. When it reached a point that she could no longer endure, Greda stayed on duty for extended periods, calling in a nurse for him.

A lack of response to the taunts confounded her sister, in whom she had confided. Fay regarded Greda's failure to reprove her husband for his extra-marital dalliance as bewildering and told her so.

Not once did she mention it, and almost never was she tempted to. Since Richard hadn't even hinted at her husband's affair, she would not either. His refraining from alluding to the event when it might have been self-serving became the precedent Greda held to in the face of the most provocative of hecklings, such as, "I've been faithful to you all my life and look what you did to me when my back was turned for but weeks. You'd do anything to have him, but you can't now, can you?" His most insufferable affront was, "How many others were there?" This would see her flee the house much to his grim delight that he had wounded her. Upon her return, the whole sorry business resumed, usually with greater intensity, until the drink gave her a reprieve.

Greda tried not to feel guilty in the face of this barrage, but accepted she had sinned, at least in that, as a married woman, she had fallen prey to loving another man. Pleading that no sexual relations outside of marriage had ever taken place was futile. Her strategy became such that she would take all the derision he threw, shouldering her 'weakness' at having succumbed to illicit affections and wondering whether there would ever be any acquittal from the scourge of his tongue.

Mental cruelty, he had told her goadingly, was a sufficient ground for divorce. A public trial of her infidelity was what he wanted. She wouldn't give him that satisfaction, as if it was the only weapon left in her armoury. With the passage of time, his taunting made Greda stronger in her resolve to go on, to relive Richard's love for her as manifested and declared in Naranam's fishing crib and in her memory of their night at Raffles.

She could but lament the fact that he would never read the thoughts of her soul. At times of desperate loneliness, if there was one thing Greda wished she could rectify, it was putting that letter into Richard's hands. When it became clear that he was a prisoner-of-war, she had sent it care of the Red Cross, the only avenue through which mail was being channelled. But, in one of those idiosyncratic events that befall those undeserving of retribution, it was returned by the postman. Someone had written on the front words to the effect that letters to British servicemen in captivity must be sent through the British High Commission in Canberra.

After less than ten months in Sydney, Greda had taken the post in Toowoomba. Her one period of meaningful private solace came each year at this time. She treasured these moments when no disordered recollections of daily life were permitted to obtrude into her reminiscences of happier times. Here was a place to store and revisit the cherished memories. Richard was the only man she had ever truly loved, and she knew with certainty he had loved her.

On this occasion, the first since her husband's passing, his malign influence had reached from the grave in the unsuspecting words of the contented young woman commiserating with her momentary lapse of composure. If she had known the real source of her grief, would it have earned any consolation? This was bitterness she hated in herself, which she tried to abolish but found it impossible so to do.

Richard was gone. It was difficult to accept that she would never see him again. His death had been announced in a list of Imperial casualties published by the *Sydney Morning Herald* nearly three years ago, confirmed unofficially by the Australian authorities and officially by the High Commission when Greda had contacted them, she still being a British subject. She had steadfastly secreted the newspaper, fearing another brace of abuse she couldn't have withstood absent a manifestation of grief.

She wondered what had happened to those of Richard's friends who would, but for last-minute events, have been instrumental in their long passage to Australia. Being more discreet, she had written to Bryan Williamson, care of the *Pelangi*, leaving the return address of her sister. When Chia responded, acquainting her with the circumstances of his death, she was stunned and couldn't conceive of how Richard had borne this silently. Suzy had a son named after his father. David Yip and his family had settled in New Zealand. Chia, Yip and Kwoli had established the North-South Shipping Company of New Zealand and were doing well, having acquired a second vessel.

Certainty that Richard had been left behind in those last cataclysmic moments of their evacuation only really solidified when, having recovered from her distress and being supported by Newton, Greda saw the shore lights fade from sight. The pall of black smoke over Singapore, evident even in the night sky, had served as a lingering reminder that he was somewhere among the anarchy that had marked their final, frantic hours in that abysmal place. Despite the trauma and her outburst at that time, she had quickly apologised. Newton became a man she greatly respected. Delivering one last shock, he revealed that Richard had voluntarily undertaken the mission to rescue Edward, the dominant reason for his being commissioned as an officer. Along with that conferment, he told her the purpose of the name 'Alderson' being gazetted.

Major Newton had disembarked from the *Empire Star* in Calcutta. Subsequent attempts to find out anything about him were thwarted at every administrative turn. Life carried on, but her memories had not faded, nor would they.

In the little bag Greda was carrying lay something she had managed to keep hidden from Edward. The candleholder survived the trek across country, the lifeboat in the Straits of Malacca and the last moments in Singapore. For the first time since coming to Picnic Point, Greda placed it on a park table. Ground air was still, but a rustle overhead invited Richard's spirit. She lit a solitary candle, its glow revealing a face tinged with gratitude for this memento.

The crickets united in full chorus as she continued to relive blissful times, before a voice superintended. Light had departed. Surely she was dreaming, as it resounded again.

"Dr Faircrossman, ahoy there. It's a good time to be out for a walk, taking in the evening and, if I was romantically inclined, even wishing on a candle."

She intuited a human presence and a polished accent. Although unexpected in this place, its blend of self-effacing humour and insight were sufficient not merely to interrupt Greda's reverie but jolt her.

"Major Newton!" she exclaimed, walking towards the uniformed figure. "It's so good to see you." She accepted his outstretched hand gently with both of hers. "What on earth are you doing here?" Then she noticed the absence of a crown. "Excuse me, I have sold you short."

The officer bore himself in much the same manner as four years ago, his moustache neatly trimmed, if mingled with grey, his full head of hair perfectly parted and dressed by a modest application of oil. "Yes, but don't apologise. It's, ah, Colonel these days," he said with humility. "A few more salutes. Still doing the same stuff up in my old patch, Singapore and the Malayan states, more so the latter. The communists have been fomenting trouble since the war ended."

"How did you know to find me here?" she asked, her thoughts pursuing sweeter recollections.

"Dr Faircrossman, you surprise me. I *am* an intelligence officer, or had that slipped your purview?"

She perceived a saponaceous rebuke creasing his face and relaxed, warming to his unique personality. "So long since I've seen you and much has happened, the war won, soldiers home. I tried to contact you through the High Commission after we returned to Sydney but couldn't get anywhere with the bureaucracy. You know all about such matters."

He stiffened, being the old bureaucrat himself, and cleared his throat before formality resumed. "First, let me say how sorry I was to hear of your husband's death."

"You're the second person in the last half an hour to extend that courtesy. It was very hard for him when we returned, his mind never the same."

"War seems to produce greater casualties after it's over," he offered in commiseration.

She read more into the comment than was intended. "Please don't regard me uncharitable, Colonel, but I'm anticipating you didn't come all this way to express your condolences."

"I sometimes think that if we recruited you into the service, several people active on the ground could be dispensed with."

Greda turned away and chewed nervously at one of her fingers. "You had a knack for identifying good recruits, I recall."

Moments passed before he continued. "You still think of him, even after four years. In the confusion at the end, some of us got out in one piece but, Dr Faircrossman, he could have left with a few of the others. Our personnel were evacuated with Percival's special approval. Perhaps in his heart he couldn't bring himself to leave, duty and all that, and, unfortunately, well, the rest, you know—"

"Oh, indeed it was unfortunate. My husband was eternally grateful, so much so that he never deigned to mention what Richard had done for him."

Acrimony entered her voice. Greda tried to wish the feeling away but was unable to repress it. Taking Richard's precious gift and shielding the flame, she began to walk, wanting the conversation to either attain some telling relevance or conclude. Initially he followed, then, as they passed another bench, he asked her to sit for a moment. Greda was annoyed at herself for allowing him access to her feelings, knowing the acerbity would have been noted.

"I saw the letter you wrote to him. A copy was made before it was sent back," he said at last.

"So now you know. I'm sure you suspected all the time. Well, you're dealing with a fallen woman who cheated on her husband. You won't entertain any explanations. It's all black and white to a man like—"

"I knew never having seen what you'd written. Richard told me on one of the last occasions I spoke to him. He slipped an envelope into my papers without informing me. It didn't turn up for months. His note inside asked me to give this letter to you personally, if I was ever in a position to do so. I'm here to finally, I suppose, fulfil that wish. It has never been opened. I haven't come all the way just for that; we had a meeting of staff officers in Brisbane."

She wondered what the point was in all of this now, passing on a letter after so many years. None of it could bring Richard back. For a moment she asked herself whether Newton was deriving voyeuristic pleasure out of inflicting more pain and gauging her reaction, then going on about it as if subtly gloating. But there was nothing she could detect in his voice, nor did his eyes, illuminated by the candlelight, reveal it. She couldn't relax, her heart pumping rapidly in anticipation at reading the words her lover had written so long ago.

"Please, may I have it?"

The Colonel stood up and reached into a side pocket, handing an envelope to her. "Here's a little torch, if you need it, but the candle seems to be holding up."

He walked off to permit some privacy, telling her he would be at his car if she wanted to speak with him. Greda eased it open.

February 1942, Singapore
My Darling Greda,

By now, if everything goes to plan, you should be well on your way to Australia. I pray that you will have a safe voyage and soon be lovingly reunited with your son.

To say goodbye to you, knowing it would be for the last time, was the hardest decision I ever had to make. I could not say it to your face.

I will never forget all of the times we spent together. Remember, 'I love you. Deeply, with the sun in my eyes.' How prescient was that? And then that night we danced, sealed forever in our hearts, gave me an exquisite sense of contentment and joy in the totality of my life. Until I met you, I had not understood what it meant to love another in that pure manner that only man and woman can share.

We did not and could not carry it through. So, it's entirely right for you to go to Sydney and for me to do my duty here. Real love cannot flourish and grow if it is built on a selfish desire that chooses to ignore the consequences to others who, by happenstance, are profoundly affected.

I am deeply sorry that things didn't work out for us. I thank you for the love with which you so richly blessed me. You must now forget 'this bloke' entirely. An innocent boy depends on you to do so. Fortunately, I have the luxury to choose to remember you for the rest of my life.

~Richard

The eclectic evening was closing as she read and re-read the words, unable to stem the flow of tears engulfing her. He had not predicted entirely the events that occurred subsequent to his penning of the note, she reflected, but they were both looking down the same pathway, and this made his thoughts so precious. A melancholic emptiness fell over her, companioning the enveloping darkness. Some stars refused to be extinguished by gathering clouds as she strained for their comfort. It felt as if there was no one there but her.

But then she saw a light peeping from the interior of a car. Newton stepped out as she approached.

"I'm indebted to your going to the trouble of finding me up here and delivering this." She paused while struggling to dam the tears that threatened to stream out again, before resuming in a quavering voice, "I, I have a request to make." Newton's head tilted and he studied her compassionately. "Can you tell me where Richard lies? He worked on the infamous death railway, the report said. I would like to visit the place where he rests, if that's possible."

"I anticipated your request but, regrettably am unable to fulfil it. Duty demands that I take the flying boat leaving tomorrow night, and if you—"

She bristled at his words, intuiting the return of the personality that had affronted her at their first meeting, and walked a few paces away from him before shooting back over her shoulder, "I don't expect *you* to make arrangements for me to get there or take me to his grave, but just tell me where he's buried. That's all I ask," came her forlorn plea.

As he failed to respond immediately, she returned to the candle.

"Greda."

Standing behind her, it was the first time Newton had uttered her Christian name. She was startled and faced him, trying to search beyond the measured mystique.

"Visiting a cemetery would be futile. My offer to take you to Singapore tomorrow stands, for *that* is where you'll find him. He is alive, Greda."

Epilogue

The familiarity of Singapore was subliminal. It seemed untroubled by its fall and occupation before the Japanese were finally driven out. There were no plumes of thick smoke, no burning buildings or ruptured oil storage tanks, or the conflagrations that had riven the island during the last hours leading to their desperate attempt to board the *Empire Star*.

He made a detour to the cricket ground and contrasted his freedom of movement with the experience on that field four years previously. O'Leary, the man who took his place and identity on the ill-fated escape attempt when dysentery intervened, was unknown to him then. Head bowed in the middle of the pitch, he spent some respectful minutes in silence for his mate.

When liberation had come, that Richard's skeletal body was capable of crabbing movement amazed even seasoned doctors. His eyes were so far lost within their sockets as to be indiscernible, thus forbidding any meaningful facial expression. If not for the feeble utterance of his name, Newton would never have recognised him.

The process of recovery proved a serious challenge. At the start he faltered, hovering between life and death as malaria sought mastery. The medical personnel were skilful and patient. Newton rarely left his side, and their friendship was decisive in Richard's painstaking rehabilitation.

After he gained his 'sea legs', as he dryly referred to their spindly and crooked efficacy that at first bore him around the hospital paths, much as once they might have on a ship's deck in a mighty gale, an honour awaited. His hair had "fined to a whiter shade of grey", Newton had remarked during a generous speech at the special ceremony conferring his new rank, "as befits a lieutenant-colonel of your standing and bravery." Thereafter, his health and stature progressed well.

Wondering what Newton needed to see him about ameliorated the discomposure he felt in anticipation of entering a place he deemed off limits. He had queried the choice of venue, while appreciating the favour in which it was held by officers of senior rank for less official discussions and social gatherings. Pastels of early evening seemed to denote benignity when Richard set foot within the Raffles precinct. The renowned hotel had resumed its vibrant sophistication so quickly after the last shot was fired that many wondered whether the war had conspired to change anything, apart from increasing its notoriety. But for a glance, he avoided the Grand Ballroom, deciding to take a tour around the upper level of the classical colonnaded building. A similarity with the Eastern and Oriental in Georgetown was another recollection he rapidly purged.

His eyes ran down the length of the structures, each running parallel to the other and divided by a delightful tropical smorgasbord of greenery. It was a verdant pleasure that entranced him, moist, fresh and lush. Fruit the size of two-gallon buckets hung prodigiously from durian trees. Bulbous mangoes streaked with entwining shades of strawberries and cream appeared ripe, and he checked whether any had already fallen. Banana trunks, some as thick as the columns supporting the building, held up bunches so compressed and full that attempts at counting the hands faltered several times over. Then there were coconut palms stretching up above the walkways on either side, so close that he could have reached out and picked a brilliant specimen. He followed one palm, arching like the neck of a giraffe from the fronds of its crown all the way down, to be met in the lower reaches of the journey by delicate orchids garlanded with colour, splashing out in mauves, pinks, blues and even golds. At ground level, a luxuriant array of low-growing herbs and delicate pansies combined to furnish this oasis within the city.

Drawn by ethereal propinquity to remember that night, the reflexive pain of the memory tenderly gave way to a joy Richard had not anticipated. He determined to make this first occasion a happy one and, after seeing Newton, would look again at the place where they had danced. A sense of endowment and privilege at being here and having lived those fantastic moments with the woman he adored inspired further exploration. In this labyrthine wandering, he reflected on what she might be doing at this precise moment.

He strolled systematically past the rooms that made this fine hotel one of the most memorable establishments in the whole of the Far East. Some of the doors bore the names of the famous people who had passed under those very lintels and he read them out dreamily to himself, from Somerset Maugham to Noel Coward and Bette Davis. It cheered him to see a name and join it with one who had touched the door handles brushed against as he ambled along.

While in hospital, every Friday patients were treated to in-house cinema. He had read some of the works of Maugham, a writer he came to much admire. Richard took a particular liking to a 1940 film starring Bette Davis and Herbert Marshall called *The Letter* from his book of the same name. Reading remained one of his most pleasurable pastimes and there was no shortage of classic works for anyone requesting books, he, of all the patients, being the most persistent applicant for more.

Recalling Greda leaving her copy of *Pride and Prejudice* for him, a familiar ache rose from the pit of his stomach and into his chest, constricting his breathing. Richard paused, gripping the ornate balustrade of the sweeping staircase, stultifying the mystical force impelling him towards loss of control. Salvation in part emanated from his watch, reminding that he was required elsewhere. The instinct to remain fixed to the spot was overcome and he descended to the Long Bar. Approaching the table that Newton had reserved, Richard strove to regain his self-possession before the Colonel's arrival.

In a matter of minutes, his once-commanding officer duly appeared with a greeting that almost did not become him, effusive and out of character. Newton was tanned and fit after his trip and eased Richard back into his chair. They had hardly shaken hands when an aide interrupted them and, amid profuse apologies, Newton left to take an urgent telephone call.

"No need to worry, sir. I'll be here when you return."

Richard resumed his reverie, a disconsolate figure to anyone who might have observed him, lost in the place where dreams lay strewn asunder like scattered shards, unable to decouple his inner self from its focus upon her. When Newton had told him of the meeting with senior staff officers in Brisbane, the thought had crossed his mind of requesting him to make a social call or something detached like that and reporting back. Of course, he wanted to be told that she had asked of him. Then he remembered that Greda did not know he survived the war and had chosen to refrain from making any enquiry. *Marriage stabilised*, he projected.

Seeking information about her would be inconsistent with his entire rationale, where even mention of her name was forbidden. The only exception concerned her arrival in Sydney, and he stopped Newton from adding anything else. Maybe now, on his first venture into Raffles, broaching other topics concerning her would be easier, but he doubted it. Even if he was to ask Newton whether she had received the letter, it would only serve to reopen wounds best left sutured. Another chest constriction came over him and, leaning on elbows, he pressed fingers to either side of his head as if by doing so he could stop this insidious emotion from gaining ascendancy over him.

A waiter materialised, having to announce himself twice before his customer noticed, and then only being met with a request for a glass of water. Richard was about to say not to bother lighting the candle, but it was accomplished before he could speak. In the still atmosphere, he contemplated the orange flame. Positioned on the left-hand side of the table gracefully robed with a white, starched linen cloth was a solitary red rose. Nothing here had changed, even after four years.

He hoped Newton's business would be transacted quickly. Try as he might, Greda would not be ousted from his mind. His chest heaved again and the resolve to stay strong was deserting him. Richard looked down, furtively brushing the tears from his face and searching for distractions. Anything must be focused on but that woman, as he fought to take hold of his emotions.

Richard had no inkling that his every action was being scrutinised. Studying him tenderly, Greda saw his features were the same chiselled ones that had waylaid her heart: his resolute square jaw; his broad shoulders, much less prominent than they used to be—she would fix that in no time; his face, desolately knotted, lined and pale; his close-cropped hair, like a first bestowal of autumn snow. He looked very distinguished and was older, much older.

Moved by the immense struggle evident within him, Greda constrained an impulse to rush over. She observed him idly revolving the candlestick. Then he became transfixed by its familiarity and lifted it through moistened eyes searching for the inscription.

"The colonel told me you're only allowed one of these," she whispered into his ear as she placed a tall Singapore Sling in his hand.

For a moment Richard swore the magnetic voice emitted from a spectre that by degrees he was conjuring up, until he drank her perfume, tasted her breath and felt her mouth on his.

Standing, his eyes fell on a heavenly sight, the soft, flickering glow of the candle enhancing her eternal beauty. Their tears were no longer stemmed. She threw her arms around him and he lifted her face to study this woman hypnotically, before meeting her lips with uninhibited intensity.

"Greda, my serene Greda! You're here. You were never really away from me in this place as I wandered. How I love you."

"Yes. I'm here forever, Richard." Their eyes locked together. "And damn the British Army and that infernal, lovable Colonel Newton," she quipped, ecstatic beyond her tears.

And there they stayed for several minutes, fixed in an embrace that wouldn't be undone, unable to speak, broken finally with another lingering kiss, followed by unrestrained expressions of love and happiness.

"You're coming home to me, Richard."

About the Author

Upon completion of a four-year apprenticeship, A. C. (Tony) Smith went to sea setting a course to become a marine engineer.

His studies were interrupted when a serious collision in Vancouver Harbour almost cut the ship on which he was serving as third engineer in half. Miraculously, the vessel stayed afloat.

Experience as a witness in the ensuing court proceedings fired an interest in the law. From that point onward, he determined to become a barrister.

Graduating from the University of Queensland with a Bachelor of Laws and admitted to the Bar in 1982, a successful legal practice followed.

Life-threatening heart disease was discovered in 2013 and, after major surgery, he ceased practising law.

Two years later, he took up writing in earnest.

Tony lives in Brisbane.